Why did Scarlett have such power over him?

For the last two weeks, since she'd left him standing on Madison Avenue with a stunned look on his face, he'd thought of nothing else. All Vin's considerable resources had been dedicated to one task: finding her.

She was in his blood. He hadn't been able to forget her. Not from the first moment he'd seen her in that bar. From the moment he'd first taken her in his arms. From the moment she'd disappeared from his bed after the best sex of his life.

From the moment she'd violently crashed his wedding and told him she was pregnant with his baby.

Scarlett Ravenwood was half-angel, half-demon. There was a reason he hadn't seduced any other woman for over eight months—an eternity for a man like Vin. He'd been haunted by Scarlett: haunted body and soul, driven half mad by memories of her naked in his arms.

Scarlett was the wo
wanted. And he int

D1188669

One Night With Consequences

When one night...leads to pregnancy!

When succumbing to a night of unbridled desire
it's impossible to think past the morning after!

But, with the sheets barely settled, that little blue line
appears on the pregnancy test and it doesn't take long
to realise that one night of white-hot passion
has turned into a lifetime of consequences!

Only one question remains:

How do you tell a man you've just met
that you're about to share more than just his bed?

Find out in:

Look for more *One Night With Consequences*
coming soon!

A RING FOR VINCENZO'S HEIR

BY
JENNIE LUCAS

First Published in Great Britain 2016
By Mills & Boon, an imprint of HarperCollins*Publishers*
1 London Bridge Street, London, SE1 9GF

© 2016 Jennie Lucas

ISBN: 978-0-263-92129-8

Our policy is to use papers that are natural, renewable and recyclable products and made from wood grown in sustainable forests. The logging and manufacturing processes conform to the legal environmental regulations of the country of origin.

Printed and bound in Spain
by CPI, Barcelona

USA TODAY bestselling author **Jennie Lucas**'s parents owned a bookstore and she grew up surrounded by books, dreaming about faraway lands. A fourth-generation Westerner, she went east at sixteen to boarding school on scholarship, wandered the world, got married, then finally worked her way through college before happily returning to her hometown. A 2010 RITA® finalist and 2005 Golden Heart® winner, she lives in Idaho with her husband and children.

Books by Jennie Lucas

Mills & Boon Modern Romance

Nine Months to Redeem Him
Uncovering Her Nine-Month Secret
The Sheikh's Last Seduction
To Love, Honour and Betray
A Night of Living Dangerously
The Virgin's Choice
Bought: The Greek's Baby

At His Service

The Consequences of That Night

Princes Untamed

Dealing Her Final Card
A Reputation for Revenge

One Night In…

Reckless Night in Rio

Unexpected Babies

Sensible Housekeeper, Scandalously Pregnant

Visit the Author Profile page at millsandboon.co.uk for more titles.

To Pippa Roscoe, editor extraordinaire.

CHAPTER ONE

"You have two choices, Scarlett." Her ex-boss's greedy eyes slowly traveled from her pregnant belly to the full breasts straining the fabric of her black maternity dress. "Either you sign this paperwork to give your baby away when it's born, and become my wife immediately, or…"

"Or what?" Scarlett Ravenwood tried to move away from the papers he was pushing toward her. But the man's overmuscled bulk took up most of the backseat of the limousine.

"Or…I'll have Dr. Marston declare you insane. And have you committed." His fleshy lips curved into a pleasant smile. "For your own safety, of course. Because any sane woman would obviously wish to marry me. And then you'll lose your baby anyway, won't you?"

Scarlett stared at him, barely seeing the gleaming buildings of Manhattan passing behind him as they drove down Fifth Avenue. Blaise Falkner was handsome, rich. And a monster.

"You're joking, right?" She gave an awkward laugh. "Come on, Blaise. What century do you think we're living in?"

"The century a rich man can do whatever he wants. To whomever he wants." Reaching out, he twisted a tendril of her long red hair around a thick finger. "Who's going to stop me? You?"

Scarlett's mouth went dry. For the last two years, she'd lived in his Upper East Side mansion as nursing assistant for his dying mother, and over that time Blaise had made increasingly forceful advances. Only his imperious mother, horrified at the thought of her precious heir lowering himself to the household help, had kept him at bay.

But now Mrs. Falkner was dead, and Blaise was rich beyond imagination. While Scarlett was nothing more than an orphan who'd come to New York desperate for a job. Ever since she'd arrived, she'd been isolated in the sickroom, obeying the sharp orders of nurses and doing the worst tasks caring for a fretful, mean-spirited invalid. She had no friends in New York. No one to take her side against him.

Except…

No, she told herself desperately. *Not him.*

She couldn't. Wouldn't.

But what if Blaise was right? What if she escaped him and went to the police, and they didn't believe her? Could he and his pet psychiatrist find a way to carry through with his threat?

When he'd crassly propositioned her at the funeral that morning—literally over his mother's grave!—she'd tried to laugh it off, telling him she was leaving New York. To her surprise, he'd courteously offered a ride to the bus station. Ignoring her intuition's buzz of warning, she'd accepted.

She should have known he wouldn't give up so easily. But she'd never imagined he'd go this far. Threatening her into marriage? Trying to force her to give her baby away?

She'd made a mistake thinking of Blaise as a selfish, petulant playboy who wanted her like a spoiled child demanded a toy he couldn't have. He was actually insane.

"Well?" Blaise demanded. "What is your answer?"

"Why would you want to marry me?" Scarlett said weakly. With a deep breath, she tried to appeal to his vanity. "You're good-looking, charming, rich. Any woman would be happy to marry you." *Any woman who didn't know you*, she added silently.

"But I want you." He gripped her wrist tightly enough to make her flinch. "All this time, you've refused me. Then you get yourself knocked up by some other man and won't tell me who." He ground his teeth. "Once we're wed, I'll be the only man who can touch you. As soon as that brat is born and sent away, you'll be mine. Forever."

Scarlett tried to squelch her rising panic. As the limo moved down Fifth Avenue, she saw a famous cathedral at the end of the block. A desperate idea formed in her mind. Could she…?

Yes. She could and she would.

It hadn't been her plan. She'd intended to buy a bus ticket south, use her small savings to start a new life somewhere sunny where flowers grew year-round and raise her baby alone. But as her own father often said when she was growing up, new challenges called for new plans.

Her new plan scared her, though. Because if Blaise Falkner was a frying pan, Vincenzo Borgia was the fire.

Vin Borgia. She pictured the dark eyes of her unborn baby's father, so hot one moment, so cold the next. Pictured the ruthless edge of his jaw. The strength of his body. The force of his will.

A shiver went through her. What if he…

Don't think about it, she told herself firmly. One impossible thing at a time. Another maxim she'd learned from her father.

As the chauffeur slowed down at a red light, she knew it was now or never. She took a deep breath, then opened her eyes with a brittle smile.

"Blaise." Scarlett leaned forward as she tightened her hidden right hand into a fist. "You know what I've always wanted to do…?"

"What?" he breathed, licking his lips as he looked down at her breasts.

"This!" She gave him a hard uppercut to the jaw. His teeth snapped together as his head knocked backward, shocking him into releasing her.

Without waiting for the limo to completely stop, she yanked on her door handle and stumbled out onto the sidewalk. Kicking off her two-inch heels, she put her hand protectively over her belly and ran with all her might, feet bare against the concrete, toward the enormous cathedral.

It was a perfect day for a wedding. The first of October, and every tree in the city was decorated in yellow, orange and red. St. Swithun's Cathedral was the most famous in New York, the place where the wealthy and powerful held their christenings, weddings and funerals. Two hundred years old, it was a towering midtown edifice of gray marble, big as a city block, with soaring spires reaching boldly into the bright blue sky.

Panting as she ran, Scarlett glanced down at the peeling gold-tone watch that had once belonged to her mother. She prayed she wasn't too late.

A vintage white Rolls-Royce Corniche was parked at the curb, bedecked with ribbons and flowers. Next to it, a uniformed driver waited. Bodyguards with dark sunglasses, scowls and earpieces stood guard on the cathedral steps and around the perimeter.

The wedding had started, then. Scarlett had been trying not to think about it for the last four months, since she'd seen the announcement in the *New York Times*. But the details had been blazed in her memory, and now she was glad, because only Vin Borgia could help her.

A bodyguard blocked her with a glare. "Miss, stand back…"

Clutching her belly theatrically, Scarlett stumbled forward on the sidewalk. "Help! There's a man chasing me! He's trying to kidnap my baby!"

The bodyguard's eyes widened behind his sunglasses. "What?"

She ran past him, calling back, "Call the police!"

"Hey! You can't just—"

Scarlett ran up the cathedral's steps, gasping for air.

"Stop right there!" A second bodyguard came toward her with a thunderous expression. Then he turned when he heard the shout of his colleague as two of Blaise's bodyguards started throwing punches at him on the sidewalk below. "What the…"

Taking advantage of his distraction, she pushed open the cathedral doors and went inside.

For a moment, she blinked in the shadows.

Then her eyes adjusted, and she saw a wedding straight out of a fairy tale. Two thousand guests sat in the pews, and at the altar, beneath a profusion of white roses and lilies and orchids, was the most beautiful bride, standing next to the most devastatingly handsome man in the world.

Just seeing Vin now, for the first time since that magical night they'd created a baby, Scarlett caught her breath.

"If anyone here today has reason," the officiant intoned at the front, "why these two may not lawfully be joined…"

She heard a metallic wrenching sound behind her, then Blaise's harsh triumphant gasp as he burst through the cathedral doors.

"…speak now, or forever hold your peace."

Desperate, Scarlett stumbled to the center of the aisle. Holding up her hand, she cried, "Please! Stop!"

There was a collective gasp as two thousand people turned to stare at her. Including the bride and groom.

Scarlett put her hands to her head, feeling dizzy. It was hard to speak when she could barely catch her breath. She focused on the only person who mattered.

"Please, Vin, you have to help me—" Her voice choked off, then strengthened as she thought of the unborn child depending on her. "My boss is trying to steal our baby!"

Unlike many grooms the night before they wed, Vincenzo Borgia, Vin to his friends, had slept very well last night.

He knew what he was doing today. He was marrying the perfect woman. His courtship of Anne Dumaine had been easy, and so had their engagement. No discord. No messy emotion. No sex, even, at least not yet.

But today, their lives would be joined, as would their families—and more to the point, their companies. When Vin's SkyWorld Airways merged with her father's Air Transatlantique, Vin would gain thirty new transatlantic routes at a stroke, including the lucrative routes of New York–London and Boston–Paris. Vin's company would nearly double in size, at very advantageous terms. Why would Jacques Dumaine be anything but generous to his future son-in-law?

After today, there would be no more surprises in Vin's life. No more uncertainty or questions about the future. He liked that thought.

Yes, Vin had slept well last night, and tonight, after he finally made love to his very traditional bride, who'd insisted on remaining a virgin until they married, he expected to sleep even better. And for every other night for the rest of his well-ordered, enjoyably controllable life.

If he wasn't overwhelmingly attracted to his bride, what of it? Passion died soon after marriage, he'd been told, so perhaps it was a good thing. You couldn't miss what you'd never had.

And if he and Anne seemed to have little in common other than the wedding and the merger, well, what difference did that make? Men and women had different interests. They weren't supposed to be the same. He would cover her weaknesses. She would cover his.

Because whatever his enemies and former lovers might accuse, Vin knew he had a few. A lack of patience. A lack of empathy. In the business world, those were strengths, but once he had children, he knew greater sources of patience and empathy would be required.

He was ready to settle down. He wanted a family. Other than building his empire it was his primary reason for getting married, but not his only. After his last sexual encounter, an explosive night with a gorgeous redhead who'd given him the most amazing sex of his life, then disappeared, he decided he was fed up with unpredictable love affairs.

So, a few months later, he'd sensibly proposed to Anne Dumaine.

Born in Montreal, Anne was beautiful, with an impeccable pedigree, certain to be a good mother and corporate wife. She spoke several languages, including French and Italian, and held a degree in international business. Best of all she came with an irresistible dowry—Air Transatlantique.

Vin smiled at Anne now, standing across from him as they waited to speak their vows. She looked like Princess Grace, he thought, blonde and grave, with a modest white gown and a long lace veil that had been handmade by Belgian nuns. Flawless. A picture-perfect bride.

"If anyone here today has reason," the archbishop presiding over their marriage said solemnly, "why these two may not lawfully be joined…"

There was a scuffle, a loud bang. Footsteps. From the corner of his eye he saw heads in the audience turn. He refused to look—that would be undisciplined—but his smile grew a little strained.

"...speak now," the minister finished, "or forever hold your peace."

"Please! Stop!"

A woman's voice. Vin's jaw tightened. Who would dare interrupt their wedding? One of his despondent ex-lovers? How had she gotten past the bodyguards? Furious, he turned.

Vin froze when he saw green eyes fringed with black lashes in a lovely heart-shaped face, and vivid red hair cascading down her shoulders, bright as heart's blood. She stood in the gray stone cathedral, his dream come to life.

Scarlett. The woman who had haunted his dreams for the last eight months. The flame-haired virgin who'd shared a single night with him he could not forget, then fled the next morning before he could get her number— or even her last name! No woman had ever treated him so badly. She'd inflamed his blood, then disappeared like Cinderella, without so much as a damned glass slipper.

She was dressed completely in black. And barefoot? Her breasts overflowed the neckline of her dress. His gaze returned sharply to her belly. She couldn't be...

"Please, Vin, you have to help me," she choked out, her voice echoing against the cool gray stone. "My boss is trying to steal our baby!"

For a moment, Vin stared at her in shock, unable to comprehend her words.

Our baby?

Our?

There was a collective gasp as two thousand people turned to stare at him, waiting for his reaction.

Vin's body flashed hot, then cold as he felt all control— over the wedding, over his privacy, over his life—ripped from his grasp. Nearby, he saw the glower of Anne's red-faced father, saw her mother's shocked eyes. Fortunately he had no family of his own to disappoint.

He turned to his bride, expecting to see tears or at least agonized hurt, expecting to have to explain that he hadn't cheated on her, of course not, that this had all happened months before they'd met. But Anne's beautiful face was carefully blank.

"Excuse me," he said. "I need a moment."

"Take all the time you want."

Vin went slowly down the aisle toward Scarlett. The people watching from the pews seemed to fall away, their faces smearing into mere smudges of color.

His heart was pounding as he stopped in front of the woman he'd almost convinced himself didn't exist. Looking at her belly, he said in a low voice, "You're pregnant?"

She met his eyes. "Yes."

"The baby's mine?"

Her chin lifted. "You think I would lie?"

Vin remembered her soft gasp of pain when he'd first taken her, holding her virgin body so hot and hard and tight against his own in the darkness of his bedroom. Remembered how he'd kissed her tears away until her pain melted away to something very different…

"You couldn't have told me before now?" he bit out.

"I'm sorry," she whispered. "I didn't…" Then she glanced behind her, and her expression changed to fear.

Three men were striding up the aisle, the leader's face a mask of cold fury.

"There you are, you little…" He roughly grabbed Scarlett's wrist. "This is a private matter," he snarled at Vin, barely looking at him. "Return to your ceremony."

Vin almost did. It would have been easy to let them go. He felt the pressure of his waiting bride, of the pending merger, of her family, of the cathedral and the archbishop and the many guests, some of whom had flown around the world to be here. He could have told himself that Scarlett was lying and turned his back on her. He could have walked back to calmly speak the vows that would bind his life to Anne.

But something stopped him.

Maybe it was the man's iron-like grip on Scarlett's slender wrist. Or the way he and his two goons were dragging her back down the aisle, in spite of her helpless struggles. Maybe it was the panicked, stricken expression on her lovely face as all those wealthy, powerful guests silently watched, doing nothing to intervene.

Or maybe it was the ghost of his own memory, long repressed, of how it had once felt to be powerless and unloved, dragged from his only home against his will.

Whatever it was, Vin found himself doing something he hadn't done in a long, long time.

Getting involved.

"Stop right there," he ordered.

The other man's face snapped toward him. "Stay out of this."

Vin stalked toward him. "The lady doesn't want to leave with you."

"She's distraught. Not to mention crazy." The man, sleek and overfed as a Persian cat, yanked on her wrist. "I'm taking her to my psychiatrist. She's going to be locked away for a long, *long* time."

"No!" Scarlett whimpered. She looked up at Vin, her eyes shining with tears. "I'm not crazy. He used to be my boss. He's trying to force me to marry him and give our baby away."

Give our baby away.

The four words cut through Vin's heart like a knife. His whole body became still.

And he knew there was no way he was going to let this man take her.

His voice was ice-cold. "Let her go."

"You think you can make me?"

"Do you know my name?" Vin said quietly.

The man looked at him contemptuously. "I have no…" His voice trailed off, then he sucked in his breath. "Borgia." He exhaled the two syllables through his teeth. Vin saw the fear in the man's eyes. It was a reaction he'd grown accustomed to. "I…I didn't realize…"

Vin glanced at his own bodyguards, who'd entered the cathedral and surrounded the other men with surgical precision, ready to strike. He gave his chief of security a slight shake of his head, telling them to keep their distance. Then he looked at the man holding Scarlett. "Get. Out. Now."

He obeyed, abruptly releasing her. He turned and fled, his two bodyguards swiftly following him out of the cathedral.

Noise suddenly rose on all sides. Scarlett fell with a sob into Vin's arms, against the front of his tuxedo.

And a young man leaped up from a middle pew.

"Anne, I told you! Don't marry him! Who cares if you're disinherited?" Looking around the nave, the stranger proclaimed fiercely and loudly, "I've been sleeping with the bride for the last six months!"

Total chaos broke out then. The father of the bride started yelling, the mother of the bride wept noisily and, faced with such turmoil, the bride quietly and carefully fainted into a puffy heap of white tulle.

But Vin barely noticed. His world had shrunk to two things. Scarlett's tears as she wept in relief against his chest. And the tremble of her pregnant body, cradled beneath the protection of his arms.

CHAPTER TWO

OUT OF THE frying pan, into the fire.

Scarlett had escaped Blaise, but at what price?

For the last hour, she'd tried to calm the fearful beat of her heart as she sat in a faded floral chair next to a window overlooking a private garden. Vin had brought her to the private sitting room in the rectory behind the cathedral and told her to wait while he sorted things out. A kindly old lady—a housekeeper of some sort?—had pushed a hot cup of tea into her trembling hand.

But the tea had grown cold. She set the china cup into the saucer with a clatter.

Scarlett didn't know which scared her more. The memory of Blaise's snarling face. Or the fear of what Vin Borgia might do now to take over her future—and her baby's.

She should run.

She should run now.

Running was the only way to ensure their freedom.

Growing up, Scarlett had lived in over twenty different places, tiny towns hidden in forests and mountains, sometimes in shacks without electricity or running water. She'd rarely been able to go to school, and when she did, she'd had to dye her red hair brown and use a different name. Things that normal kids took for granted, such as having a real home, friends, going to the same school for a whole year, were luxuries Scarlett had only dreamed of. She'd never played sports, or sung in the school choir, or gone to prom. She'd never even gone on a real date.

Until she was twenty-four. The day she'd met Vin Borgia, she'd been weak, emotional, vulnerable. And he'd caught her up like a butterfly in a net.

She looked out the window with its view of the back garden, full of roses and ivy. A secret garden, surrounded by New York skyscrapers. A strangely calm, verdant place that seemed miles from the noisy traffic and honking cabs of Fifth Avenue. Rising to her feet, she started to pace.

A frosty gray afternoon last February, she'd been picking up a medicine prescription for Mrs. Falkner when she received a text from an old Boston friend of her father's with news that had staggered her.

Alan Berry had just died in an inconsequential knife fight in a Southie bar. The man who'd betrayed her father seventeen years before, who'd cut a deal for his own freedom and forced Harry Ravenwood to go on the run with his sick wife and young daughter, had died a meaningless death after a meaningless life. All for nothing.

Standing in the drugstore, Scarlett's knees had gone weak. She'd felt sick.

Five minutes later, she'd found herself at a dive bar across the street, ordering her first drink. The sharp pungent taste had made her cough.

"Let me guess." A low, amused voice had spoken from the red leather banquette in the corner. "It's your first time."

She'd turned. The man came out of the shadows slowly. Black eyes. Dark hair. Powerful broad shoulders. A black suit. Hard edges everywhere. Five-o'clock shadow. He was like a hero—or a handsome villain—from a movie, so masculine and powerful and handsome that he'd affected her even more than the vodka shot.

"I had a…bad day." Her voice trembled.

An ironic smile lifted the corners of his cruel, sensual mouth. "Why else would you be drinking in the afternoon?"

She wiped her eyes with a laugh. "For fun?"

"Fun. That's an idea." The man had come close enough to see her red-rimmed eyes and tear-streaked cheeks in the shadowy dive bar. She'd braced herself for questions, but he just slid onto the bar stool beside her and raised his hand to the bartender. "Let's see if the second shot goes down easier."

In spite of what she knew about him now, Vin Borgia still affected her like that. When Scarlett had seen him standing at the altar with his beautiful bride, all the memories had come back of their night together in February, when he'd taken her back to his elegant, Spartan, wildly expensive penthouse. He'd seduced her easily, claiming her virginity as if he owned it. He'd made her life explode with color and joy.

She'd known Vin's name, since his doorman had greeted him with the utmost respect as "Mr. Borgia." But she'd never told Vin her last name. Some habits were hard to break.

A phone call from Mrs. Falkner's nurse had woken Scarlett when Vin still slept. Only her sense of duty had forced her to wrench herself from the warmth of his bed. She'd returned to the Falkner mansion and handed over the prescription, then dreamily looked up her one and only lover online.

That had woken her up fast. She'd been horrified by what she found.

Vincenzo Borgia was a ruthless airline billionaire who'd risen from nothing and didn't give a damn who got hurt in his pursuit of world domination. She couldn't imagine why a man like that had seduced her, when he usually had liaisons with socialites and supermodels. But she was grateful she hadn't given him her last name. She wouldn't give him the chance to hurt her.

Later, when she'd discovered she was pregnant, she'd

wondered whether she'd made the right decision. But seeing Vin's engagement announcement in the paper had clinched it.

Scarlett had never expected to see Vin again. She'd planned to raise her baby alone.

She wasn't scared to be alone. She'd grown up on the run, and her fugitive father had secretly taught her skills after her mother got too sick to notice. How to pick pockets. How to pick locks. And most of all, how to be invisible and survive on almost nothing.

Compared to what she'd already lived through, raising a child as a single parent would be easy. She wasn't a fugitive. She'd never committed any crimes. She had a marketable skill as a nurse's aide. She'd even saved some money. She no longer had to hide.

Or did she?

Scarlett stopped pacing the thick rug of the cathedral rectory, staring blankly at the faded floral furniture. Did she really want to take the chance that Vin Borgia, the man she'd read such horrible things about, could be a good father? Did she dare take that risk, just because she'd loved her own father so much?

She could see the soft shimmer of dust motes through a beam of fading golden sunlight from the window. She put her hands gently on her belly.

Vin had saved her from Blaise, but rich, powerful men all had one thing in common: they wanted to be in control. And Vin Borgia was richer and more powerful than most.

She should just leave before he returned.

Right now.

Scarlett took a step, then stopped when she remembered her suitcase and handbag were still in Blaise's limo, with her money, ID, credit card, phone. When she'd fled him in terror, those had been the last thing on her mind. But now… How could she run with no money and no passport?

She looked down glumly at her bare toes snuggled into the plush rug. She didn't even have shoes!

"What's your name?"

She whirled to face the door. Vin had entered the room, his jaw like granite as he loosened his tie. Just looking at his hard-muscled body caused a physical reaction in her, made her tremble from the inside out, with a mixture of fear and desire. Even the sleekly tailored tuxedo couldn't give him the look of a man who was entirely civilized. Especially with that hard, almost savage look in his black eyes.

She swallowed. "You know my name. Scarlett."

He glowered at her. "Your *last* name."

"Smith," she tried.

Vin's jaw tightened. Turning away, he picked up a carafe of water sitting on a tray on a nearby table. He poured water into one of the glasses. "Your last name is Ravenwood."

Her lips parted in shock. "How did you—"

Reaching into his jacket pocket, he held up her wallet, his handsome face impassive.

"How did you get that?"

"Falkner sent your purse to me. And your suitcase."

"*Sent?* You mean he dumped them in the street?"

"I mean his bodyguards personally brought them to me, neatly stacked, with his compliments."

Oh, this was so much worse than she'd feared. Scarlett breathed, "The worst man I know is afraid of you?"

He smiled grimly. "It's not unusual." He held her wallet out toward her. "Here. Seventeen dollars cash and a single credit card. With an eight-hundred-dollar limit."

"Hey!" She snatched at it. Her cheeks burned. "How do you know my credit limit?"

Picking up his glass, Vin swirled the clear water thoughtfully. "I wanted to know what I was dealing with.

An orphan who never lived anywhere for long, who came to New York for a thankless live-in job, who saved every penny for two years, who made no new friends, who worked all the time and never went out." He tilted his head, looking at her with heavily lidded black eyes as he murmured, "With one memorable exception."

A flash of heat went through her, then cold. She couldn't think about that night. Not now. "You have some nerve to—"

"The Falkners barely paid minimum wage, but you saved every penny you could. Impressive work ethic, considering your jailbird father—"

"Don't you dare call him that!" she shouted. "My dad was the kindest, best man who ever lived!"

"Are you serious?" Vin's lips curved. "He was a bank robber who became a fugitive and dragged you and your mother into a life on the run. You had no money, barely went to school, and your mother died of an illness that she might perhaps have survived with proper care. What am I missing?"

"Stop judging him," she raged. "My father gave up that life when I was a baby. But a friend of his convinced him to try for one last score. After my mother found out, she gave him an ultimatum. He gave the money back to the bank!"

"Just gave it back, hmm?"

"He left the bags of money outside the police station, then tipped them off with an anonymous call."

"Why didn't he turn himself in?"

"Because he didn't want to leave my mom. Or me." Scarlett took a deep breath. "We would have been fine, except Alan Berry was caught spending his own share of the money six months later and threw my father under the bus as the supposed mastermind of the crime! After he'd tried to do the right thing—"

"The right thing would have been for your father to turn himself in at the start," Vin said mercilessly, "instead of waiting ten years to find the courage, and dragging you and your mother through such a miserable life on the run." He calmly took a sip of water. "The only truly decent thing your father ever did was die in that plane crash after he got out of prison. Giving you that tidy multimillion-dollar settlement offered by the airline."

Scarlett nearly staggered to her knees at his easy reference to the greatest loss of her life, one that still left her grief-stricken every day—her father's sudden death, along with thirty other people, in a plane crash a year and a half before, as he was coming to New York to see her, finally free after five years in a medium-security prison.

Vin looked at her curiously. "You gave all that money away." He tilted his head. "Why?"

She was so shocked, it took her a moment to find her voice. In mere minutes, Vin Borgia had casually ripped through her privacy and exposed all the secrets of her life.

"I didn't want their blood money," she whispered. "I gave it to charity."

"Yes, I know. Cancer research, legal defense for the poor and help for children of incarcerated parents. All fine causes. But I don't understand why you'd choose to be penniless."

"Like you said, maybe I'm used to it. Anyway." She clutched her wallet. "Some things matter more than money."

"Like a baby?" Vin said coldly. He put the glass down with a *thunk* on the wooden table. "You let me seduce you and take your virginity, then snuck out while I slept. You never bothered to contact me. You waited until my wedding to spring the news on me that you were pregnant."

"I had no choice—"

"There were plenty of choices." His jaw tightened. "Tell

me the truth. If Falkner hadn't threatened you today, you never would have told me about the baby, would you?"

She stared at him for a long moment, then shook her head.

"Why?" he demanded.

The warmth from the cathedral garden was failing. Scarlett glanced at the fading afternoon light, now turning gray. She didn't answer.

"You refused to even tell me your last name that night. Why?" he pressed, coming closer. "Was it because you were also encouraging Falkner's attentions?"

"I never did!" She gaped at him. "I knew he wanted me, but I never thought he'd attack me while giving me a ride from his mother's funeral!"

"Ah. That explains the black dress." He looked down at her pale pink toenails. "But why are you barefoot?"

"I kicked off my shoes running on Fifth Avenue. I knew your wedding was here today." She looked down. "I'm sorry I ruined it."

"Yes. Well." His jaw tightened as he said grudgingly, "I suppose I should thank you."

"You didn't know your bride was cheating on you?"

"She convinced me she was a virgin and wanted to wait for marriage."

A laugh rose to her lips. "You thought she was a virgin? In this day and age?"

"Why not?" he said coldly. "You were."

Their eyes met, and Scarlett's body flooded with heat. Against her will, memories filled her of that night, of being in his arms, in his bed, his body hard and hot and slick against hers. She tried to smile. "Yeah, but I'm not normal."

"Agreed." His dark gaze seared hers. "Am I really the father of your baby, Scarlett? Or were you lying just because you needed my help?"

"Of course the baby's yours!"

He bared his teeth into a smile. "I will find out if it's not true."

"You're the only man I've ever slept with, so I'm pretty sure!"

"The only man? Ever?" For a moment, something stretched between them. Then it snapped. "So what do you want from me now? Money?"

She glared at him. "Just point me in the direction of my suitcase and I'll be on my way!"

"You're not going anywhere until this is sorted."

"Look, I'm deeply grateful for your help with Blaise, and sorry if I ruined your big wedding day, but I don't appreciate you digging into my life, then assuming that I'm either a con artist or a gold digger. I'm neither. I just want to raise my baby in peace."

"There will be a DNA test," he warned. "Lawyers."

She looked at him in horror. "Lawyers? What for?"

"So we both know where we stand."

Scarlett felt a *whoosh* of panic that made her unsteady on her feet. Her voice trembled. "You mean you intend to sue me for custody?"

"That will not be necessary." She exhaled in relief, before he finished, "Because once I have proof the baby's mine, Scarlett, you will marry me."

With those words, Vin took control over the spinning chaos of the day.

He'd been wrong about Anne Dumaine. He'd convinced himself she was modest and demure when all the while she'd been cheating on him and lying to his face. To say she'd turned out to be a disappointment was an understatement.

"Sorry," she'd whispered the last time he'd seen her, when she'd pressed the ten-carat engagement ring into his palm. But she hadn't looked sorry as she'd joyfully turned to her lover—a boy of maybe twenty-three, ridiculously shabby in a sweater, and they'd fled the cathedral hand in hand, Anne's wedding veil flying behind her like a white flag.

Leaving Vin to face the annoyed glower of her father. "If you'd bothered to show my daughter the slightest attention, she wouldn't have fallen for that nobody!"

The merger with Transatlantique was clearly off.

Vin's mistake. He'd never bothered to look beyond Anne's cool blonde exterior into her soul. Truthfully, her soul hadn't interested him. But he should have had his investigators check her more thoroughly. *Trust no one* had been his motto since he was young. Trust no one; control everything.

Scarlett Ravenwood was different. She didn't have the education or pedigree of Anne, her manners were lamentable and she had no dress sense. Her only dowry would be the child she carried inside her.

A baby. His baby. After his own awful childhood, he'd decided long ago that any child of his would always know his father, would have a stable home and feel safe and loved. Vin would never abandon his child. He'd die first.

Standing in the shabby room of the rectory, surrounded by chintzy overstuffed furniture, Vin looked at Scarlett, so vivid with her pale skin and red hair.

The dark sweeping lashes over her green eyes, the color of every spring and summer of his Italian childhood, seemed to tremble. When he'd first seen her in that bar nearly eight months ago, right before Valentine's Day, coughing over her first taste of vodka, it had been like a burst of sun after a long cold night, a sunrise as bright and red as her hair, filling him with warmth—and fire.

His mind moved rapidly. She had no fortune, but perhaps that was an advantage. No father-in-law to scream in his ear. No family to become a burden. She had nothing to offer him but their baby. And her sexy body. And the best lovemaking of his life.

He shivered just remembering that night…

It was, he reflected, not the worst way to begin a marriage. He could make of her what he wanted. She could be the perfect wife, made to his order. She had no money. She was grateful to him for saving her from that imbecile Falkner. He already had complete control.

Now she just had to realize that, as well.

"You want to marry me?" Scarlett repeated, staring at him in shock. "Seriously?"

"Yes." He waited for her to be suitably thrilled. Instead, she burst into laughter.

"Are you crazy? I'm not marrying you!"

"If the baby is mine, it is our only reasonable course of action," he said stiffly.

As if he'd told her the best joke in the world, she shook her head merrily. "You really don't want to lose your wedding deposit, do you?"

"What are you talking about?"

"Am I expected to just put on your last bride's wedding gown, and you'll let the guests know there's been a slight change in the lineup? You'll just change the color of the bride's hair on the cake topper from blond to red, and proceed as planned?"

"You think I'd marry you to avoid losing a little money?" he said incredulously.

"No?" She tilted her head, on a roll now, clearly enjoying herself. "Then what is it? Is marriage just on your schedule, and you need to check it off your to-do list before you pick up your dry cleaning and pay your electric bill?"

"Scarlett, I get the feeling you're not taking this seriously."

"I'm not!" she exploded. "Why on earth would I marry you? I barely know you!"

Vin felt irritated at her irrational response, but he reminded himself that she was pregnant, and therefore to be treated gently. "You've had a trying day," he said in the most soothing voice he could muster. "We should go to my doctor."

"Why?"

"Just to check you're doing fine. And we'll get the paternity test."

"You can't just take my word the baby's yours?"

"You could obviously be lying."

For some reason, she seemed upset by this. She glared at him. "I'm not doing some stupid paternity test, not if it causes risk to the baby—"

"The doctor just draws a little blood from your arm and mine. There's no risk to the baby whatsoever."

"How do you know that?"

Vin didn't care to explain the sordid story of the one-night stand who last February had tried to claim her baby was his, even though he'd used a condom and she'd claimed to be on the pill. It had turned out the DNA test was unnecessary as she wasn't pregnant at all. She'd just hoped he would marry her and she'd get quickly pregnant—and he'd be too stupid to do the math. That experience had left him cold.

It was ironic that after confronting that one-night stand over her lies, he'd stopped for a drink in a new bar—and, meeting Scarlett, they'd ended up conceiving a child.

Looking at Scarlett now, he felt his body tighten. She had no right to look so lovely, her riotous red curls tumbling over her shoulders, her eyes so wistful and luminous, her lips so naturally full and pink. Her breasts strained the modest neckline of the simple black dress, and her large baby bump made her even more voluptuous, more sexy.

Pregnant. With his baby.

If it was true, he would devote his life to giving this baby a very different childhood than he'd had. His child would always be safe, and loved. Unlike Vin, his child would always know who his father was.

If her child was even his, he reminded himself. She could be lying. He needed proof. He held out his hand. "Let's go."

With visible reluctance, she put her hand in his. "If I go with you to the doctor, and you get proof you're the father, then what?"

"I'll have my lawyers draw up a prenuptial agreement."

"A pre-nup?" Her voice sounded surprised. "Why?"

He gave a grim smile. "I can hardly marry you without control."

"Control of what?"

"Everything," he said honestly.

He led her through the now empty cathedral, with only rapidly wilting wedding flowers and a few despondent janitors sweeping up. Her voice trembled as she asked, "What specifically would be in the pre-nup?"

"Standard things." He shrugged. "Giving me final say on schooling and religion and where we will live. Things like that. I am based in New York but have homes all over. I am often required to travel while running SkyWorld Airways, sometimes for months at a time. I would not want to be away from my children."

"*Children?* I'm not carrying twins."

"Obviously, our child will need siblings." She made a sound like a squeak, but he ignored her, continuing, "I expect you to travel with me whenever and wherever I wish."

Her forehead furrowed. "But how would I hold down a job?"

"Money will no longer be an issue. As my wife, your only requirement will be to support me. You will be in society. You will learn to properly entertain powerful people to promote my company's best interests. You may need comportment lessons."

"What?"

"And, of course," he added casually, "in the event we ever divorce, the pre-nup will simplify that process. It will clearly spell out what happens if you cheat on me, or either of us decides to separate. You'll know what amount of money you'll be entitled to based on years—"

"Of service?"

He smiled blandly. "Of marriage, I was going to say. Naturally, I would automatically gain full custody of our children."

"What?!"

"Don't worry. You would still be allowed to visit them."

"Big of you," she murmured. As they walked down the cathedral steps to his waiting car, his bodyguards waiting beside the large SUV behind it, Scarlett abruptly stopped.

"Before we go to your doctor and have the paternity test, could you do me a favor?" She smiled prettily, showing a dimple in her left cheek, then waved helplessly at her bare feet on the sidewalk. "Could we stop at a shoe store?"

Like Cinderella, Vin thought. He was surprised how well she was taking everything. The way she was looking at him so helplessly, so prettily. She would be easy to mold and shape into the perfect wife.

"Of course," he said almost tenderly. "I'm sorry. I should have thought of that before." Picking her up in his arms, he carried her. In spite of being heavily pregnant, she seemed to weigh nothing at all. He gently set her into the waiting car, still bedecked with flowers.

The driver's eyes were popping out of his head to see Vin had left the church carrying a redhead, when he'd gone in to marry a blonde. But he wisely said nothing and just started the car.

Vin climbed into the backseat beside her. "Any preference about the shoe store?"

He expected her to name a designer store, the sorts of luxury brands that Anne had constantly yammered about, but here again Scarlett surprised him.

"Any shoes good to run in," she said demurely, her black eyelashes fluttering against her pale cheeks.

"You heard her," he told his driver.

Ten minutes later, Scarlett was trying on running shoes at an enormous athletic store on Fifty-Seventh Street. She chose her favorite pair of running shoes, along with a pair of socks, exclaiming at Vin's generosity all the while.

"Thank you," she whispered, suddenly giving him a hug. For a moment, he closed his eyes. He could smell the peppermint of her breath and breathed in the cherry blossom scent of her hair. Then she abruptly pulled back. Staring up at him wide-eyed, she bit her lip. Vin could imagine the sensual caress of those full, plump lips.

Then she smiled, and her eyes crinkled. "I'll wear the shoes starting now. Excuse me."

Vin watched her walk toward the ladies' restroom, past the displays of expensive athletic shoes and equipment. His eyes lingered appreciatively over the curve of her backside, the sway of her hips. Scarlett made even a plain black funeral dress look good.

What a wife she would make. And as for the honeymoon…he shuddered.

Determined to hurry them into the car, he turned toward the cashier. Normally his assistant would have dealt with such mundane details, but he'd left Ernest at the cathedral to handle the logistical problems of the ruined wedding—returning mailed gifts, organizing early rides to the airport for disgruntled guests, donating the expensively catered reception dinner to a local homeless shelter. So Vin himself went to pay for the shoes.

There would soon be lots of other purchases, he thought. Baby booties. A crib. A nursery. He'd have his houses baby-proofed. He'd hire a larger staff. He would buy a few more family-sized SUVs to add to his personal fleet of expensive cars. Small tasks that would distract him from building his empire, but it would be worth it to finally have a family of his own.

He'd be the parent he himself had never had. His child would never know what it felt like to be abandoned. To be used. To be neglected and alone.

Reaching into his tuxedo jacket, Vin felt for his wallet. Frowning, he looked in his pockets. Empty. Had he left it in the car, or back at the cathedral? Scowling, he motioned for one of his bodyguards to pay and told the other one to track down the wallet. Sitting down at a nearby bench, Vin called his doctor to arrange for an immediate appointment. Then he tapped his feet.

Scarlett was taking a long time.

"Go check on her," he ordered his bodyguard impatiently.

Vin paced. Checked his phone again. Stopped.

Suspicion dawned.

She couldn't. She wouldn't.

She had.

"Miss Ravenwood is nowhere to be found, boss," Larson said when he returned. "I had the bathroom checked. Empty." He hesitated. "There is a door beside it that leads to a storeroom, then out to the alley."

With a low curse, Vin strode through the sporting goods store, his two bodyguards behind him. In the back, near the ladies' restroom, he found the storeroom. Store employees shrank back at his glare as he threw open the back door with an angry bang.

Outside was an alley with graffiti-littered brick walls. Vin walked slowly past the Dumpsters to the end: busy

Madison Avenue, crowded with people and cars packed bumper to bumper. He stared around him in shock.

Scarlett Ravenwood had not only walked out on him, she'd most likely stolen his wallet. Not only that, she'd warned him first! "Shoes good to run in" indeed!

Clawing his hand back through his dark hair, he gave a single, incredulous laugh. He'd been ditched twice in one day. Lied to by two different women.

Anne's loss he could accept. That had involved only money.

Scarlett was different. He'd never stopped desiring her. And now she was carrying his baby.

Or was she? Perhaps she'd lied. He rubbed his forehead. Why would any woman run away when he'd asked her to marry him and live in luxury for the rest of her life? Unless she was afraid of the paternity test. That was the only rational explanation: the baby wasn't his. The thought caused a sick twist in his gut.

Then he remembered the angry gleam in Scarlett's green eyes.

I don't appreciate you digging into my life, then assuming that I'm either a con artist or a gold digger. I'm neither. I just want to raise my baby in peace.

Standing motionless as pedestrians rushed by him on Madison Avenue, Vin narrowed his eyes.

Either way, he had to know.

Either way, he'd find her.

And this time, she wouldn't trick him so easily. Nothing would stop him from getting what he wanted. He wouldn't listen to her excuses. Next time, he'd bend her to his will.

Barefoot, if necessary.

CHAPTER THREE

THERE WAS ONLY one thing that mattered in life, Scarlett's father had always told her as a child. Freedom.

Freedom. It was Harry Ravenwood's rallying cry every time their family had to flee in the night, tossing their belongings into black trash bags and heading blindly to a new city. At seven years old, when Scarlett accidentally left her teddy bear—her only friend—behind, she'd cried until her father comforted her with stories of Mr. Teddy backpacking around the world, climbing the Pyramids and the Pyrenees. His funny stories of her bear's adventures finally made her smile through her tears. On cold winter nights in Upstate New York, as their family shivered in unheated rooms and icy wind rattled the windows, Harry sang jaunty songs about freedom.

Freedom. Even on the bleak night when Scarlett was twelve, when her mother died in the emergency room of a hospital in a faded factory town in Pennsylvania, her father kissed Scarlett as tears streamed down his weathered face. "At least now your beautiful mother is free of pain."

Scarlett had her freedom now. From Blaise Falkner. From Vin Borgia. She and her unborn baby were free.

But it had come at a cost.

To start with, her flight two weeks ago, from Boston to London, had had a little trouble over the Atlantic.

A small fire in the cargo hold caused the plane to divert to a small airport on the west coast of Ireland. As the plane descended, she saw dark clusters of birds through her porthole window, flying rapidly past the plane. "Bird strike!" a passenger cried out, and as one flight attendant rushed toward the cockpit, another tried to murmur reassuring, unconvincing words to the passengers. Wide-eyed, Scarlett gripped her armrests as she felt the plane ominously vibrate and groan in midair.

All she'd been able to think was, she shouldn't be on this plane. Pregnant women weren't supposed to fly after their seventh month. She was nearly at eight. She'd fled from New York, with a quick stop in Boston, because she thought it was her only way to escape Vin. But now that danger seemed small when she and her child were both going to die. Just like her own father had died in that wintry plane crash a year and a half ago. *She never should have gotten on a plane.*

"Prepare for crash landing," came the pilot's terse voice over the intercom. "Brace for impact." The flight attendants repeated the words as the nose of the plane started to plummet and they rushed to buckle themselves in. "Heads down! Brace for impact! Stay down!"

Scarlett had braced herself, hugging her belly, thinking, *please don't let my baby die.*

Like a miracle, the plane had finally steadied on one engine and limped hard, landing with a heavy bang on the edge of the runway. No one was hurt, and passengers and crew alike cheered and cried and hugged each other.

Sliding off the plane on the inflatable yellow slide, Scarlett had fallen to her knees on the tarmac and burst into noisy, ugly sobs.

She never should have gotten on a plane. Any plane. After her father's death, she should have known better.

But just like when she'd accepted that limo ride from Blaise Falkner, she'd ignored her intuition and convinced herself that her fears were silly. And both she and her baby had nearly died as a result.

She'd never ignore her intuition again. From now on,

she'd listen seriously to her fears, even when they didn't make rational sense.

And above all: she would never, ever get on any plane again.

But why would Scarlett need to? She had no family in New York. No reason to ever go back. Vin Borgia had done her a huge favor, warning her in advance that he intended to rule her life and their child's with an iron fist and separate her from her baby if she ever objected or tried to leave him. She didn't feel guilty about leaving him, not at all.

She did feel guilty about stealing his wallet. Stealing was never all right, and her mother must be turning over in her grave. Scarlett told herself she'd had no choice. She'd had to cover her tracks. Vin was not only a ruthless billionaire, he owned an airline and had ridiculous connections. If she'd stepped one toe on a flight under her own name, he would have known about it.

So she'd contacted one of her father's old acquaintances in Boston to buy a fake passport. That cost money.

So she'd taken—borrowed—the money from Vin. She hadn't touched anything else in his wallet. Not his driver's license, or his credit cards, most of them in special strange colors that no doubt had eye-popping credit limits. And after she'd arrived safely in Switzerland via ferry and train from Ireland, and gotten her first paycheck at her new job, she'd mailed back Vin's wallet, returning everything as he'd left it. She'd even tossed in some extra euros as interest on the money she'd borrowed.

She'd gotten the euros from northern Italy, where she'd gone to mail back the package. She could hardly have sent Vin money in Swiss francs, letting him know where she was!

But that was all behind her now. She'd paid everything back. She and her baby were free.

Scarlett took a deep breath of the clear Alpine air. She'd been in Gstaad for over two weeks now, and finally, *finally* she was starting to relax. She just had to hope when Vin couldn't easily find her, he would forget about her and the baby, and she'd never have to worry about him again.

Scarlett passed out of the gates of the chalet, if the place could be called a chalet when it was the size of a palace, and turned her face up toward the sun.

It was mid-October, and the morning air was already frosty in the mountains around the elegant Swiss ski resort of Gstaad. The first snowfall was expected daily.

She had her own event to expect soon, too. Her hand moved over her belly, grown so large she could no longer button up her oversize jacket. Only two and a half weeks from her due date. Her body felt heavier, slower. But luckily her new job allowed plenty of opportunity for gentle morning walks.

She'd been lucky to get this job. When she'd fled the shoe store in New York, racing down the alley to hail a cab on Madison Avenue, she'd already decided exactly where to go. Her mother's best friend, Wilhelmina Stone, worked as housekeeper to a wealthy European tycoon in Switzerland. Though Scarlett hadn't seen her since her mother's funeral, she'd never forgotten the woman's hug and fierce words, "Your mother was my best friend. If you ever need anything, you come straight to me, you hear?"

Since then, she'd gotten only an occasional Christmas card. But when Scarlett had shown up uninvited and shivering at the gate of the enormous villa outside Gstaad, the plump, kindly woman had proved good as her word.

"My boss just asked me to hire a good cook for ski season. The best Southern cook in the US, he said. Can you make grits and fried chicken? Jambalaya? Dirty rice?"

Eyes wide, Scarlett shook her head. Wilhelmina sighed. "All right, he usually starts coming here in early December, after the season starts. So you've got six weeks, maybe more, to learn how to make amazing fried chicken and all the rest. I'll put you on staff payroll now. Just make sure you learn to cook for groups of ten or more, because Mr. Black always brings friends!"

For the last two weeks, Scarlett had been trying to teach herself to cook, using cookbooks and internet videos. She was still pretty bad. The security guard routinely teased her that even his dog wouldn't eat what she cooked. It was sadly true.

But she would learn. Being a specialty chef for a hard-traveling, hard-partying tycoon who was rarely around was the perfect job for any single mother with a newborn. She would be able to take a week or two off to heal after the birth, then work with her baby nearby, almost as if this were her own home.

Plus, Switzerland was the perfect place to raise a baby. Scarlett tucked her hands in her jacket pockets as she walked along the slender road. Gravel crunched beneath her soft boots as she took a deep breath of crisp mountain air smelling of sunlight and pine trees. For a brief moment, she closed her eyes, turning her face to the sun. Her heart was full of gratitude.

Then she heard a snap in the forest ahead of her.

She opened her eyes, and the smile dropped from her face.

"Scarlett," Vin greeted her coldly.

He stood ahead of her, wearing a long black coat, a sleek dark suit and a glower. She saw a sleek sports car and a black SUV parked on the road behind him. Three bodyguards lined the vehicle, an impenetrable wall of money and power.

She stumbled back from him. He was on her in seconds, grabbing her wrist.

"Don't touch me!" she cried.

His grip tightened, his eyes like black fire. "You stole from me."

"I paid all your money back—with interest!" She glanced back desperately toward the guarded gate, but it was too far. Johan would never see her. And how could one security guard take on Vin Borgia and at least three of his men?

"I wasn't just talking about the money."

She put her free hand protectively over her belly. "You're not my baby's father. I—I lied!"

"I think you're lying now."

Scarlett tried to pull her wrist from his grip. "Leave me alone!"

"I do not understand your behavior." He wrenched her closer. "Most women would find it fortunate to be pregnant by a billionaire."

"A billionaire who destroys people?" She shook her head. "You don't just take companies—you ruthlessly crush and annihilate your rivals. Their marriages, their families, their very lives!"

Silence fell in the Swiss forest. The only sound was the call of birds.

Then he spoke, his voice low and flat. "So you did some digging on the internet, did you?"

"Why do you think I never tried to contact you after our night together?" She took a deep breath. "I had a good reason to leave you that first morning. A nurse called and I was needed at the Falkner mansion. I hoped to see you again. Until I looked you up online." She glared at him. "If you think I'm going to let my precious baby be raised by a man who takes pleasure in other people's pain—"

His lip twisted contemptuously. "If you think I'm such a bastard, why did you ask for my help?"

"I was terrified of Blaise."

"And now you're terrified of me?"

"After I interrupted your wedding, I thought maybe I should give you a chance. My own father wasn't perfect, but I loved him." She narrowed her eyes. "Then you made your intentions clear."

"What are you talking about? My intention to take responsibility, marry you and be a good father?"

"If I honestly believed we could be a family, and love and trust each other, I'd marry you in a second. But I'd rather raise my baby alone than with a man who might hurt me!"

"Hurt you?" he said incredulously. "I've never hurt a woman in my life!"

"With your cold heart? I bet you've hurt plenty."

He relaxed. "Oh. You mean *emotionally*."

"Yes, emotionally," she retorted. "You don't think that counts?"

"Not really, no."

"And that's why I don't want to marry you."

He abruptly released her wrist, his eyes strangely alight. "I've never killed anyone, no matter what the rumors say. I never poisoned someone or sabotaged an engine. Nor did I hire someone else to do it. A reporter just happened to notice that during some points in my business career, some men have coincidentally had problems."

"You expect me to believe that? It was pure coincidence?"

"It's the truth. A man was discovered in an affair while doing business with me. It was hardly my fault his wife took offense and dumped poison in his morning whiskey. Another man had a heart attack from stress during my hostile takeover. He could have walked away at any time but chose to fight and take the risk. Another man chose to start a feud with his sister when she sold her shares to me. Their family was ripped apart, yes—but again, not my fault."

"Then why was Blaise so afraid of you? And you expected him to be!"

"I know the rumors about me. They're not true, but people believe them. I'd be a fool not to take advantage of it."

"And you're no fool."

"No." His jaw tightened. "So I don't appreciate that you've made me look like one. Twice."

She turned her head back again toward the distant gate of the chalet. She wished she could run. But she'd become so heavily pregnant and slow—

"I want a paternity test," Vin said coldly. "You have an appointment today with a doctor in Geneva."

"I've got my own doctor in the village, thank you."

"Dr. Schauss has a world-renowned clinic. She was obstetrician to a princess of Sweden and has delivered half the babies of the royal houses of the Persian Gulf. She's well qualified."

"I'm not gallivanting off to Geneva just because you want some extra-fancy doctor."

"The choice isn't yours to make."

"And if I refuse?"

Vin's eyes flickered. "I am acquainted with Kassius Black, the owner of this chalet." He looked up at the imposing roofline over the trees. "What would he say if I told him that your friend, his trusted housekeeper, had knowingly hired a fugitive and thief to live here, and you were both conspiring to steal from his houseguests this coming ski season?"

"You wouldn't," she gasped. "It's not true!"

He shrugged. "You are a proven thief and liar. It *could* be true. But the point is, are you willing to repay your friend's kindness in giving you a job by causing her to lose hers?"

"You are despicable."

His face hardened. "No, *cara*. You are despicable. I

have done nothing but seek to fulfill my responsibility. I am trying to do the right thing, the honorable thing. It is you who are the thief."

"I repaid every penny!"

"Yes, with interest. At an annualized interest rate of thirty percent. The money you repaid yielded a better return than many of my other investments. So it was profitable." He gave a slight, ironic bow. "Thank you for stealing my wallet."

"Oh?" she said hopefully. "So you're not—"

"Stealing my child is something else."

Scarlett's brief hope faded. What could she do? She couldn't let Wilhelmina be hurt for her loyalty and kindness.

The clinic in Geneva. That could be her escape route. Clinics had back doors. She could sneak out before her blood was even drawn.

Scarlett let her shoulders sag, scuffling her feet in the gravel, hoping she looked suitably downhearted. Her heart was beating fast. "You win."

"I always do." He gave a quick motion to the bodyguards waiting outside the black SUV with dark tinted windows, then turned back, his voice brisk. "The trip to Geneva will take two hours by car, and in your state of advanced pregnancy I am concerned this will be uncomfortable for you. I can have a helicopter here in ten minutes—"

"No!" she said a little too quickly. At his frown, she said in a calmer voice, trying to smile, "The drive will give us a chance to talk. It's so beautiful around Lake Geneva this time of year."

He stared at her for a long moment, then shrugged. "As you wish."

Five minutes later, as a bodyguard went upstairs to pack up her meager possessions, she went to the kitchen to say farewell to Wilhelmina. The older woman seemed bewildered by the sudden turn in events.

"You're quitting your job, Scarlett? Just like that?"

"I'm sorry, Wilhelmina. You came through for me, and I'm leaving you in the lurch. I'm so sorry—"

"For me it's fine. Honestly, your fried chicken still is something awful. Mr. Black would have thought I lost my mind, hiring you. You're the one I'm worried about." She looked doubtfully at Vin. "So this man is the father of your baby, but do you really want to go with him?" Her eyes narrowed in her plump face. "Or is he forcing you?"

The suspicion in the older woman's face was less than flattering to Vin, but as she was a housekeeper to Kassius Black, a man whose reputation for ferocity was even worse than his own, he could understand her lack of automatic admiration for the average billionaire. The housekeeper, like Scarlett, had obviously had enough experience with the wealthy to know the ugliness that could lie behind the glamorous lifestyle.

"I will take good care of Scarlett and her baby," he told her gravely. "I promise you."

The housekeeper stared at him, then her scowl slowly disappeared. "I believe you."

"Good." Vin gave her his most charming smile. "We intend to marry soon."

She looked accusingly at Scarlett. "You're engaged?"

Scarlett looked a little dazed. "We haven't decided anything for sure…"

"Mrs. Stone," Vin interrupted, "I appreciate your loyalty and kindness to Scarlett. Should you ever want to switch jobs, please let us know."

Handing her a card, he took Scarlett by the hand and led her out of the chalet as the bodyguards followed with her shockingly small amount of luggage: a purse and a single duffel bag. He watched as they packed it into the back of the glossy SUV. An unwelcome image floated through Vin's mind of his own meager belongings when he'd left Italy at fifteen, after his mother's devastating revelation and death, to go live in New York with an uncle he barely knew. He'd felt so alone. So hollow.

He pushed the memory away angrily. He wasn't that boy anymore. He would never feel so vulnerable again—and neither would any child of his.

Vin opened the passenger door of the red sports car, then turned to Scarlett coldly. "Get in."

"You're driving us? Yourself?"

"The bodyguards will follow in the SUV. Like you said—" he gave a hard smile "—it's a beautiful day for a drive."

Once they were buckled in, he stepped on the gas, driving swiftly out of the gate and down the mountain, to the paved road that led through the expensive village of Gstaad, with its charming Alpine architecture, exclusive designer boutiques and chalets with shutters and flower boxes. The midmorning sun glowed in the blue sky above craggy forested mountains as they looped onto the Gstaadstrasse, heading west.

Vin glanced at Scarlett out of the corner of his eye. She was dressed very casually, an unbuttoned jacket over an oversize shirt, loose khaki pants and fur-lined booties. But for all that, his eyes hungrily drank in the sight of her. Her flame-red hair fell in thick curls down her shoulders. Her lustrous eyes were green as an Alpine forest. He could remember how it had felt to have those full, pink lips move against his skin, gasping in ecstasy...

He shuddered.

Why did Scarlett have such power over him?

For the last two weeks, since she'd left him standing on Madison Avenue with a stunned look on his face, he'd thought of nothing else. All of his considerable resources had been dedicated to one task: finding her.

She was in his blood. He hadn't been able to forget her. Not from the first moment he'd seen her in that bar. From the moment he'd first taken her in his arms. From the moment she'd disappeared from his bed after the best sex of his life.

From the moment she'd violently crashed his wedding and told him she was pregnant with his baby.

Scarlett Ravenwood was half angel, half demon. There was a reason he hadn't seduced any other woman for over eight months—an eternity for a man like Vin. He'd been haunted by Scarlett, haunted body and soul, driven half mad by memories of her naked in his arms.

Scarlett was the woman for him. The one he wanted. And he intended to have her.

"How did you find me in Switzerland?" she asked him quietly now.

Lifting his eyebrow, Vin focused on the road ahead. "It was a mistake for you to mail my wallet from a small Italian village. I still have connections in that country. It was easy to track down the *postino* who'd helped you. He remembered seeing your car with Swiss plates."

"He noticed my car?"

He smiled grimly. "There are surprisingly few Swiss registrations of a 1970 Plymouth Hemi Cuda convertible in pale green. The *postino* kissed his lips when he described it. *'Bella macchina.'* He remembered you, too, a pregnant redheaded woman, very beautiful but a tragic driver. He thought the car deserved better."

"I chose that car from the chalet's garage because I thought it was the oldest," she said, sounding dazed, "so figured it was the cheapest."

"They're rare and often sell for two or three million dollars."

"Oh," she said faintly. "So if I'd taken the brand-new sedan…"

"I wouldn't have found you." Gripping the steering wheel, he looked at her. "You keep wondering if I'm trustworthy. I could wonder the same about you, except I've seen the answer. You've lied to my face, stolen my wallet. Kidnapped my child—"

"Kidnapped!"

"What else would you call it?" He looked at her. "How do I know our baby will be safe with you? The criminally minded daughter of a felon?"

"Felon!" Fury filled her green eyes. "My father never should have gone to prison. If his accomplice hadn't betrayed him—"

"Spare me the excuses," Vin said, sounding bored. "He was a bank robber."

"He returned all the money. Can you say the same?"

"What are you talking about?"

"I'm talking about you and Blaise Falkner and every other billionaire—you are the real ones who should be…"

She abruptly cut herself off.

"Go on," Vin said evenly. "You were about to accuse me of something?"

Scarlett looked him straight in the eye. "Every rich man I've ever known was heartless. My dad in his worst year was less a thief than all the corporate embezzlers and Wall Street gamblers with their Ponzi schemes, wiping out people's pension funds, their savings, their hope!"

"You're comparing me to them?"

"You wouldn't sacrifice one of your platinum cuff links—" she glanced contemptuously at his wrist "—let alone risk your life or happiness, to save someone else."

"You don't know that."

"Don't I?" She lifted her chin. Through the car window he could see the gray-and-blue shimmer of Lake Geneva behind her. "You told me yourself. You don't think twice about causing emotional pain. I bet you've never loved anyone in your life. And you asked me to marry you!"

"Love isn't necessary."

"That's a screwed-up way of looking at things. That's like saying there's no point in eating things that taste good. Marriage without love, isn't that like eating gruel for the rest of your life? Why eat gruel when you can eat cake?"

"Cake is an illusion. It all turns out to be gruel in the end."

"That's the saddest thing I ever heard." She shook her head. "I feel bad for you. A billionaire who's content to eat gruel for the rest of his life."

Vin could hardly believe this penniless girl who had nothing and had once stolen his wallet actually felt sorry for him. "Better a hard truth than the sweet comfort of lies."

"No, it's worse than that. You're a cynic who claims not to believe in the existence of love." She looked up at him through dark eyelashes. "Some woman must have hurt you pretty badly."

Yes. One woman had. But it wasn't what Scarlett thought. "Then she did me a favor. Taught me the truth about life."

"Taught you wrong." She rubbed her belly, looking out the window as they drove closer to Geneva.

"Right or wrong, once the paternity test proves I'm your baby's father, we will be celebrating our marriage."

She tossed him a glance. "No, thanks. I'm no fan of gruel."

Vin ground his teeth. "Are you trying to tell me your childish, foolish dreams of love are more important than our child's welfare? A baby deserves two parents. A stable home."

Her expression changed. "Don't you think I know that?

All I ever wanted my whole childhood was to have a real home. I don't even know what it feels like to make roots, have friends, be part of a community." Her voice cracked. "But you know what? We were still happy, even on the run. Because my parents loved each other. And they loved me."

He didn't know what that felt like, Vin thought unwillingly. He'd grown up in a derelict villa in Rome, neglected and ignored by a mother who was only interested in her love affairs. Her son was valuable for one reason only: to extort money from his father.

His *so-called* father.

Vin's shoulders tightened.

Anyone he loved, he lost. His mother had coldly used him as a bargaining chip to finance her lifestyle, before she violently died. Paid nannies left or were fired. His kindly grandfather had had a stroke when Vin was eight. He'd become estranged from his loving father and step-mother at fifteen. Sometimes he felt like he'd been alone his whole life. As alone as that Christmas Eve, when he was only eight and was left utterly alone in the villa, for-gotten in the dark—

He shook the memory away. His own child's life would be very different. And he'd make sure his child's mother was either a loving, stable, nurturing influence—or no influence at all.

"Why did you run away from New York?" he de-manded. "Because you decided to believe everything you'd read about me?"

"Are you kidding?" Scarlett looked at him in amaze-ment. "That pre-nup."

Gripping the steering wheel, he glanced at her in sur-prise. "You wanted to avoid the pre-nup?"

"Did you really think I would sign papers to give you total power over not just me, but our child? Did you think

I'd be so happy to become your trophy wife, I'd trade away my freedom for the rest of my life?"

"The pre-nup has been vetted by my lawyers to be completely fair..."

"Completely fair." For the first time since he'd known her, he heard a cynical note in her voice. "When you would get to make every decision about our lives? And if we ever decided to divorce for any reason, you would automatically get full custody of our baby?"

"Divorce is not my plan," he said sharply. "But I know I could not prevent you from leaving, if you wished it. Whatever you might think, there are no dungeons in my penthouse. The prenuptial agreement is merely a tool to minimize the impact of all your potentially bad decisions on our innocent children."

"*My* bad decisions?" She shook her head almost sadly. "And that's just the stuff in the pre-nup you told me about. Who knows what would have been buried in the fine print, a requirement that I give you five blow jobs a week?"

It was a crude comment, said matter-of-factly. There was nothing sensual or suggestive about her tone. If anything, she meant to insult him, to drive him away.

But his body's reaction was instantaneous. He turned from coldly furious to burning hot in a second, blood rushing to his groin as images went through his mind of that full rose-red mouth, hot and wet, around his hardened length... He tried to clear his head of the erotic image as he shifted uncomfortably in the leather seat of the car.

"That was not my intention." Although it sure as hell was now. Vin wondered what his lawyer's expression would be if he told him to add a blow job requirement.

Scarlett continued stubbornly, "You accuse me of being childish and foolish. But in refusing to marry you, I'm protecting our baby."

"How can you say that?" As they drove through the

outskirts of Geneva, he stopped at a red light. "I can offer both you and the baby a lifestyle you could never dream of. Six houses around the world, private schools, jewels, cars. Private jets…"

She shuddered at his mention of the jets. It seemed strange to him.

"I'm protecting our baby from a man who would only want to control us," she said softly. "Not love us."

That brought Vin up short.

As they arrived at the clinic, a modern building with clean lines on the edge of the lake, he pushed his thoughts aside. Parking the car, with the dark SUV parking nearby, he got out and opened Scarlett's door. He extended his hand to assist his very pregnant future bride.

With visible reluctance, she placed her hand in his.

Vin felt an electric jolt from the contact. As they walked together toward the front door of the clinic, he wouldn't—couldn't—let her hand go. He stopped, lifting it to his lips, and gently kissed the back of her hand. Her skin was soft. He felt her tremble.

"You could never love anyone." Her voice trembled. "Because you'll never trust anyone. Just the fact you're making me take this test…"

"I believe you, Scarlett," he said softly. "I'm only insisting on a paternity test because I've been lied to about it before."

"What?"

"A woman once claimed I was the father of her nonexistent baby, trying to get me to marry her. But this time, in my heart, I already know the truth. You're carrying my baby."

"Vin…"

Reaching out, he tucked a tendril of her red hair behind her ear. Her green eyes were wide.

"I like it when you look at me like that," he murmured.

"You are so beautiful, *cara*. Your eyes are such a deep emerald. Like a forest." He gently stroked the side of her face. "Your lips," he whispered, "are red and plump and ripe as fruit. I'll never forget—" he ran the tip of his finger along the full length of her bottom lip "—how it felt to taste them…"

Her tremble became violent. She looked so vulnerable, so stricken, so caught—she, who could have had any man she wanted with her beauty! Vin realized that he, too, was shaking.

His blood was pounding with the need to take her.

Then he remembered the bodyguards watching from the parking lot, the appointment at the clinic looming overhead.

Soon, he vowed to himself. Soon, he would satiate himself with her completely.

"You're right about one thing." He cupped her cheek. "I don't believe in love. At least not the romantic kind. But I do believe," he whispered, "in desire. I never stopped wanting you. From the moment we first met."

"But you were going to marry another…"

"Because I thought you were lost to me. I thought I couldn't have you. Now… I know I will." Vin ran the pads of his fingertips lightly along the edge of her jawline, to her earlobes, to the tumbling red waves of her hair. "I will have you, Scarlett," he growled. "At any price."

CHAPTER FOUR

"THERE CAN BE no doubt, Mr. Borgia. The baby is yours."

The Swiss doctor beamed at them. She was obviously pleased to be giving them good news.

Scarlett saw a flash of emotions cross Vin's hard, handsome features—pride, relief, joy and then, as he looked at her, anger. He hadn't forgiven her for running away.

Just you wait, Scarlett thought, giving him a bland smile.

But she'd thought she'd escape before this. Certainly before they drew the blood that they'd already tested in their in-house, state-of-the-art medical lab. She'd never intended for Vin to have the actual proof he was the father of her baby, proof he could use against her in courts of law.

But he'd never given her the opportunity. From the moment they'd arrived at the medical clinic, to the hour they'd spent waiting for the results, having lunch at a nearby elegant restaurant on the lake, Vin had never let Scarlett out of his sight. Even when she'd excused herself to use the restroom, he'd waited outside in the hallway, in an apparently courteous gesture. When she needed to get her handbag from the car, he'd insisted on sending a bodyguard to collect it.

Over lunch at the Michelin-starred restaurant, as he'd enjoyed lamb and asparagus in a delicate truffle sauce and a glass of wine, he'd expounded on what he would expect of her as his wife, each detail more outrageous than the last. He expected to dictate everything in her life, from the friends she kept to the clothes she wore!

She'd tried her best to lull his suspicions, listening meekly as she ate her lunch and sipped sparkling water. But inside, she was fuming.

Vin was so sure he'd won. He thought he could bully her into giving all her rights away—being nothing more than his indentured servant, the wife he could dominate, holding power over her future and their child's! He was as bad as Blaise!

What century do you think we're living in?

The century a rich man can do whatever he wants. To whomever he wants.

Actually, Vin was more dangerous. Because from the moment she'd met him, when he'd taken her in his arms and made her feel things she'd never felt before, pleasure and joy beyond imagining, he'd made her want to surrender to his demands. And he could do it again, if she let him.

I will have you, Scarlett. At any price.

She shivered as she remembered the hunger in his black eyes. The same hunger she felt for him.

But the price was too high. She couldn't allow herself to surrender, not when it would cost her everything!

"Do you want to know the baby's sex?" Dr. Schauss asked now in slightly accented English.

Vin's eyes were wide as he looked at Scarlett. He cleared his throat and said in an unsteady voice, "Sure."

The doctor smiled. "You're having a boy!"

A boy? Scarlett's eyes filled with tears. In just a few weeks, a sweet baby boy would be in her arms!

"A boy?" Vin's face lit up, and he looked at Scarlett. His usual hard, cynical expression fell away and he looked suddenly young and joyful. Then he turned back to the doctor. "And the pregnancy? Is Scarlett well?"

If she'd loved him, or even trusted him, she might have been touched by the anxiety in his deep voice.

The doctor nodded. "Mademoiselle Ravenwood is doing well. Her blood pressure is fine and in spite of being so close to her due date, she shows no signs of imminent labor. Though that can quickly change, of course…"

"Then we have time to be married." His expression hardened as he turned to Scarlett. "My lawyer in New York has sent the prenuptial agreement. As soon as we leave here, you will sign it, and we will marry."

Scarlett's heart fell all the way to her fur-lined boots. "I…"

Holding up his hand, he pressed his phone to his ear. "Ernest, find out where we can be married quickly. Yes, I know it's more complicated in Europe. Tonight if possible, tomorrow at the latest."

Staring at him, Scarlett instantly saw her mistake.

My God, she was stupid. She never should have let him get the legal proof that he was the father of her child. She should have screamed bloody murder rather than willingly give blood for the paternity test. Running away would be ten times harder now. He'd never give up looking for her. And he'd have the law on his side.

She rose unsteadily to her feet. "Thank you for the news, Doctor." Her teeth were chattering as she glanced at Vin, who had turned away to bark questions to his assistant, about places like Gibraltar and Denmark and even, heaven help her, Las Vegas. In another moment, he'd be arranging the plane, then he'd be back to giving her his full attention. She had only seconds.

Adrenaline pumped her heart. It was now or never.

"Mademoiselle Ravenwood—" the Swiss doctor looked at her with concern in her kindly bespectacled eyes "—are you quite all right?"

"Fine, I'm great." She forced a smile. "I just need to go to the ladies' room. If you'll excuse me."

"Of course—"

Scarlett swiftly exited the brightly lit exam room. She saw Vin's eyes look up piercingly as she closed the door.

She fled down the hall, past other beaming couples holding ultrasound photos and smiling nurses and doctors in white coats. She ran down multiple hallways, looking desperately for the back exit, since she knew that Vin's bodyguards were waiting at the front entrance of the clinic.

She found the back staircase and raced down it, one hand over her heavy belly as she scrambled to think of a coherent escape plan. She'd go back to Gstaad and beg Wilhelmina to use her influence with her boss—Kassius Black—to hide her. If that failed, she'd borrow money and hop a train for somewhere Vin had no connections at all. She scrambled to think how far she'd have to go. Samarkand? Ulaanbaatar? Vladivostok?

Scarlett burst out of the steel-framed door to the sunlight and fresh air of the wide lawn behind the clinic. She saw the shining gleam of the lake, saw a local bus approaching on a distant road. She started to run across the grass—

Then came to a screeching halt.

Vin was on the grassy hill beside the clinic, his arms folded. "Going somewhere?"

Out of earshot but watching the exchange with interest, she saw his bodyguards. Her lips parted, but she couldn't find her voice. Couldn't find a single word of explanation or excuse as he came forward, his handsome, implacable face set in stone.

She stammered, "How did you—"

"I expected you to run."

"But I didn't argue with you at all!" she gasped. "I didn't even criticize the obnoxious things you said at lunch!"

"That's how I knew." His voice was almost amused.

"The fiery woman I know would never let such a thing pass."

"It was a test?" Her voice squeaked in outrage.

He shrugged. "You seemed like you were willing to come quietly for the paternity test. I was glad to let it ride. But of course I knew." He put his hands in his pockets, looking more devastatingly handsome than ever in his tailored dark suit and long black coat. He tilted his head curiously. "Actually, I'm a little disappointed in you, trying the same trick twice. I'd like to think you had a little more respect for my intelligence."

She sucked in her breath as he came closer. His dark eyes were almost feral above the hard hungry slant of his cheekbones and rough edges of his jaw, shaded with five-o'clock shadow.

"Why are you so afraid of me?" he asked softly. "You seem to think I'm a murderous villain, merely because I seek to take responsibility for my child and marry you."

She lifted her chin furiously. "You don't *wish* to marry me. You're insisting on it! You're no better than Blaise Falkner!"

He grew dangerously still. "And now you insult me?"

"He wanted me to sign papers forcing me to give the baby away, too!"

"That's not what I—"

"At least with Blaise," she interrupted, "I knew from the start he was a monster. But I liked you. I slept with you." She hated the tears that rose in her eyes. She wiped them away furiously. "But beneath your charm, you're just the same as Blaise. Selfish to the core. You're determined to force this prenuptial agreement on me. Well, guess what, I'm not going to sign it! You can't make me marry you. We're in modern-day Europe, not the Dark Ages!"

"Oh, for…" A low mutter of hard words that she guessed to be Italian curses escaped his sensual lips. He set his jaw. "I don't have time for this. I'm due in Rome in five days. The prenuptial agreement is waiting in the car. You can read it thoroughly while we're driving to the airport."

Her stomach fell. "Airport?"

"En route to our wedding in Las Vegas."

"I'm not getting on a plane!"

"Why," he jeered, "because you're afraid I will kidnap you to some shadowy place not so civilized as Switzerland? You think so little of me. Why did you let me seduce you, let me fill you with my child, if the idea of taking my name and being under my protection and letting me provide for you is so unpalatable? If you truly believe me to be such a villain, why did you give me your body?" he said softly. "Why did you grip my shoulders and cry with joy as I made love to you again and again?"

Scarlett looked up at him, hardly able to breathe. He was so close to her. "I didn't…"

"It took a week for the nail marks to disappear from my back."

She flinched, then glared at him, folding her arms. "So you're good in bed. Big deal. I didn't have the experience to fight my desire for you then, but I do now. I won't sell myself to you and I definitely won't sell my baby."

His dark eyes narrowed. "So you prefer that our son has no father? That he is raised without my name or my protection or my love, all of which I freely offer you now?"

"Your…love?"

"Of course, you think I would not love my own child?"

Oh. Of course that was what he meant. Biting back her disappointment, angry with herself for feeling it, she said, "You're not offering me anything for free. If you were, you wouldn't make me sign those horrible documents."

"You expect me to marry you without a pre-nup? Leaving you free to take half my fortune?"

Scarlett shook her head stubbornly. "Of course not. You wouldn't want to take the risk. But neither do I. So, the answer is simple. We will not marry."

Vin stared at her in the Geneva sunlight. A soft wind rustled the autumn leaves above the grassy slope, between the modern two-story clinic and the sparkling water of the lake. She heard the soft call of a bird, the distant sound of honking and noise from the city.

"Because you're hoping to marry for love." He glared at her. "You are just like my mother was, before she died. Ignoring your responsibilities to run toward some romantic fantasy."

"I'm not! I'm running *away* from a nightmare. You!"

His lips pressed together. "Perhaps once our child is born, you will run away from him, too."

"Never!" she gasped.

"How do I know?"

"I love my baby more than anything!"

"So all you want from me is child support—is that it?"

"I don't want your money."

"You'd be the first."

"Money comes with strings, as you know perfectly well. Or you wouldn't offer it."

"So how do you expect to support our baby alone?"

"Well…" She tilted her head, thinking. "If you weren't pursuing me, and I didn't have to hide from you, I might go back to Gstaad and learn to cook fried chicken."

Vin looked at her incredulously. "You mean, instead of living in the lap of luxury as my wife, you'd pursue a career as a common cook?"

"You're such a snob! Fried chicken makes the world a better place. Can you say that about what you do?"

"Owning a billion-dollar airline?"

"Yeah, stuffing passengers like cattle into economy class, in seats the size of a postage stamp!"

He ground his teeth, letting her insult slide. "I have great appreciation for fine meals and for the talented chefs who prepare them. But according to Wilhelmina Stone, that's definitely not you."

"So I'll learn." Scarlett folded her arms. "I worked my way through a year of community college to become a nursing assistant, studying at night after working all day. I can handle it. All it takes is hard work and a willingness to do without sleep, and fortunately I've had experience with both."

Vin's dark eyes glinted so dangerously, she was almost surprised she didn't burst into flames beneath the force of his glare. "So you don't want my name, you don't want my money and you won't marry me. You prefer for our child to have no father at all while you aspire to low-paying jobs and try to survive."

Scarlett looked at him uneasily. When he put it like that, he made her sound like an idiot.

Vin looked into her beautiful eyes and a realization chilled him to the bone.

He had no leverage.

No way to force Scarlett's compliance, at least not one he felt comfortable with. This wasn't the business world, where he could offer a higher price or blackmail shareholders over their secrets in order to make them comply with his requests. The standard rules of mergers and acquisitions didn't apply.

Or did they?

He'd learned enough from his investigator to realize how little Scarlett had going for her. No family. No savings. Her savings account held the same amount one might spend for a business dinner with a few bottles of wine. She had no bachelor's degree, and worst of all, thanks to Blaise Falkner, she'd have no job recommendation.

But Falkner would suffer for that. Vin's lips lifted. He'd regret treating Scarlett so badly. He'd regret threatening Vin's future wife and child.

If Scarlett ever actually became his wife.

He didn't understand why this was so hard. Why shouldn't he be able to just buy her? He'd be willing to pay quite a bit, as long as it didn't cost something he actually cared about. Like his time. Or control. Or any requirement for him to be vulnerable.

But money? He had more than he could spend. Money was confetti to him. A way to keep score. A way to buy toys. And he wanted Scarlett Ravenwood more than any toy.

Shifting his strategy, he lifted an eyebrow. "What if I sweetened the pre-nup with a million-dollar payout for every year of our marriage?"

"No."

He frowned. "Two million?"

"Vin, you can't buy me."

"Everyone says that. But everyone has a price. Ten," he said. "My final offer. Ten million dollars for every year we stay married. Think about that."

Her eyes widened. For a moment he thought he had her. Then her chin lifted. "I told you. Not for any price." Her green eyes glittered furiously. "I'm not giving you the right to order me around like a slave—and permanent custody of our baby if I ever try to fight back. Freedom is worth more than some stupid money."

Vin stared at her, then regretfully decided he believed her. Damn it. Everything about her body language spoke of stubborn sincerity. He was dealing with an idealist, with a heart as stubborn as his own.

He had mixed feelings about it. That made her different from his own mother, which would be good for his son's happiness.

But it made Scarlett a more challenging adversary for Vin. How could he gain his objective, if money wasn't enough to sway her?

Standing on the grassy hillside behind the clinic, Vin looked at the sunlight flickering across Lake Geneva.

He wanted Scarlett as his wife, as his lover. In his bed, at his beck and call.

He also wanted his son to be safe and secure and loved, raised in the same home, with the same name. He wanted his son to have siblings. Vin wanted to know exactly where his family was and that everyone was protected, and provided for, at all times.

He looked at Scarlett. "How can I change your mind?"

"You can't," she said firmly. "The only reason to marry someone is for love. And I don't love you."

"You wanted a home. I can give you six." Or more. He couldn't quite remember which ones he'd sold or bought lately.

She looked wistful, then squared her shoulders. "A home without love isn't a home at all."

"That's the most ridiculous thing I've ever heard."

But he suddenly knew his answer. He'd use her romantic heart against her.

Scarlett cared about two things: love and freedom. All he had to do was give her both.

Or at least make her *think* he was giving them to her.

Vin had never tried to pretend to be in love before, but how hard could it be? He'd been raised by a woman who was a master at it, who'd used the pretense of emotion as a means of manipulating others.

But could he pull it off? Scarlett was no fool. Would she buy it?

He'd have to move slowly...

Vin tilted his head as if in thought, then took a deep breath and looked up almost pleadingly.

"Maybe you can show me I'm wrong. Prove to me that love isn't an illusion for fools."

Her eyes widened in surprise, then faded. "Please. You'll never give your heart to anyone. You've made it clear that to you marriage is a business deal."

"Maybe I'm wrong. Because you're different from any woman I've met." That was certainly true. "I want you as I've never wanted anyone." Also true. "You're carrying my child. I respect your intelligence, your warm heart. I need you. Want you." Clawing his hand back through his dark hair, he gave her a crooked smile. "Maybe that's how it starts."

He held his breath, waiting for her response.

"You expect me to believe that... That you could some-day love me?" She gave a harsh laugh. "Nice try. What kind of idiot do you think I am?"

"Just give me a chance," he said quietly. "To see where this could lead."

"How?"

He thought furiously. Then he knew.

His eyes pierced hers. "I'll marry you without a pre-nup."

"What?" she breathed. She shook her head in disbelief. "Like you said—you'd risk half your fortune! From the moment we spoke our vows!"

Vin watched her carefully, watched the play of conflicting emotions cross her pale, lovely face. The way her white teeth nibbled furiously at her full, pink bottom lip. "Maybe it's worth the risk."

Yes. He was taking a risk, gambling that he'd quickly make her fall in love with him, placing her securely under his thumb and willing to sign a postnuptial agreement before the ink on their marriage license was dry. Which, he thought arrogantly, was almost no risk at all.

He'd never tried to make a woman fall in love with him

before. Usually it was the opposite—getting women into bed and leaving them before any emotional attachment was formed. This would be interesting. He felt strangely excited by the challenge.

Or maybe it was just standing so close to Scarlett, beneath the golden sun, feeling the cool October breeze against his overheated skin, knowing that he would soon possess her. In this moment, he would have been almost willing to pay half his fortune just to get her in his bed.

"Will you?" he said softly, coming closer. "Will you take a chance on me, if I take one with you?"

She seemed to shudder, looking up into his eyes. Her expression was bewildered, vulnerable, as if she were fighting hope itself. "But why?" she whispered. "Why does marriage matter so much to you?"

He didn't want to answer, but the new role he was playing, that of a secretly vulnerable man who could possibly be open to love, forced him to at least partial honesty. "I know what it's like to grow up without a father. My son must have a better childhood. He must always know who his parents are."

She looked confused. "How could he not know that?"

Vin changed the subject. "Family starts with a name. With a home. Our baby must feel safe and loved. He must know where he belongs." He looked at her. "Marry me, Scarlett. Right now."

She bit her lip, visibly wavering.

He pressed his advantage. "My private plane is fueled up and waiting. We can be in Las Vegas in…"

"No!" He was surprised at the sudden vehemence of her tone. She licked her lips. "Um, Dr. Schauss said I could go into labor at any time—"

"She also said she saw no imminent signs." He looked at her pale face and added soothingly, "We can bring a doctor on board with us, just in case."

"Forget it." She swallowed. "I'm not getting on any plane."

"Why?"

She took a shuddering breath. "If I do, I'll die! We'll both die!"

"What are you talking about?"

Tears spilled over her lashes. "My father died in a plane crash…"

"Yes," he said, his voice gentle, "but that doesn't mean—"

"Two weeks ago, my own flight almost crashed." He vaguely recalled reading something about an emergency landing in Ireland for her London-bound flight. She continued, "After what happened to Dad, I should have known better than to get on a plane for any reason! I told myself I was being silly. I ignored my intuition, and it almost killed us!" Hugging her belly, she shook her head fiercely. "I'll never get on another plane—ever!"

"But, Scarlett," he said quietly, "there are, on average, a hundred thousand flights every single day. Almost every one takes off and lands safely, without incident. Statistically—"

"Shut up! Don't you quote statistics to me!"

Her voice sounded almost hysterical. He had the feeling if he pushed her, he'd lose even the small bridge of trust he'd created. So he changed tactics. "I own an airline and also have two private jets for my own use. I even have a pilot's license, should I ever need to fly a plane myself. So I can supervise the equipment check, Scarlett. I can personally guarantee you'll be safe."

Scarlett choked out a tearful laugh. "And I can personally guarantee that I'm never getting on another plane!"

He tried to think of a way to reason with her. But as he looked into her beautiful, anguished eyes, as he saw the tears streak down her cheeks, he suddenly didn't want to argue. He just wanted to make it better.

Without a word, he pulled her into his arms. She fell against him, and he wrapped her in his coat, stroking her hair and back, murmuring gentle words until her sobs quieted and she was no longer shaking.

"All right," Vin said softly. "We don't have to fly. I'll never make you do anything you don't want to do. I'll always look out for you, Scarlett. Always."

Nestled against his white button-up shirt, wrapped beneath the lapels of his long black coat, Scarlett lifted her head with a ragged breath. She looked so beautiful in the sunlight, he thought. Her tearful eyes shone like emeralds.

She was vulnerable. It was the moment Vin should have pressed his advantage, gotten her to acquiesce to his proposal, boxed her in.

Instead, he felt something twist in his heart. And instead of pouncing on her weakness, forcing her to agree to his demands, he did what he'd wanted to do since he'd first seen her standing in the New York cathedral, her red hair tumbling over her shoulders, her green eyes luminous and pleading beneath a beam of golden light.

Cupping her face in his hands, Vin lowered his head and kissed her.

CHAPTER FIVE

SHE HADN'T EXPECTED him to kiss her.

The world seemed to whirl around Scarlett, making her dizzy as Vin's lips moved against hers. The kiss deepened, his mouth becoming hard and demanding, as if she belonged to him, and he owned the right of possession. He held her tight, her rounded belly and overflowing breasts pressing against his taut stomach and the hard muscles of his chest. He wrapped her in his warmth, protecting her from the wind, and she shook as she felt a hot rough pulse of electricity course through her.

She'd forgotten what it was like to kiss him. She'd forced herself to forget. But now, as she felt the tip of his tongue flick inside her mouth, as she felt his hot mouth silky against hers, she clutched him closer, never wanting to let him go. She couldn't. Not when every night for eight and a half months, she'd ached for him, dreaming of the hot night he'd ruthlessly taken her virginity, given her mind-blowing pleasure and filled her with his child.

He'd made her feel wanted. Adored. Even…loved.

"I've wanted you so long," he whispered against her skin. Her heartbeat tripled in her chest. "Say you'll marry me, Scarlett. Say it…"

"I'll marry you."

His handsome face lit up with joy and hope, and she realized what she'd just said. With an intake of breath, she met his eyes.

"Do you mean it?"

She saw in his dark eyes that he wanted her to marry him. Desperately. And she…

She wanted to be in his arms. She wanted her baby to have a father. She wanted her child to be safe and loved and live in a comfortable home. Was she a fool? Of course she wanted those things!

But only if their marriage could be real. If she and Vin actually cared for each other, they might have a chance at happiness…

Will you take a chance on me, if I take one with you?

Vin was willing to marry her without a prenuptial agreement. He was taking the biggest risk. Was she willing to take a smaller one?

For the potential happiness—for all of them?

Yes.

"I'll marry you," she choked out and realized she was crying. She had no idea why, until he pulled her into his arms and held her tight, and she knew.

Vincenzo Borgia, so handsome and powerful, could have chosen any woman for his wife.

But he'd chosen her. Not only that, he was giving her incredible power over his life. If he could be brave enough to do that, so would she.

She'd be brave enough to make the choice based on her hopes, not her fears…

"I'd never take advantage of your trust," she whispered.

"I know," he said with a private smile, then kissed her tenderly. "You've made me so happy."

"Me, too," she said, smiling through her tears.

"Let's marry as quickly as possible." He caressed her cheek. "But the marriage laws are much stricter in Europe. My assistant says the quickest options include Gibraltar and Denmark, but at your state of pregnancy, I'm not sure you'd find a long car ride comfortable. I also have to be in Rome in five days to close a business deal."

"What deal?"

"A controlling interest in Mediterranean Airlines. After I lost the deal with Air Transatlantique so spectacularly a couple of weeks ago—" he gave a wry smile "—I'm determined to get it. It's a closely held company and the founder insisted on meeting with me before he'd sell his shares."

"So let's get married in Rome."

He hesitated, then nodded. "It'll take a little longer to get married there, with the required paperwork, but if we drive straight through, we could be in Rome by late tonight. I think I even own a house there."

She gave an incredulous laugh. "You *think* you own a house? You're not sure?"

A ghost of a smile traced the edges of his sensual lips. "I haven't been back to my birth country for twenty years. I grew up in Rome, but—" his lips twisted bitterly "—my memories aren't terribly happy there."

His voice was strained, and his jaw tightened in a way that suggested she shouldn't ask any more questions. But Scarlett was dying to ask them. It occurred to her that she knew very little about his past, or what had driven him to become a self-made billionaire who was cynical at the thought of love.

But before she could try to think of a way to formulate the question that he might actually answer, Vin took her hand and led her across the grass, back to the clinic's parking lot, where the bodyguards waited with the cars.

As they walked, Scarlett glanced down at Vin's hand holding her smaller one. Feeling the warmth of his rough palm against hers, skin on skin, his fingers wrapped so possessively around hers, made her tremble as she walked. Her lips still tingled from his kiss.

"Congratulate us." Vin brought her to the three hulking, scowling bodyguards. "Scarlett has agreed to be my bride. We'll be married in a few days."

The three bodyguards lifted up their mirrored sunglasses, and their scowls gave way to bright smiles. They looked almost human as Vin introduced each of them by name. Each man shook her hand, murmuring congratulations. It was amazing how much less scary they suddenly seemed. Scarlett couldn't help smiling back.

"You're on her protection detail now," Vin told them, "as much as mine."

The men snapped to attention. "We're on it, boss."

"Welcome to the family, Miss Ravenwood," the first bodyguard told her with a big smile. Then the sunglasses snapped back, along with the scowl. "We'll keep you safe."

"Thank you." She hid a smile. As if she needed protecting! What was she, some politician or celebrity or something? But she was willing to play along.

Vin opened the door of the red sports car for her, then spoke quietly to the bodyguards before he climbed into the driver's seat beside her. He started the engine with a low smooth roar.

To her surprise, he didn't drive back immediately to the expressway but went the other direction, with the bodyguards following them in the SUV, deeper into downtown Geneva. "Where are we going?"

Vin turned onto the exclusive Rue du Rhône. "You agreed to marry me."

"So?"

His eyes slanted sideways to her hand. "You need a ring."

An hour later, they'd left the elegant jewelry store and were crossing into the French Alps, near Chamonix and Mont Blanc, en route to Italy. The mountain scenery was breathtaking, but Scarlett couldn't take her eyes off the biggest rock she'd ever seen: the ten-carat, emerald-cut, platinum-set diamond now on her left hand.

As she moved her finger, the enormous diamond reflected sparkling prisms of sunlight against her body, against her face, against the luxurious interior of the car. Against the handsome, powerful man driving beside her.

"I didn't need such a big diamond," she said for the tenth time.

He changed gears. "Of course you need it. You're going to be my wife. You must always have the best."

The ring was spectacular, but she felt briefly troubled. She would have been fine with a plain gold band, but his desires had overridden hers. What if her original fears were proven true—that he would attempt to rule her life?

Calm down, it's just a ring, she told herself. And if she were truly honest with herself, part of her was dazzled by the huge diamond, over-the-top and impractical as it was. She tried not to think about how much it had cost. More than she'd ever earn in a lifetime, that was for sure.

The highway wound through mountains and tunnels as they headed south. As they traveled, Vin kept asking if she was comfortable, if she'd like to stop for a meal, for a break or just to stretch her legs and admire the view.

Anxious to arrive in Rome so she could be done traveling and settle in, she mostly refused, stopping only briefly at a truck stop near the Italian border.

As they crossed through Tuscany, the orange sun was lowering into the west horizon of lush autumn fields like a ball of fire, and Scarlett's stomach started to growl. "Could we stop for dinner?"

"Of course, *cara*." Vin glanced at the countryside around the highway. "There is an excellent restaurant not too far from here, in Borgierra. I often visited the town when I was young."

"Borgierra? Sounds like your last name."

"My family founded the village five hundred years ago." He paused, then mumbled, "My father still lives there."

Her jaw dropped. "Your *father*?"

"So?"

"You never mentioned him. I assumed he was...well..."

"He's not dead. I just...haven't seen him for a while. Since I left Italy."

"Wait—twenty years ago?"

"Contrary to popular opinion," he said irritably, "creating a billion-dollar airline doesn't just magically happen. I've had to work all day, every day, from the time I was fifteen and set foot in New York. Gambling every penny I had. Working until I bled."

"Don't try to distract me from the main point."

"Which is?"

"You haven't seen your father for twenty years. Why? Was he horrible? Abusive?"

Vin's hands tightened on the steering wheel. "No."

Then she didn't understand at all. "I want to meet him."

He stared stonily ahead. "We don't have time."

"We have time to stop for dinner."

"I'm not talking about this."

"Too bad, because I am." The interior of the sports car suddenly seemed very small. "Weren't you the one who insisted it would be morally wrong of me not to allow our child to be raised by a father, as well as a mother? Now you expect me to ignore his chance to have a grandfather?"

His jaw tightened.

She tried again. "You say your father is a good person, but after two decades, you seriously intend to drive right by his house without stopping?" She glared at him. "It makes me wonder..."

He glared back at her. "Wonder what?"

She looked down, twisting the enormous diamond engagement ring. "When you said family was so important, I actually believed you."

"You are my family now, Scarlett. You and our son."

"The more family, the better." She took a deep breath. "I never had any siblings or cousins. Since my parents died, I've been totally alone. Do you know how that feels?"

He didn't answer.

Their eyes locked, and Scarlett's heart twisted at something she saw hidden deep in his dark eyes. Some pain. She took a deep breath. "You should want our baby to have as much family—as much love—as he possibly can," she said quietly. "Two parents are great, but what if something happens to us? Your father is our baby's only grandparent. Why haven't you seen him in twenty years?"

"It's complicated." He stared grimly forward at the road. "My mother never married Giuseppe. She preferred more exciting men who treated her badly." He smiled grimly. "But she enjoyed keeping my father on a string, not letting him fall out of love with her, making him suffer. Most of all, she enjoyed him as a source of income to her jet-set lifestyle. Anytime he wished to see me, he had to pay her a small fortune."

Her lips parted with shock. His mother had made his father *pay* for the privilege of seeing his son? "Oh, Vin…"

"When I was ten, he finally was able to stop loving her. He married another woman, Joanne."

"A wicked stepmother?" Scarlett guessed.

He snorted, then sobered. "Not at all. She was kind to me. I spent Christmas with them when I was fifteen, when my mother was partying with her boyfriend in Ibiza. It was the best Christmas of my life, with them and my new half sister. Maria was barely more than a baby then. When I had to leave, Giuseppe and Joanne said they wanted me to come live with them full-time."

"So did you?"

Vin's gaze was unfocused as he stared ahead. Then he shook his head. "My mother refused to let me go."

Scarlett's heart broke a little at the thought of a young

boy, simultaneously ignored and used as a bargaining chip by his own mother, losing his chance to be in a stable home, safe and loved. No wonder he was so determined to be a good father to his own son.

"It doesn't matter." His voice changed. "My mother died shortly after that, and I moved to New York to live with an uncle."

"I'm sorry about your mother." She frowned. "But why didn't you go live with your father after she died? There was nothing to stop you then."

"It was all a long time ago," he said grimly.

"But—"

"Drop it, Scarlett."

She wanted to push, but something in his expression warned her. "Okay. For now." She took a deep breath. "But if we're driving by his house, can't we just stop by so I can meet him? Just for ten minutes?"

"We're on a tight schedule."

"Please…"

"They might not even be at home."

"I promise if we stop, and they're not home, then I'll quit talking about it the rest of the way to Rome."

Vin stared at her. Then, with a sigh, he picked up his phone and told the bodyguards in the SUV behind them they'd be taking a detour.

The night was growing dark as they drove through a wrought-iron gate in the Tuscan countryside. The moon was full over the trees and fragrant fields. Vin seemed to grow progressively more tense as they drove down the long, dusty road, edged on both sides by cypress trees.

At the end of the road, Scarlett gasped when she saw a gorgeous three-story villa with green shutters and yellow stucco lit up by warm golden lights in the dark night.

When they reached the top of the hill, they saw at least

forty cars parked around the circular drive and stone fountain.

"Looks like they're having a party," she said awkwardly.

Vin parked the car right by the front door and turned off the engine. For a moment he didn't move. His handsome face looked strangely bleak. She reached for his hand.

"Two minutes," he said, pulling his hand away.

"We agreed we'd stay for ten—"

At his look, she decided not to press her luck.

Moon laced through clouds, decorating the October night like bright pearlescent lace across black velvet. He walked toward the front door, looking like a man going to the guillotine. The bodyguards, after doing a quick eyeball check of the perimeter, hung back respectfully. So did Scarlett.

At the door, Vin glanced back at them, then set his jaw. He reached for the brass knocker and banged it heavily against the wood. For some moments, no one answered.

Then the door was thrown open, and light and music from inside the villa poured out around them. Scarlett saw a dignified gray-haired man standing silhouetted in the doorway.

"Buona sera," Vin began woodenly, then spoke words in Italian that she didn't understand.

But she didn't need to. He had barely spoken a sentence before the man in the doorway let out a gasp and, with a flood of Italian words, pulled Vin into his arms with a choked sob of joy.

Vin was furious.

He hadn't wanted to come here. He felt manipulated, backed into a corner. Exactly how he'd promised himself he'd never feel again: like someone else's puppet, under their control.

But Scarlett had made her threat clear, with her pointed insinuation, twisting her engagement ring, that she might change her mind about their marriage if he didn't do this. He'd barely contained his fury during their drive up the cypress-lined road. *This* was the thanks he received for striving to take good care of his pregnant soon-to-be wife, letting her have her way in everything? It still wasn't enough? Now Scarlett wanted to put her spoon into his heart and stir?

He hated her for this. Up till the very moment when he'd banged on the door.

Vin had been prepared for a servant to answer, or someone he didn't know, as there seemed to be a party. But he instantly recognized the man in the doorway.

Giuseppe Borgia had aged twenty years, with more lines on his skin and gray in his hair. But he'd known him. His father.

No. The man Vin had *believed* to be his father for his entire childhood. The man whose heart would be broken if he ever knew the truth.

The last time they'd seen each other, at his mother's funeral, Vin had been hostile and cold. Nothing like he'd been the week before, during the happy Christmas he'd stayed at this very villa, believing he'd found a place to call home and a real family who loved him.

But when he'd returned to Rome after Christmas and asked his mother if he could permanently live with his father, she'd barked out a cruel laugh.

"You're not even Giuseppe's son," Bianca Orsini had said. She'd taken a long drag off her cigarette. "It's time you knew. I got pregnant after a one-night stand with a musician I met in a bar in Rio." She smiled her brittle, hollow smile. "But I needed Giuseppe's money. So I lied."

"I have to tell him," Vin had choked out.

"Do it, and for reward, he'll just stop loving you." Her

fingers tightened around the shrinking cigarette. "Did you really think I'd let you go live with him and that British woman and give up my only source of income?"

Ironically, Bianca hadn't needed that income for long. She'd died a few days later, when, while distracting her current boyfriend with caresses of an intimate nature— at least that was what the police believed—she'd caused him to accidentally swerve his convertible off a cliff, killing them both.

Vin had barely been able to face Giuseppe and Joanne at the funeral a few days later. They'd tried to hug him, to console him, telling him to pack up and come home with them. But he'd known if they realized he wasn't really Giuseppe's child, how quickly they would have given him up. Especially since they had their own child, an adorable little girl of four, who actually deserved their love.

He couldn't wait around for them to reject him. Better that he do it first. So he'd gone to live with his mother's brother in New York, a lawyer who worked eighty-hour weeks and had little to offer his grieving, lonely nephew except his example as a workaholic.

Now Vin stared at Giuseppe in the doorway of the villa. The man he'd once believed to be his father, whose hair had since gone gray. They'd both changed so much over twenty years. Would Giuseppe even recognize him now?

"Good evening," Vin said haltingly in his native Italian. The language tasted rusty on his lips. "I apologize for the interruption. I'm not sure you'll recognize me—"

Giuseppe's lips parted. Then his eyes suddenly shone with tears.

"Vincenzo," he choked out. "My boy, my boy—you've come home at last!"

The old man's arms went around him, and he felt the force of his father's sobs. A stab went through Vin's frozen heart, as if it had painfully started beating again.

Giuseppe pulled back, wiping his eyes, and called out loudly in Italian. Suddenly there were more people at the door, including two dark-haired women, one young, the other older, both pretty and smiling.

His stepmother, Joanne, and…could that be his sister, Maria, now a young woman of twenty-four? They both hugged him with cries of joy, and Giuseppe, weeping openly, hugged all three of them in his vast arms.

Vin blinked fast, feeling like his soul was peeling.

His father. His *family*. He longed to love them again. But he didn't have the right. And if they ever knew the truth, their love would evaporate.

"But who's this?" Giuseppe said in Italian, looking past Vin's ear. He saw Scarlett fidgeting shyly behind him in the gravel driveway. Heavily pregnant and still in the same casual khakis and jacket she'd worn in Gstaad, she looked incredibly beautiful, with her red hair, chewing her pink lower lip, her green eyes uncertain.

Vin took her hand.

"This is Scarlett, Papà," he said quietly in the same language. "She's carrying my child and we're going to be wed."

His father gasped, and all the new people now flooding around them—only a few of whom he confusedly recognized—immediately began crying out their welcome and approbation.

"You brought her home to meet us?" Reaching out, Giuseppe patted her cheek.

Vin said drily, "She insisted."

"Then she is already beloved by me," the old man said.

"Scarlett doesn't speak Italian."

He smiled. "She understands." And indeed, she had a bright, joyful smile as she looked between him and Giuseppe. She thought she'd brought Vin and his father back together.

If only it was the truth. If only it were even possible.

But in this moment, surrounded on all sides by love, Vin could not fight it. He pushed away his shame about the lie. As the Borgias whisked them into the villa, it was easier to just pretend, for just a short while, that he really was their long-lost son, their long-lost brother. Easier to pretend he was actually deserving of their love and care.

"You came to my engagement party!" His dark-haired young sister said happily, slipping her arm around his as she led him through the grand hall toward the courtyard outside. "You have made this a party to remember!"

"You are engaged, Maria?" he said incredulously. "You were a toddler last time I saw you! Do you even remember me?"

Her smile broadened. "I confess my memory is not perfect, but I know you from your picture." Her smile faded. "Our father often cried over it."

"Maria…"

"But all is forgiven now you are here." Brightening, she motioned across the decorated courtyard, her eyes sparkling. "That is my fiancé, Luca."

Luca barely looked old enough to be out of college, Vin thought. Or maybe he himself was just old. Outside of Manhattan most people did not wait until they were thirty-five to be wed. And even in New York, no one waited that long to fall in love.

"Forgive me for interrupting your party. If I'd known—"

"Vincenzo, having you here is the best engagement present in the world! Did you see Papà's face? He's prayed for this. When we sent you the invitation, we never dreamed you would accept."

Vin hadn't gotten the invitation, because he'd instructed his assistant to toss anything from the Borgia family straight into the trash. "Um…"

"And now you are engaged as well, and expecting a child," Maria said, her eyes shining. "Our family is growing!"

Beneath the fairy lights of the large courtyard, guests were dancing to the music of a small band. It didn't even feel cold, with the heat lamps. A beautiful evening party, with a panoramic view of the moon-swept Tuscan countryside.

He looked back at Scarlett, already sitting at a table near the dinner buffet, a plate of food in front of her as she talked to Giuseppe and Joanne. Amid all the elegant suits and gowns, she was still wearing the same casual clothes she'd worn on her morning walk in Gstaad. But it didn't matter. Just looking at her, Vin felt a flash of heat that blocked out all other thoughts and feelings. A welcome distraction.

As if she felt his stare, Scarlett turned. Their eyes locked across the crowd, and electricity thrummed through him, as if they were the only two people in the world.

Then his stepmother rose from the table, gesturing her to follow. Finishing a last bite of dinner, Scarlett rose. Lifting her eyebrow at him with a mysterious smile, she turned and disappeared inside the villa.

It was as if clouds suddenly covered the moonlight. Clearing his throat, Vin turned back to Maria, trying to remember what they'd been saying. "Ah... I hope you'll both be very happy."

"You, too, brother." Her smile broadened. "But since you're in love, getting married and having a baby, something tells me you're about to be happier than you can even imagine."

Ten minutes later, Scarlett was staring at herself in the full-length mirror.

"Thank you," she breathed, looking at herself in the

borrowed floaty knee-length dress with charming bell sleeves. "Oh, thank you so much!"

Vin's stepmother, Joanne, beamed back at her. "It's vintage, darling. Haven't worn it in years. I'm just glad I had a dress with an empire waist!" She glanced fondly at Scarlett's belly. "How wonderful it will be—" she sighed happily "—to have a new baby in the family. Now I don't even have to pressure Maria about children for a while, because you're making me a grandmother!"

From the moment Scarlett had met Vin's parents, they'd treated her like family. While talking with them in the courtyard, Scarlett had shyly mentioned she felt woefully underdressed for the party, in wrinkled khakis.

"Your bodyguards just brought in your suitcase," Joanne had said helpfully, but Scarlett shook her head, looking down at her casual clothes with regret.

"All my clothes look like this."

"Don't worry!" Joanne had said suddenly. "I know just the thing!"

Scarlett had immediately liked the dark-haired British woman, with her obviously kind heart. Now, blinking back tears, she reached out and impulsively hugged her. "I'm so glad we're going to be family."

"Me, too, darling." Joanne smiled as she drew back, her eyes glistening with tears. "I can't remember the last time I saw Giuseppe so happy. You've put our family back together and added years to my husband's life. Now—" she shook her head briskly, wiping her eyes "—we just need to find you better shoes. I think Maria has some sparkly sandals about your size…"

After Scarlett was dressed, she brushed out her red hair and put on a bit of lipstick. Feeling nervous as Cinderella, Scarlett went back out to the noisy courtyard to join the party.

She'd hoped for a family reconciliation, but she'd never

imagined a family like Vin's—so loving, so warm, so ready to welcome Scarlett and their coming baby with open arms!

Vin's father, Giuseppe, smiled at her as she returned to the festive tables on the edge of the courtyard. He said in accented English, "I'm glad you're here. I can see the love between you and my son."

Scarlett blushed and let the remark pass. She could hardly tell Giuseppe that she and Vin had gotten pregnant by accident. They didn't love each other.

But she wanted to love him.

Yes, Vin was ruthless. But he was also honorable, determined to do the best he could—as he saw it—for their baby, and for Scarlett, too. He'd repeatedly put her needs in front of his. Agreeing to drive, instead of fly. Agreeing to introduce her to his family. Most of all, agreeing to marry her without a pre-nup! She could only imagine how his shark lawyers would have their heads blown off at that one.

"When is your wedding?" Giuseppe asked.

"I'm not exactly sure. Sometime soon in Rome. We haven't really planned it yet. But I do hope you'll all be able to come…"

Her voice trailed off as Vin saw her across the courtyard. He started pushing through the crowd toward her.

Her body felt the rhythm of the music, the beat of the dancers' pounding feet against the flagstones. But she was unable to move, unable to even breathe, captured in his dark hungry gaze.

He was breathtakingly handsome. His muscled legs were barely contained by well-tailored black trousers and his broad shoulders seemed to expand the sharp white shirt with the top button undone. But it wasn't the broadness of his shoulders or sharp line of his jaw or even the intensity of his black eyes that shook her. His sex appeal was obvious to anyone with eyes.

This was more.

Scarlett felt like she knew a secret. Something no other woman had been privileged to see. Something he hid from the world and would deny to the death if ever accused of it.

Beneath the layers of slick designer suits and hard brutal muscle, Vin secretly had a good heart.

"Scusi," he said now to his father, who smiled indulgently.

"But of course, you want to be with your future bride."

Reaching out, Vin pulled Scarlett away. Beneath his touch, her body flashed hot, then cold. As they stood together on the crowded dance floor of the villa's courtyard, as the fairy lights swayed above them in the moonlit night, her heart was pounding.

She suddenly couldn't meet his eyes. She focused on the curve of his neck. On the hair-dusted forearms casually revealed by his rolled-up sleeves. The hard edge of his unshaven jawline. The upturn of his cruelly sensual lips.

Blood was suddenly rushing in her ears. Her knees felt weak. What was happening to her?

"Cara," he said softly. "You look so beautiful in that dress." He pulled her into his arms. "Dance with me."

The slow dance was pure torture for Scarlett as she felt his hard, powerful body brush against hers. His muscles moved against her breasts and belly, and his hands slowly traced down her back.

Her full breasts felt heavy, her nipples tightening, aching to be touched. Even the barest brush of him against her was almost too much—and yet not nearly enough. Agonized desire flowed through her, twisting deep, deep inside her. She ached for him to kiss her, to stroke her naked skin, to thrust inside her, fill her fully, stretch her wide—

Her breaths came in gasps. She tried to hide her desire. She couldn't let him know that such an innocent slow dance, while surrounded by his family and friends at an engagement party, was making her insane with need. How could she be so wanton? What was wrong with her?

The song finished, and she exhaled. "Um, thanks…"

But as she tried to leave the dance floor, he held her tight, murmuring, "Don't go."

His large hands moved slowly from her hips to her lower back. He pulled her back against his body, crushing her breasts against his hard chest. Dizzy with need, she looked up at him.

He smiled down at her. Powerful. Sure of himself.

There was a lull in the music. His expression changed, became dark. Hot. His lips slowly lowered toward hers—

"Vincenzo!"

They turned as Giuseppe's voice called across the courtyard. Vin's father beamed at them, his arm around his wife's shoulders, with Maria smiling beside them.

"My son," he announced, "there is no sense in you getting married in Rome, with strangers." He gesticulated wildly. "We have decided you and Scarlett should be married right here."

"Say yes," Maria begged.

"It would make us so happy," Joanne added warmly. "What do you say?"

Having her wedding at this beautiful Tuscan villa, surrounded by Vin's family? Scarlett wanted it instantly. Holding her breath, she looked hopefully at Vin.

But his expression was strangely shut down. Scarlett didn't understand why he seemed so tense at the idea. But whatever the reason, she knew he didn't want to do it. She sensed he'd been pushed as far as he'd be pushed. But he remained stubbornly silent, forcing Scarlett to be the one to give his family the bad news.

Biting her lip, she forced herself to say apologetically, "Thank you, but we want to be wed as quickly as possible—"

"All the more reason to do it here," Joanne pointed out. "What is the point of getting married in Rome? It will just take longer to get all the paperwork done. Here, it will be quicker because Giuseppe is mayor—"

"*Sì*, mayor," he repeated proudly.

"And he'll make sure all the necessary documentation is completed as fast as humanly possible. You're both American citizens now—" Joanne glanced humorously at her stepson, as if to say *What a fool you were to trade away this beautiful country* "—so no banns are necessary."

"Please!" Maria clutched Scarlett's hands. "I'll arrange a beautiful wedding for you. It'll be good practice for planning my own. Why shouldn't you get married here? It's your home now, too, Scarlett!"

Put that way, it was impossible to refuse. Scarlett looked desperately at Vin.

He scowled. "I have connections in Rome. It can be done quickly enough."

Giuseppe snorted. "Amid strangers! What about your family? What about your bride?"

Vin's jaw tightened. "I don't—"

"Please," Scarlett whispered.

He stared at her for a long moment, then sighed.

"Va bene." His shoulders looked tense. "We will have our wedding here, since my bride wishes it." As Maria clapped her hands together with joy, he added fiercely, "But I must be in Rome within five days."

"No problem!" Joanne said.

"Easy!" Giuseppe said.

"You will see," Maria chortled. "I bet we can do it in three!"

Vin's expression said he feared three days would last an eternity. Why? Scarlett wondered. What could possibly be making him so tense? Was it cold feet? Had he changed his mind about wanting to marry her? The thought caused a shiver of nervousness to go through her. Because she was starting to not hate the idea of marrying him.

"Perhaps it's not an entirely bad idea," Vin murmured, looking down at her. His arms tightened. "If we're staying, that means no more driving tonight. Which means," he whispered, "I can take you to bed now."

Fire flashed through her, and she almost tottered on her borrowed strappy sandals. Her heart was pounding so hard and fast she felt light-headed.

Her whole world shrank down to the sensation of his body near hers, his hand supporting her arm. Did he intend to seduce her? No, surely not. She was eight and a half months pregnant. Not exactly a sexpot. She wanted him. Definitely. But she was surely imagining the dark fierce smolder in his eyes.

And part of her was afraid of what would happen if he made love to her. How much of her soul he might take, along with her body…

"My fiancée is tired," he said abruptly. "I am sorry, but we must cut our night short."

"Of course, of course," came the chorus around them in English and Italian. Everyone looked at her belly and smiled. Everyone loved a pregnant woman.

"Where can I take her to rest?"

"Follow me," his father said, waving them along. He took them through the beautiful villa, up the sweeping stairs to the quieter second floor, then triumphantly through double doors to a huge, luxurious bedroom.

"But there's only one bed," Scarlett whispered to Vin in consternation. His father heard her and chuckled.

"There is no reason for you to pretend you do not share a bedroom," he said with a laugh, eyeing her belly. "We are not so old-fashioned as to need that deception. Or so stupid as to believe it! Do not be embarrassed. We wish you only to be comfortable."

Refusing to meet Vin's eyes, Scarlett said stiltedly, "Perhaps other rooms could be found—"

"Yes, of course." His father nodded, but before she could sigh with relief, he finished, "The villa is full of party guests, but we did find rooms for your bodyguards. I appreciate your concern for them," he said approvingly. "You've chosen the right woman, Vincenzo. So thoughtful and kind. Look." He nodded toward her duffel bag and his sleek designer suitcase, stacked neatly on the closet floor. "Our staff already unpacked your clothes for you. We were hoping to convince you to stay. So now there is nothing—" his eyebrows wiggled suggestively "—to prevent you both from having a good night's sleep."

Giuseppe left, shutting the double doors behind him.

Alone in the shadowy bedroom, standing next to the enormous bed, Scarlett and Vin looked at each other.

"What now?" she whispered, shivering. "What should we—"

Before she could finish her sentence, before she could even finish her thought, Vin pulled her roughly into his arms. Claiming her lips as his own, he twined his hands in her long red hair, kissing her with deep, ferocious hunger that could not be denied.

CHAPTER SIX

VIN HADN'T FELT so emotionally out of control for a long, long time.

All night, he'd been forced to endure feelings he'd ignored for twenty years, since he'd left Italy and closed the door marked "love and family" forever in his mind.

But that door had been wrenched open. He was out of practice dealing with any feeling but anger, so staggered by conflicting emotions.

Right now, there was only one thing he wanted to feel. *This*. Kissing Scarlett, Vin stroked his hands up her arms, feeling the silky fabric of her empire-waist dress slide beneath his fingertips. Feeling the warmth of her body beneath. He could be sure of this.

And this. He deepened the kiss, teasing her with his tongue.

Her sigh was soft in his mouth, like a whimper, but he felt the way she moved, her belly hard against his, her breasts swollen and soft.

This was all he wanted to feel. What he could physically grasp. What he could hold.

Scarlett.

Distantly, he heard the raucous noise of the party downstairs in the courtyard. But here in the hush of the darkened bedroom it felt strangely private, even holy. This was a place out of time, belonging to them alone.

Vin felt her tremble against him. Her lips parted beneath his, open and ripe for the taking. The rational part of his brain disappeared. It was like he'd never kissed anyone before.

He caressed her cheek, running his hand down the back of her neck, through her long hair tumbling down her shoulders. He drew back, looking at her. She was so sexy. So impossibly desirable. Beneath the silk bodice of her dress, he could see the hard nipples of her swollen breasts.

His body was screaming to take her now, take her hard and fast.

He exhaled, forcing himself to stay in control. She was heavily pregnant with his child, so he'd have to be gentle. She would need to be on top. To set the rhythm.

Plus, she was nervous. He felt that in her hesitation, in the way she'd shyly asked for separate rooms. She was afraid of what their lovemaking would start between them.

She was right to be afraid.

He intended to use every weapon he had to make her fall in love with him. To make her acquiesce to his every desire, and give him total command.

He needed to lure her slowly. Until she wanted him so badly that she was the one pushing him back roughly against the bed, and climbing on top of his naked body, easing her soft, wet core around him, driving him hard until they both screamed, clutching each other—

He shuddered with need. Patience, though a virtue, wasn't his strong point.

But he was starting to suspect that the torture of wanting her, and waiting for her, would make this conquest the single most spectacular sexual event of his life. For that, it was worth a little self-control.

If he could keep himself from losing it…

He gentled his kiss, making his lips seductive and soft. She leaned her body against him, reaching up to twine her hands in his short dark hair, pulling his head down harder against hers. Her rough, savage kiss made him feel so, so good, his body taut, his blood rushing and pounding and spiraling with need—

With a silent curse, Vin pulled away. She wouldn't be able to resist now if he drew her to the bed. He saw that in her sweetly mesmerized face. She wasn't the problem.

He was.

He couldn't lose control. Not now. Not ever. He needed a new strategy to force himself to slow down.

Scarlett's big eyes gleamed in the shadowy room as she looked up at him, dazed with desire. Cupping her cheek, he said in a low voice, "You have had a long day, *cara*. You need some comfort. Let me take care of you." Her forehead furrowed, then smoothed as he ran his hand gently along her shoulder. "I saw a marble tub in the en suite. Shall I start you a bath?"

"A bath?" she said, sounding bewildered, and he couldn't blame her.

"A deliciously sensual bath." He smiled. "One you'll want to linger in."

"That would be lovely—if you're sure you don't mind?"

She was already sighing in anticipation. She *had* had a stressful day, he thought. Considering she'd woken up that morning a single mother, a cook working in a Swiss chalet, and now was in Italy, Vin's fiancée, the proven mother of his child, with a ten-carat diamond on her finger. She'd met his family and was about to share his bed. That was a lot of change for anyone. And more was soon to come.

He smiled down at her. "It will be my pleasure."

And it would be.

Going into the luxurious en suite bathroom, Vin turned on the water, then looked around quickly. How to make it even more romantic? Pulling fresh roses from a nearby crystal vase, he crumpled rose petals into the warm running water. But he wanted more. Digging through the bathroom cabinet, he found expensively perfumed bubble bath and triumphantly discovered four candles and a box of matches in the bottom drawer.

"Can I come in?" she called.

"Not yet." He carefully placed the candles around the white marble bathroom with its elegant silver fixtures. He checked the water temperature—not too hot—and added a few more rose petals over the bubbles for good measure. He lit the candles, then turned out the lights. "Now."

Scarlett came into the bathroom, then stopped, her mouth agape. She looked at him, her own beautiful face suddenly nervous. As well she should be, he thought smugly.

"For you, *cara*," he said innocently. "I'll leave you to it."

He did leave the bathroom. He was that much of a gentleman. In the bedroom closet, he found his clothes unpacked in a drawer and pulled off his formal white shirt and tailored black trousers, exchanging them for just one article of clothing that would be easy to take off—low-slung sweatpants. When he heard the water slosh in the bathtub, heard her sigh as she descended into the warm, fragrant water, he gave a single knock on the bathroom door and pushed it open.

The white bubbles covered Scarlett's naked body modestly in the flickering candlelight. Only the tops of her breasts and a small bit of belly protruded as she looked back at him in surprise.

Her long red hair was piled high in a topknot, but tendrils of hair fell down her neck. Her cheeks were flushed pink, her full lips red and parted.

Vin had braced himself for seeing her naked, but the image still hit him low in the gut. Very low. It wasn't like he could hide his desire, either, in the low-slung sweatpants. His chest was bare, showing his shape from hours burning off energy and rage in the boxing gym and martial arts dojo. His hard flat belly was dusted with dark hair, like an arrow pointing down to the center of his desire.

So be it. Let her look.

Let his intentions be clear.

"What are you—" Her voice came out a croak. She swallowed, then looking up at his face, she said in a steadier voice, "What do you want?"

"I told you." He came closer, giving her a sensual, heavy-lidded smile. "I want to make you feel good."

"You made me this bath."

"I can do even better," he said silkily. "If you'll let me."

For a moment, she seemed to hold her breath.

"What did you have in mind?"

Vin sat behind her, on the tiled edge of the enormous marble tub.

He knew he could reach down, turn her face to his and claim her lips. Claim all of her. But he forced himself to take it slow. To seduce her, bit by bit.

"Let me show you," he said softly.

With agonizing slowness, he lowered his hands to her naked shoulders peeking out above the bubbles. Amid the flickering shadows, he sucked in his breath at the sensual shock of feeling her warm, slippery skin beneath his fingers, and knowing that she was naked beneath the rose petals and bubbles, there for his pleasure, just waiting for him to claim her.

Closing his eyes so he wouldn't be tempted by the soft sway of the water visibly caressing her round breasts, he began to rub her shoulders. His massage was light at first, then gradually he increased the pressure.

Scarlett exhaled, as though the stress of months or years was melting beneath his touch. Using his fingertips, his thumbs, he rubbed the knots away from her shoulders and neck. She closed her eyes, her rosy face the picture of pleasure as she leaned against his hands, like a cat meeting his stroke.

After a few minutes, when her face was blissfully peaceful, his hands began to move differently. Slowly, he moved past her shoulders to her upper arms, then her neck. He brushed the tender flesh of her earlobes with the flicker of a caress.

By now, the bubbles had mostly disappeared, and he could see the curves of her naked body beneath the water. He had himself under control now—for the moment—but he was also only a man. Too much of this and he might dive headlong into the enormous bathtub with her, to make love to her against the hard marble, amid the slosh of the cooling water.

Lowering his head to the nape of her neck, Vin brushed the red tendrils of her hair aside and kissed her, his lips lingering sensually on her skin.

Scarlett felt the brush of Vin's lips against the sensitive skin of her neck, and it was like lightning sizzling through her. All peace disappeared.

The water's temperature had cooled, and more alarmingly, the bubbles had diminished, no longer providing camouflage. Her breasts were entirely visible now, gleaming wet and flicked with only a few tiny bubbles like decorative pearls. Her hard nipples were rosy beneath the water.

"Scarlett, look at me," Vin said in a low, savage voice.

She had no choice but to obey. Tilting her head, she looked at his handsome face. Her eyes unwillingly traced his half-naked body, his thickly muscled chest, the trail of dark hair that led downward from his belly to the low waistline of his dark gray sweatpants, and below that…!

Even in the soft candlelight, she could see the outline

of him, huge and hard for her. Involuntarily, she sucked in her breath with a whimper.

"I want you," he growled.

She swallowed. She wanted him, too, desperately. But she was afraid of what would happen if she surrendered to him completely. Would it be the start of a wonderful, loving, lifelong marriage? Or would it be the beginning of a lifetime of misery?

He was physically perfect. While she… She glanced back at her own body and her cheeks burned self-consciously. "But I'm so big…"

"Yes. You are." His hand reached down to cup a pregnancy-swollen breast, as if feeling the weight. It overflowed his hand as he tightened his fingers around an aching nipple. "And I want you as I've never wanted any woman."

The pleasure of his touch was so sharp and raw it made her gasp.

Lowering his head, he kissed her, his lips hot and smooth as silk. Fire flooded through her. She kissed him back, water sloshing around her as she placed her hand against his cheek.

"Oh, Vin," she breathed. "I want you, too…"

And she kissed him recklessly.

Abruptly, his arms plunged into the bathtub. Reaching around her, he lifted her naked, wet body from the cool water, carrying her against his hard bare chest as if she weighed nothing at all. He slowly set her down to stand in front of him, her naked body sliding against his, before her feet reluctantly touched the white fluffy rug.

She was eight and a half months pregnant, and standing naked in front of him. She was so heavy. How could he want her? How could any man find her sexy, let alone Vin Borgia, who was so handsome and powerful he could have had any woman on earth?

But he didn't love her. She shivered. If she surrendered now, would she regret it for the rest of her life?

"You're cold," he murmured. Grabbing an enormous white cotton towel, he gently wrapped her in it.

But she wasn't shivering from cold. Swallowing, she looked up at him, her heart in her throat.

"I'm not exactly your usual supermodel," she said, trying for levity, but her voice trembled around the edges.

"No. You're not." He ran his hands gently through her hair, loosening the topknot so the damp waves tumbled down her shoulders. "There is nothing *usual* about you, Scarlett. You are special. The most beautiful, resourceful, kindhearted woman I've ever known." Holding the towel, he pulled her closer. "But that's not why I want you in my bed."

"It's not?"

He shook his head. "My need for you is far more primitive than that." His fingertips traced the bare skin lightly from her collarbone to the hollow between her breasts. "You're in my blood, Scarlett." His voice lowered almost to a growl. "You belong to me, and I intend to have you."

The moment stretched out between them, threatening to snap.

Belong to him?

She couldn't belong to him.

Not when he didn't belong to her. He didn't love her, and she didn't know if he ever would.

Panic rose from her heart to her throat. "No—"

Ripping the towel from his grasp, she turned and fled, practically slamming the door behind her.

In the bedroom, she beat the world record for finding her oversize T-shirt and cotton panties in a drawer. Within thirty seconds, she was tucked into the enormous bed, the heavy bedcovers pulled tightly to her neck.

The bedroom was dark. Her heartbeat drummed in her

throat as she waited for Vin to come out of the bathroom. What did she hope to achieve by hiding in this bed? They were sharing the room. He'd just have to sleep on the sofa by the window, she thought.

But Vin Borgia didn't seem like the kind of man who would politely take himself off to sleep on the sofa. Not when he'd made such a ruthless declaration.

You've in my blood, Scarlett. You belong to me, and I intend to have you.

She jolted when she heard the door abruptly open, causing a trickle of light across the bed. She squeezed her eyes shut as she heard him blow out the candles in the bathroom, one by one. Then silence.

"Go sleep on the sofa!" she tried to say, but her voice wouldn't work. She heard the echo of heavy footsteps coming toward her. They stopped.

The mattress beneath her swayed. She felt his warmth, breathed in the scent of sandalwood. Nervously, she scooted to the other side of the enormous king-size bed. Her heart was pounding. Part of her yearned desperately for him to reach out and pull her into his arms—but she was oh, so afraid of giving him complete power over her!

He reached for her in the darkness, and without a word, slowly, he turned her to face him. She felt his fingertips tantalizingly trail the edge of her hair, her shoulder, her hip.

His hand cupped her full breast, his palm moving against her aching nipple through her thin white cotton T-shirt. His other hand moved lingeringly over the curve of her belly, moving lower, and lower still. She felt something pressing hard against her and realized he was naked.

Tension coiled deep inside her, a sweet ache of need that was starting to build beyond her control.

She'd thought she knew desire from their first night together, their night of escape and exploration and discovery. But this was something else. Something else entirely.

Pregnancy hormones had given a fierce edge to her sexual need that she'd never experienced before. Or maybe it was because she now wore his ring on her finger, she was sleeping in his bed, she was pregnant with his child and soon would be his wife.

She wanted him. She wanted *this*. All of it. A home with warmth and comfort. A family. But most of all she wanted something impossible: she wanted him to love her...

She pulled back, struggling to see his face in the darkness. Her eyes adjusted, and the scattered moonlight from behind the window blinds silhouetted the hard edges of his cheekbones and jawline with silver.

Could he ever love her? Or was he just seducing her into marriage, for the sake of their baby?

She yearned to ask but didn't have the courage. Instead, she whispered, "Kiss me."

She heard his intake of breath, then felt the hard, sweet taste of his mouth on hers.

He kissed her for minutes—or hours—until her cheeks felt abraded from the roughness of the dark bristles on his jawline. His mouth was hungry and hard, pushing her lips apart as he teased her with his tongue. She clutched his shoulders, electrified by the heat of his hard naked body, the strength and size of him against her. She gripped him tight as his hands roamed possessively over the curves of her breasts and thighs.

Breaking the kiss, he pushed her back against the bed and slowly kissed down her body, stroking her full breasts and the mound of her belly and her voluptuous hips through her thin cotton T-shirt until he knelt at the foot of the bed. Spreading her feet apart, he caressed the hollows of her feet, the tender skin of her ankle.

Then he started moving upward. He kissed and caressed her calves. He kissed her knees, and the hollows beneath them, with a sensual flick of his tongue. Moving inexorably toward her thighs, he pushed her T-shirt up to her hips, leaving her cotton panties exposed.

Stroking the outside of her thighs, he positioned his head between them, and she started to shake.

Using his large hands to spread her legs wide, he kissed and nibbled her inner thighs. His breath warmed her skin, causing prickles of heat and furious desire to spread like wildfire through her body.

He teased her, kissing her softly with little flicks of his tongue along the edge of her panties. He cupped her mound over the thin cotton, rubbing the most sensitive part of her with his palm, leaving her gasping with need.

Her hands gripped the bedsheet as her hips moved of their own accord, swaying beneath his touch.

He slowly pulled her cotton panties down the length of her legs, in a whisper of sensation. She held her breath, squeezing her eyes shut as he moved back to her.

Placing his large hands on her inner thighs, he lowered his head. She felt his hot breath full against her, teasing her, and she quivered beneath him.

Spreading her wide, he took a long, languorous taste.

She gave a soft cry at the immediate wave of pleasure. It was almost too much. She tried to twist her hips away, but he held her more firmly against the bed.

He flicked the tip of his wet tongue lightly against her, swirling around her hard, aching nub in a circular motion. Then he spread her wide, lapping her hungrily with the full width of his tongue. She felt wet, so wet. She gasped as he eased a finger inside her.

Sweet agony built inside her, higher and higher. Her hips started to lift off the bed. A low cry came unbidden from her lips as he worked her roughly with his tongue, and his expert fingers teased her. Gripping his shoulders, she screamed, blinded by the bright explosion of pleasure.

He did not wait. With a low growl, he pulled her upright and yanked off her flimsy T-shirt, leaving her completely naked beneath him.

Her body was still boneless and satiated as he fell beside her on the mattress, rolling her over him, so she straddled his hard, naked body, her belly huge between them. With her knees over the hard planes of his hips, she felt the intimate press of his rock-hard body. He was enormous.

Her swollen breasts were angled toward his mouth. Lifting his head, he suckled each one greedily in turn, causing her to gasp and arch her back with the new sweet sensation of his lips and tongue and teeth. With her legs spread wide over his hips, she slid against him on instinct, her body tightening as she felt him press against her slick core, demanding entry.

He lifted her, positioned himself, then slowly thrust inside her, filling her inch by inch, filling her to the hilt.

She moaned as she felt him push deep inside her. Her hips moved, swaying, quivering around him. He was so thick, so hard. So deep—

Hearing his intake of breath, she looked down at his face. His eyes were closed, his expression rapt, and she suddenly realized that if he had power over her, she had power over him.

Slowly, she began to ride him. As his lips parted in a soundless gasp, she rode him harder and faster, her breasts swaying with the rough movement.

Tension coiled and built inside her, even higher than before. She leaned forward, gripping his muscled shoulders with her fingertips. She felt him tense beneath her, heard his gasp. She felt him try to draw back, to slow down—

But she wouldn't let him withdraw. She rode him hard, pushing him until his body started to shake beneath her.

She heard his rising growl and felt him explode inside her. Only then did she let herself go, and as she heard him cry out, her own world exploded into a million sparkling colors, before going black with the savage intensity of their joy.

CHAPTER SEVEN

AWARENESS CAME SLOWLY to Vin. It seemed like hours later when he opened his eyes.

Blinking in the darkness, he remembered they were in the guest room of the villa. Scarlett moved in his arms, warm and soft. His woman. His hands tightened on her as she slept.

He'd deliberately teased her, intending to make her insane with desire, to make her love him. But she wasn't the only one who'd lost control.

Setting his jaw, Vin stared up grimly at the ceiling.

What if his lie about the possibility of falling for her hadn't been a lie?

Could he really be starting to care?

No, he told himself fiercely. No way. He enjoyed having Scarlett in his bed. It was sexual pleasure. That was all it could possibly be.

But this place was messing with his brain. All of it. Italy. This villa. Being around family again. It all reminded him of who he'd once been, when all he'd wanted was to have a real home, to be loved.

But Vin had toughened up since then. Smartened up. Home could be anywhere. He owned more houses than he could keep track of, mostly as investments but also for his convenience. They were all decorated the same, modern and Spartan in stark black and gray, devoid of many personal details or clutter. That was always how he liked his relationships, too. In his opinion, "love" was a fancy decoration, as tacky and inappropriate as pink flounces or Victorian chintz.

He put his hand to his forehead, feeling a sense of vertigo. He couldn't let himself return to the vulnerable, tenderhearted boy he'd been. The boy who'd actually cared. The boy who'd felt things. Who'd hungered for things that had nothing to do with money—

It was this *place*, he thought angrily.

No. He looked at Scarlett sleeping so trustingly in his arms. It was *her*.

He couldn't let himself lose his head. He had to keep it together. Stay cool. Stick to the plan.

They would be married soon, he told himself. All he had to do was make her love him enough to sign the postnup. That was all.

But it was hard for Vin to keep his vow.

It took four more days, not three, before they were able to wed. The Borgias had been wrong. Even with the town mayor expediting paperwork, even with copies of their birth certificates—Vin's listed paternity a glaring lie that set his teeth on edge—there were certain formalities that had to be completed, and not even political connections or deep pockets could completely circumvent them.

Four days.

Four days of spending every moment with beautiful, intuitive, keen-eyed Scarlett and the wonderful people who believed themselves to be his family. Four days of listening to Maria prate on excitedly about her plans for their wedding. A required visit to the American Consulate in Florence turned into a pleasurable day of sightseeing with Scarlett, gawking at the Duomo followed by lunch at a charming café in the Piazza della Signoria. Four days of taking long walks in the Tuscan sunshine, eating glorious food.

Four days of talking to Scarlett, of learning about her, of finding new things to admire. One rainy afternoon by the fire, she'd suddenly set down her book and on impulse offered to show him the intricacies of picking a pocket.

He appreciated the lesson and, in return, offered to teach her how to fight. "My dad already showed me," she said primly. "I tried my punch out on Blaise in New York."

"I bet you did," he said, grinning at her. "All right. Here's how to use your own body weight against an attacker who grabs you from behind. Bet your dad didn't teach that."

Vin still smiled, remembering how pleasurably those lessons had ended—in bed together.

Such a strange way to live, Vin thought. He wasn't accustomed to such a luxurious squandering of time. He usually spent eighteen-hour days in the office, and that was what he should have been doing now, nailing down the details of the upcoming Mediterranean Airlines deal.

Instead, he sent his assistant on to Rome without him. He told his staff to handle everything, promising only that he'd arrive in Rome for the face-to-face meeting required by the other company's CEO, Salvatore Calabrese.

He'd spent the last twenty years focused on work. He told himself he'd be justified to take a few days off, but this was no mere vacation. He had a clear goal: making Scarlett love him so she'd sign the postnuptial agreement giving him the permanent control he needed to protect his son.

At least that was what Vin told himself as he spent hours walking with Scarlett through brilliantly colored autumn fields, on footpaths laced with cypress trees, holding her hand as they talked about everything and nothing. Hours of lingering together over meals, midday picnics beneath the golden sunlight, evening dinners inside by the fire. Vin found out why Scarlett was such a bad cook. "The day after my mother died, I tried to cook a can of soup over an open stove and nearly burned the house down." She smiled. "My father declared he'd be in charge of meals for safety reasons. My job was to keep the house clean and focus on school, when I was able to go."

She smiled about it now, but when Vin broke down the many sources of pain in that sentence—her mother died, they had to cook over an open stove, she wasn't always able to go to school—he marveled at her resiliency. He admired her strength.

That didn't stop him from arguing about what they'd name their son. He wanted a simple name like John or Michael. She wanted an Italian name from his family. "Like Giuseppe," she'd suggested hopefully. Vin had shut that idea down fast.

But he was afraid his emotions were starting to be compromised after four solid days of getting to know her mind and heart. Four nights of utterly exploring her body.

He'd spent hours kissing Scarlett, running his hands over her lush curves and overheated skin, as they'd set their bedroom on fire. They'd made love in every possible way as he'd explored every possibility of giving her pregnant body the deepest pleasure.

All in all, they'd been days and nights he would never forget. He was almost regretful to see them end.

But his plan was working. He could see it in Scarlett's green eyes when she looked at him now.

Against her will, she was starting to love him.

Perhaps Scarlett would have fallen in love with him anyway, without him trying so hard. Most women did. It was not something he was vain about; it was simply a fact. They could not resist his sex appeal, his raw power and the underlying attraction of his billions in the bank. He didn't have to *try* with women. It was usually the opposite. He would be cold to them, and they stunningly and stupidly loved him for it.

Scarlett was different.

For one thing, she didn't lust for money. In fact, she was suspicious of it as a manipulative tool. That just proved her intelligence, which made her even more desirable.

Seducing her in bed had been easy. Winning her heart was a little more tricky.

He'd had to share his *feelings*.

His *regrets*.

He still shuddered a little, remembering their conversation as they'd walked beneath the cypress trees last night, in the cool October air.

"Why did you move to New York after your mother died?" She'd looked up at the villa, the windows gleaming with warm light in the darkness. "You were only fifteen. Why didn't you come live here?"

His body had tensed. He should have known she wouldn't let that go. He'd wanted to say something sarcastic, or tell her to mind her own business. But looking at her hopeful, vulnerable expression, he'd known he had to do better than that, at least until they were safely married and he had the signed post-nup. And as intuitive as she was, he couldn't tell her a lie, either. So he'd shaped his mouth into something he hoped looked like a smile and told her part of the truth.

"Even at fifteen, I dreamed of starting my own company. Building my own fortune. My uncle was a hard-driving corporate lawyer. I knew if I moved to New York he'd be able to help me."

And Iacopo Orsini had. When Vin was eighteen, he'd taken all the money he'd saved from constant work, and the untouched payout from his mother's life insurance, and asked his uncle to help him draw up the necessary papers to set up his first company. Iacopo had also led by example, showing Vin it was possible to work every waking hour, and avoid inconsequential things, like spending time with family and loved ones. Or even *having* loved ones.

"Oh," Scarlett had said, and the light in her eyes had faded as she bit her lip. "That makes sense, I guess."

"Flying makes me feel alive," he'd heard himself add. "It gives me a sense of control. I can go anywhere. Do anything. Be whoever I want to be."

"It's your idea of freedom."

"Yes."

"That's funny. My idea of freedom is being able to stay in one place, as long as I want, surrounded by family and friends. Freedom," she said quietly, "would be a real home, filled with love, that no one would ever be able to take from me."

Their eyes locked in the moonlight, and for one crazy moment he'd wanted to tell her everything. He'd been tempted to offer up not just his body, not just his name, but his past, his pain, his heart. His future.

But it was a risk he couldn't take.

"Come on," he'd said abruptly. "Let's go inside."

The memory of how he'd felt last night still left Vin feeling uncomfortable. Vulnerable. Exposed. He didn't like it. It was a situation he didn't intend to repeat.

He had to get the papers signed as soon as possible so he could get back to a life he recognized, a life under his control.

But first things first.

Today was their wedding day.

Vin looked at his bride now, as she stood across from him in the villa's courtyard with the view of the wide Tuscan fields, as Giuseppe, as mayor of Borgierra, spoke the words that would bind the two of them in marriage.

In the distance, Vin could hear the plaintive cry of birds as they soared across the bright blue sky, as they were watched by Joanne and Maria and the other friends and Borgia relatives who'd packed in around them.

Vin couldn't look away from Scarlett's beautiful face.

Her warm green eyes sparkled in the sun, shining with joyful tears as she smiled up at him. She was wearing a simple sheath dress in creamy duchesse satin, purchased in Milan, altered for Scarlett's advanced state of pregnancy. Her red hair tumbled down her shoulders, and she had a tiny fascinator with a single cream-colored feather and a bit of netting that his sister had selected. Large diamond studs to match her ring now sparkled in her ears, a gift from Vin. Maria had wanted her to hold a bouquet of white lilies, but on this one detail, Scarlett was firm: no lilies. "They're not just stinky, they're appallingly overpriced."

Vin smiled at the thought of Scarlett being worried about the price of flowers, when the diamonds she was wearing cost hundreds of thousands of euros.

Instead, she held a bouquet of autumn wildflowers. It was just like her, he thought. The vivid blooms were as bright as her hair, and the scent as sweet as her soul. But the wild roses still had thorns—little flashes of temper and fire.

Solemnly, Vin, then Scarlett, spoke the words that would bind them together as husband and wife. He didn't exhale until it was done and they were actually married. After everything it had taken to get her to the altar, it was surprisingly easy.

No man could now tear them asunder.

"You may kiss the bride," Giuseppe said happily.

Scarlett Ravenwood—Mrs. Scarlett Borgia now—looked up at him with joy suffusing her beautiful face.

Looking into her eyes, Vin felt dizzy with happiness. She was wearing his ring. Carrying his baby. Bearing his name. He hadn't felt like this since—

A cold chill went down his spine.

The last time he'd felt this happy had been in this very same villa, that Christmas when Giuseppe and Joanne had asked him to live with them. At fifteen, for the first time in his life, he'd felt wanted and loved. But within a week, he'd lost everything.

Looking at his wife's beautiful, joyful face, Vin felt a sharp twist in the gut, a darkness curling around his heart like a poisonous mist.

Letting himself be happy, letting himself care, was like asking for abandonment. For loneliness. *For pain.*

He couldn't let her change him. He couldn't let himself be vulnerable. He had to be tough. Strong. He had to keep his fists up.

"You can kiss her, son," Giuseppe repeated in English, smiling.

Lowering his head, Vin kissed her. The touch of her lips electrified him like a blessing—or a curse.

He heard applause and teasing catcalls from the loving, kind people around him. He wrenched away from the kiss. Staring at Scarlett, he suddenly couldn't breathe.

Giuseppe, Joanne, Maria and even, *especially*, Scarlett were so wrong to love him. If they only knew the truth—

As beaming family and friends came forward to offer their congratulations, Vin loosened the black tie of his tuxedo, feeling attacked by all the overwhelming, suffocating, terrifying love around him.

CHAPTER EIGHT

As SCARLETT SPOKE her wedding vows, looking up at Vin's dark eyes, she felt like every dream she'd ever had was coming true today.

Every day had been a new dream, from afternoons spent together in the cool autumn countryside, walking hand in hand as they talked about everything and nothing, to the deliciously hot nights they'd explored each other in bed, doing things that had nothing to do with talking. He made her feel…joyful. Sexy. Exhilarated.

He'd made her feel free. Like he accepted her just as she was. Like he…cared for her.

And she'd come to care for him, to respect and admire him. She'd started to even… But the thought scared her.

After all the romantic days and nights together, gazing into each other's eyes beneath the loggia and teasing each other with hot kisses behind the thick hedges of the garden maze, today's beautiful courtyard wedding, presided over by Vin's father, was the perfect end to such perfect days.

As she and Vin spoke their vows in the courtyard, surrounded by his family and friends, Scarlett looked up at him. She'd never seen such stark emotion in his dark eyes.

Was it possible Vin might be falling for an ordinary girl like her?

Scarlett's voice trembled as she spoke her vows, but Vin's voice was calm and steady and deep. She felt his lips brush softly against hers as a pledge of forever, and she thought she might die of happiness.

Then everything changed. The tenderness in Vin's

expression hardened, turned cold. As their family and friends came forward in the villa's courtyard to congratulate them, her brand-new husband dropped her hand as if it burned him and backed away, loosening his tie, as if he could barely stand to look at her.

What had happened? Scarlett didn't understand. She felt confused and hurt as she followed him into their wedding reception lunch, held immediately afterward in the great hall inside the villa. She tried to tell herself she was being too sensitive. They'd just gotten married, with a lifelong vow. That was what mattered. Not that he'd dropped her hand after he kissed her, and his eyes suddenly looked cold.

But it troubled her as she sat beside Vin at the head table through the elegant wedding lunch.

She looked around the great hall. Maria had outdone herself. The enormous room was filled with flowers and people and music. It was so warm with love, it barely needed the fire in the enormous stone fireplace. When the staff served a lunch of pasta and salad, Vin ate silently beside her. Scarlett smiled at him shyly.

He glowered back.

Scarlett's cheeks turned hot with embarrassment as she looked away. Maybe it was the sudden tension between them, but her lower back and belly started to ache strangely. She sipped sparkling juice instead of champagne, one hand rubbing her belly over the knee-length, cream-colored satin dress.

She told herself to relax. Whatever was bothering Vin, they had hours to work it out before they left for Rome tonight. He would close the deal with Mediterranean Airlines tomorrow morning. Vin wanted to check them into a suite at the best hotel in Rome tonight, their wedding night. While he was signing the papers, she could meet her new doctor and prepare for their baby's imminent birth.

She was trying to convince him that they should skip the hotel and go directly to live in the home he'd grown up in, but he resisted.

"It's a mess," he'd said shortly.

Now, sitting at the wedding luncheon, Scarlett sighed. Pasting a smile on her face, she turned away from Vin, who was still glowering silently at nothing, and turned to chat with Giuseppe and Joanne and Maria and her fiancé, Luca. She laughed and applauded as their friends and neighbors offered champagne toasts, half of which she couldn't understand, as they were in Italian, but they were lovely all the same. She just wished her parents could have been here to see her wedding day.

Tears rose to her eyes as her new father-in-law and mother-in-law and sister-in-law all hugged her and teased her and constantly asked if they could get her anything.

She had a family again. After all her years alone, she hated to leave them.

Rome was only three hours away, she comforted herself. She glanced at her handsome new husband. Maybe Rome would be even more amazing. The city where their baby would be born. Their first real home. It would be where their life together would begin.

Tears filled her eyes as she listened to Giuseppe's emotional toast, as he praised his son and expressed his gratitude that he'd returned to the Borgia family after so many years apart. She was still wiping her eyes and applauding at the end of his speech when Vin suddenly growled in her ear, "We need to go."

"Go?" Scarlett blinked. "But you said we could stay the entire day—"

"I changed my mind." He tossed his napkin over his empty plate. "I want to be in Rome before dark. I still have a lot of work to do. We've wasted enough time here."

Wasted? The best days of her life?

Scarlett took a deep breath, struggling not to take it personally. "All right. I understand." She was trying to understand, but her heart felt mutinous. She bit her lip, looking around. "We'll need a little time to say goodbye—"

"You have two minutes." Rising to his feet, he stalked toward the table where his bodyguards were busily flirting with two of the local girls.

Scarlett stared after him, shocked and hurt. The muscles around her pregnant belly clenched and she felt a sharp tinge in her lower back that made her leap to her feet.

"What is it?" Giuseppe said.

"I'm afraid we have to go," Scarlett said. "Vin is anxious to get to Rome. You know he has the big business deal in the morning…"

"That is a pity," Giuseppe said, rising to his feet. "You can't stay the rest of the day?"

"Thank you." Vin was suddenly beside her. He held out his hand to Giuseppe and said coldly, "It was a very nice wedding."

"You're welcome?" His father looked bemused as Vin shook his hand, then Joanne's in turn.

"You can't leave, Vin!" cried his sister. "You haven't even cut the wedding cake! I've planned activities for the rest of the day. There's a dance floor, and…"

"I'm sorry. As I told you from the beginning, I have an unbreakable appointment in Rome."

"Oh. Right." Maria looked crestfallen. Her fiancé, Luca, put his arm around her encouragingly. She bit her lip, tried to smile. "Of course, I… I understand."

Scarlett didn't understand. Why did they have to leave so soon, cutting off their wedding celebration? It seemed not just rude, but nonsensical. But she forced herself to hold her tongue.

Vin held out his hand to his sister, but the young brunette just brushed his hand aside and threw her arms around him in a hug. He stiffened, but she drew back with a smile. "We will see you soon, brother. Luca's family lives in Rome. He's trying to convince me to have our wedding there!"

"Oh?" His voice was cool.

"But we will see you sooner than that, I hope." Looking at Scarlett, she said, "Call us when the baby comes."

"Of course," she replied warmly, trying to make up for her husband's rudeness. "We will never forget all your kindness."

"Not kindness," Giuseppe insisted, patting Scarlett's shoulder. *"Family."*

She swallowed, blinking fast. "You've all been so wonderful…"

"Ciao." Vin grabbed Scarlett's wrist and pulled her away. She waved back at them, and they waved in return, until Vin and Scarlett were out of the villa and in the fresh air outside. The bodyguards were packing their luggage into the SUV.

"That was rude," Scarlett said to Vin as he helped her into the passenger side of the two-seater.

Vin's face was chilly as he climbed in beside her, starting up the engine. "You asked me to stop here for ten minutes, and we stayed for five days. What did you want, *cara*—to live here permanently?"

Without looking back, Vin pressed on the gas, driving around the stone fountain with a squeal of tires.

Twisting her head, Scarlett saw a crowd had poured out of the villa's front door to wave goodbye and cry out their good wishes. "Vin, wait!"

He ignored her, pressing down harder on the gas pedal until they were on the cypress-lined road, out of the villa's view, and all she could see were the bodyguards following in the big SUV behind them.

"What is wrong with you?" Scarlett demanded as she faced forward in her seat, folding her arms over her belly. "Why are you acting like this?"

"I'm not acting like anything. We stayed for the wedding. I thanked them for their kindness. It's time to go."

"We were rude! After everything they did for us—"

"Send them a thank-you card," he said harshly.

Gripping the wheel of the car, he made record time down the tree-lined road across the wide Tuscan fields, and they soon returned to the main road.

Scarlett was fuming. Arms folded tightly, she glared out her window, lips pressed tightly together. The interior of the car was silent for a long time, until they were back on the heavily trafficked *autostrada* headed south toward Rome.

"Stop pouting," he said coldly.

"I'm not." She continued to glare out the window at the passing Italian countryside. "I'm mad, which is something else entirely."

"Stop being mad, then." He paused. "I meant to tell you. I got you a wedding present."

Her jaw tightened, but she still refused to look at him.

"It isn't a gift that I could wrap," he continued, obviously counting on her curiosity to overcome her fury. "It's something I did for you."

"Well?" Wiping her eyes, Scarlett turned her glare on him. "What is it?"

Dodging through the increasing traffic of the highway, he said, "Blaise Falkner."

She frowned. "What about Blaise?"

Vin gave her a triumphant sideways glance. "I've ruined him." His lips spread into a grin. "He'll never be able to threaten you again. Or anyone."

Scarlett stared at Vin, feeling hollow. "What do you mean, you ruined him?"

"He's penniless, disgraced, destroyed. Abandoned by his friends. Even the Falkner mansion is getting repossessed in New York. So he's also homeless." Vin turned dark eyes on her. "I did it for you."

"I never asked for that!"

His jaw was hard as he focused on the road. "I protect what is mine."

Scarlett shivered, hearing an echo of memory.

What century do you think we're living in?

The century a rich man can do whatever he wants. To whomever he wants.

As the red car sped down the highway, she felt her belly again tighten painfully. It had been doing that with increasing frequency. Stress would do that, she told herself. It was stress. Not the early signs of labor.

She breathed, "What did you do?"

"Falkner wasn't as rich as people thought." Vin changed lanes rapidly, rather than slow down with the traffic. He gave a smug, masculine smile. "His inheritance barely covered half his debt. He refused to work and was spending thousands of dollars every night for bottle service in clubs. And women. I merely made sure his lines of credit were not extended and allowed his true financial situation to become public."

"You used your influence with the banks?"

"I'm a very good customer."

"And dropped hints to some aggressive reporter?"

He tilted his head thoughtfully. "I believe in freedom of the press."

"But how did you get his friends to abandon him?"

"Ah, that was the easiest part. Half of them only endured his company because he always footed the bill. He owed the other half money. Once he was broke—no more friends."

Scarlett might have felt bad for Blaise Falkner, if she

didn't still remember the terror she'd felt when he'd threatened to take her baby away and force her into marriage.

But still...

"Revenge is wrong," she said in a low voice.

"You're angry?" Now Vin was the one to look shocked. His expression turned hard. "He deserved it. He deserved worse."

Vin's expression scared her. He didn't look like the good-hearted man she'd come to know in Tuscany. He looked like the ruthless billionaire she'd fled in New York.

She felt tension building in her body. She put her hands on her baby bump and felt the muscles of her belly harden. Like a contraction. She took a quick breath. "You could have...just left him alone."

"I have the right to protect my family."

"We aren't in danger! We're thousands of miles away!" She took another deep breath, trying to will her body to calm down, to relax. If she could, then maybe these contractions would stop. "It was revenge, pure and simple."

"What do you want, Scarlett?" His black eyes flashed. "Should I have bought the man a pony, tucked him in with milk and cookies, thanked him for the way he threatened my wife and child? Is that what you think?"

"I think—" Her breathing was becoming increasingly difficult. She was beginning to feel shooting pains radiating from her lower spine with increasing frequency. Then—

She sucked in her breath as she felt a sudden rush, a sticky mess. She looked down at her cream satin wedding dress in dismay. At the expensive black leather seat below it.

She whispered, "I think I'm in labor."

"You—" His hard voice abruptly changed in tone. "What?"

"My water just broke."

Scarlett felt scared. Really scared. She looked at her husband. Vin stared at her, his dark eyes shocked.

Then his jaw tightened. "Don't worry, Scarlett." He grimly changed the gears of the Ferrari. "I'll get you to the hospital."

He stomped on the gas, and they thrust forward on the highway as if shot by a cannon. If she'd thought the car was going a little too fast before, now it went on wings, flying past the other cars like a bullet.

She braced herself, gripping her seat belt with one hand and her tightening belly with the other. Yet strangely, in this moment, her fear was gone.

Scarlett looked at her husband's silhouette. Through the opposite window, she saw the darkening shadows of the Italian countryside flying past in smears of purple and red. And though she had been so terrified a moment before, she suddenly knew Vin, so capable and strong, would never let anything bad happen to her or their baby. He would protect them from any harm. Even death itself…

She glanced behind them. "We lost the bodyguards."

"They'll catch up."

Scarlett held her belly as she gasped out with the pain of a bigger contraction. She felt Vin automatically tense beside her. Then she made the mistake of looking behind them again. "Oh, no—"

Vin glanced in the rearview mirror and saw flashing police lights. Scarlett saw him hesitate. She knew he was tempted to keep driving, even if every single policeman in Italy chased them.

But with a rough curse, he pulled abruptly off the *autostrada*.

The police car parked behind them. As Vin rolled down his window, the young policeman came forward, speaking in good-natured Italian. Vin interrupted, pointing at Scarlett in a desperate gesture. The man's eyes widened when he saw her sticky wedding dress, as she gripped her belly and nearly sobbed with the pain.

Five minutes later, a police car was clearing their path with siren and flashing lights as their car roared south to the nearest hospital.

Standing in the bright morning light of their private room in the new, modern hospital, Vin cradled his newborn son in his arms, staring down at him in wonder.

"I'll keep you safe," he whispered to the baby, who was gently swaddled in a soft blue baby blanket. "You'll always know I'm watching out for you."

Vin looked up tenderly at his wife, who was also sleeping. Labor hadn't been easy. She'd been too far along in her contractions to get any kind of epidural.

So her only option had been to just get through it, to breathe through each wave of agony that brought her closer to their baby being born. With each contraction, Scarlett had held Vin's hand tight enough to bruise, looking up at him pleadingly from the bed. He'd tried to stay strong for her, to hide his own anguish at seeing her pain. All he could do was hold her hand and uselessly repeat, "Breathe!"

Now Vin looked at Scarlett in wonder. She'd been so strong. He'd never seen that kind of courage. As she slept, he saw the smudged hollows beneath her eyes, dark eyelashes resting against her pale cheeks, subdued red hair spilling on the pillow around her.

He looked back down at their baby's tiny hand wrapped around his finger, and another wave of gratitude and love washed over him.

"Happy birthday," he said to his son, smiling as he touched his small cheek with his fingertips. "I'm your *papà.*"

The baby kept sleeping.

Outside the hospital room window, Vin saw a beautiful October morning, a bright blue sky. He blinked, then yawned, stretching his shoulders as much as he could without disturbing the baby. What a night it had been.

Sitting down in a chair beside the hospital bed where his wife slept, Vin held the baby for an hour, watching over them. He brushed back his baby's dark, downy hair, marveling at the tiny size of his head, his fragility. Vin could never let anything happen to his wife. Or his child.

His son would have a different childhood than he'd had. Vin's own earliest memory in life was of crying himself to sleep after his nanny locked him in his bedroom when he started crying loudly for his mother. His mother hired servants based on their cheapness, not their reliability or kindness, and he was often left to their care for weeks while she enjoyed time with her latest boyfriend in St. Barts or Bora Bora.

Except on those rare nights Vin's grandfather came to stay, no one ever comforted him when he heard a scary noise in the darkness or was frightened there was a monster under his bed. Vin had learned that the only way to survive was to be meaner than any monster. The only way to survive was to pretend not to be afraid.

But now, holding his son, Vin felt real fear. Because he knew that if this tiny baby was ever hurt, it would destroy him. It made him wonder how his own mother could have cared so much more for her momentary pleasures than her own son.

Vin took a deep breath. He'd be nothing like her. His son would always be his priority. From now on, that was his only duty. His only obligation. To keep his wife and child safe. He'd have to build an even bigger fortune, to protect them from worry or care. Vin's heart squeezed. He had a family to protect now. And he would. With his dying breath.

"Vin."

He looked up to see Scarlett's tired eyes smiling up at him. She held out her hand, and he immediately took it.

"Look at our son," he said softly. "The most beautiful baby in the world."

"You're not biased," she teased.

He shook his head solemnly. "It's not opinion. It's fact—" he smoothed back the soft edge of the baby blanket "—as anyone with eyes could see. He'll be a fighter, too."

"Just like his father."

It didn't sound like criticism, but praise; and hearing that from her made him catch his breath. The golden light of morning flooded the bed and the white tile floor, casting it in a haze as their eyes locked for a long moment. Then, leaning forward, he gently kissed her.

When he pulled away, her green eyes were luminous. Then they turned anxious. "But, Vin, what about your meeting? The deal with Mediterranean Airlines?"

Vin's jaw dropped. He'd *forgotten*. He'd totally forgotten about the meeting that was so important it had been circled in red on the calendar of his mind. He looked at the clock on the wall. He'd been so determined to get to Rome, and here he was, in a hospital just north of the city. The time was nine fifteen. The meeting had started at nine.

"Maybe you can still make it," Scarlett said. "Give me the baby. We can have Larson or Beppe meet you outside. You still—"

"No." His voice was quiet, but firm.

"Are you sure?" He could see the desperate hope in her eyes that he would stay, even as she said, "I know what this deal means to you. You should go."

He wondered what it cost her to say that. Being abandoned in an Italian hospital outside Rome, exhausted and still recovering from her physical ordeal, with an hours-old baby, couldn't be what she wanted. But she encouraged him because she wanted him to have what he desired most.

But for the first time, something compelled Vin more than his business, or money, or even power.

He couldn't leave his wife and their newborn son. Not now. Not after everything he'd just seen Scarlett endure. Not when his baby was still so tiny and fragile and new.

His place wasn't in a boardroom in Rome. His place was right here, keeping watch over the ones who depended on him far more than any employees or stockholders. The ones who really mattered. His family.

And if part of him was incredulous he was making this choice, even mocking him for it, he pushed that aside. "I'm staying." He looked back at the baby. "What shall we call him?"

She looked at him with barely concealed relief, then smiled. "A name that has meaning in your family. If not Giuseppe, what about Vincenzo?"

"After me?" Vin shuddered, then shook his head. "Our baby deserves better. He must have a name of his own." He thought for a moment, then said haltingly, "My *nonno*— my mother's father—was very kind to me. He died when I was eight, but I never forgot him. He made Christmas special." His lips quirked at the edges. "He said it was his job, because of his name. Nicolò."

She considered. "Nicolas?"

Vin looked at his baby son's face and nodded. "Nico," he said softly. "I like it."

For long moments, they held hands without speaking, Scarlett propped against pillows in the hospital bed and Vin cradling their baby in the chair beside her. He thought he'd maybe never been happier, or so at peace.

But it ended too soon as Ernest, his executive assistant, burst into the hospital room. "Sir, did you turn off your phone? I have been calling."

"Obviously," Vin said tightly, "I did not wish to be disturbed. Whatever the problem, you can handle it."

"The deal just fell apart and the other CEO stormed out when you didn't appear this morning. Everything is a shambles in the Rome office..."

As he spoke, a nurse bustled in and wanted to check over Scarlett and the baby. Nico himself began to complain that he was hungry and wanted his mother.

As Scarlett eagerly took her baby into her arms, the chaos increased as Vin heard an argument in the hallway. Ernest went to check it out, closing the room's door behind him. But the arguments only got louder through the door.

"Handle your guests, please," the nurse told Vin crisply in Italian. "This is a hospital, not a nightclub."

Vin ground his teeth, then turned to his wife with a bright smile. Kissing her forehead, he excused himself and went out into the hall.

One of his bodyguards was physically blocking a slender man in glasses who was yelling and trying to push into the private room. Ernest was trying to mollify him in a low voice.

"What is going on?" Vin demanded.

"Ah. Signor Borgia." The slight man immediately relaxed and turned to him politely. "Salvatore Calabrese sent me. He wished to convey his displeasure at your disrespect today."

"No disrespect to Signor Calabrese was meant. As you can see, I was unable to personally meet him this morning to close the deal with Mediterranean Airlines because I was called away on urgent family business."

"Signor Calabrese found your lack of commitment to the business deal very disappointing. He wished me to inform you that he is father to four children and was not present at a single one of their births."

Vin wondered that any man would brag about something like that, but he said merely, "I would be pleased to reschedule—"

"That is sadly now impossible." The man pushed up his wire-rimmed glasses. "Signor Calabrese will be exploring options with your Japanese and German competitors, many of whom have larger, more established airlines than yours. He hopes you enjoy family time," the man continued politely, "as you'll soon have much more of it. Without the expansion your airline needs, you'll soon be ripe for takeover yourself." The man gave a little bow. "Good day."

As he departed, Vin stared after him in shock.

The Japanese and German airlines who also hoped to take over Mediterranean Airlines were indeed formidable and powerful. It hadn't been easy to convince Salvatore Calabrese that SkyWorld Airways was the right choice. Vin had been forced to personally meet with him in New York and London.

"All right. I'll take a gamble with you, kid," Salvatore Calabrese had told him finally. "You remind me of myself when I was young. A shark who'll win at any cost." He'd given Vin a hard smile. "Just meet me in Rome to sign the papers. I need that mark of respect. Plus, I need to know I'm selling my baby to a man who'll always put his company first."

Now Vin clawed his hand through his dark hair, thinking of the hours, money and effort that he and his team had spent, costing millions of dollars and thousands of hours, to put the deal together. This on top of the public debacle in New York of losing the Air Transatlantique deal. The snotty little assistant had been right. Vin's rivals would start to smell blood in the water.

A stab went through him as he felt the cost of making his family the priority today. Twice now, his relationship with Scarlett had wrecked badly needed business deals. And now, just when he most needed his airline to succeed, for the sake of his family, for the sake of his son's future legacy, he was facing another failure.

"It'll be all right, boss." Ernest looked at him nervously. "Plenty of other fish in the sea. Lots of ways to expand our airline. Right, Mr. Borgia?"

His executive assistant clearly expected reassurance, but Vin stared at him blankly.

For the first time ever, he didn't know his next move.

Maybe this was what happened, Vin thought numbly. When you started choosing with your heart, instead of your head.

CHAPTER NINE

"CAN'T YOU GO SLOWER?" Scarlett pleaded.

"No." Her husband sounded annoyed.

"Just a little—"

"Scarlett, this is Rome. If we go any slower, we'll be run over."

Sitting in the backseat of their brand-new Bentley SUV, she looked anxiously at their three-day-old baby quietly tucked in his baby seat beside her, looking up at her so trustingly, with those big dark eyes like Vin's.

At least, she comforted herself, he hadn't insisted on using the sports car. The two-seater had been professionally cleaned, and Vin had donated it to the highway police. "A little gift to say thanks," he told her.

Scarlett was glad it had gone to a good home, and grateful to the kindhearted policeman who'd helped them get to the hospital so quickly.

She still remembered how terrified she'd been that day, and how awful labor had been. Her body had felt ripped apart. But already, that memory of pain was starting to fade every time she looked at her baby.

Scarlett was happy to be leaving the hospital. The hospital staff had been lovely, but she was ready to go home. Ready but also terrified. Because that meant there would no longer be medical professionals hovering to give quick advice if Nico couldn't sleep at night or didn't seem to be eating enough.

But at least Scarlett knew she had one person she could rely on. One person she could trust. The person who'd never left her side, not once, even though that choice had cost him dearly. And she loved him for it.

She loved Vin for that, and so much more.

She was totally, completely in love with him. There could no longer be any question. She'd known it when, after holding her hand uncomplainingly through long hours of labor, he'd tenderly placed their newborn baby in her arms.

"Look what you've created, Mrs. Borgia," he'd said, looking down at her with a suspicious gleam in his black eyes. "You should be proud."

"*We* created," she'd corrected, looking up at him.

"We," he'd whispered tenderly.

And that was that.

She loved Vin.

Another thing that thrilled her—and terrified her.

Heart in her throat, she looked at him, in the front seat beside their driver. Bodyguards were following in the black SUV. Vin had told her he wished to remain in Rome for the foreseeable future, in hopes of patching up the deal with Mediterranean Airlines. Scarlett had been delighted. She already adored this country, this city. How could she not?

But at the moment, her husband was looking back at her, his handsome face the picture of disbelief. "Are you sure you really want to do this?"

His tone implied she was crazy. He'd asked her the same question at least six times since their driver had picked them up from the hospital.

"I'm sure," Scarlett said calmly.

"I have reservations at the best hotel in Rome. The royal suite. We'd have an entire floor to ourselves, in total luxury with an amazing view. Room service," he added almost desperately.

Smiling, she shook her head. "That's not what I want."

Vin folded his arms, his expression disgruntled. "It's a mistake."

"It's not a mistake to want our baby to have a real home, instead of living in some hotel. I don't care how fancy it is."

"You'll care tonight, when there's no hot water and the beds are lumpy. The roof probably leaks."

"You'd really rather stay at a hotel than your own childhood home?"

"It wasn't particularly great then, and I'm sure it's worse now." He turned away as the driver drove them deeper into the city. "I've rented it out for the last twenty years, and from what my staff has told me, the tenant didn't exactly improve the situation."

"Oh, come on," Scarlett said with a laugh, rolling her eyes. "It's a villa in Rome. How bad could it be?"

The answer to that question came soon, as she gingerly entered the faded, dilapidated eighteenth-century villa, set behind a tall gate with a guardhouse and a private cobblestoned drive.

Holding the baby carrier carefully in her arms—she'd refused all offers from bodyguards and her husband to carry it, as her baby's eight pounds was precious cargo to her—Scarlett went through the enormous front door into the foyer. Stepping over the crumpled trash on the floor, she went farther into the villa.

On the high ceiling of the great room, a disco ball gleamed dully in the shadows. She stopped.

Black leather furniture, zebra and leopard print pillows, strobe lights and multiple bowls of overflowing cigarette butts decorated the room. In front of the enormous marble fireplace was a bearskin rug stained with red wine... at least she hoped it was wine. Empty liquor bottles littered every corner.

Wide-eyed, Scarlett turned to her husband, who was watching her with amusement. "I told you."

"Was your tenant a playboy?" she said faintly. "From the early seventies?"

"Styles change. People don't always change with them." Vin's lips quirked. "Luigi did live here a long time. He was quite the ladies' man, for eighty-five."

"Eighty-five! So did he move, or…?" She paused delicately.

Vin shook his head with a grin. "Decided he was finally ready to settle down. Moved to Verona and married his childhood sweetheart."

"Wow," Scarlett breathed. "Getting married. At eighty-five."

"Just goes to show it's never too late to change your life." His sensual lips lifted to a grin. "He only moved out last week. So this place hasn't been remodeled yet." He tilted his head. "The suite at the hotel is still available…"

Scarlett shook her head. "No hotels. When I was young, we didn't live in any house long enough to make memories, good or bad. Don't worry," she said brightly. "We'll make this the home of our dreams!"

He snorted. "Dream—or nightmare?"

"This house has good bones," she said with desperate hope. "Wait and see."

Later, Scarlett looked back and thought the next two months of remodeling the Villa Orsini were some of the happiest of her life.

Their first night was admittedly a little rough. The bodyguards brought in the necessary supplies, then hastily decamped to a neighboring three-star hotel. Only the bodyguard who'd lost the coin toss was forced to remain, and he chose to sleep on a cot in the foyer rather than face the rats' nests of bedrooms upstairs.

So it was just Vin and Scarlett and their baby sleeping

in the great room, where the black leather sectional sofas were in decent repair, that first night.

She and Vin heated water themselves on the old stove for the baby's first sponge bath. It was almost like camping. There were no servants hovering. No phones ringing incessantly. No television or computers, even. They just shared a takeaway picnic dinner on a blanket on the floor, then played an old board game that Vin found in a closet upstairs, before they both crashed on the sofa, with Nico tucked warmly into his portable baby car seat next to her.

Her husband was protective, insisting that Scarlett take the most comfortable spot on the sofa, offering to get her anything she needed at any moment. When the baby woke her up at two in the morning to nurse, Vin woke up as well and tucked a pillow under her aching arm that held the baby's head.

"Thank you," she whispered.

"It is nothing, *cara*." His eyes glowed in the darkness. "You are the hero."

Just the two of them, she thought drowsily, regular first-time parents, a married couple in love, with each other and with their newborn baby.

The next morning, the hiring began, of designers and architects and a construction crew to start the remodel. No expense would be spared. "If you're determined to live here," Vin told her firmly, "we'll get it done as soon as possible."

As the villa was cleared out, cleaned, and slowly began to take shape, Vin suggested that they bring in permanent house staff. He wanted two full-time nannies—one for day, one for night—and a butler, housekeeper, gardeners. After their blissful night alone together, Scarlett had been crestfallen. She'd tried to convince Vin that she could take care of the villa herself. He'd laughed.

"You want to spend your every waking hour scrubbing

floors? No. Leave that to others." He kissed her. "You have a far more important job."

"Taking care of Nico?" she guessed.

His dark eyes became tender. "Being the heart of our home." She melted a little inside. Then his smile lifted to an ironic grin. "You've got your work cut out for you, married to a ruthless bastard like me."

He was joking, of course, she thought loyally. Vin wasn't a ruthless bastard. He was a good man, and in spite of his tyrannical instincts, she knew he saw her as an equal partner. After all, he'd let her make the decisions about driving instead of flying, about remodeling the villa rather than enjoying the comfort of a hotel. And most of all, he had married her without a pre-nup. As partners, they had a chance to be happy in this marriage, she thought, really happy, for the rest of their lives.

The days passed, turned to weeks. November became December. Scarlett had pictured the Eternal City as a place of eternal sunshine, but to her surprise, winter descended on Rome.

The villa had become livable. Tacky old furnishings were removed, and the walls and floors of ten bedrooms were redone. The kitchen was expanded and modernized. Bathrooms were scrapped and remodeled, and one of the extra rooms was turned into a master en suite bathroom with walk-in closet. Vin had wanted to fly in the interior designer who'd decorated his New York penthouse, but remembering the stark black-and-gray décor from the single night she'd spent there, Scarlett had refused. She wanted to make the villa warm and bright and, above all, comfortable. She'd do the decorating herself.

She loved every minute. Each morning when the baby woke her up to be fed, Scarlett woke up with a smile on her face, stretching happily in the enormous bed. She didn't get much sleep, with the baby waking her through the night, but in spite of feeling tired, Scarlett had never been so happy. Joy washed over her like sunshine.

She had the home she'd always dreamed of. The family she'd always dreamed of. The husband she'd always dreamed of. She had everything she'd ever wanted, except one thing.

Vin hadn't told her he loved her.

But soon. Soon, she told herself hopefully. In the meantime, the villa was larger than she'd imagined her home could be, so she brought it down to size. Made it homey and inviting for family and friends.

She carefully began to add household staff. Wilhelmina Stone was the first person she hired, luring her away from Switzerland as housekeeper by doubling her salary.

"You don't need to pay me so much," Wilhelmina had grumbled. "We're practically family."

"Which is why I insist," Scarlett replied happily.

Then a few other employees were added, two maids and a gardener, but Scarlett flatly refused the idea of a butler and two full-time nannies. Instead, the kind, fiercely loyal housekeeper soon became a second grandmother to Nico.

When the guest rooms became habitable, the baby's actual grandparents, Giuseppe and Joanne, came down from Tuscany for a visit in December, bringing Maria and Luca with them. They all enjoyed a weekend of sightseeing, which was ostensibly to "show the baby the sights of Rome"—as if a five-week-old in a stroller who couldn't yet sit upright would appreciate the Colosseum, the Pantheon and the Trevi Fountain.

"Of course he appreciates them," Giuseppe said expressively, using his hands. "He is my grandson! It is in his blood!"

"He can't even taste gelato yet," Vin pointed out, rather peevishly, she thought.

It was the only discordant note to the joyful melody of Scarlett's life. Vin seemed strangely uncomfortable around his family, and the more loving they were, the more he seemed to flee. Thirty minutes into their sightseeing tour, he abruptly announced an emergency at the Rome office that seemed like an excuse to leave. But Scarlett must be mistaken, because why would he want to flee his family, who loved him so?

In spite of that small flaw, Scarlett was happy and proud to share their newly beautiful home with the family that had been so kind to her. The best moment was when Maria and Luca announced they'd picked a wedding date: the second week of January, in Rome.

"A winter wedding, in Rome," Maria had beamed, holding her fiancé's hand. "It'll be so romantic."

"*You* are romantic," Luca had said rapturously and kissed her.

Scarlett had looked at Vin, but he'd avoided her gaze.

Since his parents' visit, he'd seemed even more strangely distant, spending all his time at the office, where his company was trying to devise a new offer to interest Mediterranean Airlines' CEO, Salvatore Calabrese. But the man flatly refused to have anything to do with Vin now. It made Scarlett indignant, but she knew her husband would wear him down. No one could resist Vin for long. Scarlett knew this personally.

Except she hadn't had to resist him at all lately. At least not *personally*.

He hadn't touched Scarlett in bed since their baby was born. It had been two months now since they'd last made love. At first, healing from the birth and exhausted from waking up with their baby, sex had been the last thing on Scarlett's mind. But now her body was starting to feel normal again, though she hadn't quite lost all the baby weight, and her breasts were still very full. Did he not find her attractive anymore?

She tried to ignore the feelings of rejection. She focused on the baby, who was growing chubby and starting to babble and coo. She made friends with her neighbors and started private Italian lessons with Mrs. Spinoza, a kindly widow who lived down the street. But it hurt.

Then one day while she was despondently surfing the internet, she had an idea about how to bring them close again.

According to what she read, men's needs were simple. Food. Home. Sex.

All she had to do was turn herself into the perfect wife.

Step one. Food. A man's heart was through his stomach, according to what she read online. So Scarlett learned how to cook. She started with boiling water, but within a week, she'd graduated to simple, fresh pasta dishes, which Wilhelmina tasted and pronounced, with some surprise, to be "delicious."

Vin didn't notice, of course. He generally got home late at night and would eat whatever wrapped dinner plate he found in the fridge, by the light of his computer at the dining table at midnight, usually long after Scarlett had gone to bed. But she learned new skills when he wasn't looking.

Step two. Home. A man's house was his castle. Make it warm and comfortable, and he'd never want to leave it. She looked around their newly remodeled, redecorated home. Check.

Step three. Sex.

For Scarlett, this was the hardest thing of all.

But on Christmas Eve morning, she woke up knowing that it was now or never. Today was the day.

She felt like Vin had barely talked to her in weeks. He always made an effort to play with the baby right before work, but all Scarlett seemed to get from him were cold lectures when she evaded her security detail or told her assigned bodyguard, Larson, he didn't need to follow her. Which was exactly what she was getting this morning, too.

"Stop it." Vin glowered at her, coldly handsome in his suit and tie. "I specifically assigned Larson to keep you safe. Don't make it so hard for him to do his job."

Still wearing her nightshirt and white fluffy robe, Scarlett rolled her eyes. "You seriously think I'm going to be attacked on the streets of Rome in broad daylight while I'm pushing the stroller to Mrs. Spinoza's apartment? It's silly! How am I supposed to practice my Italian with Larson glaring at her through his sunglasses? He makes her so nervous she stutters!"

"I mean it, Scarlett," Vin replied. "Either do what I tell you and let him do his job, or…"

"Or what?"

His jaw was tight. "I can't answer for the consequences."

Then he coldly left the villa, briefcase in hand. Without so much as a goodbye kiss!

She prayed her outrageous plan would solve everything. Otherwise, she was about to make a horrible fool of herself. But she had to take the chance. As her father had always said, if you want things to change, change yourself.

The moment Vin left the villa for work, Scarlett got to work, too. The enormous tree was delivered to the great hall, along with boxes of beautiful decorations. She sent the last members of the household staff on surprise vacation, leaving Scarlett and the baby alone in the villa, with her bodyguard, Larson, at the tiny gatehouse across their private cobblestoned drive.

Holding Nico on her hip, Scarlett decorated the tree herself, talking happily to her baby, singing him Christmas songs, including one in Italian. Later, she started a roaring fire in the enormous fireplace and prepared a dinner she thought Vin would love. Leaving the sauce simmering on the stove as evening started to fall, she gave her sleepy baby his dinner and bath, changed him into his footsie pajamas and tucked him into the nursery.

After Nico was safely asleep, she went into her luxurious master bathroom and started a bath. She groomed herself as carefully as a bride on her wedding night—the wedding night they'd never actually had, since she'd gone into labor on her wedding day—and moisturized her body with lotion to make her skin soft as silk. She brushed out her long red hair until it gleamed.

She didn't get dressed. Following the advice she'd read online, she left off her clothes entirely, for maximum visual impact. Not even lingerie. Not even panties. She just covered her naked body with only an old-fashioned pinafore apron.

Then Scarlett waited, terrified and breathless, for Vin to come home from work.

Tonight, she would tell him she loved him.

And then he'd tell her he loved her, too, and their lifetime of happiness would begin.

Either that, or…

She shuddered, caught between longing and terror as she waited for the door to open.

As Vin stepped out of his chauffeured Bentley into the frosted darkness of his street, he felt bone-weary.

It was late on Christmas Eve night, almost ten o'clock. He gave a low curse as he looked at his expensive watch. "I'm sorry, Leonardo," he told his driver in Italian. "I've kept you from your family. Thank you for staying."

"No problem, Mr. Borgia." His driver beamed at him. "The Christmas bonus you sent is sending our whole family on vacation to the Caribbean next month. My wife also appreciated the delicious homemade *panettone* from Mrs. Borgia." He kissed his fingertips expressively. *"Delizioso."*

Vin stared at him blankly.

"I need to thank you, too, boss," Beppe, his bodyguard on duty, interrupted. The hulking man actually blushed. "I used the bonus to buy an engagement ring for my girlfriend. I'm giving it to her tomorrow morning. And Mrs. Borgia's *panettone* was delicious. I ate the whole cake watching last night's game."

Vin was shocked. Scarlett had learned how to bake? She'd arranged Christmas gifts for his staff? And not just the practical gift of money, but a personal gift of homemade Christmas cake? "Oh. Yes." He cleared his throat. "I'm glad you liked it."

He hadn't even known. Hadn't realized.

But then, he'd been distracted lately. As his bodyguard raced ahead to enter the security code, Vin trudged to the door. He'd really thought he'd be able to convince Salvatore Calabrese to sell him Mediterranean Airlines. But the man still wouldn't talk to him. Through his skinny assistant, he'd sent Vin a single cold message: "I'm interested in selling to sharks, not minnows." And no amount of corporate diplomacy could now convince him Vin was a shark. Not since he'd put his family's needs over a business deal.

Vin felt like he was failing. At his company. At home. Working such long hours, he barely saw his baby son an hour a day. As for his wife…

Vin shivered.

He wanted to see more of her.

Much more.

They hadn't made love since Nico's birth, and at this point, all Vin could think about when he was around her was that he wanted to throw her against the wall and take her.

But he couldn't.

After what he'd seen Scarlett go through in the hospital, he didn't know when—or even if—she'd ever want him to touch her again. He didn't even know how to broach the subject. He'd never had to struggle with this before. So rather than constantly feel sexually on edge around her, like a mindless beast with only the barest thread of self-control, it was almost easier to avoid her entirely.

Looking up at the four-story elegant villa that had become a palace beneath her magical touch, and his wife the untouchable princess living inside it, Vin felt weary.

"Go home," he told his bodyguard. "We'll be fine tonight."

Beppe looked doubtful. "That's not protocol. Especially when there's the danger of—"

"It's Christmas Eve," Vin cut him off. He didn't want to think about Blaise Falkner tonight, or the fact that the man had disappeared from New York two weeks ago and couldn't be found. Another arena in which things hadn't gone to plan. "Go home. We have the security alarm. I saw Larson in the gatehouse. He'll call you if he needs you."

"If you're sure…"

"Go home to your girlfriend."

Beppe's eyes lit up. "Thank you, Signor Borgia. *Buon Natale!*"

"Merry Christmas," Vin replied dully. Alone, he pushed open the tall oak door of the villa. He went into the foyer.

Yawning, he closed the door securely behind him, turning on the security alarm. Tossing his briefcase on a table, he hung up his long black coat. Wondering if Scarlett had already gone to bed, he walked into the great room.

And he stopped.

An enormous Christmas tree, twenty feet tall, now stood in the great room by the blazing fireplace, lit up with thousands of brilliant lights like stars beneath the wood beams of the high ceiling.

Beneath the tree, he saw something even more dazzling.

"Welcome home," his wife murmured, smiling as she held out a martini on a silver tray.

She was wearing a pretty, ruffled pinafore apron tied around her waist. And beneath that...

Vin suddenly couldn't breathe.

She wasn't wearing anything under the apron.

Nothing at all.

Eyes wide, he stared at her as all the blood rushed south from his head. He couldn't think. He gaped at her.

Scarlett tilted her head, looking up at him mischievously beneath her dark eyelashes. "Don't you want the martini? It's eggnog-flavored."

He stared at her, frozen, drinking in the vision of Scarlett's long red hair tumbling down her shoulders, to the tops of her full breasts, just visible above the ruffled top of the apron. He could see the pale curve of her naked hips around the edge of the fabric.

"No? Pity." Turning, she set the silver tray down on a nearby table. He almost fell to his knees as he got the first view of her naked backside, her lush flesh swaying, each mound perfectly shaped for his palms to cup roughly in his hands. He licked his lips.

"Where's—where's Nico?" he said hoarsely.

"Sleeping upstairs."

"And Mrs. Stone?"

"It's Christmas Eve, darling. I told her to take some time off. Gave her a first-class ticket back to see her family in Atlanta."

Vin stood in the great room, surrounded by shadows and light, dumbfounded by the vision of his wife, half-naked below the enormous, brilliantly lit Christmas tree, like the gift he'd waited for all his life.

A wicked smile traced her lips as she started to walk

toward him, slowly, deliberately, her hips swaying. She stopped directly in front of him, without touching him. He could smell the faint cherry blossom of her hair, the soft floral of her perfume.

His heart was pounding. He was afraid if he touched her, he would explode.

He was afraid he would explode if he *didn't* touch her.

"I made dinner," she murmured. "Pasta. I'm keeping it warm for you." She looked at him demurely, beneath the sweep of her black eyelashes, and tilted her hip, putting a hand on her bare, creamy skin thrusting out from the edge of her apron.

Vin didn't speak. Looking down at her, he deliberately started pulling off his tie.

Scarlett's expression, which had been flirtatious and saucy, turned wide like a deer's. She took a nervous step back.

But Vin had no intention of letting her flee. It was too late for that.

Sweeping her into his arms, he pushed her roughly against the wall, gripping her wrists and holding them firmly against the cool stone. "What else have you been keeping warm?"

"Vin," she breathed, searching his gaze. "There's something I've wanted to tell you…"

But more talking was the last thing he wanted. Cutting her off, he lowered his head, plundering her mouth in a ruthless kiss. He felt her soft, plump lips part beneath his own. Releasing her wrists, he tangled his hands in her hair, tilting her head backward to deepen the kiss.

She gave a sound like a sigh as her arms wrapped around his shoulders, pulling him closer. He stroked the sides of her body, her bare skin that wasn't covered by the prim apron. He shuddered as his fingertips and palms touched the warm, silky flesh of her hips, her tiny waist beneath the apron tie, the side curve of her voluptuous breasts. She stood on her tiptoes, straining to match the hunger in the kiss. He cupped his hands over the fleshy globes of her naked backside, feeling her sensuality, her heat—

With a low growl, he lifted her up, pushing her back against the wall, wrapping her bare legs around his hips. His rock-hard erection strained between them, with only his trousers and her thin apron separating them.

Bracing her against the wall, he held her sweet backside with one spread hand—nearly gasping with the pleasure of holding her there—and yanked open the tie of the apron. Pulling the fabric off her, he tossed it to the flagstones.

And just like that, he was holding his beautiful wife, in his arms, naked against the wall of their villa in Rome.

The flicker of warm red firelight glowed against her creamy skin, against her huge breasts with taut red nipples, her long red hair. Her red lips, swollen from the force of his kiss. Red, so red. Scarlet, like her name.

As he kissed her, Vin's body shook with need. He struggled to hold himself back. It was the first time they'd made love as man and wife, the first time since the baby was born. He should go slow. Carry her upstairs to their elegant bedroom, to the perfectly appointed king-size bed. Take his time. Be gentle. Make it last…

She pulled away from his kiss. With her naked legs wrapped around his trouser-clad hips, she leaned forward. He felt the warmth of her breath, the faint brush of her lips against the sensitive flesh of his earlobe as she whispered three little words.

He realized what she'd just said. With an intake of breath, he looked down at her.

They were alone in the great room, beneath the lights of the enormous Christmas tree that stretched toward the forty-foot ceiling. But even brighter than the lights of the tree, brighter than the orange and red flames of the fire, was the blazing glory of Scarlett's eyes.

"I love you," she repeated, as if the words had been building up so long that she could no longer keep them inside. Reaching out, she cupped his jawline, the rough bristles of his five-o'clock shadow. His whole body was shaking.

I love you.

He lost his last tendril of self-control, yanking his tailored trousers so violently that a button popped to the floor. He ripped his zipper roughly apart, tearing the fabric to shove his trousers down his taut hips.

Holding her backside with both hands, he spread her wide, and with one thrust, he pushed his thick, rock-hard length inside her, filling her hard and deep.

She gasped, clinging to him. He thrust into her again, holding her roughly against the wall, stretching her to the hilt. She gripped his shoulders, head tilted back, eyes closed in fervent need.

He watched her face as he pushed inside her a third time, slowly now, his own pleasure building as he saw the ecstasy on her face. A whimper escaped his own lips. Going slow was agony, sheer masochism, when he ached to rut into her, to explode. Her fingertips gripped deeper into his tailored white shirt, into the flesh of his shoulders. Her nails cut wickedly into his skin.

I love you. The soft hush of her words still rang through his ears. Through his heart. *I love you.*

He forced himself to be still inside her. He was so close to exploding, hard and thick and aching with need. Drawing back, he filled her again, inch by rock-hard inch. He felt her hips move against him, sucking him deeper inside her, as her full, heavy breasts swayed forward. She held her breath, her muscles tense. She suddenly threw back her head, crying out his name—

As he heard her scream her pleasure, he could no longer hold himself back. He rammed into her, fast and rough, crushing her soft breasts against his hard chest. His growl rose to a shout as he exploded inside her in pleasure so violent that, as he poured into her, for a single second his vision went black.

When he regained consciousness, emotion rose in his heart, emotion stronger than he'd ever felt, emotion that would not be repressed or denied.

"I love you."

The whisper was low, guttural, achingly vulnerable. For a moment, he didn't recognize the voice. Then Scarlett, still gripping his shoulders, looked at him with the most pure joy he'd ever seen on any human face.

And Vin realized with equal parts joy and horror that the voice had been his own.

CHAPTER TEN

HE LOVED HER.

The rhythm of those words was like the beat of Scarlett's heart, the rush of her blood.

He loved her.

She'd been terrified, waiting for him to come home. More than once, she'd changed her mind and started to get dressed. What if he rejected her? What if he laughed? What if one of the bodyguards walked in first?

But that hadn't even been her biggest fear.

What if her blatant gamble to seduce her husband back into her bed, and more important, to confess her love to him, was a total humiliating failure?

Growing up as she had, Scarlett had needed to be invisible for most of her life. But somehow, loving Vin gave her the courage to be outrageous enough to reach for her dreams.

Now they'd all come true.

Christmas morning, Scarlett woke with a smile on her face, hearing her baby's soft hungry whimper from the nursery next door. She looked at her husband sleeping beside her, and her smile became a beam of pure joy.

She loved him. And he loved her.

She blessed the internet. The crazy advice had worked better than she'd ever dreamed. After he'd taken her body so roughly against the wall, after he'd told her he loved her, Vin had wrapped her shivering body tenderly in his black jacket, and they'd gone into the enormous new kitchen to eat the dinner she'd prepared, homemade bread and *fettuccine alla carbonara*. Sitting together in the shadowy kitchen, he'd smoothed a bit of sauce off her cheek, looking at her with dark unreadable eyes, and all she could think was that she'd never been so happy.

He loved her.

Vin actually loved her.

After dinner, he'd held out his hand and led her upstairs. In their dark bedroom, he'd silently taken off his clothes and pulled her into the big bed, where he made love to her again, this time with aching gentleness. This time, as he pushed into her, their eyes locked, soul to soul. No separation. No secrets.

He loved her.

Now Scarlett shaped her lips silently into the words, tasting their sweetness again and again.

Creeping out of bed quietly, so as not to wake him, she wrapped her body in a white robe and went to the en suite nursery, where she lovingly swept their two-month-old baby into her arms. Cuddling him in the nearby glider, she fed him and rocked him back to sleep in the darkness. Once he was full and drowsy, she tucked him back in his crib.

Straightening, she looked out the window at the dark frosty dawn breaking over Rome.

She'd never been so happy. She didn't know what she'd done to deserve such happiness. Her heart was almost breaking with joy. Padding back on the soft rugs over the hardwood floor, she returned to the master bedroom, into the enormous bed that she shared with her husband. Closing her eyes, she pressed her cheek against his naked back and fell asleep.

A noise woke her.

Opening her eyes, Scarlett saw by the golden light filtering through the shades that it was midmorning. She blinked dreamily, smiling. "Merry Christmas." Then she blinked. Her eyes focused on Vin across the bedroom. "What are you doing?"

"Packing," he said tersely, tossing more clothes into the open suitcase. He was already dressed, in black tailored trousers, white shirt, a black vest and red tie. His dark hair was wet from the shower.

"Yes, I see that, but packing for what?"

Vin stopped, looking at her. His dark eyes were cold, and the gorgeous mouth that had kissed her into such uncontrollable spirals of pleasure just hours before was now pressed into a severe line. "I'm leaving on a business trip."

"When?"

"Immediately."

"What?" She sat up straight in bed. "But your parents are expecting us to drive up to Tuscany with the baby—"

"Impossible," he said flatly. "I just learned Salvatore Calabrese is in Tokyo to make a deal with another company. It's my last chance to make him sell to me instead."

"But you can't leave!" Scarlett struggled to calm her voice. She sounded like a whiny child, even to her own ears. "It's Christmas Day!"

He turned on her fiercely. "What do you expect me to do, Scarlett?" His tone was scathing. "Sacrifice my company, our son's future, just to stay here and play happy family with you over the holidays?"

Yes, that was exactly what she expected. She drew back, hurt and bewildered.

Vin stared at her for a long moment. Then he turned away to pack. "I'm not sure how long negotiations might last. It could be days. Even weeks."

"You might be gone through New Year's?"

"You'll be busy anyway. Packing for you and the baby."

"Packing for what?"

"We're moving to New York."

Scarlett's jaw dropped. Was she dreaming? She stared

at her husband in the bedroom she'd personally decorated, in the villa that, after all her devoted work, felt like home. "What are you talking about? We live here! In Rome!"

"And once we're back in New York," he continued relentlessly, "I want the baby to have another paternity test."

Scarlett sucked in her breath, feeling like he'd just punched the air out of her, falling back against the pillows. "Why would you ask that?"

He shrugged. "I want to be sure."

"Why?" Scarlett, who was not a violent woman, barely contained the impulse to leap out of bed and slap his face. "How many tests do you need? How many men do you think I've slept with? How big of a liar do you think I am?"

"It is a reasonable request. I've been lied to before."

"Not by me!"

"By others," he conceded, then glared at her. "I do not appreciate you taking this hostile tone."

"Hostile! You haven't begun to see me hostile!" Rising from the bed, she stomped across the bedroom and snatched up her white fluffy robe. Tying the belt around her, she ground out, "Nico is two months old, we've been married since October and you're suddenly wondering if he's your son?"

"Scarlett—"

"Go to hell!"

He grabbed her hands. "Stop it."

"I won't." Her breath came in angry gasps as she looked up at him with flashing eyes. "Last night you said you loved me, but now it's like you're suddenly *trying* to make me hate you. Why, Vin? Why?"

His hands tightened. His gaze fell to her lips, to the quick rise and fall of her breasts. For a moment, she thought he might kiss her. That he'd tell her what was really going on. That everything would be all right.

Instead, he abruptly let her go. "I expect you to be settled in my penthouse in New York by the time I'm done in Tokyo."

"Do you?" she retorted. "Let me guess. You already have a Manhattan doctor on standby to give Nico a few more paternity tests." She was shaking with emotion. "I'd almost think you want proof you're not his father!"

"That's not true, and you know it," he bit out. "I chased around the world to find you and my son. My intentions should be clear. I want you both in New York. We are a family." His voice was impersonal, chilly. "Furthermore, you will make sure Larson is always with you and the baby when you leave this house. I mean it, Scarlett."

"I told you, I'm fed up with having a stupid bodyguard! This is Rome! Who do you think will attack us?"

"I was attacked once in midtown Manhattan. In the middle of the day."

She exhaled. "What?"

"I was seventeen, an easy target, and the guy wanted my wallet. For twenty bucks, he sent me to the hospital." He looked at her. "When I got out, I learned how to fight. When I became a millionaire, I also hired bodyguards." His jaw was tight. "I protect what is mine, Scarlett. That now includes you and my son."

"I'm sorry about what happened to you, but that was a long time ago, and Rome is very safe…"

"I'm leaving one of the private jets for you," he continued implacably. "I expect you and Nico to be en route to New York by the end of the week."

"We're not flying anywhere!"

"Scarlett." He ground his teeth. "I own an *airline*. You need to get over it!"

Get over it?! She was quivering with rage but kept her voice calm. "No, thank you. Neither I nor my child will be getting on one of those flying death traps again."

"So let me get this straight," he ground out. "You believe the airline I've built into a multibillion-dollar business to be made entirely of *flying death traps*. You refuse to live in New York. And you intend to flout my wishes by evading the bodyguard I've hired for you, leaving both you and Nico continually at risk."

"That's pretty much it, yes."

"You have so little respect for my judgment? For my leadership?"

"Why should I listen to you, when you've made it clear you aren't listening to me?" Her arms, which had been folded angrily, fell to her sides. "I don't want to leave Rome," she whispered. "I'm learning Italian. I've made friends. Your parents live just a few hours away. Your sister's getting married here next month!"

"We can order flowers sent from New York."

"You can't be serious. She's your sister!"

"What did you think, Scarlett? That we'd live here forever?"

That was exactly what she'd thought. She'd been happy and she'd thought it would last forever. She whispered over the lump in her throat, "It's our home."

"Home?" Looking around the luxurious, comfortable bedroom, he gave an incredulous laugh. "This place isn't my home. It *was* my home, when I was a miserable child at the mercy of adults. But now, thank God, it's not." He closed his suitcase firmly. "My company is based in New York."

"I have no good memories there. None."

"You must have friends in the city."

"Blaise Falkner?"

"He's no longer in New York." His lips pressed together. "My head of security recently informed me that without money or a place to live, he's fled like the rat he is." He paused, and she got the feeling there was more he wasn't telling her. He finished, "So you have nothing to worry about."

"I know I don't. Because I'm not living there."

A knock on the bedroom door interrupted them. An unhappy-looking bodyguard appeared to collect Vin's suitcase. Scarlett whirled angrily on her husband.

"You're making Beppe work today? He was going to propose to his girlfriend!" She looked at the man miserably. "I'm sorry."

"Va bene, signora," he muttered.

Ignoring him, Vin glared at her. "I grow weary of your constant criticism."

"Oh, I see. I should just tremble and obey?"

"You're twisting my words."

"What am I, if not your partner? Am I your housekeeper? Your nanny?" Her cheeks burned. "Or just your whore?"

She had the satisfaction of seeing his eyes widen. Then they narrowed. "You're my wife. The mother of my child."

"Then how can you be so unfeeling? You said you loved me!"

Vin glanced grimly toward Beppe, now walking out with his suitcase, pretending to be deaf and blind to the whole conversation. "I am simply educating you in how it's going to be. You and the baby will fly to New York within the week. You'll be ready and willing to take the paternity test!"

Vin stalked out of the bedroom in his turn, slamming the door behind him.

Woken by the noise, their baby started crying in the nursery next door. Scarlett flashed hot, then cold. In a fury, she ran to the top of the staircase.

"We're not going anywhere!" she screamed down at him. "You can't force us!"

Vin's face was startled at the bottom of the stairs. But

he didn't answer. He didn't even pause. Just kept walking, straight out the door.

Hearing the roar of the engine as his car drove away, Scarlett slumped on the top stair, tears running down her cheeks.

How had it all gone so wrong, so fast?

Just that morning, she'd been so happy. So sure he loved her.

But he couldn't. Otherwise, how could he act like this?

He didn't love her. All her dreams came crashing down around her. Covering her face with her hands, Scarlett choked out a sob.

Then, hearing her baby's wails, she took a deep breath. Wiping her eyes, she rose from the top stair, hoping, as she went to comfort her crying child, that she could somehow comfort herself.

From the penthouse bar of his ultramodern, luxurious Tokyo hotel, Vin stared out unseeingly through floor-to-ceiling windows displaying a panorama of the city, from Hamarikyu Gardens to the illuminated Rainbow Bridge stretching across Tokyo Bay. The night sky was dazzling from the bar on the thirtieth floor.

Beautiful.

Bright.

Cold.

Vin took another gulp of his scotch on the rocks, then set it back on the gleaming bar. He leaned his forehead against his palm, feeling inexpressibly weary.

It had been two weeks since he'd last spoken to Scarlett. Two weeks since their argument. For two weeks, he hadn't seen his baby, who in his short life might already be forgetting he had a father. Vin's heart felt twisted, raw, hollow.

He tried to tell himself it was worth it. Because Mediterranean Airlines was his.

It had been a hard fight, against a worthy rival, a far larger company. But Salvatore Calabrese had been duly impressed by Vin abandoning his wife and baby on Christmas Day to spend the week through New Year's and beyond focusing only on negotiations. Vin had spent the last two weeks holed up in this hotel with lawyers.

It was fortunate the view was so nice, because other than the ride from the airport, this was all he'd seen of Tokyo.

But the deal was done. They'd signed the papers an hour ago. Mediterranean Airlines was now part of Sky-World Airways.

Vin had won.

So why didn't he feel happier?

Sitting up straight on his bar stool, he tried to shake the feeling off. Scarlett was still in Rome, stubbornly defying him. She hadn't packed a thing, according to the bodyguards, whom she also continued to evade at will. She just continued her life as before, taking care of the baby and their home, helping his family arrange the last-minute details for his sister's upcoming wedding.

His so-called *sister*.

His so-called *family*.

Vin ground his teeth. It was physically painful for him to be around the Borgias, in spite of—actually, *because of*—their love for him. If they knew the truth, that he wasn't really Giuseppe's son, that Bianca had lied to him and used him for all of Vin's childhood, they would stop loving him.

It would be subtle, of course. They'd probably claim they were "still a family." But soon they'd be making excuses not to visit. Christmas cards would grow rare. Finally, there would be no contact at all, to the unexpressed relief of both sides.

Vin was done with Rome. It was the place where he'd been forced to feel emotions he didn't want to feel.

Especially for Scarlett.

His hands tightened on his glass of scotch.

But it would all soon be over. He glanced at his black leather briefcase on the bar stool beside him.

Ten minutes after he'd left Rome, with Scarlett's hurled accusations still ringing in his ears, he'd coldly called his lawyers and had the post-nup drawn up.

He should have done it weeks ago. But after their marriage, after the birth of their son, part of his soul had recoiled from betraying Scarlett. He'd known after he tricked her into signing a post-nup, she would hate him, too. So he'd put it off, telling himself there was plenty of time.

He'd been weak. He never should have allowed himself to delay his original plan. Of course he had to make Scarlett sign the post-nup. It was the only way Vin could make sure he could always keep them safe. He had to be in control.

Without it, Scarlett would continue to blithely ignore his demands that she keep the bodyguards close.

She didn't know that when Blaise Falkner disappeared from New York, he'd left a threat behind: "You'll lose even more, Borgia."

But that was just the point. Vin shouldn't have to explain such dangers to his wife. He didn't want to scare her. He just wanted to keep her safe.

Why did she have to fight him?

He'd felt so stupidly happy in her arms on Christmas Eve, making love to her. *Stupid* being the key word.

Waking up in the cold light of Christmas morning, he'd looked down at his wife in his arms, at the sweetly trusting smile on her beautiful face as she slept. For a split second, he'd been filled with joy. Then he'd felt a suffocating panic, even worse than the day they'd wed.

Happiness led to loss. It led to pain. And the joy of love could only end two ways: abandonment or death.

He'd decided long ago that he would never love anyone. He'd never give anyone that power over him.

But had he?

I love you.

He still remembered how he'd trembled when he'd heard Scarlett say those words. When he'd heard himself say them.

I love you.

He angrily shook the memory away.

He wouldn't think of it. Wouldn't feel it. And Scarlett's love for him would evaporate, along with her trust, after he tricked her into signing the post-nup. She would hate him then.

Good.

Vin's expression hardened as he took another sip of eighteen-year-old scotch. Taking love out of the equation would make things easier all around. Safer. Because he didn't like the things Scarlett made him feel.

Desire, when he thought of her.

Frustration, when she defied him.

Fear, when he thought of a life without her.

Without even trying, his wife made him feel vulnerable, all the time, in every way. This had to end.

Staring blankly out at the Tokyo night, Vin leaned his head against his hand. He'd return to Rome, ostensibly to attend Maria's wedding, with the post-nup in his pocket. He'd get Scarlett to sign it. And then—

He'd get his life back. Well-ordered. Controlled. With Vin completely in charge, and no risk of love or being vulnerable ever again.

"Borgia. Didn't expect to find you here."

Vin was jolted by a hearty clap on his shoulder. Looking back, he saw Salvatore Calabrese, still wearing the same designer suit and bright silk tie as when he'd signed the papers selling Mediterranean Airlines.

Vin already felt like he'd spent more than enough time around the self-involved, arrogant man, but he stifled his dislike and bared his teeth into a smile. "Hello, Calabrese."

The older man slid onto a nearby stool at the glossy wooden bar and gestured to the bartender as he continued, "Glad you finally pulled yourself together to convince me you were the right man to take my airline global."

"Me, too." Wishing the man would leave, Vin looked idly down at the ice cubes in his glass, so precise and modern, as was everything about this bar, this hotel, this beautiful city.

Calabrese ordered a drink from the bartender, then sat back on the sleek leather bar stool. "You learned a valuable lesson. Never put your family ahead of yourself, kid. Take it from a man who knows."

That was true enough, Vin thought. Calabrese was supposedly estranged from all three ex-wives and his four grown children, and he'd never even met his only grandchild. He definitely didn't put his family ahead of himself.

The gray-haired man tossed some bills on the glossy wooden bar, leaving a huge tip, then glanced at Vin indulgently. "I know you'll take Mediterranean Airlines to the top."

"That's the plan." Vin wondered how to get rid of him so he could order the second scotch he wanted in peace.

"As for me, I'm going to enjoy the big payout. Take life easy for a while." He picked up his martini and looked across the room. "Maybe I'll get married again. One of those girls could talk me into it."

Following his gaze, Vin saw a trio of beautiful young

models—Asian, pale blonde, dark-skinned brunette—sitting cozily on a white leather sofa by the floor-to-ceiling windows, with Tokyo as their backdrop.

Smiling, Calabrese raised his martini glass in their direction. They giggled, rolling their eyes and whispering to each other.

"You want to get married again?" Vin said, astonished.

"Why not? A wife's cheaper than a mistress. As long as she signs a pre-nup. Always make them sign. Take my advice." He winked. "If not for your current marriage, for the next one."

Vin watched Calabrese rise from the stool, then sashay toward the young women, his martini glass held high. Vin's stomach churned as his gaze fell back on his briefcase.

He was nothing like Calabrese, he told himself fiercely. *Nothing.* Their situations were completely different.

But when Vin left Tokyo that night on his private jet, he couldn't sleep, tossing and turning on the long flight.

When he finally arrived in Rome, the January light was gray. The holidays were over, leaving only the cold comfort of winter.

His driver was waiting to drive him from the airport. When he arrived at the villa, Vin set his jaw, wondering what he'd find.

He didn't have to wait long.

"Vin!" Scarlett appeared at the top of the stairs. Her skin looked pale against her vibrant red hair, her eyes flashing emerald green. She was simply dressed in a pale silk blouse and simple trousers, but he was newly overwhelmed by her beauty. He waited, expecting her anger.

To his surprise, she rushed down the stairs and threw her arms around him.

"I'm so glad you're home," she whispered.

The feel of Scarlett's body against his, the warmth of

her, was like fresh oxygen when he hadn't realized he'd been suffocating. Vin breathed her in, inhaling the scent of cherry blossoms and soft spring flowers.

She was the one to finally pull away. Her eyes were luminous in the shadowy foyer. "I haven't been able to stop thinking about our fight. I was…I was so—" he braced himself "—wrong," she finished quietly. "I was wrong."

Her admission shocked him. Vin would never have admitted he was wrong about anything. If he ever was. Which he wasn't. "About?"

"New York." She gave him a wobbly smile. "You're right. It's your company headquarters. What am I going to do—" she gave an awkward laugh "—demand that hundreds of employees uproot their families and move to Rome, just because I love it here?" She took a deep breath, then tried to smile. "I was being selfish. I'm the one who said we should be partners. So…we should at least talk about it. I still won't take a plane, but maybe I could take a ship. Isn't marriage about compromise?"

"Yes," he lied.

"But—" Scarlett gave him a shy smile "—I'm sure you want to see the baby…"

"Yes." And he meant it.

Taking his hand, she led him upstairs. Entering the shadowy nursery, Vin looked down at his sleeping son. He heard the soft snuffle of his breath, saw the rise and fall of his chest. Nico. His precious boy. He was here. He was safe. The baby already looked different. He'd grown in two weeks. Vin hated that he'd been away so long.

Never again.

He looked at Scarlett. There could only be one person in control of his life. His home. His child. And that was Vin.

The ends justified the means, he told himself. Scarlett might hate him at first, but eventually she would thank him.

Or she wouldn't. But either way, he would get his life back. Without the chaos and messy emotion she brought.

All Vin had to do was lull her back into her previous happiness and trust in him, then once she'd lowered her guard, trick her into signing the postnuptial agreement, written in Italian, giving him every right and power over every decision.

Her love for him was her weakness.

As for his own feelings—he would not feel them. They did not exist.

The one who cared least was the one who'd win.

"I missed you, Scarlett." Vin gave her a smile so sensual that she blushed to her ears. Excellent. "I swear to you on my life," he said softly, "I'll never let us be apart so long again."

She smiled happily, not knowing his dark intentions. Taking her hand, he rubbed his thumb lightly against her palm, then kissed it, feeling her shiver.

Soon, she would be unable to defy him. His decisions would automatically prevail. She would be forced to get over her ridiculous fear of flying and travel with him when he wished. It would be good for their family. And their marriage. A flash of heat went through him as he looked down at her, at the curve of her white throat, the shape of her full breasts beneath her silk blouse.

From now on, she would have no choice but to obey. In his home. In his bed. She'd be at his command. Exactly where she belonged.

CHAPTER ELEVEN

SOMETHING HAD CHANGED in Vin. As Scarlett welcomed him back from Tokyo, she couldn't quite figure out what it was.

Their last time in bed together, on Christmas Eve, had been rough and sensual and explosive. Even when he'd been tender, as he pushed inside her, his emotion had been raw on his face.

But today, since he'd returned, she felt a distance. Even as he smiled at her, even as he held her in his arms, even as he leaned down to kiss her, his dark eyes hinting at untold delights to come later—even then, there was something hidden behind his expression.

What was he hiding?

Was she imagining it?

She puzzled over it all day as they played with the baby, then got ready to go out for the evening. When she broached the subject of moving to New York, he told her he didn't want to discuss it. "Tonight, I just want to enjoy your company, *cara*."

They went out that night to his sister's wedding rehearsal dinner at a charming restaurant not too far from the Piazza Navona. Giuseppe, Joanne and Maria were delighted when he'd arrived. They'd all missed him, too. Halfway through the dinner, when Scarlett rose to her feet and publicly toasted his success with the Mediterranean Airlines deal, everyone at the table clapped and cheered.

Vin ducked his head, looking embarrassed. After all the work he'd put into the deal, his boyish humility made her more proud of him than ever. And love him more than ever.

Finally, after they returned home, after he tucked their sleeping baby into his crib, he took Scarlett to bed, too. She relished the warmth of him, the strength of him, the feel of him beside her.

She'd missed him for those two weeks.

It scared her how much she needed him now.

This time, as Vin made love to her, he held her gently, tenderly, looking deeply into her eyes. But his own eyes were carefully blank.

He touched her as if his fingertips wished to tell her everything he could not put into words. She tried to guess. He was sorry? He regretted their fight—which had been so awful, so brutal to her heart? That he hadn't lied when he said he loved her?

He made her body explode with ecstasy as he poured into her with a groan, then afterward he held her all night, snugly against his chest, in a way he'd never done before.

Cradled against him, with his strong arms around her, Scarlett felt protected. She decided she was imagining things, creating problems where they didn't exist. They were husband and wife. They were partners in life. They were in love.

She woke up smiling for the first time in two weeks. She heard a morning bird singing outside and stretched, yawning, every bit of her body feeling deliciously satisfied. How could she be anything other than happy? Vin was home at last. And today was Maria's wedding day.

Whatever conflicts arose between her and Vin, they'd work through them. Maybe they'd live in Rome for half the year, New York the other half.

She looked over at his side of the bed, but it was empty.

Scarlett started to get out of bed in her negligee, when she heard the bedroom door kick open. Startled, she saw

Vin, wearing only a towel wrapped around his trim waist, holding a breakfast tray with a rose in a small bud vase.

"You brought me breakfast?" Scarlett said in surprise. "But you must be exhausted. You traveled so long yesterday…"

"Exactly. I left you here alone to take care of Nico and my sister's wedding and all the rest. It's time I took care of you for a change." His dark eyes crinkled as he smiled, setting the tray on her lap, over the white comforter.

"By the way," he said casually as he turned away, "I've left some papers on the tray for you to sign. They're under the rose."

Frowning, Scarlett looked down. "What kind of papers?"

"No big deal." He shrugged. "Just to officially mark that you are my wife. For the Italian authorities."

She glanced at the top sheet. It was written in Italian and did seem to say something about being his wife. But her Italian language skills, in spite of her recent study, weren't strong enough to sort through the indecipherable legalese. She hesitated. "My dad always said only a fool signs something he doesn't understand. I should get it translated before I sign it."

"Sure, whatever you want," he said carelessly as he left the room. A minute later, he returned with a carafe. Coming back to the bed, he poured steaming coffee into a china cup, adding liberal amounts of cream and sugar, then put it on her tray, smiling down at her tenderly. "From now on, I'm going to take better care of you. Treat you like you deserve. Like a princess. Like a queen."

Looking up at him, Scarlett's heart twisted with love.

"Enjoy your breakfast, *cara*." He cracked a sudden grin. "I'm going to take a shower. Feel free to join me if you're feeling—" he lifted a teasing eyebrow *"—dirty."*

With a whistle, he turned away, dropping his towel to

the floor. Scarlett's lips parted at the delicious view of her husband's muscular backside before he disappeared into the bathroom. It took several seconds before she was able to focus again.

She looked down at the papers, thinking of everything she had to do today before the evening wedding. After weeks of procrastination, she still hadn't figured out what to wear. She desperately wanted to look good at the formal event, to show her respect to Maria and the rest of Vin's family. But she dreaded the pressure of scouring the chic designer shops of Rome. She always felt like a chubby bumpkin. The thought of also going to look for an English-speaking lawyer to translate and advise her felt like one unpleasant task too many.

Besides, she was Vin's wife, the mother of his child. For better or worse. If she truly believed she was his partner, why treat him like an enemy? She didn't want to be suspicious. She wanted to trust him.

So she would. End of story.

Smiling to herself in relief, Scarlett signed the papers with a flourish, then enjoyed the delicious breakfast. She polished off the almond croissant at the exact moment she heard her baby starting to fuss in the nursery. She brought the baby back to their bedroom and was cuddling and nursing him in bed when Vin came back, wrapped in a white terry cloth robe, his dark hair wet, his black eyes smoldering.

"Did you enjoy your breakfast, *cara*?"

"It was amazing. Thank you so much." She held up the signed papers. "I have these for you."

His eyes lit up with something dark and deep. He came forward. He gently took the papers from her. Seeing her signature, he kissed her on the temple and said in a low voice, "Thank you, Scarlett."

"No problem," she said, smiling up at him. Then she

sighed. "If only I could solve the problem of what to wear tonight so easily."

His own smile widened. "*Cara*, that is one problem I can solve for you."

With a single phone call, Vin solved everything. He arranged for a team of stylists to come to the villa. Beauty specialists appeared that afternoon to do her nails, hair and makeup. As Nico rolled around on the soft pad of his baby gym nearby, cooing and batting at soft dangling toys, Scarlett sipped sparkling mineral water while clothing stylists presented thirty different gowns to choose from, each more exquisite than the last.

Then she saw one that took her breath away, long and sapphire blue. When she tried it on, it made her figure look like an hourglass, especially with the lingerie underneath, a push-up bra more outrageous than she would have ever selected for herself. It made her breasts high and huge with sharp cleavage beneath the gown's low-cut bodice. The hairdresser twisted her red hair in an elegant chignon, and the makeup artist made her lips deep red, darkening her eyes with kohl. When Scarlett finally saw herself in the mirror, she gasped. She almost didn't recognize herself.

"*Bellissima,*" her hairstylist said, kissing his fingertips expressively. Scarlett blushed.

Vin had said she'd be treated like a princess, and she felt like one. She turned anxiously to Wilhelmina, who was now holding the baby. She'd become Scarlett's trusted friend. "What do you think?"

The housekeeper looked her over critically, then smiled. "Sugar, I think that husband of yours is likely to die of pride."

Scarlett prayed she was right, and that Vin didn't think she looked like an ordinary girl playing dress-up, pretending to play the role of a glamorous, sexy, sophisticated woman.

Kissing her baby's cheeks, which were getting chubbier every day, Scarlett floated out of the master bedroom, into the hall, still trembling, wondering what Vin would say when he saw her. She paused at the top of the staircase as she heard low words from below.

"Blaise Falkner..."

The voices cut off sharply as Vin and his assistant saw her. But why would they be talking about that awful man?

Her husband's eyes widened as she came down the stairs, holding the handrail carefully so she didn't trip on her four-inch, crystal-studded high heels. He met her at the bottom of the staircase.

"You dazzle me," he murmured too softly for his assistant to hear. Taking her hand, he whispered, "Forget the wedding. Let's go back upstairs..."

Her cheeks burned pleasantly, but she bit her lip. "Were you talking about Blaise Falkner?"

Vin started to shake his head, but Ernest, his assistant, interjected, "We haven't been able to track him since he left New York."

"Track him? What do you mean?"

Vin glared at his assistant, then kissed the back of her hand. Scarlett shivered as she felt the hot press of his sensual lips against her skin. "It's nothing to worry about. He's probably just too embarrassed to show his face. Drowning his sorrows in a gutter." He looked at her. "Scarlett. You are so beautiful."

Her blush deepened. "Thanks. Um. You look nice, too."

Her praise felt woefully inadequate. His black tuxedo jacket was tailored perfectly, showing off his amazing physique from his muscular shoulders to his taut waist. His dark eyes were intense in his handsome face with a jawline and cheekbones that would cut glass. But he wasn't just superficially handsome. It was more than that. Some might think he was arrogant, but Scarlett alone knew his heart, his goodness, his love for his family. That was what she loved.

Frowning, Vin tilted his head. "You just need one thing."

"What?"

Reaching to a nearby table for a flat black velvet box, he drew out a large, dazzling diamond necklace. She gasped as she felt the cold weight of the diamonds clasped gently around her throat. Then he kissed her at the crook of her neck, and she felt a rush of heat. She whispered, "Thank you."

"Now we can go," he said softly.

They kissed their baby son good-night, leaving him happily cuddled in Wilhelmina's arms, and went out into the cold night. Vin gently draped her white stole over her shoulders as they crossed their cobblestoned driveway to the waiting limousine. The gate opened on the street, and the driver, with two bodyguards traveling behind them, whisked them off to the grand *palazzo*.

Maria and Luca's evening winter wedding was sublimely beautiful, lit with candles and white flowers in the gilded receiving room of the *palazzo*. Giuseppe walked her down the aisle, tears shining on his face. Sitting nearby, Joanne cried, as well. Scarlett watched the young couple speak their vows and her heart felt overwhelmed with joy as she looked at her husband beside her and felt all the love around them.

Afterward, they adjourned to the ballroom for a formal dinner. The young bride and groom sat at a table on a dais, with their immediate families on each side of them. That included Vin and Scarlett. She hugged the bride and groom, and then Giuseppe and Joanne. She listened to the speeches toasting the bride and groom, mostly in Italian, and tried to understand. She enjoyed the freedom to drink champagne.

But the whole time, Scarlett was aware of her husband beside her, looking down at her with his darkly sensual gaze. He kept giving quick stolen kisses on her bare shoulder above the sweetheart neckline of her strapless blue gown. He kissed her on her cheek. On the lips. She leaned against him, reveling in his nearness. It was a beautiful wedding, but she could hardly wait to get home…

"We're going to miss you," the bridegroom's father, a wealthy businessman who owned this grand *palazzo*, called across the table to Vin halfway through the third course. "My son was secretly hoping your wife would give Maria some cooking lessons."

"Papà!" the groom protested.

"Luca!" The bride tossed her head in her elegant white veil, pretending to pout. "But if I learn to cook, how would we support the restaurants? One must think of helping the economy!"

But Scarlett frowned at Luca's father. "What do you mean, you'll miss us?" She looked at her husband with dismay. "Are you going on another business trip?"

"I heard you're moving to New York," Luca's father said. "In fact, I heard you've already rented out your villa here on long lease to some Hollywood actor and bought a brand-new duplex in New York for some obscene amount. I read it in the paper—was it fifty million dollars?"

Scarlett relaxed, laughed. "I'm afraid you've heard incorrectly, Signor Farro. We are talking about New York, but we haven't decided anything. We certainly haven't rented out our…"

Her voice trailed off as she saw Vin's face. Ice entered her heart.

"You wouldn't do that," she said in a small voice. "Not without talking to me. After everything I put into our home, you wouldn't rent it out from underneath me…"

Vin's expression was closed. "The decision has already been made."

"By who?" Scarlett pulled away. "By you?"

The smiles had fallen from the faces of the bride and groom. Their parents started to look anxious. Chic guests at nearby dinner tables turned to look as their voices rose.

Vin set his jaw. "Yes, by me. You were being unreasonable."

Her lips parted in disbelief. "Unreasonable?"

"I allowed you to stay in Rome—"

"Allowed!" she cried.

"—until Maria's wedding. But I already made it clear. My headquarters is in New York. Tomorrow, we will pack a few suitcases and fly there. The rest of our things can be forwarded. It's true. I have bought a brand-new penthouse close to my office, near good private schools for Nico."

Vin sat back, looking pleased with himself, as if he expected praise. Scarlett felt numb.

"We already have a home, here in Rome," she whispered.

"You'll like New York even better when we arrive tomorrow night."

"I'm not getting on a plane."

Vin's expression changed to a glower. "You have to face your fears."

She hated his patronizing tone. "No, I don't."

"You have no choice now. You—"

"Children, children…" Vin's father broke in, his weathered face anguished. "Scarlett, my dear one, I am sure my son only meant the best. But if you do not want to leave Rome, he will not force you. He is a good man. Vincenzo, my son, you must tell her that…"

Vin stood up so fast his chair fell to the floor of the dais. The noise of the crash echoed in the suddenly silent ballroom. His voice was cold as he looked at Giuseppe.

"Stop calling me your son. I am not."

Giuseppe goggled at him. Joanne and Maria both drew back in shock.

Vin's lip curled. "You wondered why I ignored you for twenty years?" he said in a low voice. "Right before my mother died, when I asked her if I could live with you in Tuscany, she laughed in my face. She told me I was the result of a one-night stand with some musician in Rio. She lied to you, Giuseppe," he said deliberately, almost cruelly, "so you'd give her money. And you paid her. Blindly. Just as you blindly loved me all those years." He slowly looked to Joanne and Maria. "So do not presume to lecture me. You are not my family." He turned to Scarlett, his eyes like ice. "And you will do what I say. You have no choice. You signed the agreement."

"Agreement?" She was still reeling from his revelation that Giuseppe was not his father. Then she realized what he was talking about, and a sick feeling rose inside her. "Those papers this morning—"

He glanced at all the people in the ballroom, then spoke too quietly for them to hear. "I always intended to make you sign, Scarlett. Either before marriage or after."

The pre-nup he'd once threatened her with. The agreement that gave him the right to make all decisions about their baby's life, and hers. The agreement that gave Vin full custody of Nico if he ever decided to divorce her. *And she'd signed it.*

Scarlett's world was spinning, crashing, on fire. Standing up from her chair, she stared at him in horror. Then, snatching her crystal-encrusted minaudière from the table, she turned away in her four-inch heels, ducking around the waiters who'd just come pouring into the ballroom with the next course. By the time she fled the ballroom, she was crying.

How could she have been so stupid?

She should have listened to her fears, not her hopes.

Don't tell him about the baby.

Don't get a DNA test.

Don't marry him.

Don't love him.

And most of all:

Always read before you sign.

Furiously, she wiped her eyes, but tears clouded her vision as she stumbled into the empty, high-ceilinged hallway. She saw Beppe leave his post outside the ballroom door and start to follow her.

"Don't even think about it!" she barked. She'd never spoken sharply to him before. She had the unhappy satisfaction of seeing him stop, his expression hurt.

Turning away, Scarlett ran past a security guard sleeping in a chair inside the foyer. She went out the front door of the *palazzo*, through the same door where she'd arrived with such happiness on Vin's arm just hours before.

Then, the exclusive Roman street had been jammed with arriving cars, gleaming and luxurious, many driven by chauffeurs. Now, the street was dark and cold and empty.

It was so cold, the drizzle of rain had turned to soft, silent snowflakes. A small dog trotted down the street sniffing at doorways. She saw a shadow of a homeless man leaning against the corner. She shivered as snowflakes melted like ice on her bare skin. She'd been in too much of a hurry to grab her white stole. But who cared about being cold?

She'd been so happy. She swallowed against the ache in her throat. With her baby. Her home. The man she loved. So completely happy.

But it had all been an illusion. Vin baiting his trap.

She had to get out of here.

Scarlett's heart pounded as she stood alone in the darkness in front of the *palazzo*. Down the street, she saw a taxi coming her direction. She could flag it down. She could rush to the villa, grab Nico and disappear. She knew how. She'd done it before.

Her heart pounded as she watched the taxi draw closer. The thought of leaving Vin, even now, and also separating him from the baby he loved, filled her with anguish.

She tried to steel herself. She told herself she had no choice. She raised her hand to flag down the taxi.

Freedom. For her entire childhood, freedom had been her rallying cry. She had to follow her dream—

Scarlett remembered the look on her father's face the day she turned eighteen and told him she'd given up her dreams of college and ever settling down. With tears in his eyes, he told her that after all their years on the run, he was turning himself in.

"What about freedom?" she'd cried.

"We were never free," he'd said quietly. "Not once. I made a horrible mistake, Scarlett. I was a coward. Running away all these years, I ruined your life, and your mother's. But no more. You will be free now." He'd taken a deep breath. "I'm doing this so you'll be free."

"Signorina?"

The taxi driver was looking at her impatiently through his open window.

Scarlett stared at him. Then, lowering her arm, she slowly shook her head. Numbly, she watched the taxi drive off.

She'd run from Vin before. If she ran now, kidnapping her innocent baby from his father, starting life as a fugitive, she wouldn't be following a dream of freedom. Not when her only idea of real freedom was to have family, stability and a real home.

"Scarlett!"

Her shoulders tightened at Vin's angry voice behind her. With a deep breath, she turned to face him.

He stopped in front of her as gentle snowflakes flurried softly to the sidewalk in the dark, cold night. "There's no point in running away," he said quietly. "The postnuptial agreement gives total control of our baby's future to me. And since I know you'll never be parted from him—" he reached out to caress her cheek "—that gives me total control over you."

For a second, she shook with fear, with regret, with rage. Then she remembered the one thing she still had.

Love.

With a deep breath, she lifted her chin, looking straight into his eyes.

"I'm not going anywhere. I'm staying right here."

Vin looked surprised. Then he caught himself and glared at her. "Good—"

"But I'm not going to let you push me around." She put her hand over his. "I love you, Vin. And you love me. That was the whole reason for this, wasn't it?"

"What are you talking about?"

"You're afraid to love me."

He dropped his hand with a snort. *"Afraid."*

"Yes, afraid. So you tried to create a wall between us." She stepped closer, until she could see the white of her breath mingle with his in the faint light. She could see the snowflakes that had fallen in his dark hair and eyelashes. "But I'm not going to let you do it. We love each other. We belong together."

"You signed it. There's nothing you can do now."

"You're wrong." Reaching up, she gently caressed his rough cheek and whispered, "I can call your bluff."

His eyes widened, and he staggered back.

"You won't hurt me," she said. "You can't. Because you love me. And I love you."

"Stop saying that—" he said hoarsely. He clenched his hands at his sides, then turned on his heel, stalking back into the *palazzo*, leaving Scarlett standing alone on the sidewalk on the dark, quiet street.

She turned her face toward the snowflakes, relishing the feel of them, soft and cold, against her overheated skin.

She had to be right. She had to be.

If she was wrong…

Scarlett heard heavy footsteps behind her. Had Vin already returned to tell her he'd changed his mind about the postnuptial agreement? Filled with hope, she turned.

But it wasn't her husband. The scruffy-looking home-less man from the corner now stood before her.

Confused, she drew back. "Can I help you?"

The man was dressed badly, his face lumpy. But when he smiled, she suddenly choked out a gasp as she recognized his face beneath the dirt.

"Yes, Scarlett." Blaise Falkner's eyes looked crazy above his evil smile. "You can."

As Vin entered the *palazzo*, his whole body felt tight, his hands clenched at his sides. He didn't even know where he was going. He just felt sick inside. Panicked. Like he had to either fight or run.

He couldn't fight Scarlett, so he'd run. He'd never run from anything in his life.

Vin ran an unsteady hand over his forehead.

When he'd told Scarlett about the post-nup, he'd expected to feel triumph, or at least a sense of calm control.

Instead, watching the happiness in his wife's eyes melt into horror, Vin had experienced a physical reaction he'd never expected. His hands had tightened into fists. He'd instantly wanted to destroy whomever had hurt her.

Except he had no one to blame—but himself.

"Vincenzo."

Vin abruptly stopped in the gilded, high-ceilinged hallway when he saw Giuseppe waiting for him.

Just what he needed. He gave a silent curse. Another person to heap scorn on him, when he was doing a fine enough job heaping it on himself. He bit out, "What do you want?"

Giuseppe came forward, solemn in his formal tuxedo. "We have to talk."

"Make it quick."

"I always knew you weren't my biological son." He gave Vin a small smile. "Is that quick enough for you?"

He gaped at him, dumbfounded. "What?"

The older man shook his head. "Vincenzo, your mother's eyes were blue. So are mine. What are the chances we could conceive a child with eyes as dark as yours?"

After twenty years of keeping the secret, Vin was staggered. "But my mother used you for money. For years. Why didn't you tell her to go to hell, tell her I wasn't yours?"

"Because you *are* mine," he said, coming forward. "From the moment I held you as a tiny baby, Vincenzo, I was your father."

Vin thought of the first moment he'd held his own son in his arms. He knew what that felt like.

Giuseppe put his hands on Vin's shoulders. "I didn't give a damn what some DNA test might say. I loved you. You were—you *are*—my son. And you will always be."

Vin felt dizzy, like he'd gotten drunk on that one glass of champagne. The floor was trembling under him.

He'd been so wrong. He, who'd believed he could never be wrong about anything, had been wrong about everything.

He thought he'd never run away from a fight?

He'd been running for twenty years.

All these years he'd avoided Giuseppe and Joanne,

avoided emotion, avoided life. For what? For the sake of a secret that didn't matter?

His whole adult life, he'd tried to control everything, to make sure he never felt tied to anyone, so he'd never feel pain when they left. When, against his will, he'd come to care for Scarlett, it had terrified him so much he'd thought he needed to bring her to heel. To make her his slave.

Had he really thought he could rule her with a piece of paper? He was powerless where she was concerned. No pre-nup or post-nup in the world could change that.

I love you, Vin. And you love me. That was the whole reason for this, wasn't it? You're afraid to love me.

Giuseppe sighed ruefully in the hallway. "I just wish I'd known that was the reason you stayed away from us." He glanced at his wife, who'd come up behind him, followed by Maria. "We were foolish to keep silent, but we didn't want to give you more reasons to stay away."

"You knew, too?" Vin said to Joanne. She smiled, even as she wiped tears away.

"Of course I knew, darling. Giuseppe and I have been married a long time. We have no secrets."

"Well, I didn't know!" Maria cried sulkily behind her, tossing her long white veil. "No one tells me anything!"

Vin glanced at his young sister in her white wedding gown, and in that instant, his whole life came sharply into focus.

Scarlett was right. About everything.

Part of him had thought if he pushed her, she would flee, which would prove his worst beliefs and justify his actions in making her sign the post-nup.

He'd *wanted* to push her away.

You're afraid to love me. Yes, afraid. You tried to create a wall between us. But I'm not going to let you do it. We love each other. We belong together.

From the first moment he'd met Scarlett, so silly and

free in the New York dive bar, choking at her first taste of vodka, he'd been enchanted. He'd never met anyone like her, so feisty and sexy and warm.

He'd wanted her from the start, and he'd been willing to make deals to possess her—like his ridiculous fantasy that he could protect his own heart, and stay in control, by making her sign a form, or by trying to love her less, because he, the one who cared less, was the one who had the power.

But that was wrong. He saw that now.

It wasn't the one who loved less who had the power, but the one who loved more. Not because you could control the outcome, or keep from getting hurt, but because it meant you were brave enough to live without fear, hurtling yourself headlong into both joy and pain.

Being a fully alive human being, with the courage to love completely—what could be more powerful than that?

And as much as he loved his son, it wasn't the baby who'd first cracked open his heart.

It was Scarlett.

He looked at his father. "I need to go talk to my wife."

"Go, son," Giuseppe said fiercely. "Show her who you really are!"

Vin nodded, turned back down the hall.

He never should have rented their home out from under her. Another way he'd tried to push Scarlett into hating him. It had never felt like his home—until now. Scarlett had taken the sad, faded, tumbledown prison of his childhood and brought it to joyous life.

She'd done the same for him. Before they'd met, Vin had been focused on money and power, to the detriment of his own happiness. He'd been so afraid of being vulnerable that, if Scarlett hadn't shown up in the New York cathedral that day, he would have married a woman he didn't give a damn about.

If not for Scarlett, he would have turned into a man like Salvatore Calabrese: selfish, shallow and cold, too insecure to risk the only thing that mattered. His heart.

So many things Scarlett had done for him, and all she'd asked in return was for him to love her. For him to be the man he'd been born to be. The man she deserved.

Vin's walk turned into a run. Nodding at the sleepy security guard sitting inside the foyer, he pushed open the front door.

Outside the *palazzo*, the street was dark and quiet. Silent white snow fell softly to the ground. But where was Scarlett?

Then he saw her.

Still in her diamond necklace and sapphire-colored gown, her red hair looked tangled and twisted, and she had terror in her eyes.

A man was holding her. A man with a gun. A man with all kinds of darkness in his eyes.

"Vin!" she cried, struggling.

"Borgia." Blaise Falkner gave him a cold, evil smile. "I should have known you wouldn't keep away for long. You've wrecked my plan, but I'm almost glad. Now you'll see what I'm going to do to her, right in front of your eyes."

Terror ripped through Vin's heart as he looked from Falkner's face to the revolver, black as a deadly snake, held against Scarlett's forehead. For a split second, Vin's world started to go dark with fear.

Then he took a deep breath. He didn't *do* fear. Ever. And he wasn't going to start now, when his wife needed him to be strong. There was only one emotion he could let himself feel right now. He let the waves of it roll over him, like an ocean in a storm.

Rage.

CHAPTER TWELVE

WHEN BLAISE HAD pulled a gun on her in the quiet, snowy street, Scarlett had thought bitterly of how Vin had ordered her to keep a bodyguard nearby. Why hadn't she listened?

Because she'd never imagined she might need a bodyguard in the center of Rome. She'd never imagined that anyone might want to attack her…

"I've been watching your house for a week," Blaise had said, keeping his black revolver trained on her. "Hoping to get you alone."

"Why?" Her teeth chattered. "You can't still want to… to marry me?"

"Marry?" His lip had twisted scornfully as he came closer, until she could smell the sickening stench of old sweat half masked with musky cologne. "I'm way past that now. Your husband made this personal. He ruined my life. Now I will do the same to him."

Snowflakes fell softly against her skin. But that wasn't what froze her to the bone. "How?"

"He loves you."

"You heard us argue—"

"Yeah, I heard it all. It's perfect." His smile became venomous. "Now when you disappear, he'll blame himself for the rest of his life and think he drove you away. He'll always wonder. He'll never know."

"You can't!"

"Watch me." With his gun still trained on her, he snatched her crystal-encrusted clutch bag from her hand. "My car is around the corner…"

"I'm not going anywhere with you." She straightened. "Shoot me here."

"You'll go. Or my next stop will be at your house. Your baby is there, with no one but the housekeeper to protect him. Shame if they had a little accident. If the doors were blocked and the place went up in flames."

"No!" she cried, whimpering at the thought. "I'll go with you. Just leave them alone…"

"That's more like it." Blaise motioned with the revolver. "Over there, in the alley…"

But as she started to move, the front door of the *palazzo* banged open. Quick as a flash, Blaise grabbed her, placing her in front of him, holding the gun to her forehead.

Scarlett nearly cried when she saw Vin had come out of the *palazzo*. His black eyes went wide when he saw them. Then his hands clenched into fists.

"Let her go, Falkner." Vin's dark gaze focused on Blaise. "We both know I'm the one you want to hurt."

"Not just hurt. I want to destroy you. And hurting her—" he gripped into her shoulder painfully, causing Scarlett to gasp aloud "—is the best way to do that."

Vin took a step toward them. "We can talk about this. Negotiate…"

"There's nothing to negotiate, and if you take one more step, she's dead."

Vin stopped. His voice was low. "You'll die the second after she does."

Blaise gave a cackle. "You think I care? You took everything from me, Borgia. My whole life. I can never go back. And now neither can you…"

Blaise pressed the cold barrel of the revolver sharply into her skin.

Vin threw Scarlett a brief glance full of meaning. "You'd attack her from behind?"

And she remembered that rainy afternoon in October.

Here's how to use your own body weight against an attacker who grabs you from behind... She gave him a single trembling nod, and then everything happened at once.

The door of the *palazzo* banged open as Beppe and two other bodyguards rushed out. As Blaise whirled to look, Vin planted his feet, lowering his body into an instinctive crouch.

With an exaggerated sigh, Scarlett sagged as if she'd fainted. It wasn't hard at all. She was so terrified she was perilously close to fainting anyway.

Her unexpected weight broke his hold, and she fell hard to the cold, wet sidewalk.

With a loud curse, Blaise pointed the gun at her. He cocked it. She saw the deadly intention in his face.

As snowflakes whirled around her, Scarlett's life flashed before her eyes. Her mother. Her father. Her baby. All the love she'd had. And Vin. Always Vin...

As she closed her eyes, bracing herself for death, she saw a shadow fly across her field of vision. But there was no mercy. The gun went off with a jarring bang, and she flinched, gasping.

But she felt nothing.

Was this what it felt like to be dead? Scarlett's eyes opened, then she quickly ran her hands over her body. Somehow, though he'd shot her from four feet away, he'd missed her!

But Vin and Blaise were still struggling for the gun. The revolver fired once more, echoing loudly in the night.

"Die, you Italian bastard!" Blaise panted.

Vin! Scarlett scrambled to her feet, desperate to save him, terrified he'd been shot. But even as the bodyguards descended from all sides, Vin flung Blaise over his back like a sack of potatoes. For half a second, Blaise was suspended in midair with a shocked, stupid look on his face. Then he crashed hard to the concrete, where he lay still.

"The police are on the way, Mr. Borgia," Beppe said.

Scarlett heard the distant whine of a siren. She knew the steps in front of the *palazzo* would soon be covered with medical and police personnel.

Blaise lay faceup, flat on his back. Unmoving, he wheezed, "You... You..."

Vin looked down at him coldly. "You are going to prison, Falkner. For a very long time. You should pray you never get out." As bodyguards surrounded him, Vin turned to Scarlett. His expression changed. He reached for her. "Scarlett—"

"You saved me," Scarlett choked out, pressing her cheek against him. Then she drew back, frowning. "But you're wet. You..." There was a darkening patch on his right shoulder, and another on his left thigh. With a gasp, she lifted the lapel of his tuxedo jacket and saw red blooming across his white shirt, like a flower. And it was in that moment she realized why she was still alive. Vin had taken two bullets for her.

When Vin saw Falkner put his finger on the trigger, everything had become crystal clear.

He would either save his wife or die with her.

Their son would know that his father had loved his mother enough to sacrifice his own life to try to save her.

That was the best legacy any father could leave his son. The only real legacy. It had nothing to do with leaving a fortune, or a billion-dollar company. A man's true legacy was his example, of how a man should live—and how he should die. *For the ones he loved.*

"Cara." Vin pulled Scarlett into his arms, holding her like the precious treasure she was. He felt a sharp pain in his shoulder, and another in his thigh. He gritted his teeth against the pain. "He was right about one thing. If anything ever happened to you, it would utterly destroy me."

"Vin, we need to try to stop the bleeding until the paramedics…"

"Not yet," he breathed. He curved his hands around her, needing the feel of her body against his. "Everything you said was true. That's what I came to say. I was afraid to love you." He searched her gaze. "Now the only thing I'm afraid of is not having the chance to love you for the rest of my life."

She looked closely at the holes in his jacket. "It looks like this bullet went straight through your shoulder and out the back. But your leg…"

He was barely listening. "I was a coward."

"Coward? Vin, you took two bullets for me!"

"It's true," he insisted roughly. He was still shaking. It was only now that he held her, now she was safe in his arms, that he could admit how terrified he'd been. "I promised myself long ago that I'd never love anyone— never give anyone that kind of power over me. Then on Christmas Eve, after I told you I loved you, I was afraid. I was desperate to regain control."

"Control over what?"

"You, me, everything. Life."

"Oh, Vin," she whispered through cracked lips. "No one can control all that."

"I realized that today." His lips twisted as he leaned on her. He could no longer put any weight on his left leg. He wondered how much blood he'd lost. But he couldn't let her go. Not yet. "I've made so many mistakes. I just found out Giuseppe has always known he's not my biological father. He just didn't care."

"No!"

He gave a low laugh, swaying on his feet. He was starting to feel dizzy. "Control is an illusion. I understand that now. All I can control in life are the choices I make. The man I choose to be." He took her hand in his own, pressing it against his chest. "You have my heart, Scarlett. No matter if you hurt me. No matter if you leave me." Her beautiful face blurred in his vision as he whispered, "After the way I tricked you into signing those papers, I wouldn't blame you."

Paramedics and firemen and policemen were swarming the street, and inquisitive wedding guests were pouring out of the *palazzo*. But all Vin could see was Scarlett's pale, determined face.

"You listen to me, Vin Borgia," she said hoarsely. "This is something I want you to remember for the rest of your life." She took both his hands in hers. Her green eyes looked enormous. "You're safe with me, Vin. As long as I live, I'll watch out for you."

It was a strange thing to hear from a woman so much smaller than he. But as he swayed, feeling weak from loss of blood, she was beneath his arm, supporting him, the source of his strength. As he was the source of hers.

"And I know I'm safe with you," she whispered, her eyes filling with tears. "I will never leave you. I'm yours for life."

Her love washed over him like an enveloping embrace. Vin exhaled. He hadn't realized he'd been holding his breath for so long, waiting to hear those words. Years. Decades.

He breathed, "Scarlett..."

Snow fell softly in the dark January night, frosting the streets of Rome. As people swarmed all around them, Vin pulled her close. He felt new, reborn. She'd made him the man he'd been born to be.

Then he staggered back as his vision got a little hazy.

"You're losing too much blood!" She waved wildly to the paramedics. "Over here! Quick!"

The paramedics swiftly assessed Vin's injuries and worked to control the bleeding, applying pressure and bandages before leaning him into a backboard, to carry him into the ambulance. "We need to get him to the hospital, *signora*."

"Yes," she said anxiously.

"Wait." Feeling woozy, Vin looked at his wife. "We'll live in Rome."

She tried to smile. "What about the long-term lease to Mr. Hollywood?"

"Canceled. We'll stay."

She looked down at him, her tangled red hair streaked with snow and blood. "No."

"No?"

She shook her head. "That's not how marriage works. It's not my decision." Taking his hand in hers, she kissed it. "It's ours. I love you, Vin."

He looked at her, now holding nothing back, letting her see his whole heart and soul. "I love you more."

"Are you ready?"

No, Scarlett thought, biting her lip hard. She shivered, then nodded.

"Good." Vin held out his hand.

She took it and stepped onto a plane for the first time in almost a year.

"You can do this," he said.

She took a deep breath. She looked at his hand in hers, then squared her shoulders. "I know."

He smiled. "That's my girl."

The plane was tiny, a four-seater Cessna. There would be no flight attendants. Only one pilot. And only one passenger.

But it was going to be all right, Scarlett suddenly knew. Because she trusted this pilot with her life.

She sat beside him now as he pushed knobs and flicked

on switches. He moved the throttle, then glanced at her. "Maybe someday you'll get your own pilot's license."

"Ha-ha," she said, then realized he was serious.

Vin looked at her. "The best way to live is to do what scares you most. You taught me that, *cara*."

Maybe he was right, Scarlett thought suddenly. Maybe. But...

"I'll just survive being a passenger first," she said, gripping her headphones tightly.

He reached over and put his hand on her knee. "Look at my face."

She did and relaxed.

"There's no way we can crash." He sat back in the pilot's seat with an encouraging grin. "I'm safe with you, remember? You'll watch out for me."

"I meant it." She knew he wouldn't let anything happen to her, either. If anyone could keep Vin safe, it was Scarlett. If anyone could keep Scarlett safe, it was Vin.

She took a deep breath, clutching her armrests.

So much had changed in the last eight months, since the night of Maria's wedding, when he'd been shot by Blaise Falkner. Vin had spent days recovering in the hospital, where he'd also been interviewed by the police. But he'd been lucky.

"If he'd shot you a little lower in the shoulder," the doctor had told him, "the bullet would have hit you in the heart. If he'd shot you a little higher in the thigh..." He hesitated.

"I'd be done fathering children?" Vin had grinned up at Scarlett, standing by his hospital bed. "Remind me to visit Falkner in prison and thank him for his poor aim."

She didn't find it funny at all. "This is no laughing matter."

"Oh, *cara*, but it is." Vin had kissed the back of her

hand, then looked at her seriously. "One should always be joyful in the presence of a miracle."

When he finally was able to return home, he'd embraced his baby son happily swinging in his bouncy chair, who had no idea of the tragedy that had nearly taken his parents' lives. Vin had kissed his son's downy head, kissed his wife's lips, then gone straight to the study and thrown the signed postnuptial agreement into the fire.

He'd also ripped up the villa's lease to the movie star. The man had immediately threatened to sue, but Vin had solved the problem by paying for him to stay three months at a fancy hotel, and the actor quit complaining.

"Room service," Vin explained succinctly.

Vin had also insisted on paying for his sister to have a second honeymoon. It was the least he could do, he said, after ruining her wedding reception. After the young couple had returned from Tahiti, while Giuseppe and Joanne were visiting their grandson for a week, they had the whole family together for dinners and game nights.

Eventually, when Vin's wounds had healed and Scarlett felt ready, they had a farewell party to say *ciao* to Rome. They packed up what they needed most and took the train to London and, from there, a luxurious ocean liner to New York.

Scarlett had felt guilty about the six-day voyage—so much longer than a transatlantic flight—but her husband hadn't grumbled once. In fact, he'd claimed he enjoyed the vacation, and the chance to dance with his wife every night on the dance floor while Mrs. Stone kept a close eye on Nico in their lavish suite.

"In fact, I might consider a fleet of ships for my next SkyWorld expansion," he'd told Scarlett, waggling his eyebrows. She still wasn't sure if he'd been serious.

The two of them had agreed to compromise, and split their time between Rome and New York. But since they'd moved to Manhattan, Scarlett had found to her surprise that she'd come to love this rough-and-tumble city, too. Next week, when they returned to Rome, she might even miss New York. Living in their delightful two-story penthouse with a view of Central Park—which she'd decorated to be homey and comfortable—meant she often passed St. Swithun's Cathedral on Fifth Avenue.

"The place you decided to marry me," she liked to tease Vin, "in the middle of your wedding to someone else."

He grinned. "*Bella*, I know a good thing when I see her."

"I love you," she said.

"I love you more," he said seriously.

Which of them loved the other one more was, of course, not their only quarrel. They were human, after all. Sometimes Vin worked too much, or Scarlett fretted about their perfectly happy baby, who could now sit on his own and loved to giggle and was starting to talk. But even during their rare arguments, Vin would claim that Scarlett was perfect, the most wonderful woman in the world. It irritated her to no end. How could she properly fight with a man who continually insisted she was perfect?

So when Vin suggested one tiny, tiny thing she might do for his birthday, she had to listen. He asked her to take a plane ride. "I have a little Cessna parked at Teterboro. I'd be the pilot. We'd fly for fifteen minutes, tops. Short circle, totally uneventful, then we'd land." He looked at her hopefully. "What do you say?"

She hadn't wanted to disappoint him, so she'd agreed. But now…

"I can't believe you talked me into this," she breathed, as the engine noise started to build, shaking the small plane.

He grinned. "You'll love it. Trust me."

And the funny thing was, she did trust him. So maybe

he was right. Maybe she would love this. Maybe the fear that had been holding her back all this time from flying was the same one that had made him afraid to love her.

It was normal to be afraid of taking a risk. But wasn't it the point of life to find courage—even if it took a little while—and be bold enough to fly?

"Are you ready, Scarlett?" her husband asked quietly.

She felt green with fear. But she knew that if anyone could keep her safe, if anyone truly loved her, it was Vin. She took a deep breath. "Hit it."

"I love you," he said, pushing the throttle forward.

She looked at him, her heart full. "I love you more."

The Cessna started to increase speed down the runway, going faster and faster. And as the nose lifted off the ground, and their little plane soared off the runway into the bright blue sky, Scarlett knew they'd be relishing the pleasures of that argument for the rest of their lives.

* * * * *

If you enjoyed this story, look out for these other great reads from Jennie Lucas
UNCOVERING HER NINE-MONTH SECRET
NINE MONTHS TO REDEEM HIM
THE SHEIKH'S LAST SEDUCTION
THE CONSEQUENCES OF THAT NIGHT
Available now!

Also available in the
ONE NIGHT WITH CONSEQUENCES
series this month
THE SHEIKH'S BABY SCANDAL
by Carol Marinelli

"You may kiss the bride."

Mikolas revealed his bride's face—and froze.

She was beautiful. Her mouth was eye-catching, with a lush upper lip and a bashful bottom one tucked beneath it. Her chin was strong, and came up a notch in a hint of challenge, while her blue, blue irises blinked at him.

This was no girl on the brink of legal age. She was a woman—one who was mature enough to look him straight in the eye without flinching.

She was *not* Trina Stamos.

"Who the hell are *you*?"

Canadian **Dani Collins** knew in high school that she wanted to write romance for a living. Twenty-five years later, after marrying her high school sweetheart, having two kids with him, working at several generic office jobs and submitting countless manuscripts, she got 'The Call'. Her first Modern Romance novel won the Reviewers' Choice Award for Best First in Series from *RT Book Reviews*. She now works in her own office, writing romance.

Books by Dani Collins

Mills & Boon Modern Romance

Bought by Her Italian Boss
Vows of Revenge
Seduced into the Greek's World
The Russian's Acquisition
An Heir to Bind Them
A Debt Paid in Passion
More than a Convenient Marriage?
No Longer Forbidden?

The Wrong Heirs

The Marriage He Must Keep
The Consequence He Must Claim

Seven Sexy Sins

The Sheikh's Sinful Seduction

The 21ˢᵗ Century Gentleman's Club

The Ultimate Seduction

One Night With Consequences

Proof of Their Sin

Visit the Author Profile page at
millsandboon.co.uk for more titles.

THE SECRET
BENEATH THE VEIL

BY
DANI COLLINS

First Published in Great Britain 2016
By Mills & Boon, an imprint of HarperCollins*Publishers*
1 London Bridge Street, London, SE1 9GF

© 2016 Dani Collins

ISBN: 978-0-263-92129-8

Our policy is to use papers that are natural, renewable and recyclable
products and made from wood grown in sustainable forests. The logging
and manufacturing processes conform to the legal environmental
regulations of the country of origin.

Printed and bound in Spain
by CPI, Barcelona

THE SECRET
BENEATH THE VEIL

To you, Dear Reader,
for loving romance novels as much as I do.
I hope you enjoy this one.

CHAPTER ONE

THE AFTERNOON SUN came straight through the windows, blinding Viveka Brice as she walked down the makeshift aisle of the wedding she was preventing—not that anyone knew that yet.

The interior of the yacht club, situated on this remote yet exclusive island in the Aegean, was all marble and brass, adding more bounces of white light. Coupled with the layers of her veil, she could hardly see and had to reluctantly cling to the arm of her reviled stepfather.

He probably couldn't see any better than she could. Otherwise he would have called her out for ruining his plan. He certainly hadn't noticed she wasn't Trina.

She was getting away with hiding the fact her sister had left the building. It made her stomach both churn with nerves and flutter with excitement.

She squinted, trying to focus past the standing guests and the wedding party arranged before the robed minister. She deliberately avoided looking at the tall, imposing form of the unsuspecting groom, staring instead through the windows and the forest of masts bobbing on the water. Her sister was safe from this forced marriage to a stranger, she reminded herself, trying to calm her racing heart.

Forty minutes ago, Trina had let her father into the room where she was dressing. She'd still been wearing this gown, but hadn't yet put on the veil. She had promised Grigor she would be ready on time while Viveka had kept well out of sight. Grigor didn't even know Viveka was back on the island.

The moment he'd left the room, Viveka had helped Trina out of the gown and Trina had helped her into it. They had hugged hard, then Trina had disappeared down a service elevator and onto the seaplane her true love had chartered. They were making for one of the bigger islands to the north where arrangements were in place to marry them the moment they touched land. Viveka was buying them time by allaying suspicion, letting the ceremony continue as long as possible before she revealed herself and made her own escape.

She searched the horizon again, looking for the flag of the boat she'd hired. It was impossible to spot and that made her even more anxious than the idea of getting onto the perfectly serviceable craft. She hated boats, but she wasn't in the class that could afford private helicopters to take her to and fro. She'd given a sizable chunk of her savings to Stephanos, to help him spirit Trina away in that small plane. Spending the rest on crossing the Aegean in a speedboat was pretty close to her worst nightmare, but the ferry made only one trip per day and had left her here this morning.

She knew which slip the boat was using, though. She'd paid the captain to wait and Stephanos had assured her she could safely leave her bags on board. Once she was exposed, she wouldn't even change. She would seek out that wretched boat, grit her teeth and sail into the sunset, content that she had finally prevailed over Grigor.

Her heart took a list and roll as they reached the top of the aisle, and Grigor handed her icy fingers to Trina's groom, the very daunting Mikolas Petrides.

His touch caused a *zing* of something to go through her. She told herself it was alarm. Nervous tension.

His grip faltered almost imperceptibly. Had he felt that static shock? His fingers shifted to enfold hers, pressing warmth through her whole body. Not comfort. She didn't fool herself into believing he would bother with that. He was even more intimidating in person than in his photos, exactly as Trina had said.

Viveka was taken aback by the quiet force he emanated, all chest and broad shoulders. He was definitely too much masculine energy for Viveka's little sister. He was too much for *her*.

She peeked into his face and found his gaze trying to penetrate the layers of her veil, brows lowered into sharp angles, almost as if he suspected the wrong woman stood before him.

Lord, he was handsome with those long clean-shaven plains below his carved cheekbones and the small cleft in his chin. His eyes were a smoky gray, outlined in black spiky lashes that didn't waver as he looked down his blade of a nose.

We could have blue-eyed children, she had thought when she'd first clicked on his photo. It was one of those silly facts of genetics that had caught her imagination when she had been young enough to believe in perfect matches. To this day it was an attribute she thought made a man more attractive.

She had been tempted to linger over his image and speculate about a future with him, but she'd been on a mission from the moment Trina had tearfully told her she was being sold off in a business merger like sixteenth-century chattel. All Viveka had had to see were the headlines that tagged Trina's groom as the son of a murdered Greek gangster. No *way* would she let her sister marry this man.

Trina had begged Grigor to let her wait until March, when she turned eighteen, and to keep the wedding small and in Greece. That had been as much concession as he'd granted. Trina, legally allowed to marry whomever she wanted as of this morning, had *not* chosen Mikolas Petrides, wealth, power and looks notwithstanding.

Viveka swallowed. The eye contact seemed to be holding despite the ivory organza between them, creating a sense of connection that sent a fresh thrum of nervous energy through her system.

She and Trina both took after their mother in build, but Trina was definitely the darker of the two, with a rounder face and warm, brown eyes, whereas Viveka had these icy blue orbs and natural blond streaks she'd covered with the veil.

Did he know she wasn't Trina? She shielded her eyes with a drop of her lashes.

The shuffle of people sitting and the music halting sent a wash of perspiration over her skin. Could he hear her pulse slamming? Feel her trembles?

It's just a play, she reminded herself. Nothing about this was real or valid. It would be over soon and she could move on with her life.

At one time she had imagined acting for a living. All her early career ambitions had leaned toward starving artist of one kind or another, but she'd had to grow up fast and become more practical once her mother died. She had worked here at this yacht club, lying about her age so they'd hire her, washing dishes and scrubbing floors.

She had wanted to be independent of Grigor as soon as possible, away from his disparaging remarks that had begun turning into outright abuse. He had helped her along by kicking her out of the house before she'd turned fifteen. He'd kicked her off this island, really. Out of Greece and away from her sister because once he realized she had been working, that she had the means to support herself and wouldn't buckle to his will when he threatened to expel her from his home, he had ensured she was fired and couldn't get work anywhere within his reach.

Trina, just nine, had been the one to whisper, *Go. I'll be okay. You should go.*

Viveka had reached out to her mother's elderly aunt in London. She had known Hildy only from Christmas cards, but the woman had taken her in. It hadn't been ideal. Viveka got through it by dreaming of bringing her sister to live with her there. As recently as a few months ago, she had pictured them as two carefree young women, twenty-three and eighteen, figuring out their futures in the big city—

"I, Mikolas Petrides…"

He had an arresting voice. As he repeated his name and spoke his vows, the velvet-and-steel cadence of his tone held her. He smelled good, like fine clothes and spicy aftershave and something unique and masculine that she knew would imprint on her forever.

She didn't want to remember this for the rest of her life. It was a ceremony that wasn't even supposed to be happening. She was just a placeholder.

Silence made her realize it was her turn.

She cleared her throat and searched for a suitably meek tone. Trina had never been a target for Grigor. Not just because she was his biological daughter, but also because she was on the timid side—probably because her father was such a mean, loudmouthed, sexist bastard in the first place.

Viveka had learned the hard way to be terrified of Grigor. Even in London his cloud of intolerance had hung like a poison cloud, making her careful about when she contacted Trina, never setting Trina against him by confiding her suspicions, always aware he could hurt Viveka through her sister.

She had sworn she wouldn't return to Greece, certainly not with plans that would make Grigor hate her more than he already did, but she was confident he wouldn't do more than yell in front of all these wedding guests. There were media moguls in the assemblage and paparazzi circling the air and water. The risk in coming here was a tall round of embarrassed confusion, nothing more.

She sincerely hoped.

The moment of truth approached. Her voice thinned and cracked, making her vows a credible imitation of Trina's as she spoke fraudulently in her sister's place, nullifying the marriage—and merger—that Grigor wanted so badly. It wasn't anything that could truly balance the loss of her mother, but it was a small retribution. Viveka wore a grim inner smile as she did it.

Her bouquet shook as she handed it off and her fingers felt clumsy and nerveless as she exchanged rings with Mikolas, keeping up the ruse right to the last minute. She wouldn't sign any papers, of course, and she would have to return these rings. Darn, she hadn't thought about that.

Even his hands were compelling, so well shaped and strong, so sure. One of his nails looked… She wasn't sure. Like he'd injured it once. If this were a real wedding, she would know that intimate detail about him.

Silly tears struck behind her eyes. She had the same girlish dreams for a fairy-tale wedding as any woman. She wished this were the beginning of her life with the man she loved. But it wasn't. Nothing about this was legal or real.

Everyone was about to realize that.

"You may kiss the bride."

* * *

Mikolas Petrides had agreed to this marriage for one reason only: his grandfather. He wasn't a sentimental man or one who allowed himself to be manipulated. He sure as hell wasn't marrying for love. That word was an immature excuse for sex and didn't exist in the real world.

No, he felt nothing toward his bride. He felt nothing toward anyone, quite by conscious decision.

Even his loyalty to his grandfather was provisional. Pappoús had saved his life. He'd *given* Mikolas this life once their blood connection had been verified. He had recognized Mikolas as his grandson, pulling him from the powerless side of a brutal world to the powerful one.

Mikolas repaid him with duty and legitimacy. His grandfather had been born into a good family during hard times. Erebus Petrides hadn't stayed on the right side of the law as he'd done what he'd seen as necessary to survive. Living a corrupt life had cost the old man his son and Mikolas had been Erebus's second chance at an heir. He had given his grandson full rein with his ill-gotten empire on the condition Mikolas turn it into a legal—yet still lucrative—enterprise.

No small task, but this marriage merger was the final step. To the outside observer, Grigor's world-renowned conglomerate was absorbing a second-tier corporation with a questionable pedigree. In reality, Grigor was being paid well for a company logo. Mikolas would eventually run the entire operation.

Was it irony that his mother had been a laundress? Or appropriate?

Either way, this marriage had been Grigor's condition. He wanted his own blood to inherit his wealth. Mikolas had accepted to make good on his debt to his grandfather. Marriage would work for him in other ways and it was only another type of contract. This ceremony was more elaborate than most business meetings, but it was still just a date to fix signatures upon dotted lines followed by the requisite photo op.

Mikolas had met his bride—a girl, really—twice. She was young and extremely shy. Pretty enough, but no sparks of attraction had flared in him. He'd resigned himself to affairs while she grew up and they got to know one another. *Therein might be another advantage to marriage,* he had been thinking distantly, while he waited for her to walk down the aisle. Other women wouldn't wheedle for marriage if he already wore a ring.

Then her approach had transfixed him. Something happened. *Lust.*

He was never comfortable when things happened outside his control. This was hardly the time or place for a spike of naked hunger for a woman. But it happened.

She arrived before him veiled in a waterfall mist that he should have dismissed as an irritating affectation. For some reason he found the mystery deeply erotic. He recognized her perfume as the same scent she'd worn those other times, but rather than sweet and innocent, it now struck him as womanly and heady.

Her lissome figure wasn't as childish as he'd first judged, either. She moved as though she owned her body, and how had he not noticed before that her eyes were such a startling shade of blue, the kind that sat as a pool of water against a glacier? He could barely see her face, but the intensity of blue couldn't be dimmed by a few scraps of lace.

His heart began to thud with an old, painful beat. *Want.* The real kind. The kind that was more like basic necessity.

A flicker of panic threatened, but he clamped down on the memories of deprivation. Of denial. Terror. Searing pain.

He got what he wanted these days. Always. He was getting *her*.

Satisfaction rolled through him, filling him with anticipation for this pomp and circumstance to end.

The ceremony progressed at a glacial pace. Juvenile eagerness struck him when he was finally able to lift her veil. He didn't celebrate Christmas, yet felt it had arrived early, just for him.

He told himself it was gratification at accomplishing the goal his grandfather had assigned him. With this kiss, the balance sheets would come out of the rinse cycle, clean and pressed like new. Too bad the old man hadn't been well enough to travel here and enjoy this moment himself.

Mikolas revealed his bride's face and froze.

She was beautiful. Her mouth was eye-catching with a lush upper lip and a bashful bottom one tucked beneath it. Her chin was strong and came up a notch in a hint of challenge while her blue, blue irises blinked at him.

This was no girl on the brink of legal age. She was a woman, one who was mature enough to look him straight in the eye without flinching.

She was *not* Trina Stamos.

"Who the hell are you?"

Gasps went through the crowd.

The woman lifted a hand to brush her veil free of his dumbfounded fingers.

Behind her, Grigor shot to his feet with an ugly curse. "What are you doing here? Where's Trina?"

Yes. Where was his bride? Without the right woman here to speak her vows and sign her name, this marriage— *the merger*—was at a standstill. *No.*

As though she had anticipated Grigor's reaction, the bride zipped behind Mikolas, using him like a shield as the older man bore down on them.

"You little bitch!" Grigor hissed. Trina's father was not as shocked by the switch as he was incensed. He clearly knew this woman. A vein pulsed on his forehead beneath his flushed skin. "Where is she?"

Mikolas put up a hand, warding off the old man from grabbing the woman behind him. He would have his explanation from her before Grigor unleashed his temper.

Or maybe he wouldn't.

Another round of surprised gasps went through the crowd, punctuated by the clack of the fire door and a loud, repetitive ring of its alarm.

His bride had bolted out the emergency exit.

What the *hell*?

CHAPTER TWO

VIVEKA RAN EVERY DAY. She was fit and adrenaline pulsed through her arteries, giving her the ability to move fast and light as she fled Grigor and his fury.

The dress and the heels and the spaces between planks and the floating wharf were another story. *Bloody hell.*

She made it down the swaying ramp in one piece, thanks to the rails on either side, but then she was racing down the unsteady platform between the slips, scanning for the flag of her vessel—

The train of her dress caught. She didn't even see on what. She was yanked back and that was all it took for her to lose her footing completely. *Stupid heels.*

She turned her ankle, stumbled, tried to catch herself, hooked her toe in a pile of coiled rope and threw out an arm to snatch at the rail of the yacht in the slip beside her.

She missed, only crashing into the side of the boat with her shoulder. The impact made her "oof!" Her grasp was too little, too late. She slid sideways and would have screamed, but had the sense to suck in a big breath before she fell.

Cold, murky salt water closed over her.

Don't panic, she told herself, splaying out her limbs and only getting tangled in her dress and veil.

Mom. This was what it must have been like for her on

that night far from shore, suddenly finding herself under cold, swirling water, tangled in an evening dress.

Don't panic.

Viveka's eyes stung as she tried to shift the veil enough to see which way the bubbles were going. Her dress hadn't stayed caught. It had come all the way in with her and floated all around her, obscuring her vision, growing heavier. The chill of the water penetrated to her skin. The weight of the dress dragged her down.

She kicked, but the layers of the gown were in the way. Her spiked heels caught in the fabric. This was futile. She was going to drown within swimming distance to shore. Grigor would stand above her and applaud.

The back of her hand scraped barnacles and her foot touched something. The seabed? Her hand burned where she'd scuffed it, but that told her there was a pillar somewhere here. She tried to scrabble her grip against it, desperately thinking she had never held her breath this long and couldn't hold it any longer.

Don't panic.

She clawed at her veil with her other hand, tried to pull it off her hair. She would never get all these buttons open and the dress off in time to kick herself to the surface—

Don't panic.

The compulsion to gasp for air was growing unstoppable.

A hand grabbed her forearm and tugged her.

Yes, please. Oh, God, please!

Viveka blew out what little air she still had, fighting not to inhale, fighting to kick and help bring herself to the blur of light above her, fighting to reach it…

As she broke through, she gasped in a lungful of life-giving oxygen, panting with exertion, thrusting back her veil to stare at her rescuer.

Mikolas.

He looked murderous.

Her heart lurched.

With a yank, he dragged her toward a diving ramp off the back of a yacht and physically set her hand upon it. She slapped her other bleeding hand onto it, clinging for dear life. Oh, her hand stung. So did her lungs. Her stomach was knotted with shock over what had just happened. She clung to the platform with a death grip as she tried to catch her breath and think clear thoughts.

People were gathering along the slip, trying to see between the boats, calling to others in Greek and English. "There she is!" "He's got her." "They're safe."

Viveka's dress felt like it was made of lead. It continued trying to pull her under, tugged by the wake that set all the boats around them rocking and sucking. She shakily managed to scrape the veil off her hair, ignoring the yank on her scalp as she raked it from her head. She let it float away, not daring to look for Grigor. She'd caught a glimpse of his stocky legs and that was enough. Her heart pounded in reaction.

"What the *hell* is going on?" Mikolas said in that darkly commanding voice. "Where is Trina? Who are you?"

"I'm her sis—" Viveka took a mouthful of water as a swell bashed the boat they clung to. "*Pah.* She didn't want to marry you."

"Then she shouldn't have agreed to." He hauled himself up to sit on the platform.

Oh, yes, it was just that easy.

He was too hard to face with that lethal expression. How did he manage to look so action-star handsome with his white shirt plastered to his muscled shoulders, his coat and tie gone, his hair flattened to his head? It was like staring into the sun.

Viveka looked out to where motorboats had circled to see where the woman in the wedding gown had fallen into the water.

Was that her boat? She wanted to wave, but kept a firm grip on the yacht as she used her free hand to pick at the buttons on her back. She eyed the distance to the red-and-gold boat. She couldn't swim that far in this wretched dress, but if she managed to shed it…?

Mikolas stood and, without asking, bent down to grasp her by the upper arms, pulling her up and out of the water, grunting loud enough that it was insulting. He swore after landing her on her feet beside him. His chest heaved while he glared at her limp, stained gown.

Viveka swayed on her feet, trying to keep her balance as the yacht rocked beneath them. She was still wearing the ridiculously high heels, was still in shock, but for a few seconds she could only stare at Mikolas.

He had saved her life.

No one had gone out of their way to help her like that since her mother was alive. She'd been a pariah to Grigor and a burden on her aunt, mostly fending for herself since her mother's death.

She swallowed, trying to assimilate a deep and disturbing gratitude. She had grown a thick shell that protected her from disregard, but she didn't know how to deal with kindness. She was moved.

Grigor's voice above her snapped her back to her situation. She had to get away. She yanked at her bodice, tearing open the delicate buttons on her spine and trying to push the clinging fabric down her hips.

She wore only a white lace bra and underpants beneath, but that was basically a bikini. Good enough to swim out to her getaway craft.

To her surprise, Mikolas helped her, rending the gown

as if he cursed its existence, leaving it puddled around her feet and sliding into the water. He didn't give her a chance to dive past him, however. He set wide hands on her waist and hefted her upward where bruising hands took hold of her arms—

Grigor.

"Nooo!" she screamed.

That ridiculous woman nearly kicked him in the face as he hefted her off the diving platform to the main deck of the yacht. Grigor was above, taking hold of her to bring her up. What did she think? That he was throwing her back into the sea?

"Noooo!" she cried and struggled, but Grigor pulled her all the way onto the deck where he stood.

She must be crazy, behaving like this.

Mikolas came up the ladder with the impetus of a man taking charge. He hated surprises. *He* controlled what happened to himself. No one else.

At least Grigor hadn't set this up. He'd been tricked as well, or he wouldn't be so furious.

Mikolas was putting that together as he came up to see Grigor shaking the nearly naked woman like a terrier with a rat. Then he slapped her across the face hard enough to send her to her knees.

No stranger to violence, Mikolas still took it like a punch to the throat. It appalled him on a level so deep he reacted on blind instinct, grabbing Grigor's arm and shoving him backward even as the woman threw up her arm as though to block a kick.

Stupid reaction, he thought distantly. It was a one-way ticket to a broken forearm.

But now was not the moment for a tutorial on street fighting.

Grigor found his balance and trained his homicidal gaze on Mikolas.

Mikolas centered his balance with readiness, but in his periphery saw the woman stagger toward the rail. Oh, hell, no. She was not going to ruin his day, then slip away like a siren into the deep.

He turned from Grigor's bitter "You should have let her drown" and provoked a cry of "Put me down!" from the woman as he caught her up against his chest.

She was considerably lighter without the gown, but still a handful of squirming damp skin and slippery muscle as he carried her off the small yacht.

On the pier, people parted and swiveled like gaggles of geese, some dressed in wedding regalia, others obviously tourists and sailors, all babbling in different languages as they took in the commotion.

It was a hundred meters to his own boat and he felt every step, thanks to the pedal of the woman's sharp, silver heels.

"Calm yourself. I've had it with this sideshow. You're going to tell me where my bride has gone and why."

CHAPTER THREE

VIVEKA WAS SHAKING right down to her bones. Grigor had hit her, right there in front of the whole world. Well, the way the yacht had been positioned, only Mikolas had probably seen him, but in the back of her mind she was thinking that this was the time to call the police. With all these witnesses, they couldn't ignore her complaint. Not this time.

Actually, they probably could. Her report of assault and her request for a proper investigation into her mother's death had never been heeded. The officers on this island paid rent to Grigor and didn't like to impact their personal lives by carrying out their sworn duties. She had learned that bitter lesson years ago.

And this brute wouldn't let her go to do anything!

He was really strong. He carried her in arms that were so hard with steely muscle it almost hurt to be held by them. She could tell it wasn't worth wasting her energy trying to escape. And he wore a mask of such controlled fury he intimidated her.

She instinctively drew in on herself, stomach churning with reaction while her brain screamed at her to swim out to her hired boat.

"Let me go," she insisted in a more level tone.

Mikolas only bit out orders for ice and bandages to a

uniformed man as he carried her up a narrow gangplank, boarding a huge yacht of aerodynamic layers and space-ship-like rigging. The walls were white, the decks teak, the sheer size and luxury of the vessel making it more like a cruise liner than a personal craft.

Greek mafia, she thought, and wriggled harder, signaling that she sincerely wanted him to put her down. *Now.*

Mikolas strode into what had to be the master cabin. She caught only a glimpse of its grand decor before he carried her all the way into a luxurious en suite and started the shower.

"Warm up," he ordered and pointed to the black satin robe on the back of the door. "Then we'll bandage your hand and ice your face while you explain yourself."

He left.

She snorted. *Not likely.*

Folding her arms against icy shivers, she eyed the small porthole that looked into the expanse of open water beyond the marina. She might fit through it, but even as the thought formed, a crewman walked by on the deck outside. She would be discovered before she got through it and in any case, she wasn't up for another swim. Not yet. She was trembling.

Reaction was setting in. She had nearly drowned. Grigor had hit her. He'd do worse if he got his hands on her again. Had he come aboard behind them?

She wanted to cry out of sheer, overwhelmed reaction.

But she wouldn't.

Trina was safe, she reminded herself. Never again did she have to worry about her little sister. Not in the same way, anyway.

The steaming shower looked incredibly inviting. Its gentle hiss beckoned her.

Don't cry, she warned herself, because showers were

her go-to place for letting emotion overcome her, but she couldn't afford to let down her guard. She may yet have to face Grigor again.

Her insides congealed at the thought.

She would need to pull herself together for that, she resolved, and closed the curtain across the porthole before picking herself free of the buckles on her shoes. She stepped into the shower still wearing her bra and undies, then took them off to rinse them and— Oh. She let out a huff of faint laughter as she saw her credit card stuck to her breast.

The chuckle was immediately followed by a stab of concern. Her bags, passport, phone and purse were on the hired boat. Was the captain waiting a short trot down the wharf? Or bobbing out in the harbor, wondering if she'd drowned? Grabbing this credit card and shoving it into her bra had been a last-minute insurance against being stuck without resources if things went horribly wrong, but she hadn't imagined things would go *this* far wrong.

The captain was waiting for her, she assured herself. She would keep her explanations short and sweet to Mikolas and be off. He seemed like a reasonable man.

She choked on another snort of laughter, this one edging toward hysteria.

Then another wave of that odd defenselessness swirled through her. Why had Mikolas saved her? It made her feel like— She didn't know what this feeling was. She never relied on anyone. She'd never been *able* to. Her mother had loved her, but she'd died. Trina had loved her, but she'd been too young and timorous to stand up to Grigor. Aunt Hildy had helped her to some extent, but on a quid-pro-quo basis.

Mikolas was a stranger who had risked his life to preserve hers. She didn't understand it.

It infused her with a sense that she was beholden to him. She hated that feeling. She had had a perfect plan to get Hildy settled, bring Trina to London once she was eighteen and finally start living life on her own terms. Then Grigor had ruined it by promising Trina to this… *criminal*.

A criminal who wasn't averse to fishing a woman out of the sea—something her stepfather hadn't bothered doing with her mother, leaving that task to search and rescue.

She was still trembling, still trying to make sense of it as she dried off with a thick black towel monogrammed with a silver *M*. She stole a peek in his medicine chest, bandaged her hand, used some kind of man-brand moisturizer that didn't have a scent, rinsed with his mouthwash, then untangled her hair with a comb that smelled like his shampoo. She used his hair dryer to dry her underwear and put both back on under his robe.

The robe felt really good, light and cool and slippery against her humid skin.

She felt like his lover wearing something this intimate.

The thought made her blush and a strange wistfulness hit her as she worked off his rings—both the diamond that Trina had given her and the platinum band he'd placed on her finger himself—and set them on the hook meant for facecloths. He was *not* the sort of man she would ever want to marry. He was far too daunting and she needed her independence, but she did secretly long for someone to share her life with. Someone kind and tender who would make her laugh and maybe bring her flowers sometimes.

Someone who wanted her in his life.

She would *not* grow maudlin about her sister running off with Stephanos, seemingly choosing him over Viveka, leaving her nursing yet another sting of rejection. Her sister was entitled to fall in love.

With a final deep breath, she emerged into the stateroom.

Mikolas was there, wearing a pair of black athletic shorts and towel-dried hair, nothing else. His silhouette was a bleak, masculine statue against the closed black curtains.

The rest of the room was surprisingly spacious for a boat, she noted with a sweeping glance. There was a sitting area with a comfortable-looking sectional facing a big-screen TV. A glass-enclosed office allowed a tinted view of a private deck in the bow. She averted her gaze from the huge bed covered with a black satin spread and came back to the man who watched her with an indecipherable expression.

He held a drink, something clear and neat. Ouzo, she assumed. His gaze snagged briefly on the red mark on her cheek before traversing to her bare feet and coming back to slam into hers.

His expression still simmered with anger, but there was something else that took her breath. A kind of male assessment that signaled he was weighing her as a potential sex partner.

Involuntarily, she did the same thing. How could she not? He was really good-looking. His build was amazing, from those broad, bare shoulders to that muscled chest to those washboard abs and soccer-star legs.

She was not a woman who gawked at men. She considered herself a feminist and figured if it was tasteless for men to gaze at pinup calendars, then women shouldn't objectify men, either, but seriously. *Wow*. He was muscly without being overdeveloped. His skin was toasted a warm brown and that light pattern of hair on his chest looked like it had been sculpted by the loving hand of Mother Nature, not any sort of waxing specialist.

An urge to touch him struck her. Sexual desire wasn't

something that normally hit her out of the blue like this, but she found herself growing warm with more than embarrassment. She wondered what it would be like to roam her mouth over his torso, to tongue his nipples and lick his skin. She felt an urge to splay her hands over his muscled waist and explore lower, push aside his waistband and *possess*.

Coils of sexual need tightened in her belly.

Where was the lead-up? The part where she spent ages kissing and nuzzling before she decided maybe she'd like to take things a little further? She never flashed to shoving down a man's pants and stroking him!

But that fantasy hit her along with a deep yearning and a throbbing pinch between her legs.

Was he getting *hard*? The front of his shorts lifted.

She realized where her gaze had fixated and jerked her eyes back to his, shocked with herself and at his blatant reaction.

His expression was arrested, yet filled with consideration and—she caught her breath—yes, that was an invitation. An arrogant *Help yourself.* Along with something predatory. Something that was barely contained. Decision. Carnal hunger.

The air grew so sexually charged, she couldn't find oxygen in it. The rhythm of her breaths changed, becoming subtle pants. Her nipples were stimulated by the shift of the robe against the lace of her bra. She became both wary and meltingly receptive.

This was crazy. She shook her head, as if she could erase all this sexual tension like an app that erased content on her phone if she joggled it back and forth hard enough.

With monumental effort, she jerked her gaze from his and stared blindly at the streak of light between the curtains. She folded her arms in self-protection and kept him in her periphery.

This was really stupid, letting him bring her into his bedroom like this. A single woman who lived in the city knew to be more careful.

"Use the ice," he said with what sounded like a hint of dry laughter in his tone. He nodded toward a side table where an ice pack sat on a small bar towel.

"It's not that bad," she dismissed. She'd had worse. Her lip might be puffed a little at the corner, but it was nothing like the time she'd walked around with a huge black eye, barely able to see out of it, openly telling people that Grigor had struck her. *You shouldn't talk back to him*, her teacher had said, mouth tight, gaze avoiding hers.

Grigor shouldn't have called her a whore and burned all her photos of her mother, she had retorted, but no one had wanted to hear *that*.

Mikolas didn't say anything, only came toward her, making her snap her head around and warn him off with a look.

Putting his glass down, he lifted his phone and clicked, taking a photo of her, surprising her so much she scowled.

"What are you doing?"

"Documenting. I assume Grigor will claim you were hurt falling into the water," he advised with cool detachment.

"You don't want me to try to discredit your business partner? Is that what you're saying? Are you going to take a photo after you leave your own mark on the other side of my face?" It was a dicey move, daring him like that, but she was so *sick* of people protecting *Grigor*. And she needed to know Mikolas's intentions, face them head-on.

Mikolas's stony eyes narrowed. "I don't hit women." His mouth pulled into a smile that was more an expression of lethal power than anything else. "And Grigor has discredited himself." He tilted the phone to indicate the photo. "Which may prove useful."

Viveka's insides tightened as she absorbed how cold-blooded that was.

"I didn't know Grigor had another daughter." Mikolas moved to take up his drink again. "Do you want one?" he asked, glancing toward the small wet bar next to the television. Both were inset against the shiny wood-grain cabinetry.

She shook her head. Better to keep her wits.

"Grigor isn't my father." She always took great satisfaction in that statement. "My mother married him when I was four. She died when I was nine. He doesn't talk about her, either."

Or the boating accident. Her heart clenched like a fist, trying to hang on to her memories of her mother, knotting in fury at the lack of a satisfactory explanation, wanting to beat the truth from Grigor if she had to.

"Do you have a name?" he asked.

"Viveka." The corner of her mouth pulled as she realized they'd come this far without it. She was practically naked, wearing a robe that had brushed his own skin and surrounded her in the scent of his aftershave. "Brice," she added, not clarifying that most people called her Vivi.

"Viveka," he repeated, like he was trying out the sound. They were speaking English and his thick accent gave an exotic twist to her name as he shaped out the *Vive* and added a short, hard *ka* to the end.

She licked her lips, disturbed by how much she liked the way he said it.

"Why the melodrama, Viveka? I asked your sister if she was agreeable to this marriage. She said yes."

"Do you think she would risk saying no to something Grigor wanted?" She pointed at the ache on her face.

Mikolas's expression grew circumspect as he dropped his gaze into his drink, thumb moving on the glass. It was the only indication his thoughts were restless beneath that rock-face exterior.

"If she wants more time," he began.

"She's marrying someone else," she cut in. "Right this minute, if all has gone to plan." She glanced for a clock, but didn't see one. "She knew Stephanos at school and he worked on Grigor's estate as a landscaper."

Trina had loved the young man from afar for years, never wanting to tip her hand to Grigor by so much as exchanging more than a shy hello with Stephanos, but she had waxed poetic to Viveka on dozens of occasions. Viveka hadn't believed Stephanos returned the crush until Trina's engagement to Mikolas had been announced.

"When Stephanos heard she was marrying someone else, he asked Trina to elope. He has a job outside of Athens." One that Grigor couldn't drop the ax upon.

"Weeding flower beds?" Mikolas swirled his drink. "She could have kept him on the side after we married, if that's what she wanted."

"Really," Viveka choked.

He shrugged a negligent shoulder. "This marriage is a business transaction, open to negotiation. I would have given her children if she wanted them, or a divorce eventually, if that was her preference. She should have spoken to me."

"Because you're such a reasonable man—who just happens to trade women like stocks and bonds."

"I'm a man who gets what he wants," he said in a soft voice, but it was positively deadly. "I want this merger."

He sounded so merciless her heart skipped in alarm. *Gangster.* She found a falsely pleasant smile.

"I wish you great success in making your dreams come true. Do you mind if I wear this robe to my boat? I can bring it back after I dress or maybe one of your staff could come with me?" She pushed her hand into the pocket and gripped her credit card, feeling the edge dig into her palm. Where was Grigor? she wondered. She had no desire to pass him on the dock and get knocked into the water again—this time unconscious.

Mikolas's expression didn't change. He said nothing, but she had the impression he was laughing at her again.

Something made her look toward the office and the view beyond the bow. The marina was tucked against a very small indent on the island's coastline. The view from shore was mostly an expanse of the Aegean. But the boats weren't passing in front of this craft. They were coming and going on both sides. The slant of sunlight on the water had shifted.

The yacht was moving.

"Are you kidding me?" she screeched.

CHAPTER FOUR

MIKOLAS THREW BACK the last of his ouzo, clenched his teeth against the burn and set aside his glass with a decisive *thunk*. He searched for the void that he usually occupied, but he couldn't find it. He was swirling in a miasma of lascivious need, achingly hard after the way Viveka had stared at his crotch and swallowed like her mouth was watering.

He absently ran a hand across his chest where his nipples were so sharp they pained him and adjusted himself so he wouldn't pop out of his shorts, resisting the urge to soothe the ache with a squeeze of his fist.

His reaction to her was unprecedented. He was an experienced man, had a healthy appetite for sex, but had never reacted so immediately and irrepressibly to any woman.

This lack of command over himself disturbed him. Infuriated him. He was insulted at being thrown over for a gardener and unclear on his next move. Retreat was never an option for him, but he'd left the island to regroup. That smacked of cowardice and he pinned the blame for all of it on this woman.

While she stood there with her hand closed over the lapels of his robe, holding it tight beneath her throat. Acting virginal when she was obviously as wily and experienced as any calculating opportunist he'd ever met.

"Let's negotiate our terms, Viveka." From the moment she had admitted to being Trina's sister he had seen the logical way to rescue this deal. Hell, by turning up in Trina's gown she'd practically announced to him how this would play out.

Of course it was a catch-22. He wasn't sure he wanted such a tempting woman so close to him, but he refused to believe she was anything he couldn't handle.

Viveka only flashed him a disparaging look and spun toward the door.

He didn't bother stopping her. He followed at a laconic pace as she scurried her way out to the stern of the mid-deck. Grasping the rail in one hand, she shaded her eyes with the other, scanning the empty horizon. She quickly threw herself to the port side. Gazing back to the island, which had been left well behind them, she made a distressed noise and glared at him again, expression white.

"Is Grigor on board?"

"Why would he be?"

"I don't know!" Her shoulders relaxed a notch, but she continued to look anxious. "Why did you leave the island?"

"Why would I stay?"

"Why would you take me?" she cried.

"I want to know why you've taken your sister's place."

"You didn't have to leave shore for that!"

"You wanted Grigor present? He seemed to be inflaming things." Grigor hadn't expected his departure, either. Mikolas's phone had already buzzed several times with calls from his would-be business partner.

That had been another reason for Mikolas's departure. If he'd stayed, he might have assaulted Grigor. The white-hot urge had been surprisingly potent and yes, that too had been provoked by this exasperating woman.

It wasn't a desire to protect *her*, Mikolas kept telling himself. His nature demanded he dominate, particularly over bullies and brutes. His personal code of ethics wouldn't allow him to stand by and watch any man batter a woman.

But Grigor's attack on this one had triggered something dark and primal in him, something he didn't care to examine too closely. Since cold-blooded murder was hardly a walk down the straight and narrow that was his grandfather's expectation of him, he'd taken himself out of temptation's reach.

"I had a boat hired! All my things are on it." Viveka pointed at the island. "Take me back!"

Such a bold little thing. Time to let her know who was boss.

"Grigor promised this merger if I married his daughter." He gave her a quick once-over. "His stepdaughter will do."

She threw back her head. "Ba-ha-ha," she near shouted and shrugged out of his robe, dropping it to the deck. "No. 'Bye." Something flashed in her hand as she started to climb over the rail.

She was fine-boned and supple and so easy to take in hand. Perhaps he took more enjoyment than he should in having another reason to touch her. Her skin was smooth and warm, her wrists delicate in his light grip as he calmly forced them behind her back, trapping her between the rail and his body.

She strained to look over her shoulder, muttering, "Oh, you—!" as something fell into the water with a glint of reflected light. "That was my credit card. Thanks a *lot*."

"Viveka." He was stimulated by the feel of her naked abdomen against his groin, erection not having subsided much and returning with vigor. Her spiked heels were gone, which was a pity. They'd been sexy as hell, but when it came to rubbing up against a woman, the less clothes the better.

She smelled of his shampoo, he noted, but there was an intriguing underlying scent that was purely hers: green tea and English rain. And that heady scent went directly into his brain, numbing him to everything but thoughts of being inside her.

Women were more subtle than men with their responses, but he read hers as clearly as a billboard. Not just the obvious signs like the way her nipples spiked against the pattern of her see-through bra cups, erotically abrading his chest and provoking thoughts of licking and sucking at them until she squirmed and moaned. A blush stained her cheeks and she licked her lips. There was a bonelessness to her. He could practically feel the way her blood moved through her veins like warm honey. He knew instinctively that opening his mouth against her neck would make her shiver and surrender to him. Her arousal would feed into his and they'd take each other to a new dimension.

Where did that ridiculous notion come from? He was no sappy poet. He tried to shake the idea out of his head, but couldn't rid himself of the certainty that sex with her would be the best he'd ever known. They were practically catching fire from this light friction. His heart was ramping with strength in his chest, his body magnetized to hers.

He was incensed with her, he reminded himself, but he was also intrigued by this unique attunement they had. Logic told him it was dangerous, but the primitive male inside him didn't give a damn. He *wanted* her.

"This is kidnapping. And assault," she said, giving a little struggle against his grip. "I thought you didn't hurt women."

"I don't let them hurt themselves, either. You'll kill yourself jumping into the water out here."

Something flickered in her expression. Her skin was very white compared with her sister's. How had he not noticed that from the very first, veil notwithstanding?

"Stop behaving like a spoiled child," he chided.

She swung an affronted look to him like it was the worst possible insult he could level at her. "How about you stop acting like you own the world?"

"This *is* my world. You walked into it. Don't complain how I run it."

"I'm trying to leave it."

"And I'll let you." Something twisted in his gut, as if that was a lie. A big one. "After you fix the damage you've done."

"How do you suggest I do that?"

"Marry me in your sister's place."

She made a choking noise and gave another wriggle of protest, heel hooking on the lower rung of the rail as if she thought she could lift herself backward over the rail.

All she managed to do was pin herself higher against him. She stilled. Hectic color deepened in her cheekbones.

He smiled, liking what she'd done. Her movement had opened her legs and brought her cleft up to nestle against his shaft. She'd caught the same zing of sexual excitement that her movement had sent through him. He nudged lightly, more of a tease than a threat, and watched a delicate shiver go through her.

It was utterly enthralling. He could only stare at her parted, quivering mouth. He wanted to cover and claim it. He wanted to drag his tongue over every inch of her. Wanted to push at his elastic waistband, press aside that virginal white lace and thrust into the heat that was branding him through the thin layers between them.

He had expected to spend this week frustrated. Now he began to forgive her for this switch of hers. They would do very nicely together. Very. Nicely.

"Let's take this back to my stateroom." His voice emanated from somewhere deep in his chest, thick with the desire that gripped him.

Her eyes flashed with fear before she said tautly, "To consummate a marriage that won't happen? Did you see how Grigor reacted to me? He'll never let me sub in for Trina. If anything would make him refuse your merger, marrying me would do it."

Mikolas slowly relaxed his grip and stepped back, trailing light fingers over the seams at her hips.

Goose bumps rose all over her, but she ignored it, hoping her knickers weren't showing the dampness that had released at the feel of him pressed against her.

What was *wrong* with her? She didn't even *do* sex. Kissing and petting were about it.

She dipped to pick up the robe and knotted it with annoyance. How could she be this hot when the wind had cooled to unpleasant and the sky was thickening with clouds?

She sent an anxious look at the ever-shrinking island amid the growing whitecaps. It was way too far to swim. Mikolas might have done her a favor taking her out of Grigor's reach, but being at sea thinned her composure like it was being spun out from a spool.

"You're saying if I want Grigor to go through with the merger, I should turn you over to him?" he asked.

"What? *No!*" Such terror slammed into her, her knees nearly buckled. "Why would you even think of doing something like that?"

"The merger is important to me."

"My *life* is important to me." Tears stung her eyes and she had to blink hard to be able to see him. She had a feeling her lips were trembling. Where was the man who had saved her? Right now, Mikolas looked as conscience-less as Grigor.

Crushed to see that indifference, she hid her distress by averting her gaze and swallowed back the lump in her throat.

"This is nothing," she said with as much calm as she could, pointing at her face, trying to reach through to the man who had said he didn't hurt women. "Barely a starting point for him. I'd rather take my chances with the sharks."

"You already have." The flatness of his voice sent a fresh quake of uncertainty through her center.

What did it say about how dire her situation was that she was searching for ways to reach him? To persuade *this* shark to refrain from offering her giftwrapped to the other one?

"If—if—" She wasn't really going to say this, was she? She briefly hung her head, but what choice did she have? She didn't have to go all the way, just make it good for him, right? She had a little experience with that. A very tiny little bit. He was hard, which meant he was up for it, right? "If you want sex…"

He made a scoffing noise. "*You* want sex. I'll decide if and when I give it to you. There's no leverage in offering it to me."

Sex was a basket of hang-ups for her. Offering herself had been really hard. Now she felt cheap and useless.

She pushed her gaze into the horizon, trying to hide how his denigration carved into her hard-won confidence.

"Go below," he commanded. "I want to make some calls."

She went because she needed to be away from him, needed to lick her wounds and reassess.

A purser showed her into a spacious cabin with a sitting room, a full en suite and a queen bed with plenty of tasseled pillows in green and gold. The cabinetry was polished to showcase the artistic grains in the amber-colored wood and the room was well-appointed with cosmetics, fresh fruit, champagne and flowers.

Her stomach churned too much to even think of eating, but she briefly considered drinking herself into oblivion. Once she noticed the laptop dock, however, she began looking for a device to contact…whom? Aunt Hildy wasn't an option. Her workmates might pick up a coffee or cover for her if she had to run home, but that was the extent of favors she could ask of them.

It didn't matter anyway. There was nothing here. The telephone connected to the galley or the bridge. The television was part of an onboard network that could be controlled by a tablet, but there was no tablet to be found.

At least she came across clothes. Women's, she noted with a cynical snort. Mikolas must have been planning to keep his own paramour on the side after his marriage.

Everything was in Viveka's size, however, and it struck her that this was Trina's trousseau. This was her sister's suite.

Mikolas hadn't expected her sister to share his room? Did that make him more hard-hearted than she judged him? Or less?

Men never dominated her thoughts this way. She never let them make her feel self-conscious and second-guess every word that passed between them. This obsession with Mikolas was a horribly susceptible feeling, like he was important to her when he wasn't.

Except for the fact he held her life in his iron fist.

Thank God she had saved Trina from marrying him. She'd done the right thing taking her sister's place and didn't hesitate to make herself at home among her things, weirdly comforted by a sense of closeness to her as she did.

Pulling on a floral wrap skirt and a peasant blouse— both deliberately light and easily removed if she happened to find herself treading water—Viveka had to admit she was relieved Mikolas had stopped her from jumping. She *would* rather take her chances with sharks than with Grigor, but she didn't have a death wish. She was trying not to think of her near drowning earlier, but it had scared the hell out of her.

So did the idea of being sent back to Grigor.

Somehow she had to keep a rational head, but after leaving Grigor's oppression and withstanding Aunt Hildy's virulence, Viveka couldn't take being subjugated anymore. That's why she'd come back to help Trina make her own choices. The idea of her sister living in sufferance as part of a ridiculous business deal had made her furious!

Opening the curtains that hid two short, wide portholes stacked upon each other, she searched the horizon for a plan. At least this wasn't like that bouncy little craft she'd dreaded. This monstrosity moved more smoothly and quietly than the ferry. It might even take her to Athens.

That would work, she decided. She would ask Mikolas to drop her on the mainland. She would meet up with Trina, Stephanos could arrange for her things to be delivered, and she would find her way home.

This pair of windows was some sort of extension, she realized, noting the cleverly disguised seam between the upper and lower windows. The top would lift into an awning while the bottom pushed out to become the railing on a short balcony. Before she thought it through, her finger was on the button next to the diagram.

The wall began to crack apart while an alarm went off with a horrible honking blare, scaring her into leaping back and swearing aloud.

Atop that shock came the interior door slamming open.

Mikolas had dressed in suit pants and a crisp white shirt and wore a *terrible* expression.

"I just wanted to see what it did!" Viveka cried, holding up a staying hand.

What a liability she was turning into.

Mikolas moved to stop and reverse the extension of the balcony while he sensed the engines being cut and the yacht slowing. As the wall restored itself, he picked up the phone and instructed his crew to stay the course.

Hanging up, he folded his arms and told himself this rush of pure, sexual excitement each time he looked at Viveka was transitory. It was the product of a busy few weeks when he hadn't made time for women combined with his frustration over today's events. Of course he wanted to let off steam in a very base way.

She delivered a punch simply by standing before him, however. He had to work at keeping his thoughts from conjuring a fantasy of removing that village girl outfit of hers. The wide, drawstring collar where her bra strap peeked was an invitation, the bare calves beneath the hem of her pretty skirt a promise of more silken skin higher up.

Those unpainted toes seemed ridiculously unguarded. So did the rest of her, with her hair tied up like a teenager and her face clean.

Some women used makeup as war paint, others as an invitation. Viveka hadn't used any. She hadn't tried to cover the bruise, and lifted that discolored, belligerent chin of hers in a brave stare that was utterly foolish. She had no idea whom she was dealing with.

Yet something twisted in his chest. He found her nerve entirely too compelling. He wanted to feed that spark of energy and watch it detonate in his hands. He bet she scratched in bed and was dismayingly eager to find out.

Women were *never* a weakness for him. No one was. Nothing. Weakness was abhorrent to him. Helplessness was a place he refused to revisit.

"We'll eat." He swept a hand to where the door was still open and one of the porters hovered.

He sent the man to notify the chef and steered her to the upper aft deck. The curved bench seat allowed them to slide in from either side, shifting cushions until they met in the middle, where they looked out over the water. Here the wind was gentled by the bulk of the vessel. It was early spring so the sun was already setting behind the clouds on the horizon.

She cast a vexed look toward the view. He took it as annoyance that the island was long gone behind them and privately smirked, then realized she was doing it again: pulling all his focus and provoking a reaction in him.

He forced his attention to the porter as he arrived with place settings and water.

"You'll eat seafood?" he said to Viveka as the porter left.

"If you tell me to, of course I will."

A rush of anticipation for the fight went through him. "Save your breath," he told her. "I don't shame."

"How does someone influence you, then? Money?" She affected a lofty tone, but quit fiddling with her silverware and tucked her hands in her lap, turning her head to read him. "Because I would like to go to Athens—as opposed to wherever you think you're taking me."

"I have money," he informed, skipping over what he intended to do next because he was still deciding.

He stretched out his arms so his left hand, no longer wearing the ring she'd put on it, settled behind her shoulder. He'd put the ring in his pocket along with the ones she had worn. Her returning them surprised him. She must have known what they were worth. Why wasn't she trying to use them as leverage? Not that it would work, but he expected a woman in her position to at least try.

He dismissed that puzzle and returned to her question. "If someone wants to influence me, they offer something I want."

"And since I don't have anything you want...?" Little flags of color rose on her cheekbones and she stared out to sea.

He almost smiled, but the tightness of her expression caused him to sober. Had he hurt her with his rejection earlier? He'd been brutal because he wasn't a novice. You didn't enter into any transaction wearing your desires on your sleeve the way she did.

But how could she not be aware that she *was* something he wanted? Did she not feel the same pull he was experiencing?

How did she keep undermining his thoughts this way?

As an opponent she was barely worth noticing. A brief online search had revealed she had no fortune, no influence. Her job was a pedestrian position as data entry clerk for an auto parts chain. Her network of social media contacts was small, which suggested an even smaller circle of real friends.

Mikolas's instinct when attacked was to crush. If Grigor had switched his bride on purpose, he would already be ruined. Mikolas didn't lose to anyone, especially weak adversaries who weren't even big enough to appear on his radar.

Yet Viveka had slipped in like a ninja, taking him unawares. On the face of it, that made her his enemy. He had to treat her with exactly as much detachment as he would any other foe.

But this twist of hunger in his gut demanded an answering response from her. It wasn't just ego. It was craving. A weight on a scale that demanded an equal weight on the other side to balance it out.

The porter returned, poured their wine, and they both sipped. When they were alone again, Mikolas said, "You were right. Grigor wants you."

Viveka paled beneath her already stiff expression. "And you want the merger."

"My grandfather does. I have promised to complete it for him."

She bit her bottom lip so mercilessly it disappeared. "Why?" she demanded. "I mean, why is this merger so important to him?"

"Why does it matter?" he countered.

"Well, what is it you're really trying to accomplish? Surely there are other companies that could give you what you want. Why does it have to be Grigor's?"

She might be impulsive and a complete pain in the backside, but she was perceptive. It *didn't* have to be Grigor's company. He was fully aware of that. However.

"Finding another suitable company would take time we don't have."

"A man with your riches can't buy as much as he needs?" she asked with an ingenuous blink.

She was a like a baby who insisted on trying to catch the tiger's tail and stuff it in her mouth. Not stupid, but cheerfully ignorant of the true danger she was in. He couldn't afford to be lenient.

"My grandfather is ill. I had to call him to tell him the merger has been delayed. That was disappointment he didn't need."

She almost threw an askance look at him, but seemed to read his expression and sobered, getting the message that beneath his civilized exterior lurked a heartless mercenary.

Not that he enjoyed scaring her. He usually treated women like delicate flowers. After sleeping in cold alleys that stank of urine, after being tortured at the hands of degenerate, pitiless men, he'd developed an insatiable appetite for luxury and warmth and the sweet side of life. He especially enjoyed soft kittens who liked to be stroked until they purred next to him in bed.

But if a woman dared to cross him, as with any man, he ensured she understood her mistake and would never dream of doing so again.

"I owe my grandfather a great deal." He waved at their surroundings. "This."

"I presumed it was stolen," she said with a haughty toss of her head.

"No." He was as blunt as a mallet. "The money was made from smuggling profits, but the boat was purchased legally."

She snapped her head around.

He shrugged, not apologizing for what he came from. "For decades, if something crossed the border or the seas for a thousand miles, legal or illegal, my grandfather—and my father when he was alive—received a cut."

He had her attention. She wasn't saucy now. She was wary. Wondering why he was telling her this.

"Desperate men do desperate things. I know this because I was quite desperate when I began trading on my father's name to survive the streets of Athens."

Their chilled soup arrived. He was hungry, but neither of them moved to pick up their spoons.

"Why were you on the streets?"

"My mother died. Heart failure, or so I was told. I was sent to an orphanage. I hated it." It had been a palace, in retrospect, but he didn't think about that. "I ran away. My mother had told me my father's name. I knew what he was reputed to be. The way my mother had talked, as if his enemies would hunt me down and use me against him if they found me…I thought she was trying to scare me into staying out of trouble. I didn't," he confided drily. "Boys of twelve are not known for their good judgment."

He smoothed his eyebrow where a scar was barely visible, but he could still feel where the tip of a blade had dragged very deliberately across it, opening the skin while a threat of worse—losing his eye—was voiced.

"I watched and learned from other street gangs and mostly stuck to robbing criminals because they don't go to the police. As long as I was faster and smarter, I survived. Threatening my father's wrath worked well in the beginning, but without a television or computer, I missed the news that he had been stabbed. I was caught in my lie."

Her eyes widened. "What happened?"

"As my mother had warned me, my father's enemies showed great interest. They asked me for information I didn't have."

"What do you mean?" she whispered, gaze fixed to his so tightly all he could see was blue. "Like…?"

"Torture. Yes. My father was known to have stockpiled everything from electronics to drugs to cash. But if I had known where any of it was kept, I would have helped myself, wouldn't I? Rather than trying to steal from them? They took their time believing that." He pretended the recollection didn't coat him in cold sweat.

"Oh, my God." She sat back, fingertips covering her faint words, gaze flickering over her shoulder to where his left hand was still behind her.

Ah. She'd noticed his fingernail.

He brought his hand between them, flexed its stiffness into a fist, then splayed it.

"These two fingernails." He pointed, affecting their removal as casual news. "Several bones broken, but it works well enough after several surgeries. I'm naturally left-handed so that was a nuisance, but I'm quite capable with both now, so…"

"Silver lining?" she huffed, voice strained with disbelief. "How did you get away?"

"They weren't getting anywhere with questioning me and hit upon the idea of asking my grandfather to pay a ransom. He had no knowledge of a grandson, though. He was slow to act. He was grieving. Not pleased to have some pile of dung attempting to benefit off his son's name. I had no proof of my claim. My mother was one of many for my father. That was why she left him."

He shrugged. Female companionship had never been a problem for any of the Petrides men. They were good-looking and powerful and money was seductive. Women found *them*.

"Pappoús could have done many things, not least of which was let them finish killing me. He asked for blood tests before he paid the ransom. When I proved to be his son's bastard, he made me his heir. I suddenly had a clean, dry bed, ample food." He nodded at the beautiful concoction before them: a shallow chowder of corn and buttermilk topped with fat, pink prawns and chopped herbs.

"I had anything I wanted. A motorcycle in summer, ski trips in winter. Clothes that were tailored to fit my body in any style or color I asked. Gadgets. A yacht. Anything."

He'd also received a disparate education, tutored by his grandfather's accountant in finance. His real estate and investment licenses were more purchased than earned, but he had eventually mastered the skills to benefit from such transactions. Along the way he had developed a talent for managing people, learning by observing his grandfather's methods. Nowadays they had fully qualified, authentically trained staff to handle every matter. Arm-twisting, even the emotional kind he was utilizing right now, was a retired tactic.

But it was useful in this instance. Viveka needed to understand the bigger picture.

Like his grandfather, he needed a test.

"In return for his generosity, I have dedicated myself to ensuring my grandfather's empire operates on the right side of the law. We're mostly there. This merger is a final step. I have committed to making it happen before his health fails him. You can see why I feel I owe him this."

"Why are you being so frank with me?" Her brow crinkled. "Aren't you afraid I'll repeat any of this?"

"No." Much of it was online, if only as legend and conjecture. While Mikolas had pulled many dodgy stunts like mergers that resembled money laundering, he'd never committed actual crimes.

That wasn't why he was so confident, however.

He held her gaze and waited, watching comprehension solidify as she read his expression. She would not betray him, he telegraphed. Ever.

Her lashes quivered and he watched her swallow.

Fear was beginning to take hold in her. He told himself

that was good and ignored the churn of self-contempt in his belly. He wasn't like the men who had tormented him.

But he wasn't that different. Not when he casually picked up his wineglass and mentioned, "I should tell you. Grigor is looking for your sister. You could save yourself by telling him where to find her."

"No!" The word was torn out of her, the look on her face deeply anxious, but not conflicted. "Maybe he never hit her before, but it doesn't mean he wouldn't start now. And this?" She waved at the table and yacht. "She had these trappings all her life and would have given up all of it for a kind word. At least I had memories of our mother. She didn't even have me, thanks to him. So no. *I* would rather go back to Grigor than sell her out to him."

She spoke with brave vehemence, but her eyes grew wet. It wasn't bravado. It was loyalty that would cost her, but she was willing to pay the price.

"I believe you," he pressed with quiet lack of mercy. "That Grigor would resort to violence. The way he spoke when I returned his call—" Mikolas considered himself immune to rabid foaming at the mouth. He knew first-hand how depraved a man could act, but the bloodlust in Grigor's voice had been disturbing. Familiar in a grim, dark way.

And educational. Grigor wasn't upset that his daughter was missing. He was upset the merger had been delayed. He was taking Viveka's involvement very personally and despite all his posturing and hard-nosed negotiating in the lead-up, he was revealing impatience for the merger to complete.

That told Mikolas his very thorough research prior to starting down this road with Grigor may have missed something. It wasn't a complete surprise that Grigor had kept something up his sleeve. Mikolas had chosen Grigor because he hadn't been fastidious about partnering with the Petrides name. Perhaps Grigor had thought the sacrifice to his reputation meant he could withhold certain debts or other liabilities.

It could turn out that Viveka had done Mikolas a favor, giving him this opportunity to review everything one final time before closing. He could, in fact, gain more than he'd lost.

Either way, Grigor's determination to reach new terms and sign quickly put all the power back in Mikolas's court, exactly where he was most comfortable having it.

Now he would establish that same position with Viveka and his world would be set right.

"Even if he finds her, what can he do to her?" she was murmuring, linking her hands together, nail beds white. "She's married to Stephanos. His boss works for a man who owns news outlets. Big ones. Running her to ground would accomplish nothing. No, she's safe." She seemed to be reassuring herself.

"What about you?" He was surprised she wasn't thinking of herself. "He sounded like he would hunt you down no matter where you tried to hide." It was the dead-honest truth.

Dead.

Honest.

"So you might as well turn me over and save him the trouble? And close your precious deal with the devil?" So much fire and resentment sparked off her it was fascinating.

"This deal *is* important to me. Grigor knows Pappoús is unwell, that I'm reluctant to look for another option. He wants me to hand you over, close the deal and walk away with what I want—which is to give my grandfather what he wants."

"And what I want doesn't matter." She was afraid, he could see it, but she refused to let it overtake her. He had to admire that.

"You got what you wanted," he pointed out. "Your sister is safe from my evil clutches."

"Good," she insisted, but her mouth quivered before she clamped it into a line. One tiny tear leaked out of the corner of her eye.

Poor, steadfast little kitten.

But that depth of loyalty pleased him. She was passing her test.

He reached out to stroke her hair even though it only made her flinch and flash a look of hatred at him.

"Are you enjoying terrorizing me?"

"Please," he scoffed, taking up his glass of wine to swirl and sip, cooling a mouth that was burning with anticipation as he finalized his decision. "I'm treating you like a Fabergé egg."

He ignored the release of tension inside him as what he really wanted moved closer to his grasp.

"Grigor makes an ugly enemy. You understand why I don't want to make him into one of mine," he said.

"Is it starting to grate on your conscience?" she charged. "That he'll beat me to a pulp and throw me into the nearest body of water? I thought you didn't shame."

"I don't. But I need you to see very clearly that the action I'm taking comes at a cost. Which you will repay. I will not be leaving you in Athens, Viveka. You are staying with me."

CHAPTER FIVE

VIVEKA'S VISION GREW grainy and colorless for a moment. She thought she might pass out, which was not like her at all. She was tough as nails, not given to fainting spells like a Victorian maiden.

She had been subtly hyperventilating this whole time Mikolas had been tying his noose around her neck. Now she'd stopped breathing altogether.

Had she heard him right?

He looked like a god, his neat wedding haircut finger-combed to the side, his mouth symmetrical and unwavering after smiting her with his words. His gray eyes were impassive. Just the facts.

"But—" she started to argue, wanting to bring up Aunt Hildy.

He shook his head. "We're not bargaining. Actions have consequences. These are yours."

"You," she choked, trying to grasp what he was saying. "*You* are my consequence?"

"It's me or Grigor. I've already told you that I won't allow you to hurt yourself, so yes. I have chosen your consequence. We should eat. Before it gets warm," he said with a whimsical levity that struck her as bizarre in the middle of this intense, life-altering conversation.

He picked up his spoon, but she only stared at him.

Her fingers were icicles, stiff and frozen. All of her muscles had atrophied while her heart was racing. Her mind stumbled around in the last glimmers of the bleeding sun.

"I have a life in London," she managed. "Things to do."

"I'm sure Grigor knows that and has men waiting."

Her panicked mind sprang to Aunt Hildy, but she was out of harm's reach for the moment. Still, "Mikolas—"

"Think, Viveka. Think hard."

She was trying to. She had been searching for alternatives this whole time.

"So you're abandoning the merger?" She hated the way her voice became puny and confused.

"Not at all. But the terms have changed." He was making short work of his soup and waved his spoon. "With your sister as my wife, Grigor would have had considerable influence over me and our combined organization. I was prepared to let him control his side for up to five years and pay him handsomely for his trouble. Now the takeover becomes hostile and I will push him out, take control of everything and leave him very little. I expect he'll be even more angry with you."

"Then don't be so ruthless! Why aggravate him further?"

His answer was a gentle nudge of his bent knuckle under her chin, thumb brushing the tender place at the corner of her mouth.

"He left a mark on my mistress. He needs to be punished."

Her heart stopped. She jerked back. "Mistress!"

"You thought I was keeping you out of the goodness of my heart?"

Her vision did that wobble again, fading in and out. "You said you didn't want sex." Her voice sounded like it was coming from far away.

"I said I would decide if and when I gave it to you. I have decided. Are you not going to eat those?" He had switched to his fork to eat his prawns and now stabbed one from her bowl, hungrily snapping it between his teeth, but his gaze was watchful when it swung up to hers.

"I'm not having sex with you!"

"You've changed your mind?"

"*You* did," she pointed out tartly, wishing she was one of those women who could be casual about sex. She'd been anxious from the get-go, which was probably why it had turned into this massive issue for her. "I'm not something you can buy like a luxury boat with your ill-gotten gains," she pointed out.

"I haven't purchased you." He gave her a frown of insult. "I've earned your loyalty the same way my grandfather earned mine, by saving your life. You will show your gratitude by being whatever I need you to be, wherever I need you to be."

"I'm not going to be *that*! If I understand you correctly, you want to live within the law. Well, pro tip, forcing women to have sex is against the law."

"Sex will be a fringe benefit for both of us." He was flinty in the face of her sarcasm. "I won't force you and I won't have to."

"Keep. *Dreaming*," she declared.

His fork clattered into his empty bowl and he shifted to face her, one arm behind her, one on the table, bracketing her into a space that enveloped her in masculine energy.

She could have skittered out the far side of the bench, but she held her ground, trying to stare him down.

His gaze fell to her mouth, causing her abdominals to tighten and tremble.

"You're not thinking about it? Wondering? *Dreaming*," he mocked in a voice that jarred because he did *not* sound angry. He sounded amused and knowing. "Let's see, shall we?"

His hand shifted to cup her neck. The caress of his thumb into the hollow at the base of her throat unnerved her. If he'd been forceful, she would have reacted with a slap, but this felt almost tender. She trusted this hand. It had dragged her up to the surface of the water, giving her life.

So she didn't knock that hand away. She didn't hit him in the face as he neared, or pull away to say a hard *No*.

Somehow she got it into her head she would prove he didn't affect her. Maybe she even thought she could return to him that rejection he'd delivered earlier.

Maybe she really did want to know how it would be with him.

Whatever the perverse impulse that possessed her, she sat there and let him draw closer, keeping her mouth set and her gaze as contemptuous as she could make it.

Until his lips touched hers.

If she had expected brutality, she was disappointed. But he wasn't gentle, either.

His hold firmed on her neck as he plundered without hesitation, opening his mouth over hers in a hot, wet branding that caused a burn to explode within her. His tongue stabbed and her lips parted. Delicious swirls of pleasure invaded her belly and lower. Her eyes fluttered closed so she could fully absorb the sensations.

She *had* wondered. Intrigue had held her still for this kiss and she moaned as she basked in it, bones dissolving, muscles weakening.

He kissed her harder, dismantling her attempt to remain detached in a few short, racing heartbeats. He dragged his lips across hers in an erotic crush, the rough-soft texture of his lips like silken velvet.

All her senses came alive to the heat of his chest, the woodsy spice scent on his skin, the salt flavor on his tongue. Her skin grew so sensitized it was painful. She felt vulnerable with longing.

She splayed her free hand against his chest and released a sob of capitulation, no longer just accepting. Participating. Exploring the texture of his tongue, trying to compete with his aggression and consume him with equal fervor.

He pulled back abruptly, the loss of his kiss a cruelty that left her dangling in midair, naked and exposed. His chest moved with harsh breaths that seemed triumphant. The glitter in his eye was superior, asserting that *he* would decide *if* and *when*.

"No force necessary," he said with satisfaction deepening the corners of his mouth.

This was how it had been for her mother, Viveka realized with a crash back to reality. Twenty years ago, Grigor had been handsome and virile, provoking infatuation in a lonely widow. Viveka's earliest memories of being in his house had been ones of walking in on intimate clinches, quickly told to make herself scarce.

As Viveka had matured, she had recognized a similar yearning in herself for a man's loving attention. She understood how desire had been the first means that Grigor had used to control his wife, before encumbering her with a second child, then ultimately showing his ugliest colors to keep her in line.

Sex was a dangerous force that could push a woman down a slippery slope. That was what Viveka had come to believe.

It was doubly perilous when the man in question was so clearly not impacted by their kiss the way she was. Mikolas's indifference hurt, inflicting a loneliness on her that matched those moments in her life that had nearly broken her: losing her mother, being banished from her sister to an aunt who should have loved her, but hadn't.

She had to look away to hide her anguish.

The porter arrived to bring out the next course.

Mikolas didn't even look up from his plate as he said, "What is the name of the man who has your things? I would like to retrieve your passport before Grigor realizes it's under his nose."

Viveka needed to tell him about Aunt Hildy, but didn't trust her voice.

Mikolas said little else through the rest of their meal, only admonishing her to eat, stating at the end of it, "I want to finish the takeover arrangements. You have free run of the yacht unless you show me you need to be confined to your room."

"You seriously think I'll let you keep me like some kind of pirate's doxy?"

"Since I'm about to stage a raid and appoint myself admiral of Grigor's corporate fleet, I can't deny that label, can I? You call yourself whatever you want."

She glared at his back as he walked away.

He left her to her own devices and there must have been something wrong with her because, despite hating Mikolas for his overabundance of confidence, she was viciously glad he was running Grigor through.

At no point should she consider Mikolas her hero, she cautioned herself. She should have known there'd be a cost to his saving her life. She flashed back to Grigor calling her useless baggage. To Hildy telling her to earn her keep.

She wasn't even finished repaying Hildy! That hardly put her in a position to show "gratitude" to Mikolas, did it?

Oh, she hated when people thought of her as some sort of nuisance. This was why she had been looking forward to settling Hildy and striking out on her own. She could finally prove to herself and the world that she carried her own weight. She was not a lodestone. She wasn't.

A rabbit hole of self-pity beckoned. She avoided it by getting her bearings aboard the aptly named *Inferno*. The top deck was chilly and dark, the early night sky spitting rain into her face as the wind came up. The hot tub looked appealing, steaming and glowing with colored underwater lights. When the porter appeared with towels and a robe, inviting her to use the nearby change room, she was tempted, but explained she was just looking around.

He proceeded to give her a guided tour through the rest of the ship. She didn't know what the official definition for "ship" was, but this behemoth had to qualify. The upper deck held the bridge along with an outdoor bar and lounge at the stern. A spiral staircase in the middle took them down to the interior of the main deck. Along with Mikolas's stateroom and her own, there was a formal dining room for twelve, an elegant lounge with a big-screen television and a baby grand piano. Outside, there was a small lifeboat in the bow, in front of Mikolas's private sundeck, and a huge sunbathing area alongside a pool in the stern.

The extravagance should have filled her with contempt, but instead she was calmed by it, able to pretend this wasn't a boat. It was a seaside hotel. One that happened to be priced well beyond her reach, but *whatever*.

It wasn't as easy to pretend on the lower deck, which was mostly galley, engine room, less extravagant guest and crew quarters. And, oh, yes, another boat, this one a sexy speedboat parked in an internal compartment of the stern.

Her long journey to get to Trina caught up to her at that point. She'd left London the night before and hadn't slept much while traveling. She went back to her suite and changed into a comfortable pair of pajamas—ridiculously pretty ones in peacock-blue silk. Champagne-colored lace edged the bodice and tickled the tops of her bare feet, adding to the feeling of luxuriating in pure femininity.

She hadn't won a prize holiday, she reminded herself, trying not to be affected by all this lavish comfort. A gilded cage was still a prison and she would *not* succumb to Mikolas's blithe expectation that he could "keep" her. He certainly would not *seduce* her with his riches and pampering.

I won't force you and I won't have to.

She flushed anew, recalling their kiss as she curled up on the end of the love seat rather than crawl into bed. She wanted to be awake if he arrived expecting sex. When it came to making love, she was more about fantasy than reality, going only so far with the few men she'd dated. That kiss with Mikolas had shaken her as much as everything else that had happened today.

Better to think about that than her near-drowning, though.

Her thoughts turned for the millionth time to her mother's last moments. Somehow she began imagining her mother was on this boat and they were being tossed about in a storm, but she couldn't find her mother to warn her. It was a dream, she knew it was a dream. She hadn't been on the other boat when her mother was lost, but she could feel the way the waves were battering this one—

Sitting up with a gasp, she sensed they'd hit rough waters. Waves splashed against the glass of her porthole and the boat rocked enough she was rolling on her bed.

How had she wound up in bed?

With a little sob, she threw off the covers and pushed to her feet.

Fear, Aunt Hildy would have said, was no excuse for panic. Viveka did not consider herself a brave person at all, but she had learned to look out for herself because no one else ever had. If this boat was about to capsize, she needed to be on deck wearing a life jacket to have a fighting chance at survival.

Holding the bulkhead as she went into the passageway, she stumbled to the main lounge. The lifeboat was on this deck, she recalled, but in the bow, on the far side of Mikolas's suite. The porter had explained all the safety precautions, which had reassured her at the time. Now all she could think was that it was a stupid place to store life jackets.

Mikolas always slept lightly, but tonight he was on guard for more than old nightmares. He was expecting exactly what happened. The balcony in Viveka's stateroom wasn't the only thing alarmed. When she left her suite, the much more discreet internal security system caused his phone to vibrate.

He acknowledged the signal, then pushed to his feet and adjusted his shorts. That was another reason he'd been restless. He was hard. And he never wore clothes to bed. They were uncomfortable even when they weren't twisted around his erection, but he'd anticipated rising at some point to deal with his guest so he had supposed he should wear something to bed.

He'd expected to find release *with* his guest, but when he'd gone to her room, she'd been fast asleep, curled up on the love seat like a child resisting bedtime, one hand pillowing her cheek. She hadn't stirred when he'd carried her to the bed and tucked her in, leaving him sorely disappointed.

That obvious exhaustion, along with her pale skin and the slight frown between her brows, had plucked a bizarre reaction from him. Something like concern. That bothered him. He was impervious to emotional manipulations, but Viveka was under his skin—and she hadn't even been awake and doing it deliberately.

He sighed with annoyance, moving into his office.

If a woman was going to wake him in the night, it ought to be for better reasons than this.

He had no doubt this private deck in the bow was her destination. He'd watched her talk to his porter extensively about the lifeboat and winch system while he'd sat here working earlier. He wasn't surprised she was attempting to escape. He wasn't even angry. He was disappointed. He hated repeating himself.

But there was an obdurate part of him that enjoyed how she challenged him. Hardly anyone stood up to him anymore.

Plus he was sexually frustrated enough to be pleased she was setting up a midnight confrontation. When he'd kissed her earlier, desire had clawed at his control with such savagery, he'd nearly abandoned one for the other and made love to her right there at the table.

His need to be in command of himself and everyone else had won out in the end. He'd pulled back from the brink, but it had taken more effort than he liked to admit.

"Come on," he muttered, searching for her in the dim glow thrown by the running lights.

This was an addict's reaction, he thought with self-contempt. His brain knew she was lethal, but the way she infused him with a sense of omnipotence was a greater lure. He didn't care that he risked self-destruction. He still wanted her. He was counting the pulse beats until he could feel the rush of her hitting his system.

Where *was* she?

Not overboard again, surely.

The thought sent a disturbing punch into the middle

of his chest. He didn't know what had made him throw off his jacket and shoes and dive in after her today. It had been pure instinct. He'd shot out the emergency exit behind her, determined to hear why she had upended his plans, but he hadn't been close enough to stop her tumble into the water.

His heart had jammed when he'd seen her knock into the side of the yacht, worried she was unconscious as she went under.

Pulling her and that whale of a gown to the surface had nearly been more than he could manage. He didn't know what he would have done if the strength of survival hadn't imbued him. Letting go of her hadn't been an option. It wasn't basic human decency that had made him dive into that water, but something far more powerful that refused, absolutely refused, to go back to the surface without her.

Damn it, now he couldn't get that image of her disappearing into the water out of his head. He pushed from his office onto his private deck, where the rain and splashing waves peppered his skin. She wasn't coming down the stairs toward him.

He climbed them, walking along the outer rail of the mid-deck, seeing no sign of her.

Actually, he walked right past her. He spied her when he paused at the door into the bridge, thinking to enter and look for her on the security cameras. Something made him glance back the way he'd come and he spotted the ball of dark clothing and white skin under the life preserver ring.

What the hell?

"Viveka." He retraced his few steps, planting his bare feet carefully on the wet deck. "What are you doing out here?"

She lifted her face. Her hair was plastered in tendrils

around her neck and shoulders. Her chin rattled as she stammered, "I n-n-need a l-l-life v-v-vest."

"You're freezing." *He* was cold. He bent to draw her to her feet, but she stubbornly stayed in a knot of trembling muscle, fingers wrapped firmly around the mount for the ring.

What a confounding woman. With a little more force, he started to peel her fingers open.

The boat listed, testing his balance.

Before he could fully right himself, Viveka cried out and nearly knocked him over, rising to throw her arms around his neck, slapping her soaked pajamas into his front.

He swore at the impact, working to stay on his feet.

"Are we going over?"

"No."

He could hardly breathe, she was clinging so tightly to his neck, and shaking so badly he could practically hear her bones rattling. He swore under his breath, putting together all those anxious looks out to the water. This was why she hadn't shown the sense to be terrified of *him* today. She was afraid of boats.

"Come inside." He drew her toward the stairs down to his deck.

She balked. "I don't want to be trapped if we capsize."

"We won't capsize."

She resisted so he picked her up and carried her all the way through his dark office into his stateroom, where he'd left a lamp burning, kicking doors shut along the way.

He sat on the edge of his bed, settling her icy, trembling weight on his lap. "This is only a bit of wind and freighter traffic. We're hitting their wakes. It's not a storm."

There was no heat beneath these soaked pajamas. Even in the dim light, he could see her lips were blue. He ran his hands over her, trying to slick the water out of her pajamas while he rubbed warmth into her skin.

"There doesn't have to be a storm." She was pressing into him, her lips icy against his collarbone, arms still around his neck, relaxing and convulsing in turns. "My mother drowned when it was calm."

"From a boat?" he guessed.

"Grigor took her out." Her voice fractured. "Maybe on purpose to drown her. I don't know, but I think she wanted to leave him. He took her out sailing and said he didn't know till morning that she fell, but he never acted like he cared. He told me to stop crying and take care of Trina."

If this was a trick, it was seriously good acting. The emotion in her voice sent him tumbling into equally disturbing memories buried deep in his subconscious. *Your mother died while you were at school.* The landlord had made the statement without hesitation or regret, casually destroying Mikolas's world with a few simple words. *A woman from child services is coming to get you.*

So much horror had followed, Mikolas barely registered anymore how bad that day had been. He'd shuffled it all into the past once his grandfather had taken him in. The page had been turned and he never leafed back to it.

But suddenly he was stricken with that old grief. He couldn't ignore the way her heart pounded so hard he felt it against his arm across her back. Her skin was clammy, her spine curled tight against life's blows.

His hand unconsciously followed that hard curve, no longer just warming her, but trying to soothe while stealing a long-overdue shred of comfort for himself from someone who understood what he'd suffered.

He recovered just as quickly, shaking off the moment of empathy and rearranging her so she was forced to look up at him.

"I've been honest with you, haven't I?" Perhaps he sounded harsh, but she had cracked something in him. He didn't like the cold wind blowing through him as a result. "I would tell you if we were in danger. We're not."

Viveka believed him. That was the ridiculous part of it. She had no reason to trust him, but why would he be so blunt about everything else and hide the fact they were likely to capsize? If he said they were safe, they were safe.

"I'm still scared," she admitted in a whisper, hating that she was so gutless.

"Think of something else," he chided. The edge of his thumb gave her jaw a little flick, then he dipped his head and kissed her.

She brought up a hand to the side of his face, thinking she shouldn't let this happen again, but his stubble was a fascinating texture against her palm and his lips were blessedly hot, sending runnels of heat through her sluggish blood. Everything in her calmed and warmed.

Then he rocked his mouth to part her lips with the same avid, possessive enjoyment as earlier and cupped her breast and she shuddered under a fresh onslaught of sensations. The rush hurt, it was so powerful, but it was also like that moment when he'd dragged her to the surface. He was dragging her out of her phobia into wonder.

She instinctively angled herself closer, the silk of her pajamas a wet, annoying layer between them as she tried to press herself through his skin.

He grunted and grew harder under her bottom. His arms gathered her in with a confident, sexual possessiveness while his knees splayed wider so she sat deeper against the firm shape of his sex.

Heat rushed into her loins, sharp and powerful. All of

her skin burned as blood returned to every inch of her. She didn't mean to let her tongue sweep against his, but his was right there, licking past her lips, and the contact made lightning flash in her belly.

His aggression should have felt threatening, but it felt sexy and flagrant. As the kiss went on, the waves of pleasure became more focused. The way he toyed with her nipple sent thrums of excitement rocking through her.

She gasped for air when he drew back, but she didn't want to stop. Not yet. She lifted her mouth so he returned and kissed her harder. Deeper.

Her breast ached where he massaged it and the pulse between her legs became a hungry throb as he shifted wet silk against the tight point of her nipple.

His hand slid away, pulling the soggy material up from her quivery belly. He flattened his palm there, branding her cold, bare skin. His fingers searched along the edge of her waistband and he lifted his head, ready to slide his hand between her closed thighs.

"Open," he commanded.

Viveka gasped and shot off his lap, stumbling when her knees didn't want to support her. "What—no!"

She covered her throat where her pulse was racing, shocked at herself. He kept turning her into this…*animal*. That's all this was: hormones. Some kind of primal response to the caveman who happened to yank her out of the lion's jaws. The primitive part of her recognized an alpha male who could keep her offspring alive so her body wanted to make some with him.

Mikolas dropped one hand, then the other behind him, leaning on his straight arms, knees wide. His nostrils flared as he eyed her. It was the only sign that her recoil bothered him.

Contractions of desire continued to swirl in her abdomen. That part of her that was supposed to be able to take his shape felt so achy with carnal need she was nearly overwhelmed.

"You said you wouldn't make me," she managed in a shaky little voice.

It was a weak defense and they both knew it.

He cocked one brow in a mocking, *I don't have to.* The way his gaze traveled down her made her afraid for what she looked like, silk clinging to distended nipples and who knew what other telltale reactions.

She pulled the fabric away from her skin and looked to the door.

"You're bothered by your reaction to me. Why? I think it's exciting." The rasp of his arousal-husky voice made her inner muscles pinch with involuntary eagerness. "Come here. I'll hold you all night. You'll feel very safe," he promised, but his mouth quirked with wicked amusement.

She hugged herself. "I don't sleep around. I don't even know you!"

"I prefer it that way," he provided.

"Well, I don't!"

He sighed, rising and making her heart soar with alarmed excitement. It fell as he turned and walked away to the corner of the room.

She had rejected *him*, she reminded herself. This sense of rebuff was completely misplaced.

But he was so appealing with his tall, powerful frame, spine bracketed by supple muscle in the way of a martial artist rather than a gym junkie. The low light turned his skin a dark, burnished bronze and he had a really nice butt in those wet, clinging boxers.

She ought to leave, but she watched him search out three different points before he drew the wall inward like an oversize door. The cabinetry from her stateroom came with it, folding back to become part of his sitting room, creating an archway into her suite.

"I haven't used this yet. It's clever, isn't it?" he remarked.

If she didn't loathe boats so much, she might have agreed. As it was, she could only hug herself, dumbfounded to see they were now sharing a room.

"You'll feel safer like this, yes?"

Not likely!

He didn't seem to expect an answer, just turned to open a drawer. He pawed through, coming up with a pink long-sleeved top in waffle weave and a pair of pink and mint green flannel pajama pants. "Dry off and put these on. Warm up."

She waved at the archway. "Why did you do that?"

"You don't find it comforting?"

Oh, she was not sticking around to be laughed at. She snatched the pajamas from his hand, not daring to look into his face, certain she would see mockery, and made for the bathroom in her own suite. *Infuriating* man.

She would close the wall herself, she decided as she clumsily changed, even though she preferred the idea of him being in the same room with her. He was not a man to be relied on, she reminded herself. If she had learned nothing else in life, it was that she was on her own.

Then she walked out and found a life vest on the foot of her bed. When she glanced toward his room, his lamp was off.

She clutched the cool bulk of the vest to her chest, insides crumpling.

"Thank you, Mikolas," she said toward his darkened room.

A pause, then a weary "Try not to need it."

CHAPTER SIX

VIVEKA WAS SO emotionally spent, she slept late, waking with the life vest still in her crooked arm.

Sitting up with an abrupt return of memory, she noted the sun was streaming in through the uncovered windows of Mikolas's stateroom. The yacht was sailing smoothly and she could swear that was the fresh scent of a light breeze she detected. She swung her feet to the floor and moved into his suite with a blink at the brightness.

He didn't notice her, but she caught her breath at the sight of him. He was lounging on the wing-like extension from his sitting area. It was fronted by what looked like the bulkhead of his suite and fenced on either side by glass panels anchored into thin, stainless steel uprights. The wind blew over him, ruffling his dark hair.

She might have been alarmed by the way the ledge dangled over the water, but he was so relaxed, slouched on a cushioned chair, feet on an ottoman, she could only experience again the pinch of deep attraction.

He had his tablet in one hand, a half-eaten apple in the other and he was mostly naked. Again. All he wore were shorts, these ones a casual pair in checked gray and black even though the morning breeze was quite cool.

Her heart actually panged that she had to keep fighting

him. He looked so casually beautiful. It wasn't just about her, though, but Aunt Hildy.

He lifted his head and turned to look at her as though he'd been aware of her the whole time. "Are you afraid to come out here?"

She was terrified, but it had nothing to do with the water and everything to do with how he affected her.

"Why are you allowed to have your balcony open and I got in trouble for it?" she asked, choosing a tone of belligerence over revealing her intimidation, forcing her legs to carry her as far as the opening.

"I had a visitor." He nodded at the deck beside his ottoman.

Her bag.

Stunned, she quickly knelt and rifled through it, coming up with her purse, phone, passport... Everything exactly as it should be. Even her favorite hair clip. She gathered and rolled the mess of her hair in a well-practiced move, weirdly comforted by that tiny shred of normalcy.

When she looked up at him, Mikolas was watching her. He finished his apple with a couple of healthy bites and flipped the core into the water.

"Help yourself." He nodded toward where a sideboard was set up next to the door to his office.

"I'm in time-out? Not allowed out for breakfast?"

No response, but she quickly saw there was more than coffee and a basket of fruit here. The dishes contained traditional favorites she hadn't eaten since leaving Greece nine years ago.

Somehow she'd convinced herself she hated everything about this country, but the moment she saw the *tiganites*, nostalgia closed her throat. A sharp memory of asking her mother if she could cut up her sister's pancakes and pour the *petimezi* came to her. Nothing tasted quite like grape molasses. Her heart panged, while her mouth watered and her stomach contracted with hunger.

"Have you eaten?" she called, hoping he didn't hear the break in her voice. She glanced out to see he didn't have a plate going.

"Óchi akóma." Not yet.

She gave him a large helping of the smoked pork omelet along with pancakes and topped up his coffee, earning a considering look as she served him.

Yes, she was trying to soften him up. A woman had to create advantages where she could with a man like him.

"Efcharistó," he said when she joined him.

"Parakaló." She was trying to act casual, but she had chosen to start with yogurt and thyme honey. The first bite tasted so perfect, was such a burst of early childhood happiness, when her mother had been alive and her sister a living doll she could dress and feed, she had to close her eyes, pressing back tears of homecoming.

Mikolas watched her, reluctantly fascinated by the emotion that drew her cheeks in while she savored her breakfast. Pained joy crinkled her brow. It was sensual and sexy and poignant. It was *yogurt*.

He forced his gaze to his own plate.

Viveka was occupying entirely too much real estate in his brain. It had to stop.

But even as he told himself that, his mind went back to last night. How could it not, with her sitting across from him braless beneath her long-sleeved nightshirt? The soft weight of her breast was still imprinted on his palm, firm and shapely, topped with a sensitive nipple he'd longed to suck.

Instantly he was primed for sex. And damn it, she'd

been as fully involved as he had been. He wasn't so arrogant he made assumptions about women's states of interest. He took pains to ensure they were with him every step of the way when he made love to them. She'd been pressing herself into him, returning his kiss, moaning with enjoyment.

Fine, he could accept that she thought they were moving too fast. Obviously she was a bit of a romantic, flying across the continent to help her sister marry her first love. But sex would happen between them. It was inevitable.

When he had opened the passageway between their rooms, however, it hadn't been for sex. He had wanted to ease her anxiety. She had been nothing less than a nuclear bomb from the moment he'd seen her face, but he'd found himself searching out the catch in the wall, giving her access to *his* space, which had never been his habit with any woman.

He didn't understand his actions around her. This morning, he'd actually begun second-guessing his decision to keep her, which wasn't like him at all. Indecision did not make for control in any situation. He certainly couldn't back down because he was *scared*. Of being around a particular *woman*.

Then the news had come through that Grigor was, indeed, hiding debts in two of his subsidiaries. There was no room for equivocating after that. Mikolas had issued a few terse final orders, then notified Grigor of his intention to take over with or without cooperation.

Grigor had been livid.

Given the man's vile remarks, Mikolas was now as suspicious as Viveka that her stepfather had killed her mother. Viveka would stay with him whether he was comfortable in her presence or not.

Whether she liked it or not. At least until he could be sure Grigor wouldn't harm her.

She opened her dreamy blue eyes and looked like she was coming back from orgasm. Sexual awareness shimmered like waves of desert heat between them.

Yes. Sex was inevitable.

Her gaze began to tangle with his, but she seemed to take herself in hand. She sat taller and cleared her throat, looking out to the water and lifting a determined chin, cheekbones glowing with pink heat.

He mentally sighed, too experienced a fighter not to recognize she was preparing to start one.

"Mikolas." He mentally applauded her take-charge tone. "I *have* to go back to London. My aunt is very old. Quite ill. She needs me."

He absorbed that with a blink. This was a fresh approach at least.

She must have read his skepticism. Her mouth tightened. "I wish I was making it up. I'm not."

If he expected her trust—and he did—he would have to trust her in return, he supposed. "Tell me about her," he invited.

She looked to the clear sky, seeming to struggle a moment.

"There's not much to tell. She's the sister of my grandmother and took me in when Grigor kicked me out, even though she was a spinster who never wanted anything to do with children. She had a career before women really did. Worked in Parliament, but not as an elected official. As a secretary to a string of them. She had some kind of lofty clearance, served coffee to all sorts of royals and diplomats. I think she was in love with a married man," she confided with a wrinkle of her nose.

Definitely a sentimentalist.

She shrugged, murmuring, "I don't have proof. Just a few things she said over the years." She picked up her coffee and cupped her hands around it. "She was always telling me how to behave so men wouldn't think things." She made a face. "I'm sure the sexism in her day was appalling. She was adamant that I be independent, pay my share of rent and groceries, know how to look after myself."

"She didn't take her own advice? Make arrangements for herself?"

"She tried." Her shoulder hitched in a helpless shrug. "Like a lot of people, she lost her retirement savings with the economic crash. For a while she had an income bringing in boarders, but we had to stop that a few years ago and remortgage. She has dementia." Her sigh held the weight of the world. "Strangers in the house upset her. She doesn't recognize me anymore, thinks I'm my mother, or her sister, or an intruder who stole her groceries." She looked into her cooling coffee. "I've begun making arrangements to put her into a nursing home, but the plans aren't finalized."

Viveka knew he was listening intently, thought about leaving it there, where she had stopped with the doctors and the intake staff and with Trina during their video chats. But the mass on her conscience was too great. She'd already told Mikolas about Grigor's abuse. He might actually understand the rest and she really needed it off her chest.

"I *feel* like I'm stealing from her. She worked really hard for her home and deserves to live in it, but she can't take care of herself. I have to run home from work every few hours to make sure she hasn't started a fire or caught a bus to who knows where. I can't afford to stay home with her all day and even if I could…"

She swallowed, reminding herself not to feel resentful, but it still hurt. Not just physically, either. She had tried from Day One to have a familial relationship with her aunt and it had all been for naught.

"She started hitting me. I know she doesn't mean it to be cruel. She's scared. She doesn't understand what's happening to her. But I can't take it."

She couldn't look at him. She already felt like the lowest form of life and he wasn't saying anything. Maybe he was letting her pour out her heart and having a laugh at her for getting smacked by an old lady.

"Living with her was never great. She's always been a difficult, demanding person. I was planning to move out the minute I finished school, but she started to go downhill. I stayed to keep house and make meals and it's come to this."

The little food she'd eaten felt like glue in her stomach. She finished up with the best argument she could muster.

"You said you're loyal to your grandfather for what he gave you. That's how I feel toward her. The only way I can live with removing her from her home is by making sure she goes to a good place. So I have to go back to London and oversee that."

Setting aside her coffee, she hugged herself, staring sightlessly at the horizon, not sure if it was guilt churning her stomach or angst at revealing herself this way.

"Now who is beating you up?" Mikolas challenged.

She swung her head to look at him. "You don't think I owe her? Someone needs to advocate for her."

"Where is she now?"

"I was coming away so I made arrangements with her doctor for her to go into an extended-care facility. It's just for assessment and referral, though. The formal arrangements have to be completed. She can't stay where she is and she can't go home if I'm not there. Her doctor is expecting me for a consult this week."

Mikolas reached for his tablet and tapped to place a call. A moment later, the tablet chimed. Someone answered in German. They had a lengthy conversation that she didn't understand. Mikolas ended with, *"Dankeschön."*

"Who was that?" she asked as he set aside the tablet.

"My grandfather's doctor. He's Swiss. He has excellent connections with private clinics all over Europe. He'll ensure Hildy is taken into a good one."

She snorted. "Neither of us has the kind of funds that will underwrite a private clinic arranged by a posh specialist from Switzerland. I can barely afford the extra fees for the one I'm hoping will take her."

"I'll do this for you, to put your mind at ease."

Her mind blanked for a full ten seconds.

"Mikolas," she finally sputtered. "I *want* to do it. I definitely don't want to be in your debt over it!" She ignored the fact that he had already decided she owed him.

Men expect things when they do you a favor, she heard Hildy saying.

A lurching sensation yanked at her heart, like a curtain being pulled aside on its rungs, exposing her at her deepest level. "What kind of sex do you think you're going to get out of me that would possibly compensate you for something like that? Because I can assure you, I'm not that good! You'll be disappointed."

So disappointed.

Had she just said "you'll"? Like she was a sure thing?

She tightened her arms across herself, refusing to look at him as this confrontation took the direction she had hoped it wouldn't: right into the red-light district of Sexville.

* * *

"If that sounds like I just agreed to have sex with you, that's not what I meant," Viveka bit out, voice less strident, but still filled with ire.

Mikolas couldn't think of another woman he'd encountered with such an easily tortured conscience or with such a valiant determination to protect people she cared about while completely disregarding the cost to herself.

She barely seemed real. He was in danger of being *moved* by her depth of loyalty toward her aunt. A jaded part of him had to question whether she was doing exactly what she claimed she wasn't: trying to manipulate him into underwriting the old woman's care, but unlike most women in his sphere, she wasn't offering sex as compensation for making her problems go away.

While he was finding the idea of her coming to his bed motivated by anything other than the same passion that gripped him more intolerable by the second.

"Let us be clear," he said with abrupt decision. "The debt you owe me is the loss of a wife."

She didn't move, but her blue eyes lifted to fix on him, watchful and limitless as the sky.

"My intention was to marry, honeymoon this week, then throw a reception for my new bride, introducing her to a social circle that has been less than welcoming to someone with my pedigree when I only ever had a mistress du jour on my arm."

Being an outsider didn't bother him. He had conditioned himself not to need approval or acceptance from anyone. He preferred his own company and had his grandfather to talk to if he grew bored with himself.

But ostracism didn't sit well with a nature that demanded to overcome any circumstance. The more he worked at growing the corporation, the more he recognized the importance of networking with the mainstream. Socializing was an annoying way to spend his valuable time, but necessary.

"Curiosity, if nothing else, would have brought people to the party," he continued. "The permanence of my marriage would have set the stage for developing other relationships. You understand? Wives don't form friendships with women they never see again. Husbands don't encourage their wives to invite other men's temporary liaisons for drinks or dinner."

"Because they're afraid their wives will hear about their own liaisons?" she hazarded with an ingenuous blink.

Really, no sense of self-preservation.

"It's a question of investment. No one wants to put time or money into something that lacks a stable future. I was gaining more than Grigor's company by marrying. It was a necessary shift in my image."

Viveka shook her head. "Trina would have been hopeless at what you're talking about. She's sweet and funny, loves to cook and pick flowers for arrangements. You couldn't ask for a kinder ear if you need to vent, but playing the society wife? Making small talk about haute couture and trips to the Maldives? You, with your sledgehammer personality, would have crushed her before she was dressed, let alone an evening trying to find her place in the pecking order of upper-crust hens."

"Sledgehammer," he repeated, then accused facetiously, "Flirt."

She blushed. It was pretty and self-conscious and fueled by this ivory-tusked, sexual awareness they were both pretending to ignore. Her gaze flashed to his, naked and filled with last night's trance-like kiss. Her nipples pricked to life beneath the pink of her shirt. So did the flesh between his legs. The moment became so sexually infused, he almost lost the plot.

That's how he wanted it to be between them: pure reaction. Not installment payments.

He reined himself in with excruciating effort, throat tight and body readied with tension as he continued.

"Circulating with the woman who broke up my wedding is not ideal, but will look better than escorting a rebound after being thrown over. Since you'll be with me until I've neutralized Grigor, we will be able to build that same message of constancy."

"What do you mean about neutralizing Grigor?"

"I spoke to him this morning. He's not pleased with my takeover or the fact you're staying with me. You need some serious protections in place. Did you have your mother's death investigated?"

That seemed to throw her. Her face spasmed with emotion.

"I was only nine when it happened so it was years before I really put it all together and thought he could have done it. I was fourteen when I asked the police to look into it, but they didn't take me seriously. The police on the island are in his pocket. The whole island is and I don't really blame them. I've learned myself that you play by his rules or lose everything. Probably the only reason he didn't kill me for making a statement was because it would have been awfully suspicious if something happened to me right after my complaint. But stirring up questions was one of the reasons he kicked me out. Why?"

"I will hire a private investigator to see what we can find. If something can be proved and he's put in prison, you'll be out of his reach."

"That could take years!"

"And will make him that much more incensed with

you in the short term," he said drily. "But as you say, if
he's under suspicion, it wouldn't look good if anything
happened to you. I think it will afford you protection in
the long term."

"You're going to start an investigation, take care of my
aunt and protect me from Grigor and all I have to do is
pretend to be your girlfriend." Her voice rang with disbelief. "For how *long*?"

"At least until the merger completes and the investigation shows some results. Play your part well and you
might even earn my forgiveness for disrupting my life so
thoroughly."

Her laugh was ragged and humorless. "And sex?"

She tossed her head, affecting insouciance, but the
small frown between her brows told him she was anxious. That aggravated him. He could think of nothing
else but discovering exactly how incendiary they would
be together. If she wasn't equally obsessed, he was at a
disadvantage.

Not something he ever endured.

With a casual flick of his hand, he proclaimed, "Like
today's fine weather, we'll enjoy it because it's there."

Did a little shadow of disappointment pass behind her
eyes? What did she expect? Lies about falling in love?
They really were at an impasse if she expected that ruse.

Her mouth pursed to disguise what might have been a
brief tremble. She pushed to stand. "Yes, well, the alma-
nac is predicting heavy frost. Dress warm." She reached
for her bag. "I'm going to my room."

"Leave your passport with me."

She turned back to regard him with what he was starting to think of as her princess look, very haughty and
down the nose. "Why?"

"To arrange travel visas."

"To where?"

"Wherever I need you to be."

"Give me a 'for instance.'"

"Asia, eventually, but you wanted to go to Athens, didn't you? There's a party tonight. Do as you're told and I'll let you off the boat to come with me."

Her spine went very straight at that patronizing remark. Her unfettered breasts were not particularly heavy, but magnificent in their shape and firmness and chill-sharpened points. He was going to go out of his mind if he didn't touch her again soon.

As if she read his thoughts, her brows tugged together with conflict. She was no doubt thinking that the return of her purse and arrival in Athens equaled an excellent opportunity to set him in the rearview mirror.

He tensed, waiting out the minutes of her indecision. Oddly, it was not unlike the anticipation of pain. His breath stilled in his lungs, throat tight, as he willed her to do as he said.

Do not make me ask again.

Helplessness flashed in her expression before she ducked her head and drew her passport out of her bag, hand trembling as she held it out to him.

A debilitating rush of relief made his own arm feel like it didn't even belong to him. He reached to take it.

She held on while she held his gaze, incredibly beautiful with that hard-won determination lighting her proud expression. "You *will* make sure Aunt Hildy is properly cared for?"

"You and Pappoús will get along well. He holds me to my promises, too."

She released the passport into his possession, averting her gaze as though she didn't want to acknowledge the significance. Clearing her throat, she took out her phone. "I want to check in with Trina. May I have the WiFi code?"

"The security key is a mix of English and Greek characters." He held out his other hand. "I'll do it for you."

She released a noise of impatient defeat, slapped her phone into his palm and walked away.

CHAPTER SEVEN

MIKOLAS HAD SET himself up in her contacts with a selfie taken on her phone, of him sitting there like a sultan on his yacht, taking ownership of her entire life.

She couldn't stop looking at it. Those smoky eyes of his were practically making love to her, the curve of his wide mouth quirked at the corners in not quite a smile. It was more like, *I know you're naked in the shower right now.* He was so brutally handsome with his chiseled cheekbones and devil-doesn't-give-a-damn nonchalance he made her chest hurt.

Yet he had also forwarded a request from the Swiss doctor for her aunt's details along with a recommendation for one of those beyond-top-notch dementia villages that were completely unattainable for mere mortals. A quick scan of its website told her it was very patient-centric and prided itself on compassion and being ahead of the curve with quality treatment. All that was needed was the name of her aunt's physician to begin Hildy's transfer into the facility's care.

Along with Trina's well-being, a good plan for Aunt Hildy was the one thing Viveka would sell her soul for. It was a sad commentary on her life that it was the only thing pulling her back to London. She had no community there, rarely had time for dating or going out with friends.

Her neighbor was nice, but mostly her life had revolved around school, then work and caring for Aunt Hildy. There was no one worrying about her now, when she had been stolen like a concubine by this throwback Spartan warrior.

She sighed, not even able to argue that her job was a career she needed to get back to. One quick email and her position had been snapped up by one of the part-timers who need the hours. She'd be on the bottom rung when she went back. If she went back. She'd accepted that job for its convenience to home, and in the back of her mind, she'd already been planning to make a change once she had Hildy settled.

But Aunt Hildy had faced nothing but challenges all her life and, in her way, she'd been Viveka's lifeline. The old woman shouldn't have to suffer and wouldn't. Not if Viveka could help it.

And now that Mikolas had spelled out that sex wasn't mandatory…

Oh, she didn't want to think about sex with that man! He already made her feel so unlike herself she could hardly stand it. But she couldn't help wondering what it would be like to lie with him. Something about him got to her, making her blood run like cavalry into sensual battle. Sadly, Viveka had reservations that made the idea of being intimate with him seem not just ill-advised but completely impossible.

So she tried not to think of it and video-called Trina. Her sister was both deliriously joyful and terribly worried when she picked up.

"Where *are* you? Papa is furious." Her eyes were wide. "I'm scared for you, Vivi."

"I'm okay," she prevaricated. "What about you? You've obviously talked to him. Is he likely to come after you?"

"He doesn't believe this was my decision. He blames

you for all of it and it sounds—I'm not sure what's going on at his office, but things are off the rails and he thinks it's your fault. I'm so sorry, Vivi."

"That doesn't surprise me," Viveka snorted, hiding how scared the news made her. "Are you and Stephanos happy? Was all of this worth it?"

"So happy! I knew he was my soul mate, but oh, Vivi!" Her sister blushed, growing even more radiant, saying in a self-conscious near-whisper, "Being married is even better than I imagined it would be."

Lovemaking. That's what her little sister was really talking about.

Envy, acute and painful, seared through Viveka. She had always felt left out when women traded stories about men and intimacy. Dating for her had mostly been disastrous. Now even her younger sister was ahead of her on that curve. It made Viveka even more insecure in her sexuality than she already was.

They talked a few more minutes and Viveka was wistful when she ended the call. She was glad Trina was living happily-ever-after. At one time, she'd believed in that fairy tale for herself, but had become more pragmatic over the years, first by watching the nightmare that her mother's romance turned into, then challenged by Aunt Hildy for wanting a man to "complete" her.

She hadn't thought of it that way, exactly. Finding a soul mate was a stretch, true, but why shouldn't she want a companion in life? What was the alternative? Live alone and lonely, like Aunt Hildy? Engage in casual hookups like Mikolas had said he preferred?

She was not built for fair-weather frolics.

Her introspection was interrupted by a call from Hildy's doctor. He was impressed that she was able to get her aunt into that particular clinic and wanted to make arrangements to move her the next morning. He assured Viveka she was doing the right thing.

The die was cast. Not long after, the ship docked and Viveka and Mikolas were whisked into a helicopter. It deposited them on top of *his* building, which was an office tower, but he had a penthouse that took up most of an upper floor.

"I have meetings this afternoon," he told her. "A stylist will be here shortly to help you get ready."

Viveka was typically ready to go out within thirty minutes. That included shampooing and drying her hair. She had never in her life started four hours before an appointment, not even when she had fake-married the man who calmly left her passport on a side table like bait and walked out.

Not that this world was so different from living with Grigor, Viveka thought, lifting her baleful gaze from the temptation of her passport to gaze around Mikolas's private domain. Grigor had been a bully, but he'd lived very well. His island mansion had had all the same accoutrements she found in Mikolas's penthouse: a guest room with a full bath, a well-stocked wine fridge and pantry, a pool on a deck overlooking a stunning view.

None of it put her at ease. She was still nervous. Expectation hung over her. Or rather, the question of what Mikolas expected.

And whether she could deliver.

Not sex, she reminded herself, trying to keep her mind off that. She turned to tormenting herself with anxiety over how well she would perform in the social arena. She wasn't shy, but she wasn't particularly outgoing. She wasn't particularly pretty, either, and she had a feeling every other woman at this party would be gorgeous if

Mikolas thought she needed four hours of beautification to bring her up to par.

The stylist's preparation wasn't all shoring up of her looks, however. It was pampering with massage and a mani-pedi, encouragement to doze by the pool while last-minute adjustments were made to her dress, and a final polish on her hair and makeup that gave her more confidence than she expected.

As she eyed herself in the gold cocktail dress, she was floored at how chic she looked. The cowled halter bodice hung low across her modest chest and the snug fabric hugged her hips in a way that flattered her figure without being obvious. The color brought out the lighter strands in her hair and made her skin look like fresh cream.

The stylist had trimmed her mop, then let its natural wave take over, only parting it to the side and adding two little pins so her face was prettily framed while the rest fell away in a shiny waterfall around her shoulders. She applied false eyelashes, but they were just long enough to make her feel extra feminine, not ridiculous.

"I've never known how to make my bottom lip look as wide as the top," Viveka complained as her lips were painted. The bruise Grigor had left there had faded overnight to unnoticeable.

"Why would you want to?" the woman chided her. "You have a very classic look. Like old Hollywood."

Viveka snorted, but she'd take it.

She had to acknowledge she was delighted with the end result, but became shy when she moved into the lounge to find Mikolas waiting for her.

He took her breath, standing at the window with a drink in his hand. He'd paired his suit with a gray shirt and charcoal tie, ever the dark horse. It was all cut to perfection against his frame. His profile was silhouetted against the glow of the Acropolis in the distance. *Zeus*, she thought, and her knees weakened.

He turned his head and even though he was already quite motionless, she sensed time stopping. Maybe they both held their breath. She certainly did, anxious for kind judgment.

Behind her, the stylist left, leaving more tension as the quiet of the apartment settled with the departure of the lift.

Viveka's eyes dampened. She swallowed to ease the dryness in the back of her throat. "I have no idea how to act in this situation," she confessed.

"A date?" he drawled, drawing in a breath as though coming back to life.

"Is that all it is?" Why did it feel so monumental? "I keep thinking that I'm supposed to act like we're involved, but I don't know much about you."

"Don't you?" His cheek ticked and she had the impression he didn't like how much she did know.

"I guess I know you're the kind of man who saves a stranger's life."

That seemed to surprise him.

She searched his enigmatic gaze, asking softly, "Why did you?" Her voice held all of the turbulent emotions he had provoked with the act.

"It was nothing," he dismissed, looking away to set down his glass.

"Please don't say that." But was it realistic to think her life had meant something to him after one glimpse? No. Her heart squeezed. "It wasn't nothing to me."

"I don't know," he admitted tightly. His eyes moved over her like he was looking for clues. "But I wasn't thinking ahead to this. Saving a person's life shouldn't be contingent on repayment. I just reacted."

Unlike his grandfather, who had wanted to know he

was actually getting his grandson before stepping in. *Oh, Mikolas.*

For a moment, the walls between them were gone and the bright, magnetic thing between them tugged. She wanted to move forward and offer comfort. Be whatever he needed her to be.

For one second, he seemed to hover on a tipping point. Then a layer of aloofness fell over him like a cloak.

"I don't think anyone will have trouble believing we're involved when you look at me like that." He smiled, but it was a tad cruel. "If I wasn't finally catching up to someone I've been chasing for a while, I would accept your invitation. But I have other priorities."

She flinched, stunned by the snub.

Fortunately he didn't see it, having turned away to press the call button to bring back the elevator.

She moved on stiff legs to join him, fighting tears of wounded self-worth. Her throat ached. Compassion wasn't a character flaw, she reminded herself. Just because Grigor and Hildy and this *jackass* weren't capable of appreciating what she offered didn't mean she was worthless.

She couldn't help her reaction to him. Maybe if she wasn't such an incurable *virgin*, she'd be able to handle him, she thought furiously, but that's what she was and she hated him for taunting her with it.

She was wallowing so deep in silent offense, she moved automatically, leaving the elevator as the doors opened, barely taking in her surroundings until she heard her worst nightmare say, *"There she is."*

CHAPTER EIGHT

MIKOLAS WAS KICKING himself as the elevator came to a halt.

Viveka had been so beautiful when she had walked into the lounge, his heart had lurched. An unfamiliar light-heartedness had overcome him. It hadn't been the money spent on her appearance. It was the authentic beauty that shone through all the labels and products, the kind that waterfalls and sunsets possessed. You couldn't buy that kind of awe-inspiring magnificence. You couldn't ignore it, either, when it was right in front of you. And when you let yourself appreciate it, it felt almost healing…

He never engaged in rose smelling and sunset gazing. He lived in an armored tank of wealth, emotional distance and superficial relationships. His dates were formalities, a type of foreplay. It wasn't sexism. He invested even less in his dealings with men.

His circle never included people as unguarded as Viveka, with her defensive shyness and yearning for acceptance. Somehow that guilelessness of hers got through his barriers as aggression never would. She'd asked him why he'd saved her life and before he knew it, he was re-living the memory of pleading with everything in him for his grandfather—a stranger at the time—to save *him*.

Erebus hadn't.

Not right away. Not without proof.

Words such as *despair* and *anguish* were not strong enough to describe what came over him when he thought back to it.

She had had an idea what it was, though, without his having to say a word. He had seen more in her eyes than an offer of sex. Empathy, maybe. Whatever it was, it had been something so real, it had scared the hell out of him. He couldn't lie with a woman when his inner psyche was torn open that far. Who knew what else would spill out?

He needed escape and she needed to stay the hell back.

He was so focused on achieving that, he walked out of the elevator not nearly as aware of his surroundings as he should be.

As they came alongside the security desk, he heard, "There she is," and turned to see Grigor lunging at Viveka, nearly pulling her off her feet, filthy vitriol spewing over her scream of alarm.

"—think you can investigate me? I'll show you what murder looks like—"

Reflex took over and Mikolas had broken Grigor's nose before he knew what he was doing.

Grigor fell to the floor, blood leaking between his clutching fingers. Mikolas bent to grab him by the collar, but his security team rushed in from all directions, pressing Mikolas's Neanderthal brain back into its cave.

"Call the police," he bit out, straightening and putting his arm around Viveka. "Make sure you mention his threats against her life."

He escorted Viveka outside to his waiting limo, afraid, genuinely afraid, of what he would do to the man if he stayed.

As her adrenaline rush faded in the safety of the limo, Viveka went from what felt like a screaming pitch of tension to being a spent match, brittle and thin, charred and cold.

It wasn't just Grigor surprising her like that. It was how crazed he'd seemed. If Mikolas hadn't stepped in... But he had and seeing Grigor on the receiving end of the sickening thud of a fist connecting to flesh wasn't as satisfying as she had always imagined it would be.

She *hated* violence.

She figured Mikolas must feel the same, given his past. Those last minutes as they'd come downstairs kept replaying in her mind. She'd been filled with resentment as they'd left the elevator, hotly thinking that if saving a person's life didn't require repayment, why was he forcing her to go to this stupid party? He said she was under his protection, but it was more like she was under his thumb.

But the minute she was threatened, the very second it had happened, he had leaped in to save her. Again.

It was as ground-shaking as the first time.

Especially when the aftermath had him feeling the bones in his repaired hand like he was checking for fractures. His thick silence made her feel sick.

"Mikolas, I'm sorry," Viveka said in a voice that flaked like dry paint.

She was aware of his head swinging around but couldn't look at him.

"You know I only had Trina's interest at heart when I came to Greece, but it was inconsiderate to you. I didn't appreciate the situation I was putting you in with Grigor—"

"That's enough, Viveka."

She jolted, stung by the graveled tone. It made the blood congeal in her veins and she hunched deeper into her seat, turning her gaze to the window.

"That was my fault." Self-recrimination gave his voice

a bitter edge. "We signed papers for the merger today. I made sure he knew why I was squeezing him out. He tried to cheat me."

It was her turn to swing a surprised look at him. He looked like he was barely holding himself in check.

"I wouldn't have discovered it until after I was married to Trina, but your interference gave me a chance to review everything. I wound up getting a lot of concessions beyond our original deal. Things were quite ugly by the end. He was already blaming you so I told him I'd started an investigation. I should have expected something like this. I owe *you* the apology."

She didn't know what to say.

"You helped me by stopping the wedding. Thank you. I hope to hell the investigation puts him in jail," he added tightly.

He was staring at her intently, nostrils flared.

Her mouth trembled. She felt awkward and shy and tried to cover it with a lame attempt at levity. "Between Grigor and Hildy, I've spent most of my life being told I was an albatross of one kind or another. It's refreshing to hear I've had a positive effect for once. I thought for sure you were going to yell at me..." Her voice broke.

She sniffed and tried to catch a tear with a trembling hand before it ruined her makeup.

He swore and before she realized what he was doing, he had her in his lap.

"Did he hurt you? Let me see your arm where he grabbed you," he demanded, his touch incredibly gentle as he lightly explored.

"Don't be sweet to me right now, Mikolas. I'll fall apart."

"You prefer the goon from the lobby?" he growled, making a semihysterical laugh bubble up.

"You're not a goon," she protested, but obeyed the hard arms that closed around her and cuddled into him, numb fingers stealing under the edge of his jacket to warm against his steady heartbeat.

He ran soothing hands over her and let out a breath, tension easing from both of them in small increments.

She was still feeling shaky when they reached the Makricosta Olympus.

"I hate these things," he muttered as he escorted her to the brightly decorated ballroom. "We should have stayed in."

Too late to leave. People were noting their entrance.

"Do you mind if I…?" she asked as she spotted the ladies' room off to the right. She could only imagine how she looked.

A muscle pulsed in his jaw, like he didn't want her out of his sight, but after one dismayed heartbeat he said, "I'll be at the bar."

Reeling under an onslaught of gratitude and confusion and yearning, she hurried to the powder room and moved directly to the mirror to check her makeup. She felt like a disaster, but had only a couple of smudges to dab away.

"Synchórisi," the woman next to her said, gaze down as she fiddled with the straps on her shimmery black dress. Releasing a distinctly British curse she said, "My Greek is nonexistent. Is there any chance you speak English?"

Viveka straightened from the mirror, taking a breath to gather her composure. "I do."

"Oh, you're upset." The woman was a delicate blonde and her smile turned concerned. "I'm sorry. I shouldn't have bothered you."

"No, I'm fine," she dismissed with a wobbly smile. The woman was doing her a favor, not letting her dwell on all the mixed emotions coursing through her. "Not the bad kind of crying."

"Oh, did he do something nice?" she asked with a pleased grin. "Because husbands really ought to, now and again."

"He's not my husband, but…" Viveka thought of Mikolas saving her and thanking her for the wedding debacle. Her heart wobbled again and she had to swallow back a fresh rush of emotion. "He did."

"Good. I'm Clair, by the way." She offered her free hand to shake while her other hand stayed against her chest, the straps of her halter-style bodice dangling over her slender fingers.

"Viveka. Call me Vivi." Eyeing the straps, she guessed, "Wardrobe malfunction?"

"The worst! Is there any chance you have a pin?"

"I don't. Can you tie them?" She circled her finger in the air. "Turn around. Let's see what happened to the catch."

They quickly determined the catch was long gone and they were too short to tie.

"I bet a tiepin would hold it. Give me a minute. I'll ask Mikolas for his," Viveka offered.

"Good idea, but ask my husband," Clair said. "Then I won't have to worry about returning it."

Viveka chuckled. "Let me guess. Your husband is the man in the suit?" She thumbed toward the ballroom filled with a hundred men wearing ties and jackets.

Clair grinned. "Mine's easy to spot. He's the one with a scar here." She touched her cheek, drawing a vertical line. "Also, he's holding my purse. I needed two hands to keep myself together long enough to get in here or I would have texted him to come help me."

"Got it. I'll be right back."

* * *

Mikolas stood with the back of his hand pressed to a scotch on the rocks. So much for behaving mainstream and law-abiding, he thought dourly.

He was watching for Viveka, still worried about her. When she had apologized, he'd been floored, already kicking himself for bringing her downstairs at all. He could be at home making love to her, none of this having happened. Instead, he'd let her be terrorized.

There she was. He tried to catch her eye, but she scanned the room, then made for a small group in the far corner from the band.

Mikolas swore under his breath as she approached his target: Aleksy Dmitriev. The Russian magnate had logistics interests that crossed paths with his own from the Aegean through to the Black Sea. Dmitriev had never once returned Mikolas's calls and it grated. He hated being the petitioner and resented the other man for relegating him to that role.

Mikolas knew why Dmitriev was avoiding him. He was scrupulous about his reputation. He wouldn't risk sullying it by attaching himself to the Petrides name.

While Mikolas knew working with Dmitriev would be another seal of legitimacy for his own organization. That's why he wanted to partner with him.

Dmitriev stared at Viveka like she was from Mars, then handed her his drink. He removed his tiepin, handed it to her, then took back his glass. When she asked him something else, he nodded at a window ledge where a pocketbook sat. Viveka scooped it up and headed back to the ladies' room.

What the *hell*?

Viveka was thankful for the small drama that Clair had provided, but flashed right back to seesaw emotions when

she returned to Mikolas's side. He stood out without trying. He wore that look of disinterest that alpha wolves
wore with their packs, confident in his superiority so with
nothing to prove.

A handful of men in sharp suits had clustered around
him. They all wore bored-looking women on their arms.

Mikolas interrupted the conversation when she arrived.
He took her hand and made a point of introducing her.

She smiled, but the man who'd been speaking was
quick to dismiss her and continue what he was saying.
He struck her as the toady type who sucked up to powerful men in hopes of catching scraps. The way the women
were held like dogs on a leash was very telling, too.

Viveka let her gaze stray to the other groups, seeing
the dynamic was very different in Clair's circle, where
she was nodding at whoever was speaking, smiling and
fully engaged in the conversation. Her husband was
looking their way and she pressed a brief smile onto her
mouth.

Nothing.

Mikolas had been right about invisible barriers.

"This must be your new bride if the merger has gone
through," one of the other men broke in to say, frowning
with confusion as he jumped his gaze between her and
Mikolas.

I have a name, Viveka wanted to remind the man, but
apparently on this side of the room, she was a "this."

"No," Mikolas replied, offering no further explanation.

Viveka wanted to roll her eyes. It was basic playground
etiquette to act friendly if you wanted to be included in
the games. That was what he wanted, wasn't it? Was this
what he had meant when he had said it was her task to
change how he was viewed?

"I stopped the wedding," she blurted. "He was supposed to marry my sister, but…" She cleared her throat as she looked up at Mikolas, laughing inwardly at the ridiculous claim she was about to make. "I fell head over heels. You weren't far behind me, were you?"

Mikolas wore much the same incredulous expression he had when he'd lifted her veil.

"Your sister can't be happy about that," one of the women said, perking up for the first time.

"She's fine with it," Viveka assured with a wave. "She'd be the first to say you should follow your heart, wouldn't she?" she prodded Mikolas, highly entertained with her embellishment on the truth. *Laugh with me*, she entreated.

"Let's dance." His grip on her hand moved to her elbow and he turned her toward the floor. As he took her in his arms seconds later, he said, "I cannot believe you just said that."

"Oh, come on. You said we should appear long-term. Now they think we're in love and by the way, your friends are a pile of sexist jerks."

"I don't have friends," he growled. "Those are people whose names I know."

His touch on her seemed to crackle and spark, making her feel sensitized all over. At the same time, she thought she heard something in his tone that was a warning.

Dancing with him was easy. They moved really well together right out of the gate. She let herself become immersed in the moment, where the music transmitted through them, making them move in unison. He held her in his strong arms and the closeness was deliciously stimulating. Her heart fluttered and she feared she really would tumble into deep feelings for him.

"They should call it heels over head," she said, trying to break the spell. "We're head over heels right now. It means you're upright."

He halted their dance, started to say something, but off to her right, Clair said, "Vivi. Let me introduce you properly. My husband, Aleksy Dmitriev."

Mikolas pulled himself back from a suffocating place where his emotions had knotted up. She'd been joking with all that talk of love, he knew she had, but even having a falsehood put out there to those vultures had made him uncomfortable.

He had been pleased to feel nothing for Trina. He would have introduced her as his wife and the presumption of affection might have been made, but it wouldn't have been true. It certainly wouldn't have been something that could be used to prey on his psyche, not deep down where his soul kept well out of the light.

Viveka was different. Her blasé claim of love between them was an overstatement and he ought to be able to dismiss it. But as much as he wanted to feel nothing toward her, he couldn't. Everything he'd done since meeting her proved to himself that he felt *something*.

He tried to ignore how disarmed that made him feel, concentrating instead on finding himself face-to-face with the man who'd been evading him for two years.

Dmitriev looked seriously peeved, mouth flat and the scar on his face standing out white.

It's the Viveka effect, Mikolas wanted to drawl.

Dmitriev nodded a stiff acknowledgment to Viveka's warm smile.

"Did you think you were being robbed?" Viveka teased him.

"It crossed my mind." Dmitriev lifted a cool gaze to Mikolas. *When I realized she was with you*, he seemed to say.

Mikolas kept a poker face as Viveka finished the introduction, but deep down he waved a flag of triumph over Dmitriev being forced to come to him.

It was only an introduction, he reminded himself. A hook. There was no reeling in this kind of fish without a fight.

"We have to get back to the children," Clair was saying. "But I wanted to thank you again for your help."

"My pleasure. I hope we'll run into each other in future," Viveka said. Mikolas had to give her credit. She was a natural at this role.

"Perhaps you can add us to your donor list," Mikolas said. *I do my homework*, he told Dmitriev with a flick of his gaze. Clair ran a foundation that benefited orphanages across Europe. Mikolas had been waiting for the right opportunity to use this particular door. He had no scruples about walking through it as Viveka's plus one.

"May I?" Clair brightened. "I would love that!"

Mikolas brought out one of his cards and a pen, scrawling Viveka's details on the back, mentally noting he should have some cards of her own printed.

"I'd give you one of mine, but I'm out," Clair said, showing hands that were empty of all but a diamond and platinum wedding band. "I've been talking up my fundraising dinner in Paris all night—oh! Would you happen to be going there at the end of next month? I could put you on that list, too."

"Please do. I'm sure we can make room," Mikolas said smoothly. *We, our, us.* It was a foreign language to him, but surprisingly easy to pick up.

"I'm being shameless, aren't I?" Clair said to her husband, dipping her chin while lifting eyes filled with playful culpability.

The granite in Dmitriev's face eased to what might pass for affection, but he sounded sincere as he contradicted her. "You're passionate. It's one of your many appealing qualities. Don't apologize for it."

He produced one of his own cards and stole the pen Mikolas still held, wordlessly offering both to his wife.

I see what you're doing, Dmitriev said with a level stare at Mikolas while Clair wrote. Dmitriev was of similar height and build to Mikolas. He was probably the only man in the room whom Mikolas would instinctively respect without testing the man first. He emanated the same air of self-governance that Mikolas enjoyed and had more than demonstrated he couldn't be manipulated into doing anything he didn't want to do.

He provoked all of Mikolas's instincts to dominate, which made getting this man's contact details that much more significant.

But even though he wasn't happy to be giving up his direct number, it was clear by Dmitriev's hard look that it was a choice he made consciously and deliberately—for his wife.

Mikolas might have lost a few notches of regard for the man if his hand hadn't still been throbbing from connecting with Grigor's jaw. Which he'd done for Viveka.

It was an uncomfortable moment of realizing it didn't matter how insulated a man believed himself to be. A woman—one for whom he'd gone heels over head—could completely undermine him.

Which was why Mikolas firmed himself against letting Viveka become anything more than the sexual infatuation she was. The only reason he was bent out of shape was because they hadn't had sex yet, he told himself. Once he'd had her, and anticipation was no longer clouding his brain, he'd be fine.

"That was what we came for," he said, after the couple

had departed. He indicated the card Viveka was about to drop into her pocketbook. "We can leave now, too."

Mikolas made a face at the card the doorman handed him on their way in, explaining he was supposed to call the police in the morning to make a statement. They didn't speak until they were in the penthouse.

"I've wanted Dmitriev's private number for a while. You did well tonight," he told her as he moved to pour two glasses at the bar.

"It didn't feel like I did anything," she murmured, quietly glowing under his praise. She yearned for approval more than most people did, having been treated as an annoyance for most of her early years.

"It's easy for you. You don't mind talking to people," he remarked, setting aside the bottle and picking up the glasses to come across and offer hers. "Do you take yours with water?"

"I haven't had ouzo in years," she murmured, trying to hide her reaction to him by inhaling the licorice aroma off the alcohol. "I shouldn't have had it when I did. I was far too young. *Yiamas*."

Mikolas threw most of his back in one go, eyes never leaving hers.

"What, um…?" Oh, this man easily emptied her brain. "You, um, don't like talking to people? You said you hated those sorts of parties."

"I do," he dismissed.

"Why?"

"Many reasons." He shrugged, moving to set aside his glass. "My grandfather had a lot to hide when I first came to live with him. I was too young to be confident in my own opinions and didn't trust anyone with details about myself. As an adult, I'm surrounded by people who are so superficial, crying about ridiculous little trials, I can't summon any interest in whatever it is they're saying."

"Should I be complimented that you talk to me?" she teased.

"I keep trying not to." Even that was delivered with self-deprecation tilting his mouth.

Her heart panged. She longed to know everything about him.

His gaze fixed on her collarbone. He reached out to take her hair back from her shoulder. "You've had one sparkle of glitter here all night," he said, fingertip grazing the spot.

It was a tiny touch, an inconsequential remark, but it devastated her. Her insides trembled and she went very still, her entire being focused on the way he ever so lightly tried to coax the fleck off her skin.

Behind him, the lamps cast amber reflections against the black windows. The pool glowed a ghostly blue on the deck beyond. It made radiance seem to emanate from him, but maybe that was her foolish, dampening eyes.

Painful yearning rose in her. It was familiar, yet held a searing twist. For a long time she had wanted a man in her life. She wanted a confidant, someone she could kiss and touch and sleep beside. She wanted intimacy, physical and emotional.

She had never expected this kind of corporeal desire. She hadn't believed it existed, definitely hadn't known it could overwhelm her like this.

How could she feel so attracted and needy toward a man who was so ambivalent toward her? It was excruciating.

But when he took her glass and set it aside, she didn't resist. She kept holding his gaze as his hands came up to frame her face. And waited.

His gaze lowered to her lips.

They felt like they plumped with anticipation.

She looked at his mouth, not thinking about anything except how much she wanted his kiss. His lips were so beautifully shaped, full, but undeniably masculine. The tip of his tongue wet them, then he lowered his head, came closer.

The first brush of his damp lips against hers made her shudder in release of tension while tightening with anticipation. She gasped in surrender as his hands whispered down to warm her upper arms, then grazed over the fabric of her dress.

Then his mouth opened wider on hers and it was like a straight shot of ouzo, burning down her center and warming her through, making her drunk. Long, dragging kisses made her more and more lethargic by degrees, until he drew back and she realized her hand was at the back of his head, the other curled into the fabric of his shirt beneath his jacket.

He released her long enough to shrug out of his jacket, loosened his tie, then pulled her close again.

Her head felt too heavy for her neck, easily falling into the fingers that combed through her hair and splayed against her scalp. He kissed her again, harder this time, revealing the depth of passion in him. The aggression. It was scary in the way thunder and high winds and landslides were both terrifying and awe-inspiring. She clung to him, moaning in submission. Not just to him, but to her own desire.

They shuffled their feet closer, sealing themselves one against the other, trying to press through clothing and skin so their cells would weave into a single being.

The thrust of his aroused flesh pressed into her stomach and a wrench of conflict went through her. This moment was too perfect. It felt too good to be held like this, to ruin it with humiliating confessions about her defect and entreaties for special treatment. She felt too much toward him, not least gratitude and wonder and a regard that was tied to his compliments and his protection and his hand dragging her to the surface of the water before he'd even known her name.

She ached to share something with him, had since almost the first moment she'd seen him. *Be careful*, she told herself. Sex was powerful. She was already very susceptible to him.

But she couldn't make herself stop touching him. Her hands strayed to feel his shape, tracing him through his pants. It was a bold move for her, but she was entranced. Curious and enthralled. There was a part of her that desperately wanted to know she could please a man, *this* man in particular.

His breath hissed in and his whole body hardened. He gathered his muscles as if he was preparing to dip and lift her against his chest.

She drew back.

His arms twitched in protest, but he let her look at where his erection pressed against the front of his suit pants. He was really aroused. She licked her lips, not superconfident in what she wanted to do, but she wanted to do it.

She unbuckled his belt.

His hands searched under the fall of her hair. His touch ran down her spine, releasing the back of her dress.

As the cool air swirled from her waist around to her belly, her stomach fluttered with nerves. She swallowed, aware of her breasts as her bodice loosened and shifted against her bare nipples. She shivered as his fingertips stroked her bare back. Her hands shook as she pulled his shirt free and clumsily opened his buttons, then spread the edges wide so she could admire his chest.

Pressing her face to his taut skin, she rubbed back and forth and back again, absorbing the feel of him with her brow and lips, drawing in his scent, too moved to smile when he said something in a tight voice and slid his palm under her dress to brand her bottom with his hot palm.

Her mouth opened of its own accord, painting a wet path to his nipple. She explored the shape with her tongue, earned another tight curse, then hit the other one with a draw of her mouth. Foreplay and foreshadowing, she thought with a private smile.

"Bedroom," he growled, bringing his hands out of her dress and setting them on her waist, thumbs against her hip bones as he pressed her back a step.

Dazed at how her own arousal was climbing, Viveka smiled, pleased to see the glitter in his eyes and the flush on his cheeks. It increased her tentative confidence. She placed her hands on his chest and let her gaze stray past him to the armchair, silently urging him toward it.

Mikolas let her have her way out of sheer fascination. He refused to call it weakness, even though he was definitely under a spell of some kind. He had known there was a sensual woman inside Viveka screaming to get out. He hadn't expected this, though.

It wasn't manipulation, either. There were no sly smiles or knowing looks as she slid to her knees between his, kissing his neck, stroking down his front so his abdominals contracted under her tickling fingertips. She was focused and enthralled, timid but genuinely excited. It was erotic to be wanted like this. Beyond exciting.

As she finished opening his pants, his brain shorted

out. He was vaguely aware of lifting his hips so she could better expose him. The sob of want that left her was the kind of siren call that had been the downfall of ancient seamen. He nearly exploded on the spot.

He was thick and aching, so hot he wanted to rip his clothes from his body, but he was transfixed. He gripped the armrest in his aching hand and the back of the chair over his shoulder with the other, trying to hold on to his control.

He shouldn't let her do this, he thought distantly. His discipline was in shreds. But therein lay her power. He couldn't make himself stop her. That was the naked truth.

She took him in hand, her touch light, her pale hands pretty against the dark strain of his flesh. He was so hard he thought he'd break, so aroused he couldn't breathe, and so captivated, he could only hold still and watch through slitted eyes as her head dipped.

He groaned aloud as her hair slid against his exposed skin and her wet mouth took him in, narrowing his world to the tip of his sex. It was the most exquisite sensation, nearly undoing him between one breath and the next. She kept up the tender, lascivious act until he was panting, barely able to speak.

"I can't hold back," he managed to grit out.

Slowly her head lifted, pupils huge as pansies in the dim light, mouth swollen and shiny like he'd been kissing her for hours.

"I don't want you to." Her hot breath teased his wet flesh, tightening all his nerve endings, pulling him to a point that ended where her tongue flicked out and stole what little remained of his willpower.

He gave himself up to her. This was for both of them, he told himself. He would have staying power after this.

He'd make it good for her, as good as this. Nothing could be better, but at least this good—

The universe exploded and he shouted his release to the ceiling.

CHAPTER NINE

VIVEKA HUGGED THE front of her gaping dress to her breasts and could barely meet her own glassy eyes in the mirror. She was flushed and aroused and deeply self-conscious. She couldn't believe what she'd just done, but she had no regrets. She had enjoyed giving Mikolas pleasure. It had been extraordinary.

She had needed that for herself. She wasn't a failure in the bedroom after all. Okay, the lounge, she allowed with a smirk.

Her hand trembled as she removed the pins from her hair, pride quickly giving way to sexual frustration and embarrassment. Even a hint of desolation. If she wasn't such a freak, if she wasn't afraid she'd lose herself completely, they could have found release together.

Being selfless was satisfying in other ways, though. He might be thanking her for breaking up the wedding and saving him a few bucks, but she was deeply grateful for the way he had acknowledged her as worth saving, worth protecting.

The bathroom door that she'd swung almost closed pushed open, making her heart catch.

Mikolas took up a lazy pose that made carnal hunger clench mercilessly in her middle. The flesh that was hot with yearning squeezed and ached.

His open shirt hung off his shoulders, framing the light pattern of hair that ran down from his breastbone. His unfastened pants gaped low across his hips, revealing the narrow line of hair from his navel. His eyelids were heavy, disguising his thoughts, but his voice was gritty enough to make her shiver.

"You're taking too long."

The words were a sensual punch, flushing her with eager heat. At the same time, alarm bells—anxious clangs of performance anxiety—went off within her, cooling her ardor.

"For?" She knew what he meant, but she'd taken care of his need. They were done. Weren't they? If she'd ever had sex before, she wouldn't be so unsure.

"Finishing what you started."

"You did finish. You can't—" Was he growing hard again? It looked like his boxers were straining against the open fly of his pants.

She read. She knew basic biology. She knew he'd climaxed, so how was that happening? Was she really so incapable of gratifying a man that even oral sex failed to do the job?

"You can't... Men don't...again. Can they?" She trailed off, blushing and hating that his first real smile came at the expense of her inexperience.

"I'll last longer this time," he promised drily. "But I don't want to wait. Get your butt in that bed, or I'll have you here, bent over the sink."

Oh, she was never going to be that spontaneous. Ever. And for a first time? While he talked about lasting a *long* time?

"No." She hitched the shoulder of her dress and reached behind herself to close it. "You finished. We're done." Her face was on fire, but inside she was growing cold.

He straightened off the doorjamb. "What?"

"I don't want to have sex." Not entirely true. She longed to understand the mystique behind the act, but his talk of sink-bending only told her how far apart they were in experience. The more she thought about it, the more she went into a state of panic. Not him. Not tonight when she was already an emotional mess.

She struggled to close her zip, then crossed her arms, taking a step backward even though he hadn't moved toward her.

He frowned. "You don't want sex?"

Was he deaf?

"No," she assured him. Her back came up against the towel rail, which was horribly uncomfortable. She waved toward the door he was blocking. "You can go."

He didn't move, only folded his own arms and rocked back on his heels. "Explain this to me. And use small words, because I don't understand what happened between the lounge and here."

"Nothing happened." She couldn't stand that he was making her wallow in her inadequacy. "You…I mean, I *thought* I gave you what you wanted. If you thought—"

He didn't even want her. Not really. He would decide *if* and *when*, she recalled.

Good luck with that, champ. Her body made that decision for everyone involved, no matter what her head said.

Do not cry. Oh, she hated her body right now. Her stupid, dumb body that had made her life go so far sideways she didn't even understand how she was standing here having this awful conversation.

"Can you just go?" She glared at him for making this so hard for her, but her eyes stung. She bet they were red and pathetic looking. If he made her tell him, and he laughed— *"Please?"*

He stayed there one more long moment, searching her gaze, before slowly moving back, taking the door with him, closing it as he left. The click sounded horribly final.

Viveka stepped forward and turned the lock, not because she was afraid he'd come in looking for sex, but afraid he'd come in and catch her crying.

With a wrench of her hand, she started the shower.

Mikolas was sitting in the dark, nursing an ouzo, when he heard Viveka's door open.

He'd closed it himself an hour ago, when he'd gone in to check on her and found her on the guest bed, hair wrapped in a towel, one of his monogramed robes swallowing her in black silk. She'd been fast asleep, her very excellent legs bare to midthigh, a crumpled tissue in her lax grip. Several more had been balled up around her.

Rather than easing his mind, rather than answering any of the million questions crowding his thoughts, the sight had caused the turmoil inside him to expand, spinning in fresh and awful directions. Was he such a bad judge of a woman's needs? Why did he feel as though he'd taken advantage of her? She had pressed him into this very chair. She had opened his pants. She had gone down and told him to let go.

He'd been high as a kite when he had tracked her into her bathroom, certain he'd find her naked and waiting for him. Every red blood cell he possessed had been keening with anticipation.

It hadn't gone that way at all.

She'd felt threatened.

He was a strong, dominant man. He knew that and tried to take his aggressive nature down a notch in the bedroom. He knew what it was like to be brutalized by someone bigger and more powerful. He would never do that to the smaller and weaker.

He kept having flashes of slender, delicate Viveka looking anxious as she noticed he was still hard. He thought about her fear of Grigor. A libido-killing dread had been tying his stomach in knots ever since.

He couldn't bear the idea of her being abused that way. He'd punched Grigor tonight, but he wished he had killed him. There was still time, he kept thinking. He wasn't so far removed from his bloodline that he didn't know how to make a man disappear.

He listened to Viveka's bare feet approach, thinking he couldn't blame her for trying to sneak out on him.

She paused as she arrived at the end of the hall, obviously noticing his shadowed figure. She had changed into pajamas and clipped up her hair. She tucked a stray wisp behind her ear.

"I'm hungry. Do you want toast?" She didn't wait for his response, charging past him through to the kitchen.

He unbent and slowly made his way into the kitchen behind her.

She had turned on the light over the stove and kept her back to him as she filled the kettle at the sink. After she set the switch to Boil, she went to the freezer and found a frozen loaf of sliced bread.

Still keeping her back to him, she broke off four slices and set them in the toaster.

"Viveka."

Her slender back flinched at the sound of his voice.

So did he. The things he was thinking were piercing his heart. He'd been bleeding internally since the likeliest explanation had struck him hours ago. When someone reacted that defensively against sexual contact, the explanation seemed really obvious.

"When you said Grigor abused you…" He wasn't a coward, but he didn't want to speak it. Didn't want to hear it. "Did he…?" His voice failed him.

Viveka really wished he hadn't still been up. In her perfect world, she never would have had to face him again, but as the significance of his broken question struck her, she realized she couldn't avoid telling him.

She buried her face in her hands. "No. That's not it. Not at all."

She *really* didn't want to face him.

But she had to.

Shoulders sagging, she turned and wilted against the cupboards behind her. Her hands stayed against her stinging cheeks.

"Please don't laugh." That's what the one other man she'd told had done. She'd felt so raw it was no wonder she hadn't been able to go all the way with him, either.

She dared a peek at Mikolas. He'd closed a couple of buttons, but his shirt hung loose over his pants. His hair was ruffled, as though his fingers had gone through it a few times. His jaw was shadowed with stubble and he looked tired. Troubled.

"I won't laugh." He hadn't slept, even though it was past two in the morning. For some reason that flipped her heart.

"I wasn't a very happy teenager, obviously," she began. "I did what a lot of disheartened young girls do. I looked for a boy to save me. There was a nice one who didn't have much, but he had a kind heart. I can't say I loved him, not even puppy love, but I liked him. We started seeing each other on the sly, behind Grigor's back. After a while it seemed like the time to, you know, have sex."

The toaster made a few pinging, crackling noises and

the kettle was beginning to hiss. She chewed her lip, fully grown and many years past it, but still chagrined.

"I mean, fourteen is criminally young, I realize that. And not having any really passionate feelings for him... It's not a wonder it didn't work."

"Didn't work," he repeated, like he was testing words he didn't know.

She clenched her eyes shut. "He didn't fit. It hurt too much and I made him stop. Please don't laugh," she rushed to add.

"I'm not laughing." His voice was low and grave. "You're telling me you're a virgin? You never tried again?"

"Oh, I did," she said to the ceiling, insides scraped hollow.

She moved around looking for the tea and butter, trying to escape how acutely humiliating this was.

"My life was a mess for quite a while, though. Grigor found out I'd been seeing the boy and that I'd gone to the police about Mum. He kicked me out and I moved to London. *That* was a culture shock. The weather, the city. Aunt Hildy had all these rules. It wasn't until I finished my A levels and was working that I started dating again. There was a guy from work. He was very smooth. I realize now he was a player, but I was quite taken in."

The toast popped and she buttered it, taking her time, spreading right to the edges.

"He laughed when I told him why I was nervous." She scraped the knife in careful licks across the surface of the toast. "He was so determined to be The One. We fooled around a little, but he was always putting this pressure on me to go all the way. I *wanted* to have sex. It's supposed to be great, right?"

Pressure arrived behind her eyes again. She couldn't look at him, but she listened, waiting for his confirmation that yes, all the sex he'd had with his multitude of lovers had been fantastic.

Silence.

"Finally I said we could try, but it really hurt. He said it was supposed to and didn't want to stop. I lost my temper and threw him out. We haven't spoken since."

"Do you still work with him?"

"No. Old job. Long gone." The toast was buttered before her on two plates, but she couldn't bring herself to turn and see his reaction.

She was all cried out, but familiar, hopeless angst cloaked her. She just wanted to be like most people and have sex and like it.

"Are you laughing?" Her voice was thready and filled with the embarrassed anguish she couldn't disguise.

"Not at all." His voice sounded like he was talking from very far away. "I'm thinking that not in a thousand years would I have guessed that. Nothing you do fits with the way other people behave. It didn't make sense that you would give me pleasure and not want anything for yourself. You respond to me. I couldn't imagine why you didn't want sex."

"I *do* want sex," she said, flailing a frustrated hand. "I just don't want it to *hurt*." She finally turned and set his plate of toast on the island, avoiding his gaze.

The kettle boiled, giving her breathing space as she moved to make the tea. When she sat down, she went around the far end of the island and took the farthest stool from where he stood ignoring the toast and tea she'd made for him.

She couldn't make herself take a bite. Her body was hot and cold, her emotions swinging from hope to despair to worry.

"You're afraid I wouldn't stop if we tried." His voice

was solemn as he promised, "I would, you know. At any point."

A tentative hope moved through her, but she shook her head. "I don't want to be a project." Her spoon clinked lightly as she stirred the sugar into her tea. "I can't face another humiliating attempt. And yes, I've been to a doctor. There's nothing wrong. I'm just...unusually..." She sighed hopelessly. "Can we stop talking about this?"

He only pushed his hands into his pockets. "I wasn't trying to talk you into anything. Not tonight. Unless you want to," he said in a wry mutter, combing distracted fingers through his hair. "I wouldn't say no. You're not a project, Viveka. I want you rather badly."

"Do you?" She scoffed in a strained voice, reminding him, "You said *you* would decide if and when. That *I* was the only one who wanted sex. I can't help the way I react to you, you know. I might have tried with you tonight if I'd thought it would go well, but..."

Tears came into her eyes. It was silly. She was seriously dehydrated from her crying jags earlier. There shouldn't be a drop of moisture left in her.

"I wanted you to like it," she said, heart raw. "I wanted to know I could, you know, *satisfy* a man, but no. I didn't even get that right. You were still hard and—"

He muttered something under his breath and said, "Are you really that oblivious? You *did* satisfy me. You leveled me. Blew my mind. Reset the bar. I don't have words for how good that was." He sounded aggrieved as he waved toward the lounge. "My desire for you is so strong I was aroused all over again just thinking about doing the same to you. *That's* why I was hard again."

If he didn't look so uncomfortable admitting that, she might have disbelieved him.

"When we were on the yacht, you said you thought it

was exciting that I respond to you." Her chest ached as she tried to figure him out. "If the attraction is just as strong for you, why don't you want me to know? Why do you keep—I mean, before we went out tonight, you acted as if you could take it or leave it. It's *not* the same for you, Mikolas. That's why I don't think it would work."

"I never like to be at a disadvantage, Viveka. We had been talking about some difficult things. I needed space."

"But if we're equal in feeling *this* way...? Attracted, I mean, why don't you want me to know that?"

"That's not an advantage, is it?"

His words, that attitude of prevailing without mercy, scraped her down to the bones.

"You'll have to tell me sometime what that's like," she said, dabbing at a crumb and pressing it between her tight lips. "Having the advantage, I mean. Not something I've ever had the pleasure of experiencing. Not something I should want to go to bed with, frankly. So *why do I*?"

He did laugh then, but it was ironic, completely lacking any humor.

"For what it's worth, I feel the same." He walked out, leaving his toast and tea untouched.

Mikolas was trying hard to ignore the way Viveka Brice had turned his life into an amusement park. One minute it was a fun house of distorted mirrors, the next a roller coaster that ratcheted his tension only to throw him down a steep valley and around a corner he hadn't seen.

Home, he kept thinking. It was basic animal instinct. Once he was grounded in his own cave, with the safety of the familiar around him, all the ways that she'd shaken up his world would settle. He would be firmly in control again.

Of course he had to keep his balance in the dizzying teacup of her trim figure appearing in a pair of hip-hugging jeans and a completely asexual T-shirt paired with the doe-eyed wariness that had crushed his chest last night.

He couldn't say he was relieved to hear the details of her sexual misadventures. The idea of her lying naked with other men grated, but at least she hadn't been scarred by the horrifying brutality he'd begun to imagine.

On the other hand, when she had finally opened up, the nakedness in her expression had been difficult to witness. She was tough and brave and earnest and too damned sensitive. Her insecurity had reached into him in a way that antagonism couldn't. The bizarre protectiveness she already inspired in him had flared up, prompting him to assuage her fears, reassure her. He had wound up revealing himself in a way that left him mistrustful and feeling like he'd left a flank unguarded.

Not a comfortable feeling at all.

He hadn't been able to sleep. Much of it had been the ache in his body, craving release in hers. He yearned to *show* her how it could be between them. At the same time, his mind wouldn't stop turning over and over with everything that had happened since she had marched into his life. At what point would she quit pulling the rug out from under him?

"Are you taking me back in time? What is that?" She was looking out the window of the helicopter.

He leaned to see. They were approaching the mansion and the ruins built into the cliff below it.

"That is the tower where you will be imprisoned for the rest of your life." *There* was a solution, he thought.

"Don't quit your day job for comedy."

Her quick rejoinder made humor tug at the corner of his mouth. He was learning she used jokes as a defense, similar to how he was quick to pull rank and impose his control over every situation. The fact she was being cheeky now, when he was in her space, told him she was shoring up her walls against him. That niggled, but wasn't it what he wanted? Distance? Barriers?

"The Venetians built it." He gazed at her clean face so close to his, her naked lips. She smelled like tea and roses and woman. He wanted to eat her alive. "See where the stairs have been worn away by the waves?"

Viveka couldn't take in anything as she felt the warmth off the side of his face and caught the smell of his aftershave. She held herself very still, trying not to react to his closeness, but her lips tingled, longing to graze his jaw and find his mouth. Lock with him in a deep kiss.

"We preserved the ruins as best we could. Given the fortune we spent, we were allowed to build above it."

She forced her gaze to the view, instantly enchanted. What little girl hadn't dreamed of being spirited away to an island castle like in a fairy tale?

The modern mansion at the top of the cliff drew her eye unerringly. The view was never-ending in all directions and the ultracontemporary design was unique and fascinating, sprawling in odd angles that were still perfectly balanced. It was neither imposing nor frivolous. It was solid and sophisticated. Dare she say elegant?

She noticed something on the roof. "Are those solar panels?"

"*Nai.* We also have a field of wind turbines. You can't see them from here. We're planning a tidal generator, too. We only have to finalize the location."

"How ecologically responsible of you." She turned her face and they were practically nose to cheekbone.

He sat back and straightened his cuff.

"I like to be self-sufficient." A tick played at the corner of his mouth.

Under no one's power but his own. She was seeing that pattern very clearly. Should she tell him it made him predictable? she wondered with private humor.

A few minutes later, she followed him into an interior she hadn't expected despite all she'd seen so far of the way he lived. The entrance should have struck her as over the top, with its smooth marble columns and split staircase that went up to a landing overlooking, she was sure, the entire universe.

The design remained spare and masculine, however, the colors subtle and golden in the midday light. Ivory marble and black wrought iron along with accents of Hellenic blue made the place feel much warmer than she expected. As they climbed the stairs, thick fog-gray carpet muffled their steps.

The landing looked to the western horizon.

Viveka paused, experiencing a strange sensation that she was looking back toward a life that was just a blur of memory, no longer hers. Oddly, the idea slid into her heart not like a blade that cut her off from her past, but more like something that caught and anchored her here, tugging her from a sea of turbulence to pin her to this stronghold.

She rubbed her arms at the preternatural shiver that chased up her entire body, catching Mikolas's gaze as he waited for her to follow him up another level.

The uppermost floor was fronted by a lounge that was surrounded by walls of glass shaded by an overhang to keep out the heat. They were at the very top of the world here. That's how it felt. Like she'd arrived at Mount Olympus, where the gods resided.

There was a hot tub on the veranda along with lounge chairs and a small dining area. She stayed inside, glancing around the open-plan space of a breakfast nook, a sitting area with a fireplace and an imposing desk with two flat monitors with a printer on a cabinet behind it, obviously Mikolas's home office.

As she continued exploring, she heard Mikolas speaking, saying her name. She followed to an open door where a uniformed young man came out. He saw her, nodded and introduced himself as Titus, then disappeared toward the stairs.

She peered into the room. It was Trina's boudoir. Had to be. There were fresh flowers, unlit candles beside the bucket of iced champagne, crystal glasses, a peignoir set draped across the foot of the white bed, and a box of chocolates on a side table. The exterior walls were made entirely out of glass and faced east, which pleased her. She liked waking to sun.

Don't love it, she cautioned herself, but it was hard not to be charmed.

"Oh, good grief," she gasped as Mikolas opened a door to what she had assumed was a powder room. It was actually a small warehouse of prêt-à-porter.

"Did you buy all of Paris for her?" She plucked at the cuff of a one-sleeved evening gown in silver-embroidered lavender. The back wall was covered in shoes. "I hate to tell you this, but my foot is a full size bigger than Trina's."

"One of your first tasks will be to go through all of this so the seamstress can alter where necessary. The shoes can be exchanged." He shrugged one shoulder negligently.

The closet was huge, but way too small with both of them in it.

She tried to disguise her self-consciousness by picking up a shoe. When she saw the designer name, she gently rubbed the shoe on her shirt to erase her fingerprint from the patent leather and carefully replaced it.

"Change for lunch with my grandfather. But don't take too long."

"Where are you going?" she asked, poking her head out to watch him cross to a pair of double doors on the other side of her room, not back to the main part of the penthouse.

"My room." He opened one of the double doors as he reached it, revealing what she thought at first was a private sitting room, but that white daybed had a towel rolled up on the foot of it.

Drawn by curiosity, she crossed to follow him into the bathroom. Except it was more like a high-end spa. There was an enormous round tub set in a bow of glass that arched outward so the illusion for the bather was a soak in midair.

"Wow." She slowly spun to take in the extravagance, awestruck when she noted the small forest that grew in a rock garden under a skylight. A path of stones led through it to a shower *area* against the back wall. Nozzles were set into the alcove of tiled walls, ready to spray from every level and direction, including raining from the ceiling.

She clapped her hand over her mouth, laughing.

The masculine side of the room was a double sink and mirror designed along the black-and-white simplistic lines Mikolas seemed to prefer, bracketed by a discreet door to a private toilet stall that also gave access to his bedroom. Her side was a reflection of his, with one sink removed to make way for a makeup bench and a vanity of drawers already filled with unopened cosmetics.

"You live like this," she murmured, closing the drawer.

"So do you. Now."

Temporarily, she reminded herself, but it was still like trying to grasp the expanse of the universe. Too much to comprehend.

A white robe that matched the black ones she'd already worn hung on a hook. She flipped the lapel enough to see the monogram, expecting a T and finding an M. She sputtered out another laugh. He was so predictably possessive!

"Can you be ready in twenty minutes?"

"Of course," she said faintly. "Unless I get lost in the forest on the way back to my room."

My room. Freudian slip. She dropped her gaze to the mosaic in the floor, then walked through her water closet to her room.

It was only as she stood debating a pleated skirt versus a sleeveless floral print dress that the significance of that shared bathroom struck her: he could walk in on her naked. Anytime.

CHAPTER TEN

VIVEKA WASN'T SURE what she expected Mikolas's grand-father to look like. A mafia don from an old American movie? Or like many of the other retired Greek men who sat outside village *kafenions*, maybe wearing a flat cap and a checked shirt, face lined by sun and a hard life in the vineyard or at sea?

Erebus Petrides was the consummate old-world gen-tleman. He wore a suit as he shared a drink with them before they dined. He had a bushy white mustache and excellent posture despite his stocky weight and the cane he used to walk. He and Mikolas didn't look much alike, but they definitely had the same hammered silver eyes and their voices were two keys of a similar strong, com-manding timbre.

Erebus spoke English, but preferred Greek, stretching her to recall a vocabulary she hadn't tested in nine years—something he gently reproached her over. It was a pleasant meal that could have been any "Meet the Parents" occa-sion as they politely got to know each other. She had to keep reminding herself that the charismatic old man was actually a notorious criminal.

"He seems very nice," she said after Erebus had retired for an afternoon rest.

Mikolas was showing her around the rest of the house.

They'd come out to the pool deck where a cabana was set up like a sheikh's tent off to the side and the Ionian Sea gleamed into the horizon.

Mikolas didn't respond and she glanced up to see his mouth give a cynical twitch.

"No?" she prompted, surprised.

"He wouldn't have saved me if I hadn't proven to be his grandson."

Her heart skipped and veered as she absorbed that none of this would have happened. She wouldn't be here and neither would he. They never would have met. *What would have become of that orphaned boy?*

"Do you wish that your mother had told your father about you?"

"She may have. My father was no saint," he said with disparagement. "And there is no point wishing for anything to be different. Accept what is, Viveka. I learned that long ago."

It wasn't anything she didn't see in a pop philosophy meme on her newsfeed every day, but she always resisted that fatalistic view. She took a few steps away from him as though to distance herself from his pessimism.

"If I accepted what I was given, I would still be listening to Grigor call me ugly and useless." She didn't realize her hands became tight fists, or that he had come up behind her, until his warm grip gently forced her to bend her elbow as he lifted her hand.

He looked at her white knuckles poking like sharp teeth. His thumb stroked along that bumpy line.

"You've reminded me of something. Come." He smoothly inserted his thumb to open her fist and kept her hand as he tugged her into the house.

"Where?"

He only pulled her along through the kitchen and down

the service stairs into a cool room where he turned on the lights to reveal a gym.

Perhaps the original plans had drawn it up as a wine cellar, but it was as much a professional gym as any that pushed memberships every January. Bike, tread, elliptical. Every type of weight equipment, a heavy bag hanging in the corner, skipping ropes dangling from a hook and padded mats on the floor. It was chilly and silent and smelled faintly of leather and air freshener.

"You'll meet me here every morning at six," he told her.

"Pah," she hooted. "Not likely."

"Say that again and I'll make it five."

"You're serious?" She made a face, silently telling him what she thought of that. "For heaven's sake, why? I do cardio most days, but I prefer to work out in the evening."

"I'm going to teach you to throw a punch. This—" he lifted the hand he still held and reshaped it into a fist again "—can do better. And this—" he touched under her chin, lifting her face and letting his thumb tag the spot on her lip where Grigor's mark had been "—won't happen again. Not without your opponent discovering very quickly that he has picked a fight with the wrong woman."

She had been trying to pretend she wasn't vitally aware of her hand in his. Now he was touching her face, looking into her eyes, standing too close.

Somehow she had thought that giving him pleasure would release some of this sexual tension between them. Now everything they'd confessed made it so much worse. The pull was so much *deeper*. He knew things about her. Intensely personal things.

She drew away, breaking all contact, trying to keep a grip on herself as she took in what he was saying.

"You keep surprising me. I thought you were a hardened…" She cut him a glance of apology. "Criminal.

You're actually quite nice, aren't you? Wanting to teach me how to defend myself."

"Everyone who surrounds me is a strength, not a liability. That's all this is."

"Liability." The label winded her, making her look away. It was familiar, but she had hoped there was a growing regard between them. But no. He might be attracted to her sexually, last night might have changed her forever, but she was still that thing he was saddled with.

"Right. Whatever you need me to be, wherever." She fought not to let her smarting show, but from her throat to her navel she burned.

"Do you like feeling helpless?" he demanded.

"No," she choked. This feeling of being at *his* mercy was excruciating.

"Then be here at six prepared to work."

What had he been thinking? Mikolas asked himself the next morning. This was hell.

Viveka showed up in a pair of clinging purple pants that ended below her knees. The spandex was shiny enough to accent every dip and curve of her trim thighs. Her pink T-shirt came off after they'd warmed up with cardio, revealing the unique landscape of her abdomen. Now she wore only a snug blue sports bra that flattened her modest breasts and showed off her creamy shoulders and chest and flat midriff.

He was so distracted by lust, he would get his lights blacked out for sure.

He would deserve it. And he couldn't even make a pass to slake it. He'd told two of his guards who had come in to use the gym that they could stay. They were spotting each other, grunting over the weights, while Mikolas put his hands on Viveka to adjust her stance and coached her

through stepping into a punch. She smelled like shampoo
and woman sweat. Like they'd been petting each other
into acute arousal.

"You're holding back because you're afraid you'll
hurt yourself," he told her when she struck his palm. He
stopped her to correct her wrist position and traced up the
soft skin of her forearm. "Humans have evolved the bone
structure in here to withstand the impact of a punch."

"My bones aren't as big as yours," she protested. "I *will*
hurt myself in a real fight. Especially if I don't have this."
She held up her arm to indicate where he'd wrapped her
hands to protect them.

"You might even break your hand," he told her frankly.
"But that's better than losing your life, isn't it? I want you
on the heavy bag twice a day for half an hour. Get used
to how it feels to connect so you won't hesitate when it
counts. Learn to use your left with as much power as the
right."

Her brow wrinkled with concentration as she went back
to jabbing into his palms. She was taking this seriously,
at least.

That earnestness worried him, though. It would be just
like her to take it to heart that *she* should protect *him*. He'd
blurted out that remark about liability last night because
he hadn't wanted to admit that her inability to protect herself had been eating at him from the moment he'd seen
Grigor throw her around on the deck of a stranger's yacht.

He'd hurt her feelings, of course. She'd made enough
mentions of Grigor's disparagement and her aunt's indifference that he understood Viveka had been made to feel
like a burden and was very sensitive to it. That heart of
hers was so easily bruised!

The more time he spent with her, the more he could

see how utterly wrong they were for each other. He could wind up hurting her quite deeply.

I do want sex. I just don't want it to hurt.

Her jab was off-center, glancing off his palm so she stumbled into him.

"Sorry. I'm getting tired," she said breathlessly.

"I wasn't paying attention," he allowed, helping her find her feet.

Damn it, if he didn't keep his guard up, they were both going to get hurt.

Viveka was still shaking from the most intense workout of her life. Her arms felt like rubber and she needed the seamstress's help to dress as they worked through the gowns in her closet. She would have consigned Mikolas firmly to hell for this morning's punishment, but then his grandfather's physiotherapist arrived on Mikolas's instruction to offer her a massage.

"He said you would need one every day for at least a week."

Viveka had collapsed on the table, groaned with bliss and went without prompting back to the gym that afternoon to spend another half hour on the wretched heavy bag.

"You'll get used to it," Mikolas said without pity at dinner, when she could barely lift her fork.

"Surely that's not necessary, is it?" Erebus admonished Mikolas, once his grandson had explained why Viveka was so done in.

"She wants to learn. Don't you?" Mikolas's tone dared her to contradict him, but he wasn't demanding she agree with him in front of his grandfather. He was insisting on honesty.

"I do," she admitted with a weighted sigh, even though

the very last thing she ever wanted was to engage in a fistfight. She couldn't help wondering if Grigor would have been as quick to hit her if she'd ever hit him back, though. She'd never had the nerve, fearing she'd only make things worse.

Mikolas's treatment of her in the gym, as dispassionate as it had been, had also been heartening. He seemed to have every confidence in her ability to defend herself if she only practiced. That was an incredibly compelling thought. Empowering.

It made her grateful to him all over again. And yes, deep down, it made her want to make him proud. To show him what she was capable of. Show herself.

Of course, the other side of that desire to be plucky and capable was a churning knowledge that she was being a coward when it came to sex. She wanted to be proficient in that arena, too.

The music was on low when they came into the lounge of his penthouse later, the fire glowing and a bottle of wine and glasses waiting. Beyond the windows, stars sparkled in the velvet black sky and moonlight glittered on the sea.

Had he planned this? To seduce her?

Did she want to be seduced?

She sighed a little, not sure what she wanted anymore.

"Sore?" he asked, moving to pour the wine.

"Hmm? Oh, it's not that bad. The massage helped. No, I was just thinking that I'm stuck in a holding pattern."

He lifted his brows with inquiry.

"I thought once Hildy was sorted, I would begin taking my life in hand. Trina was supposed to come live with me. I had some plan that we would rent a flat and take online quizzes, choose a career and register for classes…" She had been looking forward to that, but her sister's life had skewed off from hers and she didn't even have the worry of Hildy any longer. "Instead, my future is a blank page."

On Petrides letterhead, she thought wryly.

"I'll figure it out," she assured herself. "Eventually. I won't be here forever, right?"

That knowledge was the clincher. If it had taken her twenty-three years to find a man who stirred her physically, how long would it take to find another?

She looked over to him.

Whatever was in her face made him set down the bottle, corkscrew angled into the unpopped cork.

"I keep telling myself to give you time." His voice was low and heavy, almost defeated. "But bringing you into my bed is all I can think about. Will you let me? I just want to touch you. Kiss you. Give you what you gave me."

Her belly clenched in anticipation. She couldn't imagine being *that* uninhibited, but she couldn't imagine *not* going to bed with him. She wanted him *so much* and she honestly didn't know how to resist any longer.

Surrender happened with one shaken, "Yes."

He kind of jolted, like he hadn't expected that. Then he came across and took her face in his two hands, covering her lips with his hot, hungry mouth. They kissed like lovers. Like people who had been separated by time and distance and deep misunderstanding. She curled her arms around his neck and he broke away long enough to scoop her up against his chest, then kissed her again as he carried her to his bedroom.

She waited for misgivings and none struck. Her fingers went into his hair as she kissed him back.

He came down on the mattress with her and she opened her eyes only long enough to catch an impression of monochromatic shades lit by the bluish half-moon. The carpet was white, the furniture silver-gray, the bedspread black.

Then Mikolas tucked her beneath him and stroked without hurry from her shoulder, down her rib cage, past her waist and along her hip.

"You can—" she started to say, but he brushed another kiss over her lips, lazy and giving and thorough.

"Don't worry," he murmured and kissed her again. "I just want to touch you." Another soft, sweet, lingering kiss. "I'll stop if you tell me to." Kissing and kissing and kissing.

It was delicious and tender and not the least bit threatening with his heavy hand only making slow, restless circles where her hip met her waist.

She wanted more. She wanted sex. It wasn't like the other times she'd wanted sex. Then it had been something between an obligation and a frustrating goal she was determined to achieve.

This was nothing like that. She wanted *him*. She wanted to share her body with Mikolas, feel him inside her, feel close to him.

Make love to me, she begged him with her lips, and ran her hands over him in a silent message of encouragement. When she rolled and tried to open the zip on her dress, he made a ragged noise and found it for her, dragging it down. He lifted away to draw her sleeve off her arm, exposing her bra. One efficient flick of his fingers and the bra was loose.

With reverence, he eased the strap down her arm, dislodging the cup so her breast thrust round and white, nipple turgid with wanton need.

Insecurity didn't have time to strike. He lowered his head and tongued lightly, cupped with a warm hand, then with another groan of appreciation, opened his mouth in a hot branding, letting her get used to the delicate suction before pulling a little harder.

Her toes curled. She wanted to speak, to tell him this was good, that he wouldn't have to stop, but sensation rocked her, coiling in her abdomen, making her loins weep with need. When his hand stroked to rub her bottom, she dragged at her skirt herself, earning a noise of approval as she drew the ruffled fabric out of the way.

He teased her, tracing patterns on her bare thighs, lifting his head to kiss her again and give her his tongue as he made her wait and wait.

"Mikolas," she gasped.

"This?" He brought his hand to the juncture of her thighs and settled his palm there, letting her get used to the sensation. The intimacy. "I want that, too," he breathed against her mouth.

She bit back a cry of pure joy as the weight of his hand covered her, hot and confident. He rocked slowly, increasing the pressure in increments, inciting her to crook her knee so she was open to his touch. Eyes closed, she let herself bask in this wonderful feeling, tension climbing.

When he lifted his hand, she caught her breath in loss, opening her eyes.

He was watching her while his fingertips traced the edge of her knickers, then began to draw them down her thighs.

The friction of lace against her sensitized skin made her shiver. As the coolness of the room struck her damp, eager flesh, she became starkly aware of how her clothing was askew, her breast exposed, her sex pouted and needy, her body trembling with ridiculously high desire.

For a moment anxiety struck. She wanted to rush past this moment, rush through the hard part, have done with this interminable impasse. She lifted her hips so he could finish skimming them away, but when he came down beside her again, he only combed her hair back from her face.

"I just want to feel you. I'll be gentle," he promised, and kissed her lightly.

Yes, she almost screamed.

Embarrassment ought to be killing her, but arousal was pulsing in her like an electrical current. And when he cradled her against him this way, she felt very safe.

They kissed and his hand covered her again. This time she was naked. The sensation was so acute she jolted under his touch.

"Just feel," he cajoled softly. "Tell me what you like. Is that good?"

He did things then that were gorgeous and honeyed. She knew how her body worked, but she had never felt this turned on. She didn't let herself think, just floated in the deep currents of pleasure he swirled through her.

"Like that?" He kept up the magical play, making tension coil through her so she moaned beneath his kiss, encouraging him. Yes, like that. Exactly like that.

He pressed one finger into her.

She gasped.

"Okay?" he breathed against her cheek.

She clasped him with her inner muscles, loving the sensation even though it felt very snug. She was so aroused, so close, she covered his hand with her own and pressed. She rocked her hips as he made love to her with his hand and shattered into a million pieces, cries muffled by his smothering kiss.

CHAPTER ELEVEN

THEY WERE GOING to kill each other.

Mikolas was fully clothed and if she shaped him through his pants right now, he would explode.

But oh, she was amazing. He licked at her panting lips, wanting to smile at the way she clung to his mouth with her own, but weakly. She was still shivering with the aftershocks of her beautiful, stunning orgasm.

He caressed her very, very gently, coaxing her to remain aroused. He wanted to do that to her again. Taste her. Drown in her.

She made a noise and kissed him back with more response, restless hands picking at his shirt, looking for the buttons.

He broke them open with a couple of yanks, then shrugged it off and discarded it, too hot for clothes. On fire for her.

She pulled her other arm free of her dress and held up her arms for him to come back. Soft curves, velvety skin. He loved the feel of her against his bare chest and biceps. Delicate, but spry. So warm, smelling of rain and tea and the drugging scent of sexual fulfillment.

Her smooth hands traced over his torso and back, making him groan at how good it felt on skin that was taut and sensitized. She tasted like nectarines, he thought, opening his mouth on the swell of her breast. He tongued her nipple, more aggressive than he had been the first time.

She arched for more.

He was going too fast, he cautioned himself, but he wanted to consume her. He wanted her dress out of the way, he wanted her hands everywhere on him—

She arched to strip the garment down.

He slid down the bed as he whisked the dress away, pressing his lips to her quivering belly, blowing softly on the fine hairs of her mound, laughing with delight at finally being here. He was so filled with desire his heart was slamming, pulse reverberating through his entire body.

"Mikolas," she breathed.

Her fingers were in his hair like she was petting a wolf, tugging hard enough to force him to lift his head before he'd barely nuzzled her.

"Make love to me."

A lightning rod of lust went through him. He steeled himself to maintain his control when all he wanted was to push her legs apart and rise over her.

"I am." He was going to make her scream with release.

"I mean really." Her hand moved to cradle his jaw, her touch light against the clenched muscle in his cheek. Entreaty filled her eyes. "Please."

She had come into his life to destroy him in the most subversive yet effective way possible.

He could barely move, but he drew back, coming up on an elbow, trying to hold on to what shreds of gentlemanly conduct he possessed.

"Do you ever do what's expected of you?"

"You don't want to?" The appalled humiliation that crept into her tone scared the hell out of him.

"Of course I *want* to." He spoke too harshly. He was barely hanging on to rational thought over here.

She tensed, wary.

He set his hand on her navel, breathed, tried to find something that passed for civilized behavior, but found only the thief he had once been. His hand stole lower, unable to help himself. His thumb detoured along her cleft, finding her slick and ready. Need pearled into one place that made her gasp raggedly when he found it, circling and teasing.

Her thighs relaxed open. She arched to his touch. "Please," she begged. "I want to know how it feels."

He was only human, not a superhero. He pulled away, hearing her catch back a noise of injury.

Her breath caught in the next instant as she saw he was rising to open his pants. He stripped in jerky, uncoordinated movements, watching her swallow and bite her bottom lip. He made himself take his time retrieving the condom so she had lots of opportunity to change her mind.

"I'll stop if you want me to," he promised as he covered himself, then settled over her. He would. He didn't know how, but he would.

Please don't make me stop.

It would really happen this time. Viveka's nerves sizzled as Mikolas covered her. He was such a big person compared with her. He *loomed*. She skimmed her fingertips over his broad shoulders and was starkly aware of how much space his hips and thighs took up as he settled without hesitation between her own.

She tensed, nervous.

He kissed her in abbreviated catches of her mouth that didn't quite satisfy before he pulled away, then did it again.

She made a noise of impatience and wiggled beneath him. "I want—"

"Me, too," he growled against her mouth. Then he lifted

to trace himself against her folds. "You're sure?" he murmured, looking down to where they touched.

So sure. "Yes," she breathed.

He positioned himself and pressed.

It hurt. So much. She fought her instinctive tension, tried to make herself relax, tried not to resist, but the sting became more and more intense. He seemed huge. Tears came into her eyes. She couldn't hold back a throaty noise of anxiety.

He stilled, shuddering. The sting subsided a little.

"Viveka." His voice was ragged. "That's just the tip—" He hung his head against her shoulder, forehead damp with perspiration, big body shaking.

"Don't stop." She caught her foot behind his thigh and tried to press him forward.

"*Glykia mou*, I don't want to hurt you." He lifted his face and wore a tortured expression.

"That's why it's okay if you do." Her mouth quivered, barely able to form words. It still hurt, but she didn't care. "I trust you. Please don't make me do this with someone else."

He bit out a string of confounded curses, looking into the shadows for a moment. Then he met her gaze and carefully pressed again.

She couldn't help flinching. Tensing. The stretch hurt a lot. He paused again, looked at her with as much frustration as she felt.

"Don't try to be gentle. Just do it," she told him.

He wavered, then made a tight noise of angst, covered her mouth, gathered himself and thrust deep.

She arched at the flash of pain, crying out into his mouth.

They both stayed motionless for a few hissing breaths.

Slowly the pain eased to a tolerable sting. She moved her lips against his and he kissed her gently. Sweetly.

"Do you hate me?" His voice was thick, his brow tense as he set it against hers. His expression was strained.

He didn't move, letting her get used to the feel of a man inside her for the first time. And he held her in such protective arms, her eyes grew wet from the complete opposite of pain: happiness.

She returned his healing kiss with one that was a little more inciting.

"No," she answered, smiling shakily, feeling intensely close to him. She let her arms settle across his back and traced the indent of his spine, enjoying the way he reacted with a shiver.

"Want to stop?" he asked.

"No." Her voice was barely there. Tentatively she moved a little, settling herself more comfortably beneath him. "I'm not sure I want you to move at all," she admitted wryly. "Ever."

His breath released on a jagged chuckle. "You are going to be the death of me."

Very carefully, he shifted so he was angled on his elbow, then he made a gentling noise and touched where they were joined.

"You feel so good," he crooned in Greek, gently soothing and stimulating as he murmured compliments. "I thought nothing could be better than the way you took me apart with your mouth, but this feels incredible. You're so perfect, Viveka. So lovely."

The noise that escaped her then was pure pleasure. He was leading her down the road of stirred desire to real excitement. It felt strange to have him lodged inside her while her arousal intensified. Part of her wanted him to move, but she was still wary of the pain and this felt so good. The way he stretched her accentuated the sensations. She grew taut and deeply aroused. Restless and—

"Oh, Mikolas. Please. Oh—" A powerful climax rocked her. Her sheath clenched and shivered around his hard shape with such power she could hardly breath. Stars imploded behind her eyes and she clung to him, crying out with ecstasy. It was beautiful and selfish and heavenly.

As the spasms faded, he began to pull away. The friction felt good, except sharp. She wasn't sure she could take that in a prolonged way, but then he was gone from her body and she was bereft.

"You didn't, did you?" She reached to find his thick shaft, so hard and hot, obviously unsatisfied.

He folded his hand over hers and pumped into her fist. Two, three times, then he pressed a harsh groan into her shoulder, mouth opening so his teeth sat against her skin, not quite biting while he shuddered and pulsed against her palm.

Shocked, but pleased, she continued to pleasure him until he relaxed and released her. He removed the condom with a practiced twist, then rolled away and sat up to discard it. Before he came back, he dragged the covers down and pulled her with him as he slid under them.

"Why did you do that?" she asked as he molded her to his front, stomach to stomach.

"So we won't be cold while we sleep." He adjusted the edge of the sheet away from her face.

"You know what I mean." She pinched his chest, unable to lie still when it felt so good to rub her naked legs against his and nuzzle his collarbone with her lips.

"Learn to speak plainly when we're in bed," he ordered.

"Or what?" She was giddy, so happy with being his lover she felt like the sun was lodged inside her.

"Or I may not give you what you want."

They were both silent a moment, bodies quieting.

"You did," she said softly, adjusting her head against his shoulder. "Thank you."

He didn't say anything, but his hand moved thoughtfully in her hair.

A frozen spike of insecurity pierced her. "Did *you* like it?"

He snorted. "I have just finessed my way through initiating a particularly delicate virgin. My ego is so enormous right now, it's a wonder you fit in the bed."

Viveka woke to an empty bed, couldn't find Mikolas in the penthouse, realized she was late for the gym and decided she was entitled to a bath. She was climbing out of it, a thick white towel loosely clutched around her middle, when he strolled in wearing his gym shorts and nothing else.

"Lazy," he stated, pausing to give her a long, appreciative look.

"Seriously?" Before that bath, she had ached *everywhere*.

His mouth twitched and he came closer, gaze skimming down her front. "Sore?"

She shrugged a shoulder, instantly so shy she nearly couldn't bear it. The things they'd done!

She blushed, aware that her gaze was coveting the hard planes of his body, and instantly wanted to be close to him. Touch, feel, kiss…more.

She wasn't sure how to issue the invitation across the expanse of the spa-like bathroom, but he wasn't the novice she was. He took the last few laconic steps to reach her, spiky lashes lowering as he stared at her mouth. When his head dipped, she lifted her chin to meet his kiss. Her free hand found his stubbled cheek while her other kept her towel in place.

"Mmm…" she murmured, liking the way he didn't rush, but kissed her slowly and thoroughly.

He drew back and tried taking the towel in his two hands.

She hesitated.

"I only want a peek," he cajoled.

"It's daylight," she argued.

"Exactly."

If she had feared that having sex would weaken her will around him, the fear was justified. She wanted to please him. She wanted to offer her whole self and plead with him to cherish her. Her fingers relaxed under the knowledge she was giving up more than control of a towel.

As he opened it, however, and took a long eyeful of her sucked-in stomach and thrust-out breasts, she saw desire grip him with the same lack of mercy it showed her. He swallowed, body hardening, jaw clenched like he was under some kind of deep stress.

"I was only going to kiss you," he said, lifting lust-filled eyes to hers. "But if you—"

"I do," she assured him.

He let the towel drop and she met him midway, moaning with acquiescence as he pressed her onto the daybed. Her inhibitions about the daylight quickly burned up as his stubble slid down her neck to her breast where he sucked and made her writhe. When he slid even lower, scraping her stomach then her thighs as he knelt on the floor, she threw her arm across her eyes and let him do whatever he wanted.

Because it was what she wanted. Oh, that felt exquisite.

"Don't stop," she pleaded when he lifted his head.

"Can you take me?" he growled, scraping his teeth with mock threat along her inner thigh.

She nodded, little echoes of wariness threatening, but

she couldn't take her eyes off his form as he rose and moved to the mirror over his sink, found a condom and covered himself.

When he came back and stood over her, she stayed exactly as he'd left her, splayed weakly with desire, like some harem girl offered for his pleasure.

His hands flexed like he was struggling against some kind of internal pain.

"Mikolas," she pleaded, holding out her arms.

He made a noise of agony and came down over her, heavy and confident, thighs pressing hers wide as he positioned himself. "I don't want to hurt you." His hand tangled in her hair. "But I want you so damned much. Stop me if it hurts."

"It's okay," she told him, not caring about the burn as she arched, inviting him to press all the way in. It hurt, but his first careful thrusts felt good at the same time. The friction of him moving inside her made the connection that much more intense. She rose to the brink very quickly, climaxing with a sudden gasp, clinging to him, shocked at her reaction.

He shuddered, lips pressed into her neck, and hurried to finish with her, groaning fulfillment against her skin.

She was disappointed when he carefully disengaged and sat up, his back to her.

She started to protest that it was okay, holding him in her didn't hurt anymore, but she was distracted by the marks on his back. They were pocked scars that were visible only because the light was so bright. She'd seen his back on the yacht, but in lamplight she hadn't noticed the scars. They weren't raised, but there were more than a dozen.

"What happened to your back?" she asked, puzzled.

Mikolas rose and walked first to his side of the room,

where he scanned around his sinks, then went across to her vanity, where he found the remote for the shower.

"We should set some ground rules," he said.

"Leave the remote on your side?" she guessed as she rose. She walked past her discarded towel for her white robe, wondering why she bothered when she was thinking of joining him in the shower. She wanted to touch him, to close this distance that had arisen so abruptly between them.

"That," he agreed. "And we'll only be together for a short time. Call me your lover if you want to, but do not expect us to fall in love. Keep your expectations low."

She fell back a step as she tied her robe, giving it a firm yank like the action could tie off the wound he'd just inflicted.

But what did she think they were doing? Like fine weather, they were enjoying each other because they were here. That was all.

"I wasn't fishing for a marriage proposal," she defended.

"So long as we're clear." He aimed the remote and started the shower jets.

Scanning his stiff shoulders, she said, "Is this because I asked about your back? I'm sorry if that was too personal, but I've told you some really personal things about me."

"Talk to me about whatever you want. If I don't want to tell you something, I won't." He spoke with aloof confidence, but his expression faltered briefly, mouth quirking with self-deprecation.

Because he had already shared more than made him comfortable?

"There's nothing wrong with being friends, is there?"

He glanced at her, his expression patient, but resolute.

"You don't have friends," she recalled from the other

night, thinking, *I can see why*. "What's wrong with friendship? Don't you want someone you can confide in? Share jokes with?"

His rebuff was making her feel like a houseguest who had to be tolerated. Surely they were past that! He'd just enjoyed *her* hospitality, hadn't he?

"They're cigar burns," he said abruptly, rattling the remote control onto the space behind the sink. "I have more on the bottoms of my feet. My captors used to make me scream so my grandfather could hear it over the phone. *There was more than one call*. Is that the sort of confiding you're looking for, Viveka?" he challenged with antagonism.

"Mikolas." Her breath stung like acid against the back of her throat. She unconsciously clutched the robe across her shattered heart.

"That's why I don't want to share more than our bodies. There's nothing else worth sharing."

Mikolas had been hard on Viveka this morning, he knew that. But he'd been the victim of forces greater than himself once before and already felt too powerless around her. The way she had infiltrated his life, the changes he was making for her, were unprecedented.

Earlier that day, he had risen while she slept and spent the morning sparring, trying to work his libido into exhaustion. She had to be sore. He wasn't an animal.

But one glance at her rising from the bath and all his command over himself had evaporated. At one point, he'd been quite sure he was prepared to beg.

Begging was futile. He *knew* that.

But so was thinking he could treat Viveka like every other woman he'd slept with. Many of them had asked about his back. He'd always lied, claiming chicken pox had caused the scars. For some reason, he didn't want to lie to Viveka.

When he had finally blurted out the ugly truth, he'd seen something in her expression that he outwardly rejected, but inwardly craved: agony on his behalf. Sadness for that dark time that had stolen his innocence and left him with even bigger scars that no one would ever see.

Damn it, he was self-aware enough to know he used denial as a coping strategy, but there was no point in raking over the coals of what had been done to him. Nothing would change it. Viveka wanted a jocular companion to share opinions and anecdotes with. He was never going to be that person. There was too much gravity and anger in him.

So he had schooled her on what to expect, and it left him sullen through the rest of the day.

She wasn't much better. In another woman, he would have called her subdued mood passive-aggressive, but he already knew how sensitive Viveka was under all that bravado. His churlish behavior had tamped down her natural cheerfulness. That made him feel even more disgusted with himself.

Then his grandfather asked her to play backgammon and she brightened, disappearing for a couple of hours, coming back to the penthouse only to change for the gym.

Why did that annoy him? He wanted her to be self-sufficient and not look to him to keep her amused. Later that evening, however, when he found her plumping cushions in the lounge, he had to ask, "What are you doing?"

"Tidying up." She carried a teacup and plate to the dumbwaiter and left it there.

"I pay people to do that."

"I carry my weight," she said neutrally.

He pushed his hands into his pockets, watching her

click on a lamp and turn off the overhead light, then lift a houseplant—honest to God, she checked a plant to see if it needed water rather than look at him.

"You're angry with me for what I said this morning."

"I'm not." She sounded truthful and folded her arms defensively, but she finally turned and gave him her attention. "I just never wanted to be in this position again."

The bruised look in her eye made him feel like a heel.

"What position?" he asked warily.

"Being forced on someone who doesn't really want me around." Her tight smile came up, brave, but fatalistic.

"It's not like that," he ground out. "I told you I want you." Admitting it still made him feel like he was being hung by his feet over a ledge.

"Physically," she clarified.

Before the talons of a deeper truth had finished digging into his chest, she looked down, voice so low he almost didn't hear her.

"So do I. That's what worries me," she continued.

"What do you mean?"

She hugged herself, shrugging. Troubled. "Not something worth sharing," she mumbled.

Share, he wanted to demand, but that would be hypocritical. Regret and apology buzzed around him like biting mosquitoes, annoying him.

It had taken him years to come to this point of being completely sure in himself. A few days with this woman, and he was second-guessing everything he was or had or did.

"Can we just go to bed?" Her doe eyes were so vulnerable, it took a moment for him to comprehend what she was saying. He had thought they were fighting.

"Yes," he growled, opening his arms. "Come here."

She pressed into him, her lips touching his throat. He sighed as the turmoil inside him subsided.

Every night, they made love until Viveka didn't even remember falling asleep, but she always woke alone.

Was it personal? she couldn't help wondering. Did Mikolas not see anything in her to like? Or was he simply that removed from the normal needs of humanity that he genuinely didn't want any closer connections? Did he realize his behavior was hurtful? Did he know and not *care*?

Whenever she had dreamed of being in an intimate relationship with a man, it had been intimacy across the board, not this heart-wrenching openness during sex and a deliberate distance outside of it. Was she saying too much? *Asking* too much?

She became hypersensitive to every word she spoke, trying to refrain from getting too personal. The constant weighing and worrying was exhausting.

It was harder when they traveled. At least with his grandfather at the table, the conversation flowed more naturally. As Mikolas dragged her to various events across Europe, she had to find ways to talk to him without putting herself out there too much.

"I might go to the art gallery while you're in meetings this morning. Unless you want to come? I could wait until this afternoon," was a typical, neutral approach. She loved spending time with him, but couldn't say *that*.

"I can make myself available after lunch."

"It's an exhibition of children's art," she clarified. "Is that something you'd want to see?" Now she felt like she was prying. Her belly clenched as she awaited rejection.

He shrugged, indifferent. "Art galleries aren't something I typically do, but if you want to see it, I'll take you."

Which made her feel like she was imposing on his time,

but he was already tapping it into his schedule. Later he paced around the place, not saying much, while she held back asking what he thought. She wanted to tell him about her early aspirations and point to what she liked and ask if he'd ever messed around with finger paints as a child.

She actually found herself speaking more freely to strangers over cocktails than she did with him. He always listened intently, but she didn't know if that was for show or what. If he had interest in her thoughts or ambitions, she kept thinking, he would ask her himself, but he never did.

Tonight she was revealing her old fascination with art history and Greek mythology. It felt good to open up, so she shared a little more than she normally would.

"I actually won an award," she confided with a wrinkle of her nose. "It was just a little thing for a watercolor I painted at school. I was convinced I'd become a world-famous artist," she joked. "I've always wanted to take a degree in art, but there's never been the right time."

It was small talk. They were nice people, owners of a hotel chain whom she'd met more than once.

Deep down, she was congratulating herself on performing well at these events, remembering the names of children and occasionally going on shopping dates. Tonight she had found herself genuinely interested in Adara Makricosta's plans for her hotels. That's how her own career goals had come up. Adara Makricosta was the CEO of a family-owned chain and had asked Viveka about her own work.

Viveka sidestepped the admission she was merely a mistress whose job it was to create this warming trend Mikolas was enjoying among the world's most rich and powerful.

"Why didn't you tell me that before?" Mikolas asked

when Adara and Gideon had moved on. "About wanting to study art," he prompted when she only looked at him blankly.

Viveka's heart lurched and she almost blurted out, *Because you wouldn't care*. She swallowed.

"It's not practical. I thought about taking evening classes around my day job, but I always had Hildy to look after. And I knew once I was in this position, looking to my own future, I would need to devote myself to a proper career, not dabble in something that will never pay the bills."

She ought to be thinking harder about that, not using up all her brain space trying to second-guess the man in front of her.

"You don't have bills now. Sign up for something," he said breezily.

"Where? To what end?" Her throat tightened. "We're constantly on the move and I don't know how long I'll be with you. No. There's no point." It would hurt to see that phoenix of a dream rise up from the ashes only to fly away.

Or was he implying she would be with him for the long term?

She did the unthinkable and searched his expression for some sign that he had feelings for her. That they had a future.

He receded behind a remote mask, horribly quiet for the rest of the night and even while they traveled back to Greece, adding an extra layer of tension to their trip.

Viveka was still smarting over Mikolas's behavior when she woke in his bed the next morning. They were sleeping late after arriving in the wee hours. She stayed motionless, naked in the spoon of his body, not wanting to move and wake him. She often fell asleep in his arms, but she never woke in them. This was a rare moment of closeness.

It was the counterfeit currency that all women—like mother like daughter—too often took in place of real regard.

Because, no matter how distanced she felt from Mikolas during the day, in bed she felt so integral to him it was a type of agony to be anywhere else. When he made love to her, it felt like love. His kisses and caresses were generous, his compliments extravagant. She warmed and tingled just thinking about how good it felt to join with him, but it wasn't just physical pleasure for her. Lying with him, naked and intimate, was emotionally fulfilling.

She was falling for him.

His breathing changed. He hardened against her backside and she bit her lip, heartened by the lazy stroke of his hand and the noise of contentment he made, like he was pleased to wake with her against him.

Such happiness brimmed in her, she couldn't help but wriggle her butt into his hardness, inviting the only affection he seemed to accept, wanting to hold on to this moment of harmony.

His mouth opened on her shoulder and his hand drifted down her belly into the juncture of her thighs. He made a satisfied noise when he found her wet and ready.

She gasped, stimulated by his lazy touch. She stretched her arm to the night table, then handed a condom over her shoulder as she nestled back against him, eager and needy. He adjusted her position and a moment later thrust in, sighing a hot breath against her neck, setting kisses against her nape that were warm and soft. Caring. Surely he cared?

She took him so easily now. It was nothing but pleasure, so much pleasure. She hadn't known her body could be like this: buttery and welcoming. It was almost too good. She was so far ahead of him, having been thinking about this while he slept against her, she soared over the top in moments. She cried out, panting and damp with sweat, overcome and floating, speechless in her orgasmic bliss.

"Greedy," he said in a gritty morning voice, rubbing his mouth against her skin, inhaling and calling her beautiful in Greek. Exquisite. Telling her how much he enjoyed being inside her. How good she made him feel.

He came up on his elbow so he could thrust with more power. His hand went between her legs again, ensuring her pleasure as he moved with more aggression.

She didn't mind his vigor. She was so slick, still so aroused, she reveled in the slap of his hips into her backside, hand knotting in the bottom sheet to brace herself to receive him, making noises close to desperation as she felt a fresh pinnacle hover within reach.

"Don't hold back," he ground out. "Come with me. *Now.*"

He pounded into her, the most unrestrained he'd ever been. She cried out as her excitement peaked. An intense climax rolled through her, leaving her shattered and quaking in ecstasy.

He convulsed with equal strength, arms caging her, hoarse shout hot against her cheek. He jerked as she clenched, continuing to push deep so she was hit by wave after wave of aftershocks while he thrust firmly into her, like he was implanting his essence into her core.

As the sensual storm battered them, he remained pressed over her, crushing her beneath his heavy body. Finally, the crisis began to subside and he exhaled raggedly as he slid flat, his one arm under her neck bending so he could cradle her into his front. They were coated in perspiration. It adhered her back to his front and she could feel his heart still pounding unsteadily against her shoulder blade. Their legs were tangled, their bodies still joined, their breaths slowing to level.

It was the most beautifully imperfect moment of her life. She loved him. Endlessly and completely. But he didn't love her back.

Mikolas had visited hell. Then his grandfather had accepted him and he had returned to the real world, where there were good days and bad days. Now he'd found what looked like heaven and he didn't trust it. Not one little bit.

But he couldn't turn away from it—*from her*—either.

Not without feeling as though he was peeling away his own skin, leaving him raw and vulnerable. He was a molting crab, losing his shell every night and rebuilding it every day.

This morning was the most profound deconstruction yet. He always tried to leave before Viveka woke so he wouldn't start his day impacted by her effect on him, but the sweet way she'd rubbed herself into his groin had undone him. She had gone from a tentative virgin to a sensual goddess capable of stripping him down to nothing but pure sensation.

How could he resist that? How could he not let her press him into service and give himself up to the joy of possessing her. It had been all he could do to hold back so she came with him. Because she owned him. Between the sheets, she completely owned him. Right now, all he wanted in life was to stay in this bed, with her body replete against his, her fingertips drawing light patterns on the back of his hand.

Don't *want*.

He made himself roll away and sit up, to prove himself

master over whatever this thing was that threatened him in a way nothing else could.

She stayed inside him, though. In his body as an intoxicant, and in his head as an unwavering awareness. And because he was so attuned to her, he heard the barely discernible noise she made as he pushed to stand. It was a sniff. A lash. A cat-o'-nine-tails that scored through his thick skin into his soul.

He swung around and saw only the bow of her back, still curled on her side where he'd left her. He dropped his knee into the mattress and caught her shoulder, flattening her so he could see her face.

She gasped in surprise, lifting a hand to quickly try to wipe away the tears that stood in her eyes. Self-conscious agony flashed in her expression before she turned her face to hide it.

His heart fell through the earth.

"I thought you were with me." He spoke through numb lips, horrified with himself. He could have sworn she had been as passionately excited as he was. He had felt her slickness, the ripples of her orgasm. Was he kidding himself with how well he thought he knew her?

"You have to tell me if I'm being too rough," he insisted, his usual command buried in a choke of self-reproach.

"It's not that." Her expression spasmed with dismay. She pushed the back of her wrist across her eye, then brushed his hand off her shoulder so she could roll away and sit up. "I used to be so afraid of sex. Now I like it."

She rubbed her hands up and down her arms, the delicacy of her frame striking like a hammer between his eyes. Her nude body pimpled at the chill as she rose.

"I'm grateful," she claimed, turning to offer him a smile, but her lashes were still matted. "Take a bow. Let me know what I owe you."

Those weren't tears of gratitude.

His heart lurched as he found himself right back in that moment where he had impulsively told her to pursue her interests and she had searched for reassurance that she would be with him for the long haul.

I don't know how long I'll be with you.

It had struck him at that moment that at some point she would leave and he hadn't been able to face it. He skipped past it now, only saying her name.

"Viveka." It hurt his throat. "I told you to keep your expectations low," he reminded, and felt like a coward, especially when her smile died.

She looked at him with betrayal, like he'd smacked her.

"Don't," he bit out.

"Don't what? Don't like it?"

"Don't be hurt." He couldn't bear the idea that he was hurting her. "Don't feel *grateful*."

She made a choking noise. "Don't tell me what to feel. That is where you control what I feel." She pointed at the rumpled sheets he knelt upon, then tapped her chest and said on a burst of passion, "In here? This is mine. I'll feel whatever the hell I want."

Her blue eyes glowed with angry defiance, but something else ravaged her. Something sweet and powerful and pure that shot like an arrow to pierce his breastbone and sting his heart. He didn't try to put a name to it. He was afraid to, especially when he saw shadows of hopelessness dim her gaze before she looked away.

"I'm not confusing sex with love, if that's what you're worried about." She moved to the chair and pulled on his shirt from the night before, shooting her arms into it and folding the front across her stomach. She was hunched as though bracing for body blows. "My mother made that mistake." Her voice was scuffed and desolate. "I won't. I know the difference."

Why did that make him clench his fist in despair? He ought to be reassured.

He almost told her this wasn't just sex. When he walked into a room with her hand in his, he was so proud it was criminal. When she dropped little tidbits about her life before she met him, he was fascinated. When she looked dejected like that, his armored heart creaked and rose on quivering legs, anxious to show valor in her name.

Instead he stood, saying, "I'll send an email today. To ask how the investigation is coming along. On your mother," he clarified, when she turned a blank look on him.

She snorted, sounding disillusioned as she muttered, "Thanks."

"Your head is not in the game today," Erebus said, dragging Viveka's mind to the *távli* board, where he was placing one of his checkers on top of hers.

Were they at *plakoto* already? Until a few weeks ago, she hadn't played since she and Trina were girls, but the rules and strategies had come back to her very quickly. She sat down with Erebus at least once a day if she was home.

"Jet lag," she murmured, earning a *tsk*.

"We don't lie to each other in this house, *poulaki mou*."

Viveka was growing fond of the old man. He was very well-read, kept up on world politics and had a wry sense of humor. At the same time, he was interested in *her*. He called her "my little birdie" and always had something nice to say. Today it had been, *"I wish you weren't leaving for Paris. I miss you when you're traveling."*

She'd never had a decent father figure in her life and

knew it was crazy to see this former criminal in that light, but he was also sweetly protective of her. It was endearing.

So she didn't want to offend him by stating that his grandson was tearing her into little pieces.

"I wonder sometimes what Mikolas was like as a child," she prevaricated.

She and Erebus had talked a little about her aunt and he'd shared a few stories from his earliest years. She was deeply curious how such a kind-seeming man could have broken the law and fathered an infamous criminal, but thought it better not to ask.

He nodded thoughtfully, gesturing for her to shake the cup with the dice and take her turn.

She did and set the cup within his reach, but he was staring across the water from their perch outside his private sitting room. In a few weeks it would be too hot to sit out here, but it was balmy and pleasant today. A light breeze moved beneath the awning, carrying his favorite *kantada* folk music with it.

"Pour us an ouzo," he finally said, two papery fingers directing her to the interior of his apartment.

"I'll get in trouble. You're only supposed to have one before dinner."

"I won't tell if you don't," he said, making her smile.

He came in behind her as she filled the small glasses. He took his and canted his head for her to follow him.

She did, slowly pacing with him as he shuffled his cane across his lounge and into his bedroom. There he sat with a heavy sigh into a chair near the window. He picked up the double photo frame on the side table and held it out to her.

She accepted it and took her time studying the black-and-white photo of the young woman on the one side, the boy and girl sitting on a rock at a beach in the other. They were perhaps nine and five.

"Your wife?" she guessed. "And Mikolas's father?"

"Yes. And my daughter. She was… Men always say they want sons, but a daughter is life and light. A way for your wife to live on. Daughters are love in its purest form."

"That's a beautiful thing to say." She wished she knew more about her own father than a few barely recollected facts from her mother. He'd been English and had dropped out of school to work in radio. He'd married her mother because she was pregnant and died from a rare virus that had got into his heart.

She sat on the foot of Erebus's bed, facing him. "Mikolas told me you lost your daughter when she was young. I'm sorry."

He nodded, taking back the frame and looking at it again. "My wife, too. She was beautiful. She looked at me the way you look at Mikolas. I miss that."

Viveka looked into her drink.

"I failed them," Erebus continued grimly. "It was a difficult time in our country's history. Fear of communism, martial law, censorship, persecution. I was young and passionate, courting arrest with my protests. I left to hide on this island, never thinking they would go after my wife."

His cloudy gray eyes couldn't disguise his stricken grief.

"The way my son told me, my daughter was crying, trying to cling to their mother as the military police dragged her away for questioning. They knocked her to the ground. Her ear started bleeding. She never came to. Brain injury, perhaps. I'll never know. My wife died in custody, but not before my son saw her beaten unconscious for trying to go back to our daughter."

Viveka could only cover her mouth, holding back a cry of protest.

"By the time I was reunited with him, my son was twisted beyond repair. I was warped, too. The law? How could I have regard for it? What I did then, bribes, theft, smuggling… None of that sits on my conscience with any great weight. But what my son turned into…"

He cleared his throat and set the photo frame back in its place. His hands shook and he took a long time to speak again.

"My son lost his humanity. The things he did… I couldn't make him stop, couldn't bring him back from that. It was no surprise to me that he was killed so violently. It was the way he lived. When he died I mourned him, but I also mourned what should have been. I was forced to face my many mistakes. The things I had done caused me to outlive my children. I hated the man I had become."

His pain was tangible. Viveka ached for him.

"Into this came a ransom demand. A street rat was claiming to be my grandson. Some of my son's rivals had him."

Her heart clenched. She was listening intently, but was certain she wouldn't be able to bear hearing this.

"You want to know what Mikolas was like as a child? So do I. He came to me as an empty shell. Eyes this big." He made a circle with his finger and thumb. "Thin. Brittle. His hand was crushed, some of his fingernails gone. Three of his teeth gone. He was *broken*." He paused, lined face working to control deep pain, then he admitted, "I think he hoped I would kill him."

She bit her lip, eyes hot and wet, a burn of anguish like a pike spreading from her throat to the pit of her stomach.

"He said that if the blood test hadn't been positive, you

wouldn't have helped him." She couldn't keep the accusation, the blame, out of her voice.

"I honestly can't say what I would have done," Erebus admitted, eyes rheumy. "Looking back from the end of my life, I want to believe my conscience would have demanded I help him regardless, but I wasn't much of a man at the time. They showed me a picture and he looked a little like my son, but…"

His head hung heavy with regret.

"He begged me to believe he was telling the truth, to accept him. I took too long." He took a healthy sip of his ouzo.

She'd forgotten she was holding one herself. She sipped, thinking how forsaken Mikolas must have felt. No wonder he was so impermeable.

"He thinks I want him to redeem the Petrides name, but *I* need redemption. To some extent I have it," Erebus allowed with deep emotion. "I'm proud of all he's accomplished. He's a good man. He told me why he brought you here. He did the right thing."

She suppressed a snort. Mikolas's reasons for keeping her and her reasons for staying were so fraught and complex, she didn't see any way to call them wholly right or wrong.

"He has never recovered his heart, though. All the things he has done? It hasn't been for me. He has built this fortress around himself for good reason. He trusts no one, relies on no one."

"Cares about no one," she murmured despondently.

"Is that what puts that hopeless expression on your face, *poulaki mou*?"

She knocked back her drink, giving a little shiver as the sweet heat spread from her tongue to the tips of her limbs. Shaking back her hair, she braced herself and said, "He'll never love me, will he?"

Erebus didn't bother to hide the sadness in his eyes. Because they didn't lie to each other.

Slowly the glow of hope inside her guttered and doused.

"We should go back to our game," he said.

CHAPTER TWELVE

Mikolas glanced up as Viveka came out of the elevator. She never used it unless she was coming from the gym, but today she was dressed in the clothes she'd worn to lunch.

She staggered and he shot to his feet, stepping around his desk to hurry toward her. "Are you all right?"

"Fine." She set a hand on the wall, holding up the other to forestall him. "I just forgot that ouzo sneaks up on you like this."

"You've been *drinking*?"

"With your grandfather. Don't get mad. It was his idea, but I'm going to need a nap before dinner. That's what he was doing when I left him."

"This is what you two get up to over backgammon?" He took her arm, planning to help her to her room.

"Not usually, no." Her hand came to his chest. She didn't move, just stared at her hand on his chest, mouth grave, brow wearing a faint pleat. "We were talking."

That sounded ominous. She glanced up and anguish edged the blue of her irises.

Instinctively, he swallowed. His hand unconsciously tightened on her elbow, but he took a half step back from her. "What were you talking about?"

"He loves you, you know." Her mouth quivered, the corners pulling down. "He wishes you could forgive him."

He flinched, dropping his hand from her arm.

"He understands why you can't. Even if you did reach out to him, I don't think he would forgive himself. It's just…sad. He doesn't know how to reach you and—" She rolled to lean her shoulders against the wall, swallowing. "You won't let anyone in, ever, will you? Is this really all you want, Mikolas? Things? Sex without love?"

He swore silently, lifting his gaze to the ceiling, hands bunching into fists, fighting a wave of helplessness.

"I lied to you," he admitted when he trusted his voice. "That first day we met, I said my grandfather gave me anything I wanted." He lowered his gaze to her searching one. "I didn't want any of those things I asked for."

He had her whole attention.

"It was my test for him." He saw now the gifts had been his grandfather's attempts to earn his trust, but then it had been a game. A deadly, terrifying one. "I asked him for things I didn't care about, to see if he would get them for me. I never told him what I really wanted. I never told anyone."

He looked at his palm, rubbed one of the smooth patches where it had been held against a hot kettle, leaving shiny scar tissue.

"I never tell anyone. Physical torture is inhuman, but psychological torture…" His hand began shaking.

"Mikolas." Her hand came into his. He started to pull away, but his fingers closed over hers involuntarily, holding on, letting her keep him from sinking into the dark memories.

His voice felt like it belonged to someone else. "They would ask me, 'Do you want water?' 'Do you want the bathroom?' 'Do you want us to stop?' Of course I said yes. They never gave me what I wanted."

Her hand squeezed his and her small body came into

the hollow of his front, warm and anxious to soothe, arms going around his stiff frame.

He set his hands on her shoulders, resisting her offer of comfort even though it was all he wanted, ever. He resisted *because* it was what he wanted beyond anything.

"I can't—I'm not trying to hurt him. But if I trust him, if I let him mean too much to me, then what? He's not in a position to be my savior again. He's a weakness to be used against me. I can't leave myself open to that. Can you understand that?"

Her arms around him loosened. For a moment her forehead rested in the center of his chest, then she pressed herself away.

"I do." She took a deep, shaken breath. "I'm going to lie down."

He watched her walk away while two tiny, damp stains on his shirt front stayed cold against his skin.

"Vivi!" Clair exclaimed as she approached with her husband, Aleksy.

Viveka found a real smile for the first time all night. In days, really. Things between her and Mikolas were more poignantly strained than ever. She loved him so much and understood now that he was never going to let himself love her.

"How's the dress?" Viveka teased, rallying out of despondency for her hostess.

"I've taken to carrying a mending kit." Clair ruefully jiggled her pocketbook.

"I've been looking forward to seeing you again," Viveka said sincerely. "I've had a chance to read up on your foundation. I'm floored by all you do! And I have an idea for a fund-raiser that might work for you."

Mikolas watched Viveka brighten for the first time in

days. Her smile caused a pang in his chest that was more of a gong. He wanted to draw that warmth and light of hers against the echoing discord inside him, finally settling it.

"I saw a children's art exhibit when we were in New York. I was impressed by how sophisticated some of it was. It made me think, what if some of your orphans painted pieces for an auction? Here, let me show you." She reached into her purse for her phone, pausing to listen to something Clair was saying about another event they had tried.

Beside him, Aleksy snorted.

Mikolas dragged his gaze off Viveka, lifting a cool brow of inquiry. He had let things progress naturally between the women, not pursuing things on the business front, willing to be patient rather than rush fences and topple his opportunity with the standoffish Russian.

"I find it funny," Aleksy explained. "You went to all this trouble to get my attention, and now you'd rather listen to her than speak to me. I made time in my schedule for you tomorrow morning, if you can tear yourself away…?"

Mikolas bristled at the supercilious look on the other man's face.

Aleksy only lifted his brows, not intimidated by Mikolas's dark glare.

"When we met in Athens, I wondered what the hell you were doing with her. What *she* was doing with *you*. But…" Aleksy's expression grew self-deprecating. "It happens to the best of us, doesn't it?"

Mikolas saw how he had neatly painted himself into a corner. He could dismiss having any regard for Viveka and undo all her good work in getting him this far, or he could suffer the assumption that he had a profound weakness: *her*.

Before he had to act, Viveka said, "Oh, my God," and

looked up from her phone. Her eyes were like dinner plates. "Trina has been trying to reach me. Grigor had a heart attack. He's dead."

Mikolas and Viveka left the party amid expressions of sympathy from Clair and Aleksy.

Viveka murmured a distracted "thank you," but they were words that sat on air, empty of meaning. She was in shock. Numb. She wasn't *glad* Grigor was dead. Her sister was too torn up about the loss when she rang her, expressing regret and sorrow that a better relationship with her father would never manifest. Viveka wouldn't wish any sort of pain on her little sister, but she felt nothing herself.

She didn't even experience guilt when Mikolas surmised that Grigor had been under a lot of stress due to the inquiries Mikolas had ordered. He hadn't had much to report the other day, but ended a fresh call to the investigator as they returned to the hotel.

"The police on the island were starting to talk. They could see that silence looked like incompetence at best, bribery and collusion at worst. Charges were sounding likely for your mother's murder and more. My investigator is preparing a report, but without a proper court case, you'll probably never have the absolute truth on how she died. I'm sorry."

She nodded, accepting that. It was enough to know Grigor had died knowing he hadn't got away with his crimes.

"Trina will need me." It felt like she was stating the obvious, but it was the only concrete thought in her head. "I need to book a flight."

"I've already messaged my pilot. He's doing his preflight right now. We'll be in the air as soon as you're ready."

She paused in gathering the things that had been unpacked into drawers for her.

"Didn't I hear Aleksy say something about holding
an appointment for you tomorrow?" She looked at the
clothes she'd brought to Paris. "Not one thing suitable for
a funeral," she murmured. "Would Trina understand if I
wore that red gown, do you think?" She pointed across
the room to the open closet.

No response from Mikolas.

She turned her head.

He looked like he was trying to drill into her head with
his silvery eyes. "I can rebook with Aleksy."

So careful. So watchful. His remark about coming with
her penetrated.

"Do you need to talk to Trina?" she asked, trying to
think through the pall of details and decisions that would
have to be made. "Because she inherits? Does his dying
affect the merger?"

Something she couldn't interpret flickered across his
expression. "There will be things to discuss, yes, but they
can wait until she's dealt with immediate concerns."

"I wonder if he even kept her in his will," she murmured, setting out something comfortable to travel in,
then pulling off her earrings. Gathering her hair, she
moved to silently request he unlatch the sapphire necklace he'd given her this evening. "Trina told me he blamed
me for everything, not her, so I hope he didn't disinherit
her. Who else would he leave his wealth to? Charity?
Ba-ha-ha. Not."

The necklace slithered away and she fetched the velvet box, handing it to him along with the earrings, then
wormed her way out of her gown.

"Trina better be a rich woman, after everything he put
her through. It doesn't seem real." She knew she was bab-

bling. She was processing aloud, maybe because she was afraid of what *would* be said if she wasn't already doing the talking. "I've never been able to trust the times when I've thought I was rid of him. Even after I was living with Hildy, things would come up with Trina and I'd realize he was still a specter in my life. I was so sure the wedding was going to be *it*. Snip, snip, snip."

She made little scissors with her fingers, cutting ties to her stepfather, then bounced her butt into the seat of her jeans and zipped. Her push-up bra was overkill, but she pulled a T-shirt over it, not bothering to change into a different one.

"Now it's really here. He's dead. No longer able to wreck my life."

She made herself face him. Face *it*. The truth she had been avoiding.

"I'm finally safe from him."

Which meant Mikolas had no reason to keep her.

Mikolas was a quick study, always had been. He had seen the light of the train coming at him from the end of the tunnel the moment her lips had shaped the words, *He's dead*.

He had watched her pack and change and had listened to her walk herself to the platform and he still wasn't ready when her pale, pale face tilted up to his to say goodbye.

I can rebook with Aleksy. That was as close as he could come to stating that he was willing to continue their affair. He wasn't offering her solace. She wasn't upset beyond concern for her sister. God knew she didn't need *him*. He had deliberately stifled that expectation in her.

She looked down so all he could see of her expression was her pleated brow. "If you could give me some time to work out how to manage things with Aunt Hildy—"

He turned away, instantly pissed off. *So* pissed off. But he was unable to blame anyone but himself. He was the one who had fought letting ties form between them. He'd called what they had chemistry, sexual infatuation, protection.

"We're square," he growled. "Don't worry about it."

"Hardly. I'll get her house on the market as soon as I can—"

"I have what I wanted," he insisted, while a voice in his head asked, *Do you?* "I'm in," he continued doggedly. "None of the contacts I've made can turn their backs on me now."

"Mikolas—" She lowered to the padded bench in front of the vanity, inwardly quailing. *Don't humiliate yourself,* she thought, but stumbled forward like a love-drunk fool. "I care for you." Her voice thickened. "A lot." She had to clear her throat and swallow. Blink. Her fingers were a tangled mess against her knees. "If you would prefer we stay together…just say it. I know that's hard for you, but…" She warily lifted her gaze.

He was a statue, hands fisted in his pockets, immobile. Unmoved.

Her heart sank. "I can't make an assumption. I would feel like I'm still something you took on. I have to be something…" *You want.* Her mouth wouldn't form the words. This was hopeless. She could see it.

Mikolas's fists were so tight he thought his bones would crack. The shell around his heart was brittle as an egg's, threatening to crack.

"It's never going to work between us," he said, speaking as gently as he could, trying so hard not to bruise her. "You want things that I don't. Things I can't give you."

He was trying to be *decent*, but he knew each word was a splash of acid. He felt the blisters forming in his soul. "It's better to end it here."

It happens to the best of us.

What about the worst? What about the ones who pushed it away before they knew what they were refusing?

What about the ones who were afraid because it meant succumbing to something bigger than themselves? Because it meant handing someone, *everyone*, the power to hurt him?

The room seemed to dim and quiet.

She nodded wordlessly, lashes low. Her gorgeous, kissable mouth pursed in melancholy.

And when she was gone, he wondered why, if the threat of Grigor was gone, he was still so worried about her. If he feared so badly that she would hurt him, why was her absence complete agony?

If all he had wanted from her was a damned business contact, why did he blow off his appointment with Aleksy the next morning and sit in a Paris hotel room all day, staring at sapphire jewelry he'd bought because the blue stones matched her eyes, willing his phone to ring?

"You're required to declare funds over ten thousand euros," the male customs agent in London said to Viveka as they entered a room that was like something off a police procedural drama. There was a plain metal table, two chairs, a wastebasket and a camera mounted in the ceiling. If there was a two-way mirror, she couldn't see it, but she felt observed all the same.

And exhausted. The charter from the island after Grigor's funeral had been delayed by weather, forcing her to miss her flight out of Athens. They had rebooked her, but on a crisscross path of whichever flight left soonest in the general direction of London. She hadn't eaten or slept and was positively miserable.

"I forgot I had it," she said flatly.

"You forgot you're carrying twenty-five thousand euros?"

"I was going to put it in the bank in Athens, but I had already missed my connection. I just wanted to get home."

He looked skeptical. "How did you come by this amount of cash?"

"My sister gave it to me. For my aunt."

His brows tilted in a way that said, *Right*.

She sighed. "It's a long story."

"I have time."

She didn't. She felt like she was going to pass out. "Can I use the loo?"

"No." Someone knocked and the agent accepted a file, glancing over the contents before looking at her with more interest. "Tell me about Mikolas Petrides."

"Why?" Her heart tripped just hearing his name. Instantly she was plunged into despair at having broken off with him. When she had left Paris, she had told herself her feelings toward Mikolas were tied up in his protecting her from Grigor, but as the miles between them piled up, she kept thinking of other things: how he'd saved her life. How he'd brought her a life jacket, and said all the right things that night in Athens. How he'd taught her to fight. And make love.

Tears came into her eyes, but now was not the time.

"It looks like you've been traveling with him," the agent said. "That's an infamous family to truck with."

"The money has nothing to do with him!" That was a small lie. Once Viveka had spilled to her sister how she had come to be Mikolas's mistress, Trina had gone straight to her father's safe and emptied it of the cash Grigor had kept there.

Use this for Hildy. She's my aunt, too. I don't want you in his debt.

Viveka had balked, secretly wanting the tie to Mikolas. Trina had accused her of suffering from Stockholm syndrome. Her sister had matured a lot with her marriage and the death of Grigor. She had actually invited Viveka to live with them, but Viveka didn't want to be in that house, on that island, with newlyweds being tested by Trina's reversal of fortunes, since Grigor had indeed left Trina a considerable amount of money. Truth be told, Trina and Stephanos had a lot to work through.

So did Viveka. The two weeks with her sister had been enormously rejuvenating, but now it was time to finally, truly, take the wheel on her own life.

"Look." She sounded as ragged as she felt. "My half sister came into some money through the death of her father. My aunt is in a private facility. It's expensive. My sister was trying to help. That's all."

"Are you sure you didn't steal the money from Petrides? Because your flight path looks like a rabbit trying to outrun a fox."

"He wouldn't care if I did," she muttered, thinking about how generous he'd always been.

The agent's brows went up.

"I'm kidding! Don't involve him." All that work on his part—a lifetime of building himself into the head of a legitimate enterprise—and she was going to tumble it with one stupid quip? *Nice job, Viveka.*

"Tell me about your relationship with him."

"What do you mean?"

"You slept with him?"

"Yes. And no," she rushed on, guessing what he was going to say next. "Not for twenty-five thousand euros."

"Why did you break it off?"

"Reasons."

"Don't be smart, Ms. Brice. I'm your only friend right now. What was the problem? A lover's tiff? And you helped yourself to a little money for a fresh start?"

"There was no tiff." He didn't love her. That was the tiff. He would never love her and *she loved him so much*. "I'm telling you, the money has nothing to do with him. *I* have nothing to do with him. Not anymore."

She was going to cry now, and completely humiliate herself.

Mikolas was standing at the head of a boardroom table when his phone vibrated.

Viveka's picture flashed onto the screen. It was a photo he'd taken stealthily one day when creeping up on her playing backgammon with his grandfather. He'd perfectly caught her expression as she'd made a strong play, excited triumph brightening her face.

"Where's Vivi?" his grandfather had asked when Mikolas returned from Paris without her.

"Gone."

Pappoús had been stunned. Visibly heartbroken, which had concerned Mikolas. He hadn't considered how Viveka's leaving would affect his grandfather.

Pappoús had been devastated for another reason. "Another broken heart on my conscience," he'd said with tears in his eyes.

"It's not your fault." *He* was the one who had forced her to stay with him. He'd seduced her and tried not to lead her on, but she'd been hurt all the same. "She liked you," he tried to mollify. "If anything, you gave her some of what I couldn't."

"No," his grandfather had said with deep emotion. "If I hadn't left you suffering, you would not be so damaged. You would be able to love her as she's meant to be loved."

The words stung, but they weren't meant to be cruel. The truth hurt.

"You have never forgiven me and I wouldn't deserve it if you did," Pappoús went on. "I allowed your father to become a monster. He gave you nothing but a name that put you through hell. That is my fault." His shaking fist struck his chest.

He was so white and anguished, Mikolas tensed, worried his grandfather would put himself into cardiac arrest.

"I wasn't a fit man to take you in, not when you needed someone to heal you," Pappoús declared. "My love came too late and isn't enough. You don't trust it. So you've rejected her. She doesn't deserve that pain and it comes back to me. It's my fault she's suffering."

Mikolas had wanted to argue that what Viveka felt toward him wasn't real love, but if anyone knew how to love, it was her. She loved her sister to the ends of the earth. She experienced every nuance of life at a level that was far deeper than he ever let himself feel.

"She'll find love," Mikolas had growled, and was instantly uncomfortable with the idea of another man holding her at night, making her believe in forever. He hated the invisible man who would make her smile in ways he never had, because she finally felt loved in return.

"Vivi is resilient," his grandfather agreed with poignant pride.

She was very resilient.

When Mikolas had received the final report on Grigor's responsibility for her mother's death, he had been humbled. The report had compiled dozens of reports of assault and other wrongdoings across the island, but it was the unearthed statement made by Viveka that had destroyed him.

How much difference was there between one man pulling his tooth and another bruising a girl's eye? Mikolas had lost his fingernails. Viveka had lost her *mother*. He had been deliberately humiliated, forced to beg for air and water—death even—until his DNA had saved him. She had made her way to a relative who hadn't wanted her and had kept enough of a conscience to care for the woman through a tragic decline.

Viveka would find love because, despite all she had endured, she was *willing* to love.

She wasn't a coward, ducking and weaving, running and hiding, staying in Paris, saying, *It's better that it ends here.*

It wasn't better. It was torment. Deprivation gnawed relentlessly at him.

But the moment her face flashed on his phone, respite arrived.

"I have to take this," Mikolas said to his board, voice and hand trembling. He slid his thumb to answer, dizzy with how just anticipating the sound of her voice eased his suffering. "Yes?"

"I thought I should warn you," she said with remorse. "I've kind of been arrested."

"Arrested." He was aware of everyone stopping their murmuring to stare. Of all the things he might have expected, that was the very last. But that was Viveka. "Are you okay? Where are you? What happened?"

Old instincts flickered, reminding him he was revealing too much, but in this moment he didn't care about himself. He was too concerned for her.

"I'm fine." Her voice was strained. "It's a long story and Trina is trying to find me a lawyer, but they keep bringing up your name. I didn't want to blindside you if it winds up in the papers or something. You've worked so hard to get everything just so. I hate to cast shadows. I'm really sorry, Mikolas."

Only Viveka would call to forewarn him and ask nothing for herself. How in the world had he ever felt so threatened by this woman?

"Where are you?" he repeated with more insistence. "I'll have a lawyer there within the hour."

CHAPTER THIRTEEN

MIKOLAS'S LAWYER LEFT Viveka at Mikolas's London flat, since it was around the corner from his own. She was on her very last nerve and it was two in the morning. She didn't try to get a taxi to her aunt's house. She didn't have the key and would have to ask the neighbor for one tomorrow.

So she prevailed upon Mikolas *again* and didn't bother trying to find bedding for his guest room. She threw a huge pity party for herself in the shower, crying until she couldn't stand, then she folded Mikolas's black robe into a firm hug around her and crawled into his bed with a box of tissues that she dabbed against her leaking eyes.

Sleep was her blessed escape from feeling like she'd only alienated him further with this stupid questioning. The customs agents were hanging on to the money for forty-eight hours, because they could, but the lawyer seemed to think they'd give it up after that. She really didn't care, she was just so exhausted and dejected and she missed Mikolas so bad...

A weight came onto the mattress beside her and a warm hand cupped the side of her neck. The lamp came on as a man's voice said, "Viveka."

She jerked awake, sitting up in shock.

"Shh, it's okay," he soothed. "It's just me. I was trying not to scare you."

She clutched her hand across her heart. "What are you doing here?"

His image impacted her. Not just his natural sex appeal in a rumpled shirt and open collar. Not just his stubbled cheeks and bruised eyes. There was such tenderness in his gaze, her fragile composure threatened to crumple.

"Your lawyer said you were in Barcelona." She had protested against Mikolas sending the lawyer, insisting she was just informing him as a courtesy, but he'd got most of the story out of her before her time on the telephone had run out.

"I was." His hooded lids lowered to disguise what he was thinking and his tongue touched his lip. "And I'm sorry to wake you, but I didn't want to scare you if I crawled in beside you."

She followed his gaze to the crushed tissues littering the bed and hated herself for being so obvious. "I was being lazy about making up the other bed. I'll go—"

"No. We need to talk. I don't want to wait." He tucked her hair back from her cheek, behind her ear. "Vivi."

"Why did you just call me that?" She searched his gaze, her brow pulled into a wrinkle of uncertainty, her pretty bottom lip pinched by her teeth.

"Because I want to. I have wanted to. For a long time." It wasn't nearly so unsettling to admit that as he'd feared. He had expected letting her into his heart would be terrifying. Instead, it was like coming home. "Everyone else does."

A tentative hope lit her expression. "Since when do you want to be like everyone else?"

He acknowledged that with a flick of his brow, but the tiny flame in his chest grew bigger and warmer.

"Since when do I tell you or anyone what I want? Is

that what you're really wondering?" He wanted so badly to hold her. Gather all that healing warmth she radiated against him and close up the final gaps in his soul. He made himself give her what she needed first. "I want *you*, Vivi. Not just for sex, but for things I can't even articulate. That scares me to say, but I want you to know it."

She sucked in a breath and covered her mouth with both hands.

This can't be real, Viveka thought, blinking her gritty eyes. She pinched herself and he let out a husk of a laugh, immediately trying to erase the sting with a gentle rub of his thumb.

His hand stayed on her arm. His gaze lifted to her face while a deeply tender glow in his eyes went all the way through her to her soul.

"I was terrified that if I let myself care for you, someone would use that against me. So what did I do? I pushed you away and inflicted the pain on myself. I was right to fear how much it would hurt if you were out of my reach. It's unbearable."

"Oh, Mikolas." Her mouth trembled. "You inflicted it on both of us. I want to be with you. If you want me, I'm right here."

He gathered her up, unable to help himself. For a long time he held her, just absorbing the beauty of having her against him. He was aware of a tickling trickle on his cheek and dipped his head to dry his cheek against her hair.

"Thank you for saying you want me," she said. Her slender arms tightened until she pressed the breath from his lungs. "It's enough, you know." She lifted her red eyes to regard him. "I won't ask you to say you love me. But I should have said it myself before I left Paris. I've been sorry that I didn't. I was trying to protect myself from being more hurt than I was. It didn't work," she said ruefully. "I love you so much."

"You're too generous." He cupped her cheek, wiping away her tear track with the pad of his thumb, humbled. "I want your love, Vivi. I will pay any price for that. Don't let me be a coward. Make me give you what you need. Make me say it and mean it."

"You're not a coward." Fresh tears of empathy welled in her eyes, seeping into all those cracks and fissures around his heart, widening them so there was more room for her to come in.

"I was afraid to tell you I was coming," he admitted. "I was afraid you wouldn't be here if you knew. That you wouldn't let me try to convince you to stay with me."

Viveka's heart was pattering so fast she could hardly breathe. "You only have to ask," she reminded.

"Ask." Mikolas smoothed her hair back from her face, gazing at her, humbly offering his heart as a flawed human being. "I can't insult you by asking you to *stay* with me. I must ask you the big question. Will you be my wife?"

Viveka's heart staggered and lurched. "Are you serious?"

"Of course I'm serious!" He was offended, but wound up chuckling. "I will have the right woman under the veil this time, too. Actually," he added with a light kiss on her nose, "I did the first time. I just didn't know it yet."

Tears of happiness filled her eyes. She threw her arms around his neck, needing to kiss him then. To hold him and *love* him. "Yes. Of course I'll marry you!"

Their kiss was a poignant, tender reunion, making all of her ache. The physical sparks between them were stronger than ever, but the moment was so much more than that, imbued with trust and openness. It was expansive and scary and uncharted.

Beautiful.

"I want to make love to you," he said, dragging his mouth to her neck. "*Love*, Vivi. I want to wake next to you and make the best of every day we are given together."

"Me, too," she assured him with a catch of joy in her voice. "I love you."

EPILOGUE

"PAPA, I'M COLD."

Viveka heard the words from her studio. She was in the middle of a still life of Callia's toys for the advanced painting class she'd been accepted into. Three years of sketching and pastels, oils and watercolors, and she was starting to think she wasn't half bad. Her husband was always quick to praise, of course, but he was shamelessly biased.

She wiped the paint off her fingers before she picked up the small pink jumper her daughter had left there on the floor. When she came into the lounge, however, she saw that it was superfluous. Mikolas was already turning from his desk to scoop their three-year-old into his lap.

Callia stood on his thigh to curl her arms around his neck before bending her knees and snuggling into his chest, light brown curls tucked trustingly against his shoulder. "I love you," she told him in her high, doll-like voice.

"I love you, too," Mikolas said with the deep timbre of sincerity that absolutely undid Viveka every time she heard it.

"I love Leo, too," she said in a poignant little tone, mentioning her cousin, Trina's newborn son. She had cried when they'd had to come home. She looked up at Mikolas. "Do you love Leo?"

"He spit up on my new shirt," Mikolas reminded drily, then magnanimously added, "But yes, I do."

Callia giggled, then began turning it into a game. "Do you love Theítsa Trina?"

"I've grown very fond of her, yes."

"Do you love Theíos Stephanos?"

"I consider him a good friend."

"Did you love Pappoús?" She pointed at the photo on his desk.

"I did love him, very much."

Callia didn't remember her great-grandfather, but he had held her swaddled form, saying to Viveka, *She has your eyes*, and proclaiming Mikolas to be a very lucky man.

Mikolas had agreed wholeheartedly.

Losing Erebus had been hard for him. For both of them, really. Fortunately, they'd had a newborn to distract them. Falling pregnant had been a complete surprise to both of them, but the shock had quickly turned to excitement and they were so enamored with family life, they were talking of expanding it even more.

"Do you love Mama?" Callia asked.

Mikolas's head came up and he looked across at Viveka, telling her he'd been aware of her the whole time. His love for her shone like a beacon across the space between them.

"My love for your mother is the strongest thing in me."

* * * * *

MILLS & BOON®

EXCLUSIVE EXCERPT

Dario Di Sione's triumph in retrieving his family's earrings is marred by the discovery that his traitorous wife Anais has kept their child a secret! But Anais's return to his side casts a new light on past events, and now it's not the child he just wants to claim...

Read on for a sneak preview of
THE RETURN OF THE DI SIONE WIFE
the fourth in the unmissable new eight book Modern series
THE BILLIONAIRE'S LEGACY

Dario froze.

For a stunned moment he thought he was imagining her.

Because it couldn't be *her*.

Inky black hair that fell straight to her shoulders, as sleekly perfect as he remembered it. That lithe body, unmistakably gorgeous in the chic black maxidress she wore that nodded to the tropical climate as it poured all the way down her long, long legs to scrape the ground. And her face. *Her face.* That perfect oval with her dark eyes tipped up in the corners, her elegant cheekbones and that lush mouth of hers that still had the power to make his whole body tense in uncontrolled, unreasonable, *unacceptable* reaction.

He stared. He was a grown man, a powerful man by any measure, and he simply stood there and *stared—*

as if she was as much a ghost as that Hawaiian wind that was still toying with him. As if she might blow away as easily.

But she didn't.

"Hello, Dare," she said with that same self-possessed, infuriating calm of hers he remembered too well, using the name only she had ever called him—the name only she had ever gotten away with calling him.

Only Anais.

His wife.

His treacherous, betraying wife, who he'd never planned to lay eyes on again in this lifetime. And who he'd never quite gotten around to divorcing, either, because he'd liked the idea that she had to stay shackled to the man she'd betrayed six years ago, like he was an albatross wrapped tight around her slim, elegant neck.

Here, now, with her standing right there in front of him like a slap straight from his memory, that seemed less like an unforgivable oversight. And a whole lot more like a terrible mistake.

Don't miss
THE RETURN OF THE DI SIONE WIFE
by Caitlin Crews

Available October 2016